THE
WHITNEY
CHRONICLES

THE
WHITNEY
CHRONICLES

JUDY BAER

Steeple
Hill
Café

Published by Steeple Hill Books™

STEEPLE HILL BOOKS

ISBN 0-7394-4804-8

THE WHITNEY CHRONICLES

For Adrienne
(who gives invaluable feedback—thanks, honey!)
and Aaron—all my love

So be very careful how you live. Do not live like those who are not wise. Live wisely. I mean that you should use every chance you have for doing good, because these are evil times. So do not be foolish with your lives, but learn what the Lord wants you to do.

—*Ephesians* 5:15-17

SEPTEMBER

CHAPTER I

September 14

spin·ster: **1.** A woman who spins. Alfred the Great in his will, called the female part of his family the spindle side. In Saxon times, it was believed that a woman wasn't ready to marry until she'd spun her own table, bed and body linens. Any maiden or any unmarried woman was considered a spinner, or spinster. **2.** An unmarried woman; an old maid.

My name is Whitney Blake and not only is today my birthday, but it's also the day I outgrew my fat pants. My friend Kim Easton told me the most depressing day of her life was the day she realized she'd outgrown her maternity clothes and she wasn't even pregnant. I feel her pain.

Kim told me—and she had it from a good source, Oprah, maybe—that keeping a journal is an important part of knowing oneself. She says it will be especially good for me because, at thirty, I'm unmarried and currently stuck somewhere between death and puberty. It is also proof that I'm actually learning and maturing over the course of my life. I'm starting my journal today because I need proof that by this time next year I'll have learned or accomplished something. My goal is not to be a useless leech on the crust of the earth.

Turning the big three-oh was more of a shock than I'd expected. Last year I was in total denial about the inevitability of this birthday. I didn't reach a single goal I'd set for myself. "Lose ten pounds" turned into "lose fifteen." "Exercise daily" became "exercise monthly." And "meet a nice Christian man" should have been "meet a breathing one."

Kim gave me this journal as a birthday gift. She had the words *The Whitney Chronicles* printed in gold on the cover. She hopes that will intimidate me into using it.

Well, here goes.

Goals for my thirtieth year:

Today: Begin a journal in which I will give a daily account of my life and how I am improving mentally, spiritually and physically and progressing toward my year-end goals. (*That's* pompous-sounding… Oh, well.)

This week: Give check to children's ministry so as not to be tempted to spend it like I did last month. (Note—give double this month.) Wax my legs. Bleach my teeth. Floss daily. Return black blouse (unneeded, as I already have three). Put myself on a budget. Follow it for a change. Be the perfect employee no matter what my boss, Harry, throws at me. Continue practice of adding words to my vocabulary, e.g., "spinster."

My mother is sure that if I don't get in gear soon, I'm in dire jeopardy of becoming one. Although I'm not worried about spending the rest of my life making tablecloths and bedding, I don't want to end up alone in a high-rise condominium brushing a crotchety Pekinese and wondering if, when my Prince Charming *does* come, I'll be able to find my bifocals and upper plate.

This month: Lose six…no, four…no, two…no, four…okay, *five* pounds sensibly. Then, in three months, I can wear all the clothes in my closet again. Exercise. Do not let my mother drive me crazy (a particularly difficult project). Get organized. Start by cleaning closets. Quit falling for every organizing gadget on the market. No more hanging shoe racks, drawer dividers or file cabinets. And, under no circumstances, another set of plastic drawers on wheels. Have friends over for dinner. Read my Bible more. Pray more, obsess less.

This year: Lose fifteen pounds, make a career step (preferably upward). Learn how to change a tire. Find a new hairstyle. Quit thinking of self as chubby. Become less of a couch potato and more of a social butterfly. Give up being an introvert. Become a raging extrovert. Meet and date a nice Christian man….

Clarification! Meet but *do not* date a nice Christian man— I do not need a man to make my life complete or to feel whole. Besides, Kim says diffidence is the best way to catch a guy anyway.

And, like my monthly goal, ditto on Bible reading and prayer.

This decade: See above, plus get married, have a baby and/or become a marketing consultant genius and get rich and famous. (If so, I can always marry after.) It might be fun to be a philanthropist instead of a parent for a few years. Besides, I am in no rush to meet a man (note yearly goals).

I weighed myself this morning and couldn't believe what I saw—even when I stood on the scale with my palms on the bathroom counter. Unless I learn to levitate, it is very clear that I have to go on a diet. I've heard the body clings harder to excess weight the older one gets. I just didn't think it would cling so hard so fast....

Anyway, I was already late for work by the time I discovered the waist-expansion issue (my euphemism for disgusting fat). Although being marketing coordinator at Innova Computer Solutions—ICS—allows me to dress casually, I doubt belly bloat oozing out of my zipper is allowed.

Rather than search my closet for a larger pair of pants (impossible anyway, because I refuse to buy a pair), I hooked the waistband together by looping a ponytail holder through the buttonhole and stretching it over the button (a trick I learned from Kim in the early days of her pregnancy). With a long shirt, tails out, and a jacket, I hoped no one would notice the bulge. I did, however, suddenly begin to wonder about the quality of the rubber used in hair bands. A few deep knee bends loosened the fabric, which had obviously shrunk in the wash, and I was on my way. I spent most of the day treading the fine line between mandatory shallow breathing and hyperventilation.

If only solving problems at work (*work*—is there a way to indicate a shudder on paper?) were so easy!

My boss, Harry Harrison, went mental on us today. He discovered an upcoming trade show at which it was imperative that Innova be represented with a booth and marketing people. Unfortunately the show is next week, and I usually need a lead time of two months to prepare. Harry didn't seem to care that *he* was the one who forgot to inform the marketing department of this vital trade show. Harry is a computer genius, but not the most organized man in the world. Frustrated, too, probably. I'd hate to be a balding man named Harry Harrison. But I digress....

The good news at work today was that I calculated that banging one's head against a wall uses at least 125 calories an hour. That meant I earned 500 extra calories for my birthday dinner.

In spite of my newfound caloric knowledge, I had to go to my parents' house for dinner. Mother's pork chops and onion gravy should be applied directly to my thighs, because that where they'll end up anyway. The mashed potatoes with a life raft of butter floating in the center settled directly on the flubber keeping my pants open. (I'm going to write a thank-you note to the rubber-band manufacturer tomorrow.) And the minimal calories in the "I-realize-angel-food-cake-isn't-your-favorite-but-I-know-you-are-dieting" birthday cake balanced the mounds of whipping cream covering it.

Mother, at a hundred and one pounds and a metabolism that won't quit, has never gotten the hang of dieting. A cruel trick of nature if ever there was one. No matter how thin I am, at five-eight, with broad shoulders, a potentially slim waist and size nine shoes, I'm always referred to in the family as "the big one." It's a wonder I'm as sane as I am.

I knew it was going to be a bad evening when Mom opened the door with her shirttails tied in a knot over her belly button and a tiny battery-operated fan in her hand. It wouldn't be so traumatic if menopause had crept up on her slowly, so Dad and I could grow accustomed to it over time. Instead, it was like a door flying open and quickly slamming shut—one moment she was on one side of the door and the next she was on the other. If she'd had a choice, she would have picked the prize behind any other door. She has a good attitude toward this new phase of her life, however. She says the hair on her legs grows much more slowly now, and she doesn't have to shave so often.

"Come in, darling," she said, scraping damp hair away from her forehead. "Daddy is in the kitchen opening the windows. How can you stand to have those heavy clothes on in this weather?" She reached for my lightweight sweater, but

I crossed my arms and hung on. The air conditioner was running full blast.

"Hi, Pumpkin." Daddy crossed the room to give me a hug. No matter how old I get, I'll always be his little girl.

"How are you?"

"Getting along, despite the fact my back has started going out more than I do."

"Quit with the old-age jokes, Frank. You're in the prime of life!" Mom gave him a glare that should have melted steel.

Daddy winked at me and headed for the table. He was, as he always said, "being a duck." That's how he and Mom had managed to be married all these years and still be happy. When I was growing up, every time my feelings were hurt, he'd tell me, "Be a duck, Whitney, let it roll off you like water rolls off a duck's back. Ducks have oil in their top feathers that keeps their under-feathers dry. You need to grow a few oily feathers. Don't let mean words or insensitive comments make you uncomfortable. Let them roll right off."

If I ever marry, I think that's one piece of advice that will come in very handy.

"Tell me, Whitney, have you heard from that nice young man from church?" Mother asked as she held an ice cube to her temple and stirred the gravy. It had a quarter-inch of shimmering grease on top.

That "nice young man" is forty-five if he's a day and very adept at evading eligible single women and their match-making mothers. If the church had a football team, he would be their halfback.

I performed my own punt, pass and kick maneuvers. "Cake looks great, Mom. So, Dad, how about those Vikings?"

My mother has a knack for entertaining. She once took a class on twenty ways to fold a napkin, and we've never had a flat napkin since. Tonight they were shaped into little hats with "Happy Birthday" stickers all over them. She'd made a centerpiece of chopsticks, ribbons and cutouts from egg cartons that looked amazingly like a bouquet of balloons. She uses her "good" china for every meal. My "good" china consisted of a collection of Rainbow Bright glasses and the wicker holders for paper plates.

We sat down at the table and began the same conversation we've had every year since I quit having little friends over to play on my birthday. It involves Mother recounting the entire day of my birth, from the saga of when her water broke, through the race to the hospital during which Dad's car ran out of gas, right into the delivery room. These stories give me far more details than I ever wanted to know. I am deliriously grateful that Dad did not have the presence of mind to bring a video camera into the delivery room.

Then, as is their custom, they wandered into their own childhoods and reminisced about wax lips, Black Jack gum, drive-in movies and sodas that came in glass bottles. Sooner or later they would remember whose birthday it was and start regaling me with stories of my own life—usually the ones I've tried for years to forget. Like the time I wet my pants in Sunday school and tried to sneak the damply incriminating evidence home wrapped in a picture I'd colored of David and Goliath. Or the time I "borrowed" a trinket from the drugstore without paying for it and Mom made me take it back and apologize. And the Sunday school Christmas program when, in a fit of shyness, I tried to hide and got my head stuck between the spindles on the altar railing, bottom out toward the congregation. My only consolation is that I had ruffles on my panties.

My presents—always an exercise in surprise—were quite nice this year. I got a savings bond from Grandma (who hasn't really accepted that I'm no longer in grade school), a new outfit from Mom and the traditional money folded in a card identical to the one I get every year. Mom purchased the box of cards several years ago when the local band was trying to earn enough money to go to Epcot Center. She says the cards are too ugly to give to anyone except family. No exercise equipment this year (apparently she'd found the Thighmaster I'd received for my twenty-eighth birthday unused in my garage). And thankfully there were no books by Martha Stewart on how to plan a wedding or notes indicating Mom would be willing to pay for a preliminary visit to a dating service and their introductory offer promising five dates or my money back.

I escaped with my birthday gifts in tow and more advice about how to meet a "nice single Christian man." In my life experience—at least lately, "nice *single* Christian man" is an oxymoron. I don't want to be cynical, but things are beginning to look bleak. Maybe God doesn't have someone ready for me yet. Or perhaps *I'm* not ready for *him*. Even though I trust things will turn out right, Mother feels that I'm duty-bound to do my part in the search.

Unfortunately, she's willing to help me.

Tonight's Bible verse:

> *The Lord doesn't make decisions the way*
> *you do! People judge by outward appearance,*
> *but the Lord looks at a person's thoughts*
> *and intentions.*
>
> —1 Samuel 16:7

And Samuel should know, being a prophet who wanted to keep his heart pure before God. God loves me for what's inside me. I must organize my thoughts as well as my life, set my priorities and always put Him first. If our thoughts and intentions were as visible to others as our designer jeans, what would people see in me?

Must add kindly thoughts and good deeds to my goals ASAP.

September 15

blame·storm·ing: My officemates sitting in the coffee room discussing what's going on in the office and whose fault it is.

Day two of diet. Felt as though small animals were clawing at my insides. Two slices of dry toast and an apple helped somewhat. Must make a note to myself never to drink coffee on an empty stomach again. Good thing I had Bible study after work. It's something to look forward to while Harry has a nervous breakdown. The trouble is, he's a carrier, the Typhoid Mary of insanity. When he's cracking, it spreads through the office like wildfire.

The office manager, Betty Nobel, has worked at Innova since its inception seven years ago. She's practically attached to Harry at the hip, and whatever he feels, she feels. That must be like riding a broken roller coaster in the carnival fun house in the dark after eating junk food all day. Wretched.

The amazing part is that she's often more unreasonable than Harry. Betty's the one who came up with the latest guidelines for employee absences. As far as Kim and I can figure out, we're not allowed to go to any family member's funeral except our own, and that, of course, with several weeks' notice so Betty and Harry can hire a replacement and we can train them ourselves. My assistant, Bryan Kellund, once brought in an emergency-room bill to prove he'd really been ill. Betty didn't buy that either. She said if he'd gotten as far as the hospital, the office was only a couple more blocks away, and if he'd really *cared* about his work…

Just thinking about office politics made me want to eat my lunch early—a nice tuna salad with low-fat mayo on endive and bibb lettuce. Also some insignificant hard candies and a few M&M's I discovered under the tissue box in my top drawer. Must work on problematic issue of depending on food to comfort me—tomorrow.

Fortunately my friend and co-worker in marketing is always calm. When things get hairy (because of Harry?), Kim does the deep-breathing technique she learned in Lamaze class before she delivered her baby last year. We're usually hyperventilating by the time Harry's crisis is over.

Example: I turned in the cost estimates for new marketing materials that Harry had asked to see. I was hoping to have it ready for our next show, which would be in Lost Wages…er, Las Vegas. It even surprised me a little. I'd expected double the estimate on our old booth, but apparently paper, cardboard and pressed-wood prices are volatile, and it was nearly triple the original bid. When Harry came to me with that irate grizzly-bear expression on his face, cracking his (hairy!) knuckles, I knew I had a problem. Actually, knuckle cracking is just that—a bubble of gas bursting. And Harry was a whole bunch of gas about to blow up. Nasty.

I managed to circumvent the problem for the moment, but *I* was about to explode by the time he returned to his own office. Fortunately, I discovered the rest of my M&M's— a two-pound bag, wedged at the back of my office drawer. Devouring it took the edge off my nerves.

Bryan has the best crisis-management solution. He simply leaves for the rest room at the first sign of trouble and doesn't return until it's over. He either has great hearing or an amazing sixth sense. I've also speculated about the seemingly minimal capacity of his bladder. Bryan is allergic to conflict and can smell it coming a mile away. I'm convinced he knows how to dematerialize and turn up again in the spot farthest from the action. He even has an ethereal look about him with his mushroom-colored hair, pale, pasty complexion and enormous gray eyes that never look straight at me.

Mitzi, who has no known use at all in the office as far as Kim and I can figure out, delights in conflict. It stirs up her juices. It also gives her something to do—rile Harry so he'll explode. Usually when Mitzi opens her mouth, it's to change feet. Mitzi came to work at Innova to see how the "other half" lives. Her husband is a very wealthy podiatrist. She says he owes it all to strapless high heels. I think flat, sensible Birkenstocks make him a little nervous. Mitzi could stay home and count her glass slippers, but no, she comes in every day—sometimes early—just to torment us.

One of her most evil schemes involves chocolate. Mitzi is the only woman I've ever met who doesn't like chocolate. Therefore, she brings chocolate delicacies to the office at least three times a week just to see Kim and me salivate. Kim's still trying to get rid of baby weight. I'm trying to prevent having someone ask me when my baby is due.

Today it was éclairs with frosting a half-inch thick. Be still, my heart.

Kim's one-year-old, Wesley, got a new tooth today, a molar. You'd have thought he'd erupted an oil well in his mouth, the way she carried on. Other than her blow-by-blow reporting of Wesley's every grin, burp and bowel movement, Kim is a great friend—the best, actually. We have the same rather skewed sense of humor and similar goals—getting a raise, for one. She doesn't need a husband because she already has one—and a nice Christian one at that. Kurt is an over-the-road semitruck driver/late-in-life student who wants to be either an accountant or a pastor, no matter what it takes. Those two professions don't seem to have much in common, but I know for sure he'd be a *very* trustworthy accountant. Right now, between classes and over-the-roaders, he's fully occupied.

Kim's also a Christian. That makes all the difference.

Mitzi was lying in wait for me as I left the office. She always does that on Tuesdays, when she knows I leave promptly at five. Otherwise she's gone so fast that her desk chair is still spinning when we hear the door slam.

"There are *sooo* many éclairs left that you'll have to take them home." She waved the open box holding five fat beauties, chocolate frosting glistening. Like she'd ever offer me anything *useful,* like help around the office. Oh, no, Mitzi was only generous when it served her depraved purposes, one of which is to make me weigh more than she does.

"Thanks a lot, but I'm on a diet."

"No wonder there were so many left today. Then take them for your neighbors. You *do* have neighbors, don't you?" She smiled sweetly.

"Thankfully, yes. They did not all move away when they discovered I was living nearby." Sarcasm is wasted on Mitzi, but it made me feel better. What on earth goes through that perfectly groomed brunette head of hers?

"Well, I'm sure they'll love these." Somehow she managed to transport the box into my hands, pick up her purse and escape before I could argue. At least I'd have goodies to share at Bible study.

As so often happens on the freeway, the drive to the church brought up the subject of Christian ethics. I'm a Christian. What does that mean in my everyday life? If I believe it, I have to live it. Every choice I make, every word I speak, needs to be done through that filter of faith. So here's my question. What is it with rude drivers?

As I left the parking lot, a woman shot up behind me and stuck the nose of her SUV into my back bumper. Even though the street was practically empty, she followed me as closely as she could without driving into my trunk.

I'm a fanatic about being polite in traffic. It seems to me that's where most people lose track of walking the Christian walk—or, in this case, driving the Christian drive. I'm no saint, but I usually don't expose my sinful nature when I'm driving two tons of rolling metal.

Anyway, this woman (definitely not a "lady") *honked* at me when I didn't turn fast enough for her. She had her nose in the air as she sailed around me without even a wave. I had several uncharitable thoughts but guiltily dropped back as if I'd been the one speeding and followed her to…the church parking lot.

Now, what I want to know is this—if you profess to be a Christian, if you want to let God's light shine through you— where do you get off being rude behind the wheel? Isn't part of the Christian life about behaving as Christ would behave? Would He have run the light, tailgated until the person ahead of Him was a wreck, honked His horn and broken the speed limit—all to get to *Bible study* on time?

I don't think so.

I'm going to buy a bumper sticker I saw last week for my rear bumper: Are You Following Jesus This Closely?

That's one thing I've learned since I found God and He found me. It's easy to *talk* Christianity, but not so easy to *walk* it. Fortunately, I lost track of Ms. Speedy in the church. By the time Bible study was over, I even felt like praying for her. ("Oh, Lord, keep that nutcase off the streets…." *Just kidding!!!*)

Ironically, I know lots of people who will spend hours at the gym so they can live longer—and then drive thirty miles an hour over the speed limit to make up for all the time they wasted doing it.

Thoughtlessly, I ate one of the éclairs to soothe my nerves.

I had four calls on my answering machine when I got home. Three from my mother—"Whitney, you forgot the dishrags I knitted for you out of scrap yarn." (Now how did *that* happen?) "Whitney, do you want me to invite that nice young man from church and his mother over for dinner?" (As if she could even *catch* him!) And, "Whitney, I don't know where my mind is these days. I'm so forgetful. Did I tell you that you forgot your dishrags at my house?"

Menopause can be brutal. I know now why women over fifty shouldn't have babies. They'd lay them down and forget where they put them.

The fourth call was from Eric Van Horne. He's a very special man in my life. We've been friends for years, and I don't know if a more good-natured man exists. We dated for a while, and I really thought Eric might be the one for me. He's brilliant, but impulsive and completely undependable. I spent many nights wondering if he had actually asked me out and, if so, where was he? I knew from the outset that no matter whom Eric dated, she'd have to agree to take second place to his love for airplanes. News of an air show in a neighboring state would drive everything else from his mind. He'd jump into his car, sniff the air and head in the direction of jet fuel. And on Monday he'd remember we'd had plans for the weekend.

Ardor fades quickly after sitting by the phone for a few weeks waiting for a call. Actually, we came to the decision together that until either I learned to love madcap spontaneity or he learned to be dependable and predictable, we'd just be friends. So far we've managed to navigate the bumpy waters of remaining friends and seeing each other socially.

"Hi, Whit! Sorry I didn't call sooner. Wanted to tell you about the great air show I attended. You should see my photos!"

"I don't know if I can stand being dumped for a crop duster again, Eric."

"What a kidder you are, Whit. I took a picture of a woman and the plane she uses for acrobatics. She reminded me of you."

"At least you thought of me." I can't be too hard on him. Eric is darling, but has what Kim calls "zero mac." He enjoys life too much to be cool and is way too exuberant to be macho.

Actually, that may be his best quality.

The Bible verse that comes to mind when I think of Eric is Proverbs 18:24: "Some friends may ruin you. But a real friend will be more loyal than a brother."

Mitzi may be in the first category. Kim and Eric are in the second. While Mitzi spends the day making snide remarks about my age (as if she'll ever see thirty-five again!), Eric called a second time to apologize for standing me up. He says he just "lost track of time."

Somehow, I believe him. I've known from the start that Eric has the attention span of a flea, a heart of gold and a bloodhound's nose for airplanes, and I wasn't going to change him no matter what I did. I've never gone into a relationship with that rehab-attitude. I take a guy for what he is, not for what I think he could become.

Eric is actually a much better friend than he is a date. A girl could get old waiting around for a guy like him.

I was too exhausted to cook supper, so I just heated a family-size ready-made lasagna in the oven. It was so big, I figured it would last me for days. Tasty, too. Then I started thinking about work. Ate a little more lasagna. As I put away the pan, I realized I'd eaten quite a little more. Now there's just one measly portion left for lunch tomorrow.

Tomorrow! I'll restart my diet, *seriously* this time. I'll count calories. To make sure I didn't forget, I dug out my old calorie counter from previous diets.

I can't believe a measly portion of lasagna has 230 calories. That would mean the rest of my frozen dinner would have…1840 calories! Feeling a little sick, but driven to find out exactly what kind of havoc I'd wreaked, I did today's math.

Breakfast: two slices dry toast—140 calories
1 apple—81 calories
Lunch: tuna salad with low-fat mayo on bibb and endive lettuce—150 calories
6 hard candies—125 calories
1 ounce M&M's—140 calories

Snack:	other 31 ounces of M&M's—4,340 calories
Accident:	1 éclair—500 calories
Dinner:	7 portions of an 8-portion heat-and-serve lasagna—1840 calories
Snack:	Tums—0 calories (medicinal, don't count)

Seven thousand three hundred and sixteen calories?

I have to stay calm. Running screaming into the street would not help. I ran by it again.... I'm on a 1200-calorie-a-day diet; 7316 divided by 1200 equals...six days. That means I can't eat again until September 21!

Stay calm. Start over. Tomorrow will be a clean slate. I'll utilize all I've learned so that I don't make those mistakes again. Can rubber bands stretch enough to compensate for today?

My prayers for tonight: *For a successful trip to Las Vegas, for my boss and officemates (as undeserving as they may be—just kidding!), Mom's hot flashes, Dad's sanity, Eric's memory and my life as a thirty-something. Where do You want me in this new decade of my life, Lord? And gratitude—for all of the above and for Your Son, Who loved me more than I can ever imagine.*

Humbly,
Whitney

CHAPTER 2

God wants everyone to eat and drink and be
Happy in His work. These are gifts from God.
—Ecclesiastes 3:13

September 20

I'm getting the hang of this journal thing. It's like telling a close personal friend about my day. I haven't made much progress in the self-improvement area other than managing to get the zipper closed on my fat pants.

I returned the black blouse. Since I'd put the blouse on my credit card, I didn't really feel I'd spent any money—or gained any when I returned it. So, being financially even, I went shopping, bought shoes and, naturally, charged them. There is something to be said for the tactile quality of cash. It is definitely much harder to pry out of my hand than plastic.

My feet are pretty much the only things on my body that don't change size. Of course, my mother did tell me if I didn't wear shoes, my arches would fall and I'd be flat-footed for the rest of my life. She also taught me that if I didn't quit crossing my eyes, they would freeze that way, and if I drank coffee, it would stunt my growth. It's a wonder I'm alive today considering all the risks I took.

September 21

Dad has begun hiding out to get away from Mother and her wildly fluctuating body temperature. He offered to come over and fix my plumbing (which isn't broken), build me a piece of furniture (something he's never done before in his life) and repaint my ceilings. He is one desperate man, so I invited him over for a visit. I thought I might cheer him up.

"Have you got something for me to do?" were his first words. "Please?"

"What's Mother up to today?"

"Cleaning closets. She rented a Dumpster and is emptying everything we own into it. I expect to go home to an empty house."

"Don't worry. There's probably a lot of junk you needed to get rid of by now."

Dad scowled at me. "It's only 'junk' until you throw it away. Have you noticed that as soon as the garbagemen leave the neighborhood, we have to replace everything we never thought we'd use again? Your mother is going to send me into bankruptcy!"

"It can't be that bad. What harm can she do? Try to be more open-minded about this phase of her life," I encouraged.

"'Open-minded?' Whitney, if I'm any more open-minded where your mother is concerned, my brains will fall out!"

I have the greatest father in the world. He's odd, unique and one of a kind, but he's also tenderhearted and very patient where his "little girl" and his wife are concerned. Mom is wonderful, but she can be opinionated, single-minded, stubborn and, these days, totally off-the-wall. If their strengths and weaknesses were blended together, they'd make one amazing parent—and one delightfully wacky one. They met as teenagers and it was love at first sight—on my dad's part. Mom had taken longer to come around. Tiny, extroverted and beautiful, she'd had men circling her like planes over Dallas, and it had taken her a while to fit Dad onto her radar screen. Dad said she was the most popular girl on campus. Another thing I can't relate with Mom about....

"Coffee, Dad?"

"Are you kidding? It's two o'clock in the afternoon! Do you want me to be up all night? Do you know what caffeine does to me? Combine that with your mother jumping up to turn on the air conditioner and me having to go to the bathroom...." He shook his head so dismally, my heart nearly broke.

"It's not that bad, Dad. She'll get over this, things will be better soon. Don't think of your glass as half empty. Think of it as half full."

He gave me a wry grin. "Yeah, and before long I'll have my teeth floating in it."

September 22

I thought Harry (and, by association, Betty) would become hysterical when Kim and I outlined the plans for getting a late booth into the technology show in Las Vegas. The ideas were feasible, even downright brilliant...but also expensive. Unfortunately, Harry's hobby is pinching pennies until they scream. I had to pay full price for airline tickets, and coach was booked, which meant an upgrade to first class. There was only one room left in the conference hotel, and that was a suite. Add to that the cost of the booth, getting signage and entertaining a client list (who, being called at the last moment, would need to be treated with extra—read expensive—care) and Harry might as well have invested in a small gold mine. But you can't pull something together in a week for the cost of something planned months in advance. Unfortunately we who already knew this had to suffer right along in Harry's learning curve.

The good news is that his tantrum was short-circuited by an incredibly handsome new client arriving at the office between "Do you know how much this is going to cost" and— my favorite—"Next time plan ahead for these unplanned surprises."

Handsome Client had a great smile, dark brown hair and eyes so green they remind me of the Emerald Isle. (The one I've seen in travel magazines. I want to see it in person soon— add that to Yearly Goals.) And he was six feet tall, athletically slim and wore the best suit I've seen outside of *GQ.* I found myself wondering if he was *nice, Christian* and *single.* Mother would have been so proud.

Harry called me into his office to introduce me to Matthew Lambert, CEO of a small but successful firm that roasts peanuts, pecans and the like. Lambert also makes nut butters, glazed and candied nuts and a dozen other calorie-laden items.

Matthew Lambert must have noticed me licking my lips in response to his job description, because he commented on my apparent enthusiasm for the project. Actually, all I'd had for lunch was a pathetic pile of tuna and three slices of melba toast.

Lambert is building a completely automated and computerized plant and wants Harry to design some specialized software. Apparently he wants a computer that can roast peanuts. If technology can provide a way to burn CDs, it seems like roasting a peanut should be a snap.

Harry always calls me in for the preliminaries. This is usually best for all concerned, as I have some social graces. I take over while Harry disappears with his stable of computer geeks to work his software magic. He has a deft hand on a mouse and the ability to memorize all of the numbers in a phone book. I, on the other hand, have a personality.

While I was dreaming up a way to ask Mr. Lambert if he wanted to discuss his new alliance with Innova over coffee, his cell phone rang and he was summoned away. It's my mother's fault. She filled my head with all that talk about "nice young men." (I did glance at his ring finger first, though. It was bare. Promising…)

It wasn't until I got back to my desk that the cell phone thing began to annoy me. How do people justify thinking they're so important that they have to be accessible to every-one, everywhere at all times? Humans are so vain. Men in gyms run on treadmills and talk into their cells. I've heard women in toilet stalls making luncheon dates and others in dressing rooms at the mall counseling their friends on the lat-est jerk they dated. Just last week I pulled up at a stoplight beside a guy on a Harley. He was talking on a cell phone and there was a bumper sticker on his bike that said, Thugs Are People Too. Go figure.

September 22, later

Eric has been calling. This boy/girl stuff can ruin a great friendship. Still, if he asks me, I wouldn't mind going out for an evening. It's been months since I've seen a movie that wasn't on television.

Just the thought of an evening out inspired a rush of adren-aline through my system. Having recently traded my exercise bike (obscenely expensive clothes rack with wheels) for a bookcase, a yoga mat and a lava lamp, I decided to wax my legs.

Three minutes into the project I remembered why I hate waxing my legs.

Rather than scald off my skin by overheating the wax in the microwave, I heated it on the stove. I forgot about it for just a moment when I spied some leftover potato chips (very rare at my house). Not wanting to waste food (starving chil-dren in Beverly Hills and all that), I stuffed them into my mouth before I remembered my goal to lose fifteen pounds. Occasionally I worry about my memory. Some days the only thing I seem able to retain is water.

I tried spitting the chips out into the sink, but accidentally spluttered them into the hot wax instead.

Deciding that the potato chips wouldn't hurt either the wax or my legs, I carried the pan to the bathroom. Sitting on the edge of the tub, I began frosting my hairy legs with chip-speckled yellow wax. The wax went from being too hot to too cold in a nanosecond. I didn't dare toddle back into the kitchen to return it to the stove as I was afraid the wax would harden on my legs and become a permanent part of my flesh.

I edged my fingernails under the globby sheet of goo and pulled upward. A rush of tears filled my eyes as hairless pink skin shined up at me. If someone told me I *had* to do this, I'd call it abuse. As it is, I inflict it on myself and call it grooming.

Since my legs were sticking together anyway and I couldn't walk, I decided to call my mother.

"Whitney! How are you? Isn't this weather something?"

"It's been raining, Mom."

"But *warm* rain. I've been wearing shorts all day." I didn't tell her that I expect she'll have them on in January, too.

When I broke the news to her that I'm going to Las Vegas for a trade show, she was not happy.

"Sin City? How can your employer send a young girl like you there?"

"I'm thirty, Mom. And I've always traveled with my job."

"It's a den of iniquity, darling. Tell him you can't go."

Kim, on the other hand, was in love with the idea. "Bring me something, will you?"

"I promised Mother I wouldn't leave the hotel for purposes of a touristy nature," I reminded her.

"Something from the hotel, then. With rhinestones."
So much for the good influence of friends.

September 23

I've been inundated with plans for the trade show. Whitney's my name, Creativity's my game. At least that's what Harry thinks. Only Bryan knows that today, between brilliant zaps of originality and ingenuity, I figured out which was the longest word I could type with my left hand—*stewardesses* (a travel-related exercise accomplished while being left on hold by a travel agent who went shopping and had a face-lift before getting back to me). And—this one is big—when you rearrange the words *slot machines,* you can make the words *cash lost in 'em.*

Of course, after foisting the Las Vegas trade-show problem on to me, Harry promptly forgot about it and began trolling for bigger fish. In this case it was someone from whom he'd already had a nibble but wanted to land completely, Matthew Lambert, the nut-roasting magnate I'd fondly begun referring to as Mr. Peanut.

As I walked toward Harry's office this morning, Bryan—wearing that panicked look he so often does—raised his eyebrows and pointed frantically toward Harry's door. Figuring my assistant was trying to indicate that Harry was out of sorts, I strode in expecting to see a man who hadn't yet had his sixth cup of coffee today. What I did see nearly knocked me flat.

Harry had gotten himself a permanent. Though not yet bald, his hair is thinning except for the thick assortment of hairs that halo his head in the traditional style of medieval monks.

I took a deep breath and attempted to quash the image of an unevenly growing Chia Pet on Harry's head. No wonder Bryan had looked as though he was about to faint. He'd probably been under his desk laughing himself silly.

"Are you busy tomorrow evening, Whitney?" Harry leaned back in his chair, put his hands behind his neck and fingered the tight curls at his collar.

A working *dinner?* With *Harry?* Harry never paid for anything he didn't have to, and he was married, so this wasn't a social dinner. Had his permanent given him so much aplomb that he was asking me out on a frivolous whim or were the newly tight curls on his head squeezing his brain? My relief was actually physical when he added, "I'm having dinner with Matt Lambert, and I'd like you to come along. What do you say?"

I was so happy I didn't have to dine alone with Harry and be forced to admire his Chia Pet scalp that I agreed immediately. That Matthew Lambert would be there didn't hurt either.

It wasn't until I was back at my desk that I realized that I was not in any way prepared to go anywhere or do anything with a hunky, *single* man. I'm a woman who—as recently as six days ago—was holding her clothing together with rubber bands. I had nothing to wear. Visions of pilled and holey sweatpants, stained T-shirts, too-tight jeans and my work clothing—mostly interchangeable black and beige separates and low-heeled pumps—danced in my head. I usually go into a shopping frenzy the week before a big date. It was clearly apparent that I hadn't had a frenzy—or a date—for quite some time.

It wasn't until noon that I could discuss the emergency with Kim.

"Don't you have a 'fat dress'?" she asked. "I always keep one of those empire-waist corduroy or cotton things on hand for a crisis."

"Then I might as well pitch a pup tent in the middle of the restaurant and stick my head through the top to eat. I want to look *good* for this...."

Kim, the least vain person on the planet, puzzled that one over. "Your mom has been on your case again, hasn't she? All that stuff about meeting a man?"

"She's worried about me," I admitted weakly.

"And she has her own subscription to *Bride's* magazine just for the fun of it. Get real, Whitney, she's a wedding planner waiting to happen."

"I know, I know, but I still want to look nice tomorrow night."

"'Nice?' You're already gorgeous! Sometimes I wonder if you ever look in a mirror. That dark hair of yours, those eyes, and no matter how many times you say you're 'fat' you know there are women who would give a front tooth for your curves!"

A *front* tooth? Scary thought. But that's part of why I cherish Kim. She actually believes I'm beautiful and isn't afraid to say it. Bless her heart.

"I know, I know, but I still need to look stunning tomorrow night."

"Then how about that wonderful black jumpsuit we bought last time you were pre-diet?"

I love Kim's tactfulness. I grabbed her cheeks between my palms and gave them a squeeze. "You are brilliant. Problem solved."

She nodded benignly. "Now that we've settled that, let's discuss Harry's hair."

I couldn't help it. I had to go shopping anyway.

When I don't really have anything to shop for, my default is always shoes. The good news is that there are finally cute shoes that are actually comfortable. The bad news is that nothing looks all that cute on my size nine feet. Granted, they match my five-eight height, and I'm nicely proportioned. I think of myself as the new-and-improved, more-for-your-money package.

I found a great pair of black shoes with strappy backs. These are not to be confused with my black shoes with the little bow, my black shoes with the flat heels, my black patent leathers, my black sandals, flip-flops or slippers or my several pairs of black pumps and my black running shoes. These were *different*—not different enough, however, that anyone but me would notice. And, of course, they were still black.

After a rip-roaring internal debate, I decided to buy a purse instead. No danger of falling into the I-think-I'll-buy-it-in-black trap there. Purses have personality these days—flashy colors, weird shapes, sequins and rhinestone thingamabobs dangling off them. My question is, who buys these things? Seems to me a precious little bag that's shaped like a para-keet, decorated in yellow and green sequins and holds a tis-sue and a tube of lipstick is doomed to extinction.

Uh-oh. Were those my mother's thoughts coming out of *my* mind?

I settled on a slightly larger bag shaped and decorated like a seashell because it would also hold my keys and a credit card and had pretty turquoise sequins. Who buys these things? Me, apparently.

Eric called tonight. He's so charmingly disorganized that I've gotta love him. Today he spent two hours looking for his dry cleaning. Not in the house, mind you, but in his car. He'd dropped off his clothes on the way to an appointment, and when he returned to pick them up, he realized he couldn't remember exactly which cleaner he'd used. Unfor-tunately, he'd done a few dozen other errands in the same trip and had a ten-mile radius within which his clothing could be waiting. While he was out scouting for his Laurens and his Hilfigers, he managed to hit an estate sale and a going-out-of-business blowout. It cost him a hundred and seventy-five dollars in unnecessary purchases to find his clothing.

"It's okay, though," he justified cheerfully. "I was really hop-ing to find an Andirondack chair and an Arts and Crafts floor lamp someday. I just ran across them sooner than I expected." Unfortunately, while we were on the phone, his dog, Otto, managed to chew through the cord on the floor lamp and one leg of the chair.

It's Eric's own fault, really. He loves that dog so much that he's afraid to hurt his feelings by scolding him. I'm not sure Otto *has* feelings. Bulldogs rarely appear to be in touch with their emotions. Still, Eric is crazy about him, and there is something rather sweet about an airplane buff and his dog Otto-Pilot.

I couldn't get Eric and Otto-Pilot out of my mind while I was doing my Bible readings tonight, so I looked up Job 12:7-9. "But ask the animals, and they will teach you; the birds of the air, and they will tell you; ask the plants of the earth and they will teach you; and the fish of the sea will declare to you. Who among all these does not know that the hand of the Lord has done this?" I have a real passion for His creatures. After all, if God set aside two full days of creation—the fifth to create fish and birds and the sixth to fashion animals (including the man and woman kind)—then why don't we realize how important they must be to Him—and therefore, to us?

Ironic, isn't it, that of all the creatures on the face of the earth, only humans don't seem to realize who and what they are. Animals behave like animals, plants like plants and fish like fish. Only we try to behave as if we're God.

I like it that Eric cares so much for that dog even if Otto does digest furniture the way other dogs do kibble. Tomorrow night, I'll have to remember to ask Mr. Peanut if *he's* fond of animals.

September 24

I think I'm in love! Or, at least, I have a serious case of "like."

Matthew Lambert is one handsome, charming man. When he looked at me with those Irish eyes tonight, I turned into a human puddle—and, unfortunately had to spend the rest of the night mopping up. Okay, so I'd already reached my objective of meeting a really nice man. My other goal was not to get into any foolish entanglements in the dating scene. Unfortunately the edges of my determination are crumbling already. Why did I set a stupid goal like that anyway?

I knew I was in trouble when I saw him coming across the restaurant in a stunning black suit and pristine white shirt that had been laundered and starched within an inch of its life. His tie was so red and professional-looking, it hurt my eyes to stare at it. If my mother had been there, she would have labeled him "the one" for me without hearing a word out of his mouth. She'd always dreamed I'd marry a doctor, so she'd have someone in the family with whom to discuss her various and ever-changing "symptoms," but a peanut salesman who looked like this would run a close second.

"So good to see you again, Ms. Blake."

For a moment I didn't respond. I'd forgotten my name and didn't realize he was talking to me. Then he did this corny thing and picked up my hand and kissed it. That was when I forgot my entire family history and where I'd parked my car. Until that moment, I'd always thought *giddy* was an unlikely word since I hadn't had a giddy moment in my life. Now I know the definition and it's a doozy. Matthew Lambert oozed charm like a broken toothpaste tube might ooze… Well, wow, am I bad at metaphors or what? Fortunately, Harry arrived, and from then on it was all business.

We spent the evening talking about the nut-roasting software. Harry did his usual computer-babble, and I efficiently and succinctly translated it into understandable English. (And Mom thought I needed to take Spanish to become fluent in a foreign language!) We make a pretty good team, Harry and I, even though all night I couldn't make eye contact with him because I kept having the urge to water the top of his head to make it grow.

There was an awkward moment when our meals were served. I used to hate it when my parents bowed their heads to pray in restaurants. I wanted to look like everyone else chowing directly into my meal. It takes some maturity to realize that there's no way this food would be on our plates without God's help. Frankly, what others think of me is no longer my concern. Only God's opinion counts.

Harry is not a Christian. I pray for him and am optimistic that he is a work-in-progress along with some of my other co-workers. At work, I try to witness by my actions. Matthew 5:15 is my verse there. "Let your light shine before others, so that they may see your good works and give glory to your Father in heaven." Christians should always be the brightest bulbs. Harry often calls whoever isn't agreeing with him the "dimmest bulb in the pack." Someday I pray he'll see the real Light.

What I'm really trying to say is that Harry has learned to tolerate my praying and not look so embarrassed when I do it. To me, that's progress. Matt, however, gave no indication what he felt about my attitude of gratitude. That's the trouble with people who have impeccable manners—they never let you see them sweat.

Matt and I really connected. He laughed at my jokes and I at his. He winked at me in that conspiratorial way men have with the women they love. Or maybe he had a tic in his eye. How do I know? I'm only describing *my* fantasy here, not his. There were no unwelcome advances, (if I don't count that hand-kissing thing, which was not at all unwelcome) no stupid pick-up lines, no improprieties, only flawless manners and irresistible charm.

When I think of the stupid pick-up lines I've experienced with other men, including, "Excuse me, may I look at the tag on your dress? I'm sure it says 'Made in Heaven,' just like you," there was no way the evening could have been a failure. In fact, the night would have been absolutely perfect if I hadn't had to use the ladies' room.

After eating, I got up to walk a bit, as my jumpsuit had somehow shrunk while hanging in my closet—probably due to the excessive humidity caused by recent rain showers. Anyway, I needed to jiggle the food beyond my waistband, so I excused myself and went for a stroll.

If my mother's famous teaching—"Always use the bathroom when you have the opportunity. You never know when you'll find another"—weren't indelibly engraved in my head, I wouldn't have gotten into trouble.

Still, I learned something, albeit the hard way. Never, *ever* wear a jumpsuit anywhere that you might have to use a rest room. One, you must practically undress to use the facilities. Two (here's where I goofed), you must keep the top half of the suit out of the toilet while you're using it. Actually, only one arm of my suit fell into the water, and that was after I flushed, so it could have been worse—but not much.

I spent five minutes squirming back into the soggy thing and another fifteen with my arm under the hand dryer. I had no idea how slow those things are—no wonder you always come out of the rest room hoping no one notices that you're drying your hands on your clothes.

Anyway, the ridiculousness of the whole situation got the best of me, and I did what I often do under stress. I giggled. And guffawed. And hee-hawed and ho-hoed until my stomach hurt. Every time some innocent lady walked through the bathroom door, it got funnier and funnier until tears were streaming down my face. At one point, there were four of us in there holding our sides and gasping for air. Pretty soon they were telling me all their bathroom stories, too—like getting the hems of their skirts caught in their waistbands, walking through the restaurant and wondering why everyone was staring or dragging a long piece of toilet paper through the room on the heels of their shoes. I made some new friends, but it was the weirdest bonding experience I've ever had.

As I was coming out of the ladies' room with bits of the toilet paper that I'd used to soak up water still sticking to my suit (thousands of polyesters died for this outfit), Harry and Matt were loudly asking a waitress to go in after me.

"...she's been gone a long time...."

"...maybe she isn't feeling well...."

"...you could ask her if she needs help...."

It was *not* my best moment. I've always dreamed of being a damsel in distress saved by a knight in shining armor. Being rescued by a human Chia Pet and a man I had now upgraded to Mr. Cashew because I'd wasted a half hour fishing my clothing out of a toilet was just not the same. I am also positive that this is not what Jesus meant by "All who exalt themselves will be humbled, and all who humble themselves will be exalted." This wasn't humbling. It was humiliating—never mind that in a few years it will be a great story to tell my friends.

For the rest of the evening Harry kept looking at me with beetled brows, as if he expected me to do something ridiculous at any moment. Matt, however, acted as though he knew lots of women who spent time washing clothes in the toilet. Still, at the end of the evening I was thankful to escape, and relieved that Matt didn't offer to drive me home.

September 25

Harry and I couldn't meet each other's eyes today. I was unable to look at his head and he couldn't meet my eyes after the rest-room fiasco. About four o'clock he sauntered past my desk and told me I could "wrap it up" for the day.

I asked him twice if he'd meant what he'd said. He never encourages anyone to leave early. Sometimes I feel like the Bob Cratchitt of the software world.

"Sure. You're going to Las Vegas soon, aren't you? Isn't there something you need to pick up?"

"I could use a few new binders and highlighters," I stammered.

"There you are. See you tomorrow." Then he paused and turned back as if there was something he'd forgotten to mention. I waited for the other shoe to drop.

"By the way, Matt Lambert told me last night that he'd be attending the Las Vegas trade show as a customer." Harry scowled. "I hope he doesn't have any ideas of shopping around and replacing us." He stared at me. "But *you'll* be there to make sure that doesn't happen, right?"

My heart sank into my gut. Was there no justice? Why, after publicly humiliating myself in front of this man, do I ever have to see him again? If Harry thinks I'd be good at preventing Lambert from jumping ship to another company, he wasn't looking very closely last night when Matt gawked at my wet, paper-encrusted arm.

I couldn't go to the bathroom without a disaster. Who knew what might happen when I was sent to Las Vegas, of all places, to save a corporate account?

"Harry, I can't—"

But he would have none of it. "You'd better leave now and get those binders."

Mitzi did not like my leaving before she did. She gave me a scorching glare as I headed for the door. Sailing in late and dashing out early are traditionally her domain, and she was sorely miffed. I smiled widely at her as I left. Kim gave me a thumbs-up as I passed.

I had my paycheck in my pocket and an extra hour in my life. What else was there to do but shop? Unfortunately my sensible gene kicked in before I got to Ann Taylor, so I went to a department store to look for much-needed, long-over-due bedding. I inherited my sheets from my mother, and they're paper-thin in the sunlight. Last night, after tossing and turning over the jumpsuit debacle, I put my toe between the threads and ripped the sheet in half trying to untangle myself. That, combined with a "Got To See It To Believe It" white sale, seemed like a sign. I didn't count, however, on the determination and stamina of women in need of cheap sheets.

They were standing in front of the shelves like gatekeepers, determined not to let anyone past until they had found the perfect white sheet with a faint ribbon of blue running through it. I bent down to pull an interesting-looking bed-in-a-bag ensemble from the bottom shelf and nearly got my fingers crushed.

I'd been too optimistic about this run-in, grab-some-sheets and run-out thing. After twenty-five minutes I'd determined there were no sheets that fit my bed. The bottoms were all fitted kings except for a huge stack of twins. The flat sheets were all regulars but for two queens, one in some orange and yellow design and one in dirt blue and tonsil pink that could have scared the paint off walls. I backed out of my spot disconsolately, and a woman with a designer handbag leaped into my place with the grace of a jaguar. Amazing.

I drove home vowing to sleep on the mattress pad until that ripped, too, after which I would order something off the Internet.

I complained to my mother about my shopping misadventure but, as usual, she couldn't relate. She doesn't buy sheets—she sends Dad out for them. Mother's version of shopping is sailing into what I call the itty-bitty section of the store. She picks out what she wants, slides it over her head to try it on, takes a twirl and pulls out her credit card. She's done shopping and in a coffee shop waiting before I find any two matching pieces in my size, the most popular and picked-over in America—which shall remain unmentioned.

September 27

dep·ri·va·tion: Deficiency, lack, scarcity, withdrawal, need, hardship, distress.

"I thought you were doing something about those snug pants," Mother said with her usual lack of diplomacy when I arrived at their door today.

"I am. Sort of."

"Are you still sneaking around in rubber bands, Whitney?"

"Maybe I'll join a class, something that meets every week and gives me encouragement."

"There's one at church," Mom offered. "I'll go with you if you don't want to go alone the first night."

My diversion hadn't worked. "Mother, you'd be run out of the room. No woman on a diet wants so see an entire human being who's the size of someone's thigh."

She sighed. "All right then, go alone. Here, let me read you the information." She picked up the bulletin, which she'd no doubt kept handy just for this purpose. "'Join us as we gather to support one another in our weight-loss goals, experience fun, fellowship and new recipes. For more information, call—'"

"What's the name of this group?" I interrupted.

"It doesn't say. Maybe they don't have a name. If you went, you could suggest something."

Mother thinks that I should be able to take over any meeting by receiving all the information I need about the entire group by osmosis as I wander through the room on my initial visit. She also believes the well of my creativity is artesian. Strangely enough, however, a name *did* pop into my mind. Ecclesiastical Eaters Anonymous Training. EEAT. If that wasn't the name of this group, it should be. At least that way, when I told someone I was going to EEAT, they'd think I was going out for dinner.

"By the way, Whitney," my mother continued, "your father came home from church council last night with some very exciting news. We're hiring a new youth pastor."

"What's wrong with the other one? Did he outgrow his youth?"

"Don't be flippant, dear. He's staying. Our youth program is expanding so quickly that the council decided we needed a second pastor."

"Super. That's very exciting." I'd chaperoned more than a few sleepovers at the church myself. It's good news that interest is on the rise.

"But that isn't all."

The hairs on the back of my neck began to tingle. Mom had switched tones. She was no longer talking church business.

"He's single."

"Motherrrrrr!"

"And quite nice-looking. I think you'd make a lovely couple."

"Have you discussed this with him yet? Or is the call committee using me as bait?"

"I'm serious, Whitney. This could be your big break."

"Mom, you sound like this man is a job opportunity! Is he taking résumés?"

"Just consider it, dear. You *are* thirty, you know."

"All too well, Mom. All too well."

September 29

I'm already feeling guilty. EEAT met and I didn't go. (No matter what the name of the group, it will always be EEAT to me.) Kim talked me out of it. "Are you kidding? Start a diet when you're leaving for Las Vegas—buffet capital of the world?"

"Maybe it would keep me from falling on my face in a chocolate display and eating my way out," I suggested timidly.

"Nonsense. Start trying to lose weight when you get back. I tried to diet on a cruise once, and my sister found me at the midnight buffet, clinging to a loaf of bread shaped like a swan and whimpering, 'Give me butter and jelly.'"

Smiling, I succumbed to the wisdom of her experience. Still, I will be aware of what I eat at every moment. To do that, I'm leaving my rubber bands at home. There will be no way out.

September 30

Church was great today. I felt so energized and lifted by the music. The typos in the bulletin didn't hurt, either.

There was an announcement about the upcoming Spiritual and Physical Health and Wellness Seminar.

Don't let stress kill—let the church help.
You will hear a top-notch presenter and heave a delicious lunch.

The sermon, however, seemed written for me alone. It was based on the parable of the sower. The parables have always fascinated me. They are so childishly simple and yet so profound that once you understand them, they can rock your world. The sun that melts ice hardens clay. The parables are like that—they have different effects on people, depending on where their hearts are.

I'm blessed that my parents raised me off the path where the seed couldn't root and grow. Nor was I grown in shallow soil that couldn't support my faith. My family and my church offered me rich, dark earth in which to send the roots of my faith downward and grow a system that is firm and healthy. But there's always the danger of weeds springing up to choke out healthy plants and make them die.

It's so easy to be distracted by life—work, money, greed,

busyness—that I'm in danger of forgetting that what I have is to be used for God's causes, not my own. I imagine myself pulling up weeds in my life one by one—the weed of laziness, which prods me to sleep in on Sundays, the weed of ungratefulness, which reminds me of what I don't have rather than what I do, the weed of jealousy, which makes me miserable and cranky—and the weed of greed. That one makes me put my energy into earning money to buy things I don't need to get results I don't want.

Put weeding my heart on my goal list—to be done often and with thoroughness.

As we were singing our closing hymn today, it occurred to me that Christians are economical with the truth when they sing. As I sat in the pew paging through the hymnal, I began to read the words of the hymns. I mean, to *really* read them....

"Where He leads me I will follow..." Sometimes He leads us through deep water and we resist—big-time.

"I lay my sins on Jesus..." But we keep picking them up again.

Or "I surrender all...." *All?* That's a pretty inclusive word. From now on, I'm going to sing those words and mean it.

OCTOBER

CHAPTER 3

October 3

I've never decided which I like less, packing or flying. I'm green with envy over those sleek, designer-clad, *Vogue*-toting businesswomen, who, after dropping off their Hermès luggage at the counter, walk nonchalantly to the gate, onto the plane and into the first-class section without ruffling a hair. I bring every possibility with me. The weather may be bad and I may not fit into the wardrobe I'd planned. Then again, the clothes may fit after all and maybe I'll have time to exercise/run/shop/lie by the pool. My logic is that I'll make my decisions once I get to my destination. *And,* because I want to be comfortable on the trip, I chug into the airport in tennis shoes, linen draw-string pants and an unstructured jacket, dragging the largest suitcase made, its little wheels splaying outward from the weight inside. I also have a large shoulder bag filled with all the reading and work I plan to get done while I'm gone.

Since I'll be in a new environment, I assume that I'll be able to do heroic things, so I bring everything from magazines dated six months prior, to recipes I want to recopy on cute cards and put into a matching book. That's particularly interesting, because I rarely cook. There are also the sixteen letters I need to write, those three books that are almost due at the library and the cuticle emollient I'm planning to wear to bed every night until my hangnail is history. And my purse—with PalmPilot, cell phone, gum, breath mints, emery board, lipstick, package of powdered diet shake, apple… It isn't pretty. And that's not even considering the condition of my linen suit by the time I arrive at my destination looking like an unmade bed.

And I'm even worse at flying—at least, I used to be. Every noise was a wheel falling off. Every takeoff or landing was a walk to the gas chamber. If flying is so safe, I wondered, why do we have to come and go from a *terminal?*

It wasn't until I could visualize God in control of my life wherever I am, on the ground or in the air, but always cupped in the palm of His hand, that I conquered my fear. If He can keep the sun and the moon up in the heavens, then He can handle a little old airplane.

I trundled through to first class, and as I searched for my seat got a major surprise.

"Whit! Hey, Whitney!" It was Eric. The lady behind me bowled into me with her carry-on, and I stumbled into Eric's otherwise empty row.

"What are *you* doing here?" I greeted him. Dressed in tailored trousers and a polo shirt, Eric looked downright handsome. Immediately realizing I may have sounded less than gracious, I amended, "I mean, hi."

"Hi, yourself. Dad called yesterday," Eric explained. "He bought me a ticket to fly to Las Vegas to meet him for an air show. It's only vintage planes and will be so cool. They're having 1941 deHavilland Tiger Moths—both the Canadian and

Australian models, a 1946 Piper J-3 and a Piper '37 J-2. Piper discontinued that model in 1937." A light dawned in his hazel eyes. "And you're going to a trade show." His expression brightened. "I can get you a ticket to the air show if you have time. You'd love it."

"Thanks, but I've got to work. By the time I get done manning the Innova booth and contacting clients, I'll be a zombie." My hip bumped against my carry-on. "And I brought work from home."

"Dinner then?"

"Sure, sounds good." Then I eyed him suspiciously. "You *will* remember that you asked me, right?"

"Aw, Whitney, are you ever going to let me live that down? So I've been late a few times...."

"Three months late?"

"I meant to call. You know that. I was helping a buddy restore a plane. The money was good, and I just got so engrossed...."

As always, my heart softened. No doubt Eric slept on a cot at night to be near the plane and ate every meal out of a take-out carton and was completely true-blue. I knew he wasn't seeing anyone else. He just wasn't seeing *me,* either. If anything with wings passed by, he was off trailing that.

"Okay, I forgive you. We'll have dinner. But no mushy stuff. I want you as a friend. You're far too unreliable for anything else."

He seemed delighted by the idea. "Friends?"

"Friends." I glanced around the almost-full plane. "I'd better go find my place."

"What's your seat number?"

"Row twenty, seat B."

"Welcome. I'm seat A." He patted the chair beside him, and I dropped into it gratefully. Then he turned and looked me straight in the eye. "And, someday, maybe, if things work out, could we renegotiate that friend thing?"

My stomach did a little flip-flop. I knew what he was asking and it scared me. Why, I wasn't sure. Maybe it was because I knew how easy it would be to love Eric. He saw the deer-in-headlights look in my eyes and drew back.

"Never mind. Just friends."

I couldn't say for sure, but I'm ninety percent positive he added under his breath, "For now."

As we walked out of the Las Vegas terminal, waves of heat shimmered up from the concrete. I felt as if I'd stepped into a life-size toaster oven. The linen I didn't think could wilt any further did, like a lettuce leaf in boiling water. My shoulder-length hair is thick and heavy. (Mom calls it my "crowning glory.") Unfortunately I didn't put it up for the trip, and as soon as I hit the heat, it clung to my neck and forehead, making me look as though someone had dumped a glass of water on my head. I was not in great shape to see Eric's father, who was there to pick him up.

Mr. Van Horne is the polar opposite of his son. Eric is casual, wears his light brown hair just a tad longer than normal, so he always looks like he has bed-head, shops only at the GAP and believes God would have done us all a favor if we were simply *born* wearing tennis shoes. His dad wore black trousers, a white shirt and a camel-colored jacket that oozed expensive. His hair was styled, his shoes polished to a high gloss and I'm almost positive his nails had been professionally manicured. Eric and his father did, however, share the same boyish charm.

Unfortunately, they didn't share the same taste in automobiles. Eric drives a ten-year-old Jeep with cargo room for an entire apartment. His dad drives a brand-new BMW meant to hold nothing more than a briefcase and golf clubs.

How humiliating. My luggage appeared larger than the car by which it was piled. But never underestimate a man. Thanks to good breeding, excellent manners and a lot of grunting, groaning and pushing, they got it inside the car and were still smiling.

"Here you are." Mr. Van Horne pulled around the spouting volcano to drop me off at the front door of my hotel.

"I'll call you and we'll set a time for dinner." Eric patted the piece of paper in his pocket containing my phone number.

Then they left me to the perils of Sin City. How dangerous could it be, surrounded as I was with what looked like the entire population of the Midwest? Grandpas, grandmas, mothers pushing strollers and fathers carrying toddlers swarmed around me like locusts as I made my way to the reception desk. I tried to count how many fanny packs I saw and finally decided it would be easier to count the people who *didn't* have them on.

I tipped the bellhop double for hauling my weighty bags to my room, a cavernous arena with a great tub and blackout curtains. With room service, I wouldn't have to leave for a month—if the trade show weren't such an interruption, of course. I flung myself onto the bed to make sure the mattress was up to my standards and debated the question of showering and changing before or after I checked on how the booth setup was progressing. Occasionally the people I hire to help me with logistics don't show up on time and I'm stuck doing it alone. Not showering and changing clothes first was, of course, the totally wrong decision.

I put the final touches on the trade-show booth—the laptop that would give my PowerPoint presentation, a bouquet of flowers just for color and a dish of imported chocolates in case some of the participants needed an extra incentive to hang around my booth. If I'd been thinking about my diet, I would have given away toothbrushes.

Hot, I'd mopped my forehead on my arm—makeup and all—tied my hair back with a piece of string I'd found in one of the shipping boxes and removed my shoes when Matt Lambert found me.

"So you *are* here! Harry told me you would be."

I spilled a bottle of water on my lap and tried to dissolve into the floor, but unlike the Wicked Witch of the West, I discovered liquid did nothing for me. "Oh, hi, Matt. What a surprise to see you!" I'll bet he was surprised to see *me,* too, especially looking like something drooping off the end of a fishing line.

But he never flinched. What a great guy. What élan, what sophistication, what finesse, what…was he blind?

He *must* have selective vision, because he asked me out for dinner. Since the show was only open for a couple hours that evening and the big event really started the next day, I jumped at the chance. If I could pull myself together and show him that I didn't always look like a bag lady, I could trade in my rumpled image for something more…dare I say it?…glamorous.

"It's three in the afternoon. I have to be here from seven to nine, but I'm free after that."

"I'll be here at nine. I know just the place we can eat. There's a little French hideaway within walking distance." He gave me a look that was half James Bond and half Indiana Jones and that made my fingertips tingle…then he was gone. Okay, so maybe my imagination was on overdrive and my hand had fallen asleep, but what's the fun in that?

The hotel spa was full, so I settled for a shower, an hour ironing the crumpled clothes in my suitcase and a bag of pretzels from the hotel minifridge for which I would pay a minifortune when my bill arrived.

The first time Kim stayed at a hotel that provided stocked refrigerators, she assumed everything was free and decided to eat it all. She's almost got the loan paid off on the hotel bill.

My hair still wrapped in a towel, I sat down to leave messages for clients with whom I needed to touch base. I'd just hung up from the last call when my phone rang. It was the salon. A masseuse had had a cancellation. If I still wanted to have a massage, she could bring a table to me. The luxury was irresistible. My mouth said "yes, yes" as my checkbook screamed "no, no." As usual with me, the mouth won.

A tiny woman arrived toting a portable massage table and a gym bag full of towels, oils and a tiny CD player. Practically before I could say "Come in," she had everything set up and music playing. Discreetly she turned her back as I slid under the sheets and lay back with a deep sigh.

"Do you like a light massage or deep?"

I gave her the once-over. She was smaller than my mother and looked less robust. "Deep," I said, wanting my money's worth.

And, oh boy, did I get it. Looks are deceiving. I was a loaf of bread being kneaded, a meat loaf being pounded into shape, a potato being squeezed through a ricer. While my masseuse had looked a little like David with his unobtrusive slingshot when she'd walked into the room, she massaged like Goliath.

When she left me lying on the table while she went into the bathroom to wash her hands, I took my thumb and index finger and pried open one eye. My muscles refused to go back to work. Eventually I slithered to a chair and sprawled there until the masseuse returned.

"Feeling better?" she asked. "Be sure to drink lots of water tonight."

I nodded and handed her a check with a large tip, my "mad" money for the rest of the month. But I rationalized that I'd be too limp to go shopping for a couple weeks anyway.

The show was typical of such events, with somber businessmen and computer geeks roaming the aisles. As closing time neared, I saw Matt strolling down the aisle toward me. I recalled the old commercials where a man and a woman run toward each other across a vast field in slow motion, arms out, faces blissful, eyes locked in a gaze of love. But Matt

wasn't running in slow motion or in a field or looking blissful. He did, however, have me in an eye-lock that made my
heart pound. The man was *gorgeous.*

"You look lovely," he complimented me.

Anything was an improvement over this afternoon.

"I hope you like French food," he said as we entered a darkened cavern lit with flickering candles. I nodded, but he probably couldn't see me in the shadows. He led me, stumbling,
to our table. I've never been good about entering a movie theater after the feature's begun, and this was no different. Blind
as a bat was not how I'd wanted to start the evening.

My eyes finally grew accustomed to the dimness, and I
began to appreciate the opulence of my surroundings. Even
more, I prized the play of light and dark on Matt's features
that made him appear craggy, manly and very French. I
pinched my thigh as my hand rested on my lap. Was this for
real, or had the masseuse sent too much blood to my brain?

Matt and the waiter had a spirited conversation in French.
I knew he was ordering our meal, because I heard the only
two French words I know—*escargots* and *pâté.* Snails and
liver, the two things I was most terrified of as a child. When
he took my hand, however, and looked into my eyes, I decided that eating bottom feeders and giblets was a small price
to pay to spend an evening with this man.

I was pretty pulled together for the encounter, if I do say
so myself. My hair went the direction I'd aimed it, my dress
still fit after dinner and even though I hadn't anticipated a show
of affection, I didn't burst out laughing when he kissed me.
It was just a gentle peck on my forehead, but I hadn't expected
it (fantasized, maybe—expected it, no). If I didn't get a single
client nibble this trip, it still would be a roaring success.

Clients. Falling under Matt's influence almost made me forget why I was here. I retrieved voice messages and wrote
notes to every potential or current client in the hotel to con-

firm our appointments, took a steamy bath that used up all the bath bubbles in my little complementary basket and oiled my cuticles.

Lord, thank You for safe travel, my job, my family and my friends. I pray for our country's leaders and for those people I read about in the headlines of the newspaper. Sometimes the haunted eyes of those hurting people stay with me for days. I may be flippant at times, but I know for sure that believing in You is a life-and-death issue. I ask that You touch the heart of every unbeliever so that they may know You as I do.

And, although it seems a pretty shallow request compared to the last, I pray for wisdom. I'm thirty years old and falling under my mother's questionable influence. She wants me happy but she also wants me married. Is there a fabulous, Christian man out there for me, Lord? And when You send him, will You put a big label on him, please, so I don't miss him?

With thankfulness that I have You to talk to,
Whitney

October 7

Today was a blur. I had breakfast, morning coffee, late-morning coffee, lunch, early afternoon coffee and late-afternoon coffee with clients while intermittently checking on the booth. The rest of the time I spent in the bathroom relieving myself of all that coffee. I drummed up enough business, however, to keep Harry happy into the next century. I feel a bonus coming on.

I found time to buy souvenirs for everyone, including the most spangled, outrageous T-shirt I could find—studded with rhinestones and in electric blue. Kim will love it, especially since I got a baby-size one for Wesley in the same color. I looked for a long time before I found something for Mom and Dad and finally settled on matching T-shirts that said His and Hers. Each has an arrow pointing across the shirt, supposedly to the person standing alongside you. It will give them something to do, trying to figure out if they have their arrows pointed in the right direction. I didn't recall until later that there have been a number of recent examples of Dad's trying not to claim Mom at all. Hopefully she'll start leaving that little battery-operated fan at home when they wear the shirts.

Unfortunately, the evening did not go as smoothly as the rest of the day. I'd forgotten how territorial men could be, mostly because it never happens to me—until Eric and Matt faced off in the lobby outside the show.

While waiting for Eric near the exit, I was surprised to see Matt also approaching.

"Whitney, I know this is spur of the moment, but I was wondering if you'd like to have dinner at Spago? Sorry I didn't ask you sooner, but my schedule…" Matt held his hands out helplessly. "I'm sure it's been equally busy for you today."

"Hiya, Whit. Ready for dinner?" Eric gave Matt the once-over, and his eyes narrowed.

"Eric, I'd like you to meet Matthew Lambert. Matt, this is Eric…."

I explained as best I could that Eric and I had made plans on the plane. Matt said, "I understand. It was nice to meet you, Eric," and if he'd just stopped there, we'd have been okay. Unfortunately he added, "At least we had *last night* together" in a breathy voice that made Eric's eyebrows go straight up into the thatch of sandy-brown hair tumbling over his forehead.

I didn't know Eric had a jealous bone in his body. Apparently he has quite a few, and Matt managed to bruise them all. For the rest of the night, he studied me like a bug under a microscope, as if amazed that I had enough pheromones to attract anyone but him.

There were a dozen roses in my room when I returned and a note from Matt saying "Sorry we couldn't talk business tonight—catch you later." Later, room service arrived with a large pepperoni pizza. "From somebody named Eric," the waiter said. "He told me he wanted you to have this in the morning because he knows cold pizza is your favorite breakfast."

How could I ever choose between two men who know me as well as that?

October 9

Not one moment to myself today. My bladder is feeling flabby from being stretched to the max. Had most of a pot of coffee for breakfast and didn't get to the ladies' room until noon. Oh, the pain.

I leave the hotel tomorrow at 5:00 a.m. No time to see either Matt or Eric again. It's probably for the best. I can't face either one quite yet, since I have no idea what's going on in their minds—or in my own.

October 10

Up at 3:30 a.m., in the air at seven, into the office by eleven, manic by lunchtime. No one could accuse me of not jumping right into an office frame-of-mind upon my return.

Mitzi gave me a dirty look as I entered, as if I'd been on vacation instead of working 24/7. Betty peered at me through those half-glasses middle-aged people who insist they don't really need glasses use and told me in an accusing tone that I'd let mail stack up on my desk. And the cruelest cut of all, Bryan, sadist that he is, produced a large, heavy bond envelope addressed to me in calligraphy scrolls and embellished with a wax seal and one of those "Love" stamps that sell by the millions around Valentine's Day and during the bridal season.

"Wipe that smirk off your face, Bryan," I ordered, immediately out-of-sorts, "or I'm going to ask you to be my escort to this wedding. Then you'll be the one having to dance with Whitney dressed as a human omelette in egg-yolk yellow satin and dyable shoes straight from the Marquis de Sade collection."

Fear flickered on his face and he tried to retrieve the wedding invitation, but it was too late. He'd already made my shortlist of potential escorts.

Why couldn't my friend Leah Carlson, who'd worked with the rest of us in this office until she'd earned parole, have had her bridesmaids wear something black and slinky? Wasn't that the fashion now? Of course, Leah had an insecure streak, and in order to make sure that, as the bride, she was not outshone by anyone else, she'd made sure the rest of us looked utterly ridiculous, with puffy sleeves and large straw hats laden with silk flowers, ribbons and probably a resident parakeet. The only thing that cheered me about this designer fiasco was that Kim was also in the wedding, and she insisted that she looked even worse in yellow than I did. Misery *does* love company. So do women who are forced to look like chubs of butter rolling down an aisle.

"Need to get out for lunch?" Kim smiled knowingly at the invitation in my hand and tipped her head toward the door. "I'll buy."

"One lettuce leaf, one stalk of celery, one cherry tomato and water with a slice of lemon so thin as to be transparent, please."

"I thought you were going to cut back. Doesn't a cherry tomato have a calorie or two? Have you considered what it will do to your thighs?"

"Har, har, *so* not funny." We went into the little luncheonette two doors down from our office building and I ordered "the usual" without opening my menu. Sad, isn't it, when every waitress on every shift knows my "usual." Of course, it's not that hard to remember a house salad and a slice of dry toast.

"Other than the dress, are you excited about the wedding?" Kim, ever the optimist, assumed such a thing was possible.

"My mother has offered to make me a queen-size quilt of all the bridesmaids' dresses I've ever worn. I'm sad to say she already has enough fabric to do the quilt *and* shams. This wedding will provide enough ugly fabric for the bed skirt."

Kim leaned down to sip her Coke from the straw and looked up at me through her long, dark eyelashes. "This is not totally about the dress, you know."

"I do know. It's those torture implements they call shoes. They'll dye them yellow, I'll wear them until my eyes water and my feet blister and turn color. Then I'll kick them off, destroy my nylons and have my toe broken by Leah's four-hundred-pound uncle at the reception. And she wants us to put our hair up. Kim, I'll look like Marie Antoinette!"

"It really bugs you that she's getting married and you haven't got a glimmer, doesn't it?"

I hate it when she does that. Am I that transparent?

"I didn't think so, but between this wedding and my mother's fixation on marrying me off, I guess I'm a little sensitive right now." The waitress came by with my house salad with a side of dry toast. "It's crazy, too, because I've had more male attention in the past week than in the past four months."

Kim listened with rapt attention as I told her my Eric/Matthew experiences in Las Vegas.

"What do you make of it?" she probed.

"Absolutely nothing. I can't figure out what's going on."

"Because one man likes you, you've become more interesting to all the others—at least until you commit to one and take yourself out of the market."

I really do believe that someday God will send a man into my life. I just hope that when he arrives, I won't be too old to recognize him.

October 15

Mitzi must go. Away. Far, far away. Soon.

Annoying, maddening, irritating, infuriating, exasperating, trying, aggravating, frustrating, irksome, grating, galling, vexing. It's so hard to decide which word describes her best. She is the burr under the saddle of my life, the twist in my undies, the mosquito trapped in my bedroom that won't let me sleep.

She's always most exasperating the week she receives her women's-magazine subscriptions. That's when she brushes up on what's new, cool and trendy in the world and distills it into a *Cliff's Notes* kind of report meant to either a) shame us into getting with the program or b) just shame us. She's a pop-psychology junkie and living breathing proof that a little knowledge is a dangerous thing. She has very little knowledge, all of it dangerous.

This morning she greeted me with the words, "You can't have it all, you know."

"I don't want it all. I just want my coffee, black."

"You know what I mean. You'll have to give up something in life in order to devote time and energy to what is most important to you. Obviously you've given up meaningful, loving relationships with the opposite sex and the chance at a family in order to stay at this midlevel schlepping job."

Now try that one on before you've had coffee!

"You've said 'yes' to being a lonely, pathetic single woman with a job that cannot fulfill you completely and 'no' to having the love of a man and the joy of children in your life."

Really? I had no idea. I thought it was "yes" to earning a living and "no" to jumping into bad relationships just so I could have a man on my arm.

"Which magazines came yesterday, Mitzi? *Depression Digest? Deadbook? Failures Illustrated* and *Family Triangle?*"

"Don't mock me, Whitney. You could learn a great deal from keeping up on the latest trends and polls. Why, do you even know that carbohydrates are out again?" She gave me the once-over. "Obviously not."

"What's this leading up to, Mitzi? You've got something on your mind." I could see Bryan making his way to the rest room and Betty Nobel sitting a little straighter, her nose twitching with interest.

Mitzi pushed a photocopied page from a magazine across the desk toward me. The headline blared at me like a demented trumpet: Are You Doomed To Be A Spinster? Under it was a quiz, dolled up in graphics of cartwheeling brides and one forlorn damsel sitting on an upturned briefcase. That, no doubt, was me.

"Thanks, Mitzi, but no thanks. I'm not even sure why you're more upset about my being single than *I* am."

She shook her head at me as if to say, "Poor, deluded darling," and pushed on the quiz until I picked it up.

Mission accomplished, Mitzi turned back to her computer and brought up the diet program on the Web into which she fed her list of foods consumed yesterday. With a few clicks, she had the calorie count, fat grams, fiber content and a tally of which vitamins and minerals she was low on that day. Come to think of it, I can't really remember the last time I've seen Mitzi do anything that resembled work. But apparently she types a million words a minute, because Harry keeps her around.

I stuffed the quiz in my pocket, poured myself a cup of coffee, watered my plants, checked my e-mail and then went to knock on the men's bathroom door. Bryan must have fallen asleep in there, or he would have heard that Mitzi and I had avoided a confrontation. I was right. When he stumbled out, there was a flat pink spot on his cheek where he'd laid his head against the side of the stall. I gave him a list of things I needed done and turned my attention to touching base with potential customers I'd collected at the trade show.

For a long time, I ignored the hole being burned in my pocket before I furtively took out the ridiculous survey on single women. By spreading it out on my desk with a half-dozen other magazine articles on Innova software, it seemed to blend right in. One by one, I read the questions:

WILL YOU MARRY OR ARE YOU SINGLE FOR LIFE?

Which is more important to you?
- an IRA
- PMS
- MSG

(Depends on whether I'm in a Chinese restaurant or not.)

What is your most important undergarment?
- A push-up bra
- A body shaper
- Full cut panties large enough to cover those supreme pizzas you eat alone on weekends

(No contest there.)

What is your favorite store?
- Victoria's Secret
- Ann Taylor
- GAP
- Banana Republic
- Relax the Back
- The Hemorrhoid Shop

(I have to choose just one when all six are so appealing?)

What is your favorite dog?
- A neurotic dog that weighs less than five pounds, wears bows in its fur, eats only off your plate and can pierce eardrums with its bark
- A black Lab, the son of the son of the son of your beloved childhood pet
- A glistening Doberman that salivates at the sight of cats, rabbits and short men

(Hmmmm…)

What is your favorite food?
- Yogurt pops
- Sugar-free breath mints
- Endive
- A favorite? How can anyone pick just one?

(What, no éclairs?)

What is your favorite novel?
- The latest Chick Lit on the racks
- Teach Yourself Pilates
- The History of Elizabeth I: Look Ma, No Man!

(I see they forgot "How to Cook Nutritiously for One.")

What is your favorite flower?
- Roses—by the dozen
- Bird-of-Paradise
- Violets—in those cute little plastic-lined baskets like Grandma used to have

(Violets. Definitely violets. Ha!)

What do you think about cats?
- Sneaky snakes with feet and fur
- Actually tiny women in little fur coats
- You simply can't have too many

(I like the little-women theory. It explains a lot.)

What's your most useful kitchen tip?
- Too many ice cubes make a smoothie watery
- Don't use regular dish soap in lieu of dishwasher detergent
- Alphabetizing spices makes cooking so much more pleasant

(I've experienced the first two. Hope never to know the truth about the third.)

What is your attitude toward computers?
- How did my parents and grandparents live without them?
- I buy everything from groceries to clothing online
- Highly overrated

(Finally, a question I could answer with complete honesty! I love my computer.)

What is your favorite pastime?
- Spending a day at the beach
- Cooking gourmet meals
- Shopping
- Reviewing those articles I cut out of magazines and put into plastic sleeves for future reference

(Definitely not tanning. I'm a fake-bake girl myself.)

What do you consider your personal fashion statement?
- Black. I only wear black
- Those catchy little designer purses that cost an arm and a leg but are definitely worth it
- I'm still using my 1999 fashion statement. The clothing hasn't worn out yet.

I threw the paper down on my desk and snarled. So what if I haven't had a new wardrobe for a while? I love the clothes I bought in '99. What's so bad about that? Still, for some reason the dumb thing was a little unsettling.

CHAPTER 4

October 16

"Whitney, Whit!" Kim's voice was low and urgent. She looked into my office with eyes the size of saucers. "Can we have lunch?"

"Of course. Don't we always?" Her color resembled the ream of copy paper on my desk—whiter than white. "What's wrong?"

She glanced around before answering. "We'll talk then."

"Where do you want to go?"

"Someplace private. Emilio's, maybe. Or the steak house across the street."

I knew immediately that something was seriously wrong. Kim *never* spends big money on lunch. She prefers to buy toys and clothing for Wesley with her disposable income. To suggest the dark, private booths of Emilio's or the steak house, which has a very small lunch crowd and a very hefty price list, told me that whatever it was Kim had to say, it needed to be said in private.

We waited until one o'clock when the lunch crowd was ebbing. There were plenty of booths and Kim requested the most secluded. Initially, she'd babbled nonstop about Wesley's latest venture. Not only has he discovered he's a boy but he's taken to checking every so often to make sure that his status hadn't changed. It's becoming embarrassing to Kim and Kurt. I told her it was only a phase, but thought to myself that there was no way *I'd* want to take that child out in public until he discovered something else to play with—like Tonka trucks or Matchbox cars.

She was decidedly not herself. When she talked, her voice bordered on the hysterical. Then she lapsed into deep dense silences that nothing I said would penetrate. I was beginning to feel a bit panicked myself by the time we'd ordered and we were alone in our little corner of Emilio's.

"Okay, what's up?"

"Something happened this morning."

"You and Kurt?" I prepared myself to be shocked. Kim rarely complains about her husband other than that perhaps he's *too* laid-back. To think of them fighting blew my mind. Kurt is as faithful to Kim as the day is long, so it couldn't be lipstick on his collar. He's also very meticulous, so I doubted she'd discovered that the trash hadn't been taken out on collection day.

"No, he'd already gone to work when I found it."

"Found what?"

"A lump in my breast." Her voice was a strangled whisper.

I opened my mouth to speak but nothing came out. Perhaps that was fortunate, as anything I might have said would have sounded trite or placating. A cold sweat washed over me and I stammered, "A doctor…have you…"

"I'm getting a mammogram after work. They squeezed me in."

Squeezed. My irrepressible and unruly sense of humor jumped in the driver's seat of my brain. How appropriate to be *squeezed* in for that particular test. Shock and denial do strange things to one's mind.

"I'll see the doctor in the morning. Someone Kurt knew years ago."

"That's quick," I managed to say, searching for words that would comfort Kim even though I knew there were none. She'd have to see this through and take it one day at a time.

"He said he didn't want me to have to wait and worry over the results."

"I didn't know doctors worked like that anymore."

"He's special. Kurt knew him in high school and says he's always been thoughtful and caring. Besides, he said it would save me a lot of stress if everything is fine, and if it isn't—" I saw her choke back her panic "—then we should be getting into action anyway."

Kim looked at me bravely, and then, in slow motion, I saw the bravery dissolve into something more elemental. "Oh, Whitney, what about Wesley? He's just a baby. I want to see him grow up."

"Wait a minute. You've gone from finding a lump in your breast to making Wesley grow up without a mother, and completely leaped over the fact that it might be nothing or, if it is something, that it can be treated. Wouldn't it be better not to assume the worst?"

She scrubbed at her eyes and took a breath. At that moment the waiter appeared with our sandwiches…er…sandwich. The plan was for me to eat half the sandwich. Kim was to have the other half and the fries. Being a stress eater, I had five fries in my mouth before I remembered the arrangement.

"You're right, of course." She dumped ketchup on a plate between us. "You keep me sane. That's why you have to go with me for my appointment and my mammogram."

Huh?

"I've already told Betty that I'd be gone and that it was important for you to be with me. My appointment is at ten. We'll be back at work by noon."

"We will?"

"Betty wanted to know what it was about, but I told her that I wasn't free to discuss it yet. Paranoid as she is, I think she believes we're going on some sort of covert mission for Harry. I don't want to go into it until I know something. I'm hoping tomorrow to tell her I had a false alarm."

"What about Kurt? Don't you want *him* to go with you?"

"He has class—a big test that he can't miss. Besides, the nurse had to help him twice in my room during labor. By the time Wesley was actually born, Kurt was sitting in a chair breathing into a paper bag. Having him with me wouldn't be much of a comfort."

A comfort. "Kim, we've got to pray."

"I haven't stopped since I found this thing. I was in the shower. I usually do my exam on the first of the month, but somehow it just slipped by me this time...."

I'd never seen her so upset. Kim is often my strength, the one who reminds me that everything works out, that no matter how bleak things might look, God is still in control. Now it's my turn.

I took her hands in mine and felt her fingers trembling. We prayed silently, knowing God could hear us no matter what the volume.

As we escaped the dark walls of the restaurant, it was as though I'd stepped into an alternate universe. Granted, it had been dim inside Emilio's, but it wasn't the light that made me blink, it was the color. Everything seemed so much brighter than when we'd gone inside. A glossy golden retriever wearing a vivid blue collar and leash walked by carrying a bright red ball in his teeth. His master, a college-age man, did a little shuffling dance step to the music on his headphones. I could hear snippets of music as he passed. The sky was cerulean blue and a woman in a lime-green jacket and a black skirt almost bumped into me in the crosswalk. What was going on?

Then it hit me. Leaving Emilio's had been like walking out of a womb and into a reality I was suddenly seeing through new eyes. I had been rudely reminded of the fragility and unpredictability of life. No matter how much planning for and dreaming about the future we did—Wesley's high-school graduation, the size eight jeans hanging in my closet, the end of Mother's menopause—all we had was now, and we were fools not to enjoy every moment of it: the colors, the sounds, the people.

The afternoon went slowly. I kept glancing at Kim, who had her gaze determinedly fixed on the papers on her desk. But, eventually, time has to pass. I didn't have to look up from my desk to know when it was five o'clock. I felt the whoosh of moving air as Mitzi moved by me on her way to the door. Whoever says humans can't travel at the speed of light has not worked with Mitzi. (It isn't that she *works* fast, it's just that she *leaves* fast.)

Now, I'm not all that crazy about mammograms myself, but I recently had a baseline done. My dad's sister had breast cancer years ago and my doctor recommended it. My mother didn't help a bit. She likened the test to lying on a cold concrete garage floor and having someone drive over the targeted area with the wheel of an automobile. My attitude was not good going in, but as it turned out, everything went fine.

To my dismay, Kim didn't want me to leave her side. I knew she was going to be fine as soon as I saw the hot-water bottle warming the X-ray equipment. These people knew what they were doing. Fortunately, the nurse shooed me back into the hall before the actual procedure.

As I paced back and forth in front of the door, an incredibly good-looking blond man in a dark suit, crisp white shirt and, incongruously, a Popeye and Olive Oyl cartoon tie, walked up to me.

"Is something wrong? Can I help you?" He looked so genuinely concerned that I actually felt tears scratching at the backs of my eyes, the tears I'd wanted to cry for Kim and didn't dare.

"No. My friend is having a mammogram and we're both a little nervous, that's all."

"I see." And I believe he actually did. "If either of you needs anything, just say so."

Frantically, I searched my mind for something, anything, I needed. Of course I came up blank.

"I hope your friend's test turns out well." His eyes were a kind of inky yet brilliant blue, like a brand-new crayon fresh from a box of sixty-four—indigo, I think. When he smiled, gentle, pleasant lines radiated from the corners. The term "golden boy" must have been coined for this guy. But before I could think of something intelligent to say, he tipped his head and turned away.

I wondered if he was an administrator at the clinic—he was definitely a great asset to public relations. But what did I know? Most everything I know about health I've learned from my mother, the medical encyclopedia of misinformation.

The door opened and Kim appeared next to me. "Hi."

"Hi, yourself. How was it?"

"Fine. Easy. It would have been a breeze if I could quit conjuring up worst-case scenarios." She sighed. "I asked the technician how things looked, and she said the doctor would tell me. I wouldn't have asked her if I wanted to wait for that. Don't tell me she hasn't looked at enough of those things to see what's going on in there."

"Think of it this way," I soothed her, "by noon tomorrow, you will have seen the doctor and this will be over."

"I hope so," Kim said gloomily. It was weird, but I felt chilled all the way to my bones as she spoke, as if she knew something I didn't.

Feeling troubled, I decided to stop at my parents' house. My dad is always able to calm me down when I'm upset. It's his quiet, self-effacing way, the mild-mannered exterior of a man with so much wisdom and love for me that I choke up just thinking about it.

Dad was in the yard. He'd paused with his hands resting on the top of his rake to look out at the flower garden. When he saw me drive up, his face broke into a grin. I felt better immediately.

"Hi, Daddy, how's it going?"

For once he didn't just say, "Fine."

"I had to get outside for a bit. It's a little—" he paused for just the right word "—'twitchy' in there."

"That's a new one."

"Your mother never ceases to amaze."

"What's she up to now?"

"Oh, she's looking for the money I gave her to buy herself some new clothes."

"What do you mean, 'looking for'?"

"She put it someplace 'safe,' somewhere no robber would think to look."

"Uh-oh."

"Apparently *no* one would think to look in her hiding place—including her. So far she's been through all the drawers, three closets and half the kitchen with no luck. If she doesn't locate it by bedtime, I may have to sleep at your house. She's not going to stop until she finds it."

"What if it's lost forever?"

I'm almost positive he shuddered.

"Tough week?" I asked with all the sympathy I could muster, which was plenty. "Has Mom been moody?"

He rolled his eyes.

"Snappish?"

"Like a turtle."

"Unfocused?"

"Have you been eavesdropping on us, Whitney?"

"No, but I do read women's magazines. There isn't one in existence that isn't discussing the topic. You know how it was for Grandma when she was in what she euphemistically called 'The Change.'" There had been apocryphal stories about that time whispered around the family for years.

I rubbed his shoulders and was surprised at how small he felt. When I was a little girl, he was a giant...and now he's just a man.

Dad and I were walking arm in arm toward the house when Mother burst through the front door waving a wet Baggie full of money.

"I found it! Oh, Frank, aren't you glad?" She was panting a little, and her hair looked as if it had been electrified, but it occurred to me how attractive my mom is. If she hadn't been my mother, I would have marveled at how young she looks. As it is, I take her for granted much too often.

"Why is it in a Baggie? And why is it wet?"

"You know I wanted to put it where no one would think to look for it. It was a stroke of genius, really. I bagged it up and put it inside the toilet tank. It's been there all along. All I have to do is dry it out a little, and I can go shopping...."

"You put it in the *toilet?*" my dad said.

"Not the bowl, Frank, the tank. No one would think to look there!"

"Including you, Mom."

"I'm good, aren't I?"

We followed Mom to the house and watched her dry her money with a hair dryer. As we talked, I told them my news. They were very upset about Kim as well, but Mom tried to accentuate the positive.

"This is a disease that can be caught in time now," she assured me. "Why, there must be a dozen or more women at church who have had breast cancer and are doing marvelously today."

"I know, but that doesn't make it less scary. And, of course, Kim thinks of Wesley."

"I'll notify our prayer chains at church and bring it up at Bible study," Mom promised. "The couples' group is meeting at the Bakersfields' tonight."

Dad perked up. "Really? Isn't she the one who makes peach pie?"

"Yes, dear, and she said she was having a light supper beforehand, so don't start snacking now."

Dad's face relaxed considerably. I wasn't sure if his improved mood was the result of Mom's finding the money or the thought of pie on the horizon, but I was happy for him either way.

October 17

Kim's clinic isn't far from the office. It sits near a manmade pond, and the lawns are manicured to perfection. I've heard a great plastic surgeon has offices here. She won't admit it, but I think Mitzi has already started getting things lifted and tucked. I know for sure that Betty has. No one's eyebrows should ride that high on a person's forehead. If she were bald, she could just let them grow and comb them backward for hair. And Betty has this continually surprised look that makes her look like a wide-eyed kid at the circus.

I was so busy looking at the artwork on the walls (original, I think) and the cherry-wood furnishings that looked a thousand percent better than anything in my living room, that it took me a moment to realize Kim's name had been called. She took my sleeve in her hand and tugged frantically.

"Kim, I can't go in with you!"

"I'm not going if you don't," she said, and she meant it. "Listen, Whitney, I can't do this alone."

"Kurt should be with you."

"If this is serious, he'll get plenty of chances."

If the tables were turned, I'd want someone there with me. Someone other than my mother, I think. Unless I could get her to quit reading medical books. If a side effect of a medication is shortness of breath or growing hair on one's chest, Mom's sure she has it. She pores over health magazines and reads medical thrillers voraciously. Being healthy as the proverbial horse, I've been such a disappointment to her—not an appendix scar or a root canal or even a mild case of acid reflux.

And she's nothing compared to my grandmother, who grieved for months when *Dr. Kildare* and *Ben Casey* went off the air. (Never saw 'em, never had to—anyone over fifty can give you the lowdown, especially in my family.) She ultimately came out of her depression long enough to find other medical shows on TV—now we all know enough never to call her during *E.R.*

"Okay," I said. "Although I don't know that I'll be much help."

"Just your being with me is all the help I need," Kim assured me. "That and prayer."

"I can handle that."

The doctor's office was as warm and inviting as the waiting room. Dr. Chase Andrews, Internal Medicine, said the sign on the door. Inside, there were huge banks of cherry-wood cabinets to hide those unsightly files and models of human organs that came apart like puzzle pieces for demonstration purposes. There were no body charts on the walls delineating the veins, arteries, bones and muscles either. Nice as this place was, I decided Kim's doctor probably used a PowerPoint presentation on a big-screen TV if a patient needed to be educated. And there was classical music coming from hidden speakers. How much did this guy charge, anyway? Kim said he was *the best.* Maybe he was giving her a deal, having been a friend of Kurt's and all.

Kim perched on the edge of her seat, lifted her heels and began that annoying little bounce that nervous people often do. I walked behind her to massage the knots from her shoulders. I couldn't think of a thing to say. "Everything will be all right" was not necessarily true and we both knew it.

Kim and I have a deal—no prevarication. We trust each other for complete honesty, the truth and nothing but the truth. What a liberating concept that is! I know there's at least one person on the planet who will tell me if I have a streak of bed-head running down the back of my scalp or bad breath. After all, how can you fix things you don't know about?

The door whispered open so quietly that I didn't realize at first that the doctor had entered the room. It wasn't until I saw him from the corner of my eye that I knew we were no longer alone.

Dr. Andrews stretched out his hand to Kim. "Hello, Mrs. Easton, I'm Chase Andrews. I'm glad we finally get to meet. Your husband is a great guy."

"He says the same about you," Kim ventured, her shoulders relaxing.

When he turned to me, I felt my legs turn into Gummi Bears. It was the dazzling man from the hall yesterday. *This* was Kim's doctor? I felt immediately better. Just looking at him could probably cure a dozen diseases. His sandy hair was shot with gold, and as I looked down at the floor to break his mesmerizing gaze, I noticed that in his finely crafted leather slip-ons, he wore Mickey Mouse socks.

The doctor moved to a cabinet to the left of his desk and opened a set of double doors that revealed a backlit display. From the top of his desk, he took an envelope containing Kim's films and clamped them to the screen. Not her most attractive angle, I thought wildly. I was losing my mind. Maybe I'd feel better without it.

"This is your right breast and this is your left," Dr. Dreamboat said. "As you notice, there is a considerable difference in the tissue between the two. If you'll look right here…"

He used his pen as a pointer and circled a spot on the X ray that looked alarmingly out of place. Before he said another word, I knew Kim was in trouble. Dr. Andrews's words jumbled together as I focused my full attention on the spot to which he was pointing.

"…rather large…doesn't appear to be a cyst…biopsy will tell us for sure…think it should be done right away…tomorrow…any questions?"

Questions? All I had was questions! I looked at Kim. She had a stunned look on her face and was curling her shoulders forward into a fetal position.

Dr. Andrews moved around the burnished cherry desk and angled one hip against it until he was half sitting, half standing in front of her. His posture was relaxed and somehow comforting. He gave off waves of "I am competent. I'll help you. You're safe with me."

I wondered how he did it. He must have learned it somewhere other than medical school, because if it could be taught, it would be a required class. The muscles in my own shoulders relaxed when I saw Kim shift in her chair.

"Do you think it's…?"

"It could be," he answered, without her having to say the word, "but it looks well contained, which is a good sign." He looked at Kim with so much compassion and understanding that I felt tears forming in my own eyes.

"Maybe we should wait and see…." Kim grasped at straws.

"We could," he agreed pleasantly, "but the reality is, it's here. Why not take care of it? Get on with whatever we need to do and be done with it. You have a life to live—why waste time worrying about something we can do something about right now?"

I saw Kim lift her chin and square her shoulders.

You have a life to live…. She did. She knew it, I knew it and the doctor knew it. This was a hurdle she had to move past, but Dr. Andrews was the man to help her.

I looked at him and knew immediately that he'd chosen his words with intention. He was confident that he could do what needed to be done. His competence and assurance enveloped both of us and radiated optimism and peace right into our cells.

While he and Kim were going over the details of the next step, I called Betty and told her that I'd be late and Kim wouldn't be coming in today. Then I called Kurt and left a message suggesting he meet us.

It was after two o'clock by the time I got back to the office, and it was like walking into a tree full of vultures, hunched with anticipation, sharp eyes scanning my face for clues, hungry for every detail. Mitzi, of course, was the most vulture-like of the batch. Bryan hung back to see if whatever I had to say would be of interest to him or if he'd have to disappear into the men's room until it blew over.

Betty jumped to her feet when I walked in, but I held up a hand. "I'll be back in a minute, I have to see Harry."

He was, as usual, riveted to his computer screen. There were pencils behind both ears and one even stuck into his Chia Pet "do." He'd rolled up his sleeves, loosened his tie and filled the candy dish by his mouse with Hot Tamales. That meant Harry was doing some *serious* work—he never ate Hot Tamales unless the project was really important. There were usually jelly beans in the dish, unless he'd had an easy day and had dug into his enormous stash of dried-up Peeps left over from Easter. I can't explain why he loved those sugary, pastel-colored marshmallow chicks, but he did. He sent me out to gather up all I could find right after the holiday and made them last most of a year. I guess that was how we'd come up with the terminology for the tranquil days when Harry was out of the office—that was "a Peep kind of day."

"Hi, Harry."

He looked up from his screen with a bemused expression that told me he'd been completely immersed in his work.

He stared at me for a moment until he recognized me—he really went away when he was creating—and demanded, "Where were you this morning? Matthew Lambert called three times and wanted to talk to you. Said nobody else could help him, not even me."

"Harry." I dropped into the chair across from him. "Kim wanted me to give you a message." I told him what had transpired and that Kim would be gone for the rest of the week.

To my surprise, Harry didn't hesitate for a moment. "Tell her she can take all the time she needs. We'll fill in. Mitzi isn't doing anything important these days, is she?"

Never has, never will. "I don't think so."

"Teach her to do Kim's job."

Me? Things were going to be worse than I thought.

"There's quite a bit to it," I ventured.

"Do the best you can. What Mitzi can't do, I'm sure you can."

Uh-huh. I *can.* Do I want to? No. Will I? You bet.

"And send her some flowers from us, too," he added.

"Really?" I was blown away. Harry was thinking of everything.

"Yes, really." He looked annoyed. "This is a big deal, you know." His gaze drifted over the photos on his desk. "My mother and sister both went through it."

"I had no idea. How are they?" Maybe I shouldn't ask.

"Mom's gone…"

"I am so sorry."

"…to Arizona for the winter and she feels great. Sis is fine, too, but she watches her daughters like a hawk. Has them do all those self-exams and stuff. She's not taking any chances." He looked at me somberly. "Is Kim going to be all right?"

I could have hugged Harry at that moment. He really cared about the answer.

"She's got a great doctor. He's very kind, and I asked a few people about him and have heard nothing but praise. And maybe this won't turn out to be anything...." But even as I said it, I had an odd, foreboding sense that it wasn't true.

Betty, Bryan and Mitzi were troupers. Bryan immediately went to the computer to educate himself about Kim's condition, and Betty clicked her tongue in sympathy and looked more motherly than I imagined she could. She was searching the Yellow Pages for a florist before I could say petunia.

Mitzi, of course, responded in a typically Mitzi manner. "If it had been her feet, my husband could have helped."

"I'm sure he could have." I picked up a file from Kim's desk. It was marked Urgent. "But if he can't help, I'm sure you can. This needs to be done ASAP."

"Don't be so callous, Whitney. How can you think about work at a time like this?"

She missed my double take as she made plans for Kim's recovery. "I'll buy her new pajamas. Turquoise is a good color for her, don't you think? And my manicurist will do anything for me. I'll have her go to Kim's house and do her nails."

"This is a biopsy, Mitzi."

"True, but we have to be ready. You know what the doctor said."

"It's not like she's going to a reception at the White House," I pointed out.

"*After* the surgery, silly. To keep her spirits up. A positive attitude is very important to healing."

For once I had to bow to Mitzi's superior wisdom.

Eric was waiting for me at my front door when I arrived home from work. He was holding a bag of potatoes and a raw chicken.

"Are you and your friend out for a stroll?" I unlocked the door and he followed me inside.

"There was a sale on this stuff at the market by my apartment. I was wondering if *you* knew how to cook a chicken."

"I suppose I could figure it out. The question is, why?"

"I got us a whole meal for less than five bucks!" He looked pleased at first, then ducked his head as if embarrassed. "I'd rather take you out to someplace fancy, but I just paid for aviation ground school and I'm out of cash until my next paycheck." As a jack-of-all-trades at a private airport, he wasn't exactly rolling in money. He held the chicken in the air. "So here I am!"

"So here you are." I put my purse and keys on the counter, glad I'd tidied up this morning. My place is nothing fancy, but it's mine, from the *Phantom of the Opera* poster on the wall to the overflowing shelves of self-help books to the afghan my grandmother made for me when she was in her purple and orange period.

He flushed beneath that shaggy thatch of hair and looked like a five-year-old holding an apple for his teacher. "I messed up, Whit. I've been thinking about how patient you've been with me when I get hooked on one of these tangents of mine and don't call for a month at a time. I know you're fed up with it—and probably me, but I'd like to make it up to you.

"If it's not too late, I'd like to, like, maybe…date you once in a while." His cheeks were as red as those of a baby with diaper rash.

I resisted the temptation to stick a finger in my ear and see if it was plugged. "Eric, you are the sweetest man on the planet. I love you, but you are impossible to date! I thought we were going to be *friends.*"

"Can we go out once in a while and still be friends?"

In an ideal world, maybe. "It's not likely. You know how…tangled up…relationships can get." This was an unusual twist—me, turning down a chance at a relationship just when I was worried about being alone.

"No strings? You can see anybody else you want. Just for fun, Whitney."

"*Only* for fun? And I can date others as much as I want?" *As if there were any standing in line!*

"Right." He held out his chicken with a pleading, eager look. How could I resist? Besides, it would get my mother off my back about dating. The single men at church should send Eric thank-you cards.

"You *do* understand that this will not turn into anything other than friendship, right?" *Those words actually came out of my mouth. Me!*

"I'm not saying that for myself, Whitney, but you call the shots."

Amazed at the twists and turns my life was taking, I grabbed the chicken and escorted it to the kitchen for a tour of my oven.

When it rains, it pours.

Our dinner—rosemary chicken, a creamy baked potato and steamed broccoli with cheese—impressed even me. When Eric left, believing he'd already pushed his luck about as far as it would stretch, I listened to my answering machine.

There was one message from Matthew Lambert. "Hello, Whitney." The way he said it made me feel as if we were intimate friends, not peanut-roasting collaborators. "I received the preliminaries you sent me, and things look great. I have a few questions. I see by my calendar that I have tomorrow evening free. I put in a quick call to that new place downtown and made reservations. How about a working dinner? At seven?"

A "working dinner" at seven? Uh-uh. In my protocol, unless I'm under orders from Harry otherwise, my workday ends between five and six. The seven o'clock hour means something totally different in my book—*date.*

What was going on here? I hadn't changed perfume or moved the part in my scalp to the other side of my head— I hadn't even experimented with a new deodorant. Yet suddenly men were coming out of the woodwork. Well, maybe not so very many men, but it felt that way to me, coming off a long dry spell as I was.

When I returned Matt's call, he immediately wanted to confirm my availability for dinner. "Possibly," I said coolly. I didn't want him hearing me grovel in gratitude or anything. "What things were you planning to discuss?"

There was a long pause. "Nothing big, just general information. Maybe you can tell me where Harry's at in the process."

Translation: "Nothing I couldn't pick up the phone for and find out in two minutes by calling the office. I just want to spend a couple hundred bucks and three or four hours with you, and this is as good an excuse as any."

I eyed the chicken carcass on my counter and decided I could use a meal that didn't involve my having to do dishes. "Sure. I'll meet you there."

"I'll swing by and pick you up. See you a couple minutes before seven." The phone line was dead before I had time to make a counteroffer. Interesting.

CHAPTER 5

October 18

Kim woke me with a phone call at 6:00 a.m. "Hi, it's me. Can you help me out?"

"Anything," I mumbled. I'm at my most expansive when unconscious.

"I'm having the biopsy this morning."

I sat straight up, recalling our trip to the doctor yesterday. So it hadn't been a bad dream.

"Wesley's still sleeping and we don't want to wake him. I couldn't bear to drop him off at day care this time of day. Chase Andrews said Kurt could bring him along, and that he'd arrange somewhere for them to wait."

"Helps to have old friends in high places, huh?"

"Dr. Andrews couldn't be more wonderful. Could you come over and sit with Wesley until he wakes up? He'll probably need a bath before you bring him to Kurt."

"Why don't I just stay at your house with him and go to work late?"

There was a pause on the other end of the line, and I knew Kim was gathering her thoughts and her words. "Dr. Andrews believes that it's going to be a long procedure. If it's what he thinks it is, he's going to go ahead and do whatever surgery is necessary. I may not get home today."

Suddenly I was totally awake and hearing her with terrifying clarity. "Isn't that a little quick? I mean, don't you have to think about these things? Make decisions?"

"We have. Kurt and I decided together after reading the information and doing some heavy-duty praying. If it needs to be done, we've given the doctor permission to do a lumpectomy. If surgery is necessary, I won't have to be anesthetized twice. We talked to Chase a long time about this last night."

"You sound...ready."

"I am. Chase is right. I have my life to live. I want to get on with it. So, will you stay with Wesley and bring him to the hospital later? I want to know he'll be there when I wake up."

Now, much as I love Kim, I rarely baby-sit for her. First, she wants to spend all the time she can with her little boy when she is home, and second, I'm a little insecure about the whole idea. When I was growing up, I was the youngest in the neighborhood. Therefore, sitting opportunities were limited to the occasional "watch the kids in the yard while we visit" scenario. Also, there was that time...okay, two times... when I did get hired to sit and all the flowers in the owners' front yards got trampled by firemen, policemen and gawkers. But that's another story.

I prayed all the way to Kim's house that Wesley would sleep late, wake up pleasant, let me dress him quickly and return him to his parents before anything exciting happened.

Kurt met me at the front door with a hug. "Thanks so much, Whitney. It eases Kim's mind that Wesley is in good hands."

I'm "good hands"? My confidence inched upward a notch.

Kim, looking remarkably collected, handed me a list of things to feed and to do with Wesley.

"I'll be bringing him to see you in just a few hours," I assured her as I crumpled the paper and stuffed it into my pocket in a show of self-assurance. "I don't need all these instructions. We'll be fine."

I reminded myself of that foolish comment later when I was trying to dig the instruction sheet out of my pocket, avoid projectile burping, mop what had escaped a diaper off my skirt and heat a bottle with one had tied behind my back. Actually, the arm was tied to Wesley, who wouldn't let me put him down. Same thing.

Anyway, after I waved Kim and Kurt away, feeling cocky, I poured myself a cup of coffee and settled at the kitchen table to do the crossword puzzle. I had filled in 1A and 1D when I heard my summons from the other room. Wesley had lasted only ten minutes after his parents left the house before waking.

Still in a deluded haze of competency and assuredness, I peeked into the baby's room. He was standing up in his crib on wobbly legs, sucking his thumb intently. His soft brown hair looked like a halo, sticking out, as it was, in every direction. His cheeks were round and rosy, and his eyes lit at the sight of me. And the room smelled like a barn that hadn't been mucked out in a month. How could anything so beautiful create a smell like that?

Gamely, I crossed the room, cooing, "Hi, big boy. Aren't you handsome this morning! You're so snuggly in your little blue sleeper...." He gave a high-wattage grin and flashed those white little razors that his mother calls teeth. He thought for a moment, looked at the thumb he pulled from his mouth and held out his arms to be picked up.

When I gathered him up, he curled into my body, laid his head on my chest and poked the thumb back into its orifice. My maternal instincts kicked in so quickly I didn't realize at first that Wesley was much more…squishy…than he'd been the last time I'd held him. The hand that held his little bottom felt as though it was holding a water balloon, which, of course, it was.

"We'd better change you, big guy," I said more cheerfully than I felt. Morning diapers were considerably more demanding than others I'd changed. As I laid him on his changing table, I noticed that not only was his bottom squishy, but so was his entire back, an oddly slimy texture inside his one-piece sleeper. It wasn't until my fingers ran into something smooth and warm at the nape of his neck that I realized what had happened.

Wesley had filled his diaper to overflowing. It was not only running down the back of his legs, it had mooshed itself upward and oozed out the neck of his sleeper as well. No wonder the room smelled like a barn. And he grinned at me with the angelic, innocent smile of a Botticelli angel.

I did the best I could to clean him up with baby wipes, but ran out before I could take off more than a couple of layers, so I wrapped Wesley in a cotton blanket and carried him into the bathroom. Kim said he loved baths. Good thing.

He squealed like a monkey and kicked his little feet into my gut when I started running water and wouldn't quit until I'd perfected the temperature and set him on the towel I'd thrown on the bottom of the tub to keep him from skidding around. I mopped him off until the water had a murky, sickish look, emptied the tub, refilled it and went at it again. By the third rinse even his hair was back to its proper color.

I'd ditched my jacket when I realized that the sleeves were covered with Wesley residue, and my blouse was sopping wet down to my bra. My skirt was soggy and my stockings and shoes damp by the time I got the baby dried off, rediapered and dressed in a little red romper with a train chugging across the front. Even my hair was wet and limp. My makeup had run and the mascara beneath my eyes made me look like a

raccoon. That, perhaps, was why Wesley liked me so much—
I resembled a sweet little forest creature.

Kim's clothes were too tight for me, but I did find a lumpy
cotton dress in the back of her closet to wear while my clothes
were in the washer and dryer. I also put on a pair of her white
gym socks and one of Kurt's old zippered and hooded sweat-
shirts to keep my arms warm. I was beyond caring. I didn't even
flinch when Wesley urped toddler peaches onto my bosom.

That, of course, was when the doorbell rang.

Hoping our visitor would go away, I hunkered down behind the kitchen door and closed my eyes. It didn't work.
The bell just kept ringing. So I hoisted Wesley onto my hip,
scraped my fingers—toddler peaches and all—through my
hair and stomped toward the front of the house.

"Whatever it is, we don't want any…." I began. Then my
throat constricted and my diaphragm collapsed. I couldn't
breathe. Wesley, on the other hand, clapped delightedly and
held out his hands for Matthew Lambert to hold him.

"Whitney?" He stared at me, a train wreck of a woman,
who'd opened the door and had done something dastardly
to the Whitney he knew. Who was this impostor trying to
take her place? When he didn't reach for Wesley, the baby
promptly threw himself back on my chest and clutched one
of my breasts proprietarily, as if to say "Mine, all mine."

"Matt, what are you doing here?" I wished Kim's lumpy
dress were any other color but green. I look terrible in green.

"I stopped by your place, and your dad was there. Said he
was fixing your plumbing and that you'd come over here. He
thought it was all right to come by. I wanted to give you
these." He held out a bouquet of tiger lilies, asters, mums,
daisies, minicarnations and ripe, golden wheat.

In his excitement, Wesley passed gas.

Not even caring if Matt wondered who'd been responsible for *that,* I stood back and let him inside. My back ached
from cocking my hip at this for-mothers-only angle, my

teeth ached from the frozen smile I had on my face and my hair ached because Wesley was pulling on it.

"Come in. Dad isn't fixing my plumbing—unless you call pouring Drano down the pipes fixing the plumbing. He's really hiding out from my mother. She read somewhere that women in England have lovely skin because of the extra moisture in their air. Now she runs a humidifier in every room, and Dad says he's starting to rust."

"I see."

But did he? I thought not. There was no way to really "get" my family or my current situation. Even I, who lived it, didn't understand.

"Wesley's mom is having surgery today. I'm watching him for a few hours before taking him up to the hospital to see his mommy."

"You really throw yourself full force into this, don't you?" He was gawking at my dress and my anklets. All I needed was Keds and a few bobby-pin curls in my hair to look as if I'd popped out of the fifties.

"I got wet." The dryer bell rang. I thrust Wesley into Matt's arms and dashed for the dryer. I didn't want my clothes to get more wrinkled, because I was not about to do any ironing. Who knew what kind of trouble I could get into with a hot weapon like that in my hands?

When I returned in my newly dried clothing, Matt was lying on his back on the couch letting Wesley jump on his rock-hard abs. They were both laughing, one low, rumbly chuckle and one delighted, piercing squeal—what beautiful music they made. An unfamiliar rush of maternal, housewifey feelings came over me. Matt held the baby, hands tucked beneath tiny armpits, and raised and lowered Wesley toward his belly. When Wesley's bent knees were in range, the baby straightened them out and kicked off Matt's stomach as if it were a trampoline. Then both of them roared as if they were the funniest thing since Bob Hope. I watched them until Matt noticed me.

"You're back. And in new clothes."

"Sorry about the way I answered the door. I've had a hard morning."

He was gentleman enough not to agree with my assessment.

"You two are having fun." I felt a little breathless, seeing Matt that way, playful and messy rather than sophisticated and debonair. Being more on the playful, messy side myself, I liked it.

"He's a great little kid. What a personality. He could fill a whole room with charm."

And a whole diaper with something else.

"How's his mom doing?"

"We're going to the hospital now. Kim wanted Wesley there when she woke up, and the doctor said it was okay. He and her husband, Kurt, are old high-school buddies, so he's making sure that things go smoothly for them."

"Are we still on for tonight?"

"Sure."

He gently put the baby in my arms, kissed me on the forehead and whispered, "See you at seven."

Okay, so I did stand in the doorway for a few moments, holding Wes on my hip and imagining that Matt was my husband and he'd just left for work. That I was a lovely, slim, stay-at-home mom who had nothing better to do than arrange play dates, direct the housekeeping staff, the chef and the gardener and get my nails done. (I have very rich tastes in my fantasies. I usually have a butler and a chauffeur, too.) But eventually I did remember why I was at Kim's house and why Wes was burying his nose in my neck and blowing bubbles against my skin—I'd taught him.

"We'd better get going, baby, or your mom will be out looking for us."

Wesley burped in agreement.

By the time I got to the hospital, I felt as though I'd lived two lifetimes just that morning, but it was all worth it to see

Kurt grab his little son and hug him. Kurt looked terrible, but the sight of Wes seemed to heal something inside him. His face appeared haggard and older than his thirty-six years. His nose was red, his hair rumpled and his eyes faintly unfocused.

"What's going on? You don't look very well...." I dropped the diaper bag on the floor and stared at him.

"They went ahead with the bigger surgery, Whitney. It's what Chase was concerned about. The nurse called from the operating room and said Kim would be in recovery in a couple hours."

"What more can I do?" I'd never felt so helpless.

"Go back to work. I'll call to give you an update once I know more." His eyes darkened. "And pray. She's going to need you later. She loves you like a sister, Whitney, you'll have to help her through this."

It's a big order, but I'll do my best. Abandoning my best friend to the mysterious world of medicine, I went to work to tell Harry what was up.

"How is she?" Harry asked the minute I walked into his office.

"It's what everyone was afraid of."

Harry looked genuinely grieved. "Why don't you send out a memo calling an office meeting. We'll meet tomorrow morning to plan how to cover for Kim."

"It might be a while. I don't know how long these things take to heal or if she'll need more treatment...."

"You tell her that we will make do until she's ready to come back."

"Thanks, Harry. I know that will relieve her mind." I feel better and better about my boss. I'm even beginning to love his hair.

On the way to my apartment, I heard the familiar clicking that I often notice from the apartment two doors down.

Mrs. Clempert was locking her door. Locking, unlocking and relocking, actually. She's the dearest woman in the world but for one small quirk—I think she's obsessive-compulsive about locks. I have a hunch she thinks she's left them open and has to check to make sure. Click open, click shut, click open and shut. Did I mention she has eight locks on her door? She probably watches too much news on television. Pretty soon it won't matter if you live in a secured apartment building or a house in the suburbs. The crime rate in Los Angeles or Washington, D.C., begins to feel like it's in your own neighborhood.

Granted, I have plenty of locks on my own door—five, in fact—left by the elderly man who lived here before me. At one time, this must have been a very nervous building. I lock only three of the five, so anyone trying to break in will always be locking one or two locks while opening the others. I wonder if they've thought of this technique at Fort Knox.

Although I'd been pushing it back all day and despite my worry over Kim, my excitement about the upcoming evening with Matt finally exploded. The butterflies in my stomach grew wings the size of pterodactyls, while I did the Ultimate Grooming. Floss, brush, polish, gargle. Wash, condition, dry and curl. Bath, manicure, pedicure, oil. I used more products for this procedure than are carried in stock by many stores. And I've learned a few things the hard way. *Never* do a facial or eyebrow wax the day of a Big Date.

Kurt called to say that Kim was resting comfortably and that his mother had come to get Wesley. Dr. Andrews had arranged for a roll-away to be brought into Kim's room so Kurt didn't have to leave her.

If he's as first-rate a surgeon as he is a person, Kim is in good hands with her doctor.

Mom called. I'd let it slip that I had a date, and she was craving details.

"Is he nice? How old is he? Is he a Christian?"

When I hesitated, she added, "He is, isn't he?"

"It's never really come up," I admitted. Why not? That's a top-priority issue for me. Why hadn't I discussed it with Matt? Was it because I was afraid the answer might be no?

"I have wonderful news."

"Oh?" I innocently took the bait.

"I was at the church this morning, and guess who I saw?"

I remained silent, sure she was going to tell me anyway.

"The new youth pastor!"

Uh-oh.

"He's very nice. So energetic and enthusiastic. The kids—and you—will like him."

I searched for something banal to say, and the most idiotic, inane question popped out of my mouth. "What color is his hair?"

There was a long pause on Mother's end of the line, which I immediately translated. "He's bald?"

"Thinning, dear. His head has a lovely shape. If he shaved it like so many do these days, he'd be positively handsome."

A well-shaped head. I like that in a man.

"Don't discount him, dear. Never judge a book by its cover."

Or lack of one. "Mom, I'm sure he's great. I just don't want to be fixed up with anyone right now."

For once, I have plenty of my own men—and I can't even figure out what to do with them!

"I didn't 'fix you up.' But you'll like him, Whitney, I know you will."

I didn't argue. I didn't have time. Mom was determined to fix me up whether I wanted fixing or not. "Listen, we'll sort this out later. Love you, Mom. Bye."

I was looking pretty good by five to seven—as long as I looked in the mirror from the shoulders up. EEAT is at the top of my to-do list—after dinner with Matt.

He was prompt. The doorbell rang just as the hand on my kitchen clock hit seven. I glided as well as one can in for-looks-only shoes to the door. Then I shuffled my shoulders into place for good posture and, casually, as if I might be surprised at who was on the other side, opened the door.

Just when I thought it was not possible for him to look any better, he did. The man must have his own tanning bed, barber, manicurist and wardrobe designer. Suddenly the French manicure I'd wasted ninety minutes giving myself seemed pointless. No one would ever get past him to see me.

Then he endeared himself to me as a grin spread across his face. "You look amazing!" He was so sincere I decided to believe him.

We went to a trendy Italian restaurant near the Xcel Center in St. Paul. Even with high ceilings, a packed house and the noisy chatter around us, Matt managed to make me feel as though we were stranded together on a desert island without another person in a hundred miles. And, true to my imaginary-island theme, ordered lobster for both of us. At market price. Without asking the waitress what that might be. Talk about living on the edge. Granted, lobsters are the vacuum cleaners of the sea, but I could overlook that. Especially tonight.

When I thought I couldn't eat another thing, he ordered tiramisu and a fudgy layer cake that was out of this world. Dieting only entered my head when I had more difficulty squeezing out from behind the table than I had getting in.

The best part, though, had nothing to do with food. There must be a beautiful-girl magnet installed inside the restaurant, because there were more of them there than I'd ever seen before except in a lingerie catalog. And still Matt only had eyes for me. This created a burning philosophical question for me. *Why?*

My suspicious, analytical side woke up about halfway through dinner. Granted, I am reasonably attractive, no matter what my self-esteem says, but this mad rush to sweep me off my feet was so foreign that I felt wary. An annoying little voice in the back of my head kept asking, "What's this all about?" Once I decided to put a gag on the voice and send it out to play in the street, the evening was much more pleasurable.

Sometime during dinner Matt had slipped a tiny, wrapped package to my side of the table. I didn't notice it until the dishes were removed and we were waiting for dessert. It was wrapped in silver foil and embellished with a thin silver cord.

"What's this?" It was too small to be a household appliance but big enough to hold a piece of jewelry—just the kind of package I like.

"Something for one of the smartest women I've ever met. It's a thank-you for what you've created for my company."

"That's not me alone," I demurred. "Harry and Betty and…" In all honesty, I couldn't say much about Mitzi, who had typed a few letters of copy and whined the entire time. She never whines to Harry or Betty, but Bryan and I have had to develop invisible coats when whine-showers were in the forecast.

Matt's gift was a pin, a tiny amethyst pin that looked suspiciously like a peanut. "It's what we give our salesperson of the year," Matt explained. "Very coveted in the company because it's a symbol of a person who's gone the extra mile for Lambert Industries. Like you."

Peanut or not, I loved it. It was perfect—thoughtful, symbolic and not too personal. It would have been difficult to accept a diamond brooch as a thank-you gift from a client, but a peanut seemed in the realm of appropriate. And who was I to look a gift peanut in the mouth?

As we left the restaurant, I floated on both cloud nine and my size nines. Then I saw a billboard posted at the intersection near the restaurant. It showed one of those simple pink ribbons that symbolize the fight for breast cancer and urged women to get mammograms. Immediately my mind went to Kim.

Matt must have felt me stiffen. He took a firmer grip and steered me toward his car. "We'll stop at the hospital before I take you home, if you like."

I could have hugged him. I probably could have hugged him anyway, since I'd been thinking about doing so half the evening, but now the impulse had true emotion behind it. "Thank you. It would mean a lot to me."

He opened the door to his BMW Z-4 and gestured me inside. "Hop in. I know a shortcut."

I was feeling all gooey and weepy by the time we arrived at the hospital, partly because Matt was so considerate, partly because Kim was inside and partly—well, gooey and weepy were currently my default emotion. I even cried at a television ad yesterday, and I haven't done that in ages.

"I'll pick up a *Wall Street Journal* in the gift shop and read in the lobby," Matt said. "You should spend time alone with your friend. Come down when you're ready."

Could he get any better than this?

Hospitals must all get their cleaning supplies from the same manufacturer. Or, at least they all use the fragrance eau-de-nausea. Kurt was in the hall when I arrived, pacing back and forth in front of Kim's door. A big, strapping man with a ruddy complexion who, if one didn't know he was a student/truck driver, might be mistaken for a lumberjack, Kurt looked surprisingly small and pale in the stark light of the hallway.

"What's up?" I put my hand on his arm to call him back from wherever his thoughts had taken him.

"Chase is in with her right now." Kurt ran his thick fingers through his hair. He has hands like my father's—callused, sturdy and reliable.

"How's she holding up?"

"It's her faith that's keeping her together right now. There are so many unknowns to deal with that she's had to turn it over to God. Who else could handle it anyway?"

Kurt had come to Christ in high school, and although he wasn't ostentatious about it, there was no doubt that he lived his life in accordance with his faith. I shot a brief prayer of thanks to God for giving Kim this man, the one just right for this difficult time.

"Kim says you don't like hospitals."

"I hate them. But I love her more." He sighed and grinned. "So I'm here, with a barf bag close at hand."

"Good man. And her doctor is a friend of yours...." I threw my line in the water to see what I'd catch.

"Chase is an absolute gift, Whitney. It's a miracle that we connected. We hadn't been in contact for years, and then, out of the blue he called me. He said he did it on an impulse. We were on a golf team together in high school and decided to pick up where we left off. Then I heard what a good doctor he is." He spread his hands and looked stunned. "And here we are."

God does provide in the most amazing ways. Who knew He liked to use high-school yearbooks?

At that moment, Dr. Andrews emerged from Kim's room. He was dressed casually tonight, in chinos and a light denim shirt. I hadn't noticed before that his sandy-gold hair was prematurely grayed at the temples. It did something disquieting and alluring to the color of his eyes.

He greeted us but turned immediately to Kurt to give his report. Kim was doing fine, resting now and talking about Wesley. As they softly discussed the treatment to come—radiation—I began comparing Chase Andrews to all the other men who'd recently appeared in my life. He had Eric's beguiling charm in a less loopy sort of way—and the same wonderful smile lines at the corners of his eyes, a sure sign of easy laughter. In addition, he boasted Matt's urbane, sophisticated flair, as if he could handle anything with grace. He also had the undivided attention of every nurse in the hall. The older ones were more discreet, but a couple of young aides nearly walked into a meds cart the charge nurse was pushing down the hall. Amazingly, he appeared oblivious to it all.

I'm sure I had a ga-ga look of my own. It was a badly timed lapse, because I caught Matt's eye as he exited the elevator.

I made introductions all around and managed to stammer out Dr. Andrews's name like a starstruck groupie. Matt was cordial but strained, and I noticed he had me firmly in the curve of his arm as we said good-night. In most instances, this would have been sheer bliss, but I felt Dr. Andrews's and Kurt's eyes on my back as we moved away, and wished Matt had been slightly less proprietary.

CHAPTER 6

October 27

With all the stress I've had in my job, juggling Eric and Matt, Kim's health and my mother's obsession over hooking me up with the new youth pastor, I'm eating nonstop. That, of course, adds more stress. My rubber band snapped today and left a little red welt on my abdomen, so, despite my misgivings, I went to EEAT.

Self-consciously, I strolled into the meeting room pretending I really belonged in the Sunday school teachers' meeting and entertained my invisible-shrinking-woman fantasy until I convinced myself no one would notice me. In reality, I might as well have lit a flare on my head while everyone in the room stared at the odd woman squirming uncomfortably in her chair. Worse yet, I realized that not only did I belong there, but I'm overdue. Granted, it's fifteen pounds, not fifty that I'm fighting, and I'm glad for that. Still, I'm not willing to carry fifteen pounds of pork chops around with me every day because, besides being smelly and weird, it could be a lot of work. I'm carrying fifteen pounds of my own pork around. That, too, is a lot of work, so why do it anymore?

The church basement was never so dark and unwelcoming or the air more dank and heavy. The fluorescent lights, always unflattering, threw lumps and bulges into stark relief and made everyone's lips a ghastly shade of blue. Or maybe those feelings were inspired by my mood, which was equally dismal.

So it had come to this. There I was, perched on an ice-cold folding chair in a former Sunday-school room smiling fixedly at a room half-full of women who had to lose even more weight than I did. The other half was nauseatingly pert and perky, already approaching the magic objective—*Goal Weight*. What a contrast. They smiled and bantered. Their hair looked good and their clothes even better. They wore their blouses *tucked in!* And that could be me in a few short weeks. That, at least, is what our fearless leader, Tansy Kohl, said.

I smiled weakly at the woman next to me. She twitched one lip in a grimace that I took for a smile. Tansy, or maybe one of her clones, bounced up to us and welcomed us to EEAT.

"Welcome!" She grabbed my hand, pumped it and beamed a megawatt smile on me. "I haven't met you before."

"I'm Whitney. This is my first night here."

"You will just *love* this. It is so *great*. I mean, I was so *fat*. Like almost *a hundred and thirty*, and now…" She did a pirouette to show off her size zero waist. Remarkable. I weighed more than her when I was born. Still, her smile was warm and welcoming and she did give me hope.

"I know this program will encourage you. 1 Corinthians 10:31 has been especially meaningful to me. 'So whether you eat or drink, or whatever you do, do everything for the glory of God.' That's what got me through."

Ouch. That hit me where it hurt. There wasn't much glory in eating cold pizza and drinking flat cola at 2:00 a.m. because

I couldn't sleep. I'd never really thought about food that way before. She's right. Whatever I do should be to the glory of God. Maybe this was more significant than I'd realized....

"We have remarkable success at EEAT. We're glad you're here. Where do you work, Whitney?"

Her enthusiasm was catchy. My heart raced with more than nerves. Excitement. Hope. Anticipation. The thought that I could squeeze back into my old jeans. And something more, something I don't have a handle on yet. I told her about Innova and then asked, "Where do you work, Tansy?"

"I'm in marketing, too—alternative advertising." I must have looked confused, because she added, "I work for a company that provides signage in public rest rooms—you know, the advertisements on posters on the back sides of doors in toilet stalls."

"Cool," I blurted. "I've read a lot of your work."

When the meeting started, one by one the big losers (and I mean that in the best possible sense) danced to the front and gave their enthusiastic testimonials. "Once I really decided to do this, it was easy," "I *never* crave sugar anymore," "I've replaced all sweets with pickles and green peppers, and I feel so much better" and so on. If we hadn't been meeting at church, I wouldn't have believed a word of it.

Maybe it was the idea of a pickle sundae or a green-pepper cookie that held me back—or, more likely, I just didn't want to give myself fully to the process. Frankly, I *like* to eat. Not only does food taste good, but it also feels good—for a few minutes, at least. It's a delicious transgression, a place I'd never even considered turning over to God. I wonder why not.

The hard, cold folding chairs were beginning to get uncomfortable, but no one except me seemed to notice. They were all busy taking notes as Tansy spoke. If I were to do as Tansy said and drink ten or more glasses of water a day, I'd be hiding out in the rest rooms as much as Bryan. But everyone guaranteed me that not only would I be less hungry but also my complexion would become dewy and smooth.

I don't know about that. Dewy or just plain soggy?

There were plenty of scriptures that tweaked my conscience and made me realize how casually I've treated what I put into my mouth. I collected the recipes everyone was offering, writing them all on the deposit slips in my checkbook. I left feeling thinner, the decision made, the course set. Even so, it took everything in me not to stop for a root-beer float on the way home.

The other big tip for EEAT shoppers is to shop only the perimeter of the grocery store. Instead of getting the root-beer float, I decided to stop at the store and try it for myself.

Tansy said that I could live and eat perfectly well if I only shopped the outside aisles of the store and never ventured down a center lane. Oh, sure, if all I wanted to buy were *fresh* fruits and vegetables, *fresh* seafood and meat, cheese, dairy and eggs, products made with whole grains and, of course, toilet paper. Now, who can live like that? I mean, who'd want to? What about mayonnaise, Oreos, TV dinners and boxed cake mixes? Didn't EEAT know anything about the basic food groups—tortilla chips, ice cream and chocolate?

Of course, avoiding the middle of the store also eliminated the opportunity to buy rice cakes, rye crisps, puffed wheat and canned tuna. There is a silver lining in every cloud.

Eric met me at the door to my apartment. It appeared he'd been camping there by the dog-eared thriller, empty Snickers wrappings and a bag of deep-fried pork rinds next to him as he sat on the floor (Tansy would have had a field day with him). As I approached, he jumped to his feet, gave me a bearlike hug, planted a kiss on my cheek and grabbed my grocery bag…containing a head of cabbage and a carton of cottage cheese.

"Got anything good to eat?" he asked as he placed the bag on the counter. The man is a human garbage machine. Fortunately I understand how Eric works. He just gave me his ultimate offer of affection—a hug and kiss *before* he asked for food.

"See for yourself." As he pawed through my refrigerator, I slid my EEAT manual under a chair cushion, not in the mood for questions.

"Hey! There's no food in here!"

"Sure there is. Have a carrot."

"Did you buy a rabbit?"

"Not that I know of. Eat a cup of yogurt if you're hungry."

"No animal crackers? No red licorice or Almond Joys? There's not even a can of corned-beef hash in here. What do you plan to live on?"

"I'm going to start cooking healthy meals, thank you very much."

He leaned against the counter and crossed his nicely muscled arms over his even more nicely muscled chest. "You don't have to diet for me, Whit. I think you're perfect just the way you are."

He caught my hand and pulled me toward him. "Whit, I'm not the kind of guy who is good at mushy, lovey-dovey stuff. You know that. But what I feel for you is…different. You're a great friend and so much more. Do you think you can hang on until I grow up and figure it all out?"

His face was so open and vulnerable and his words so honest that tears prickled at the backs of my eyes. Here was a wonderful, great-looking guy who thought I was perfect, who loved me just the way I was. He offered everything a girl could want, including permission to eat herself into a stupor and still know that what he'd said was true. He did like, maybe even love me.

So why wasn't I happier? Because of our history together, I suppose. I do learn from my mistakes, eventually. Though it's easy to be more casual about it now, Eric's pattern of benign neglect and absentminded inattention had once hurt. He'd proven to be completely undependable as well as utterly lovable. He'd also made me very cautious by disappointing me once too often.

"Eric, I've heard it before. It doesn't matter how perfect you might think I am if I can't count on you. You've said you'd call and not called. You tell me you're crazy about me and then you vanish. You're a roller-coaster ride, Eric."

He raked his fingers through his hair until it stood on end. "I know, I know. I realize that I have to rebuild your trust in me." He brightened. "But it's not like I'm seeing other women…."

I gave a wry laugh and recited the litany: "Piper, Cessna, Jenny, Spitfire, Kitty Hawk. They all sound like pretty stiff competitors to me. Besides, we might ruin a perfectly good friendship."

I gave him a squeeze and kicked him out of the apartment. "Go home," I said, "and don't tempt me. I have to stick to this diet no matter how mouthwatering you find me."

Eric paused at the doorway and looked down into my eyes. "What a fool I've been, Whit. Now you've given up on me."

"I haven't given up on you, Eric. I just don't understand you. Actually, I don't understand pilots in general. Tell me again why kamikaze pilots wore helmets…."

Still, I let him kiss me on the forehead before I closed the door on him. I *do* love Eric. I'm even fond of old Otto-Pilot. But I also have the gnawing sense that this particular man-dog combination isn't the right one for me.

Then Matt Lambert's face loomed in my mind. I quashed that thought too and stomped for the bathroom. From no men to too many men—no wonder I was losing my mind!

October 28

It's been weird at the office since everyone learned about Kim. No one says much, but we're all worried. Maybe it's the proximity. Kim is one of us. If she's sick, any of us could be.

Lord, thank you for good health—my own and that of my family. And forgive me for not being grateful when things are going well. Why does it always take a trauma to make me realize how good I have it? Give me a grateful heart every day, Lord, not just when I see how really wrong things can go.
Awestruck,
Whitney

Mitzi, whose home address is 100 Denial Street, seems hardest hit. She likes her body the way it is and even the *thought* of losing part of it puts her in a foul mood. Today was the worst. She screamed at Bryan for wearing Aqua Velva aftershave because it made the office smell like her grandfather and reminded her of nursing homes. Poor Bryan was just trying to use up a sample he'd received in the mail. I knew Mitzi had made him angry when I found him at his desk aiming the laser pointer I use in sales meetings toward her desk, trying to set it to stun.

Mitzi has never been one to hold back, but she's been totally out of control lately. Betty got in trouble for moving Mitzi's pencils to make room for a pile of papers, and I did the ultimate wrong by digging into a juicy orange at lunchtime and squirting juice onto her faux-leather skirt.

We are the victims of office rage. I hear a lot about road rage, but Mitzi enjoys her Mercedes too much to take any chances with that. She obviously doesn't like her officemates nearly as well, because she has no qualms whatsoever about letting us have it. We've chalked up her outbursts to stress over

Kim and have taken precautions not to invade her space, which, I might add, is currently occupying most of the office.

It didn't help that Matt sent me flowers. Mitzi is normally the only one in the office who receives bouquets. The Prince of Shoes, Corns and Bunions is either madly in love, has a great secretary who remembers to order flowers for his wife or has a standing order at the greenhouse. It's fine for Mitzi not to be able to see beyond her desk because of the flora blooming there, but when *I* had a measly two dozen of the most gorgeous roses ever grown on the planet crowding *my* desk, she went ballistic.

"You can't work with all that stuff on your desk!"

What stuff? I had a notebook and a pencil on my desk, and, of course, *The Flowers.*

She waved her hand in the direction of the gorgeous mass as if it were a terra-cotta pot full of earthworms.

"I think it's gross. Unprofessional. You should take them home."

Not on your life. Jealous Witch!

Then God tweaked my conscience and told me to behave.

"You're really upset about Kim, aren't you?" I asked. The words came out of my mouth with no conscious thought or effort. Obviously they weren't mine, but were the idea of Someone Higher.

To my amazement, she started to cry.

Mitzi doesn't cry any prettier than I do, I discovered. "She's too young! She's not supposed to have anything serious happen to her!" Translation: *Or me, either.*

"Kurt says the doctor is very upbeat. He says they caught it early."

"Still…if it could happen to her…" She didn't have to finish the sentence. I knew exactly what she meant. We all felt more vulnerable now that this illness had invaded our office.

"I won't, of course, be able to visit her in the hospital," Mitzi announced, as if this was something I should already know.

"Why not?"

"Because I don't *do* hospitals. They smell funny, and your shoes squeak on the tile."

"Your husband is a doctor. I thought you'd hang out with medical types all the time."

"At conferences, yes. In the trenches, no. You'll have to give Kim this from me." She pulled a small, elegantly wrapped box from her desk drawer. "They're earrings. I thought it might help draw attention to Kim's face."

And away from her chest? Ah, Mitzi, always thinking.

"Give it to her yourself." I shoved the box back to her.

"What?"

"You heard me. Give it to her yourself. If you can't go to the hospital, visit her at home. She needs people to support her—that means your presence as well as you presents."

"I can't, Whitney. It makes me so uncomfortable...."

"But this isn't about you, Mitzi. It's about Kim."

Mitzi scowled sourly, unaccustomed to not getting her way. "Then you'll have to go with me."

That should be fun—an outing to the hospital with a woman who doesn't like hospitals, illness or human beings in general. Still, I had to take my own advice. *This wasn't about me.*

We made a date for tomorrow after work.

October 29

I stopped at the hospital early this morning to see how Kim was doing. She was in a chair eating what hospitals attempt to pass off as breakfast. How anyone can make yellow eggs, brown bacon and beige oatmeal look all the same color is a mystery to me. Of course, everything else in the room had the pasty blue-gray tinge, too, including the walls, her hospital-issue gown and Kim's complexion.

Her face lit up when I entered the room. "Hey! Am I glad to see you!"

"Why are you still in here, anyway? I thought you'd be home by now." We gave each other air kisses and smiled.

"Chase is watching a couple things—I'm a little anemic and my blood pressure is elevated. I'll go home tomorrow. I can hardly wait. I talk to Wesley on the phone, and all he says is 'Mama, mama, mama.'" Her expression was so full of longing that even I felt the ache.

"Just wait, you'll have something to get your mind off Wesley later today."

Kim eyed me suspiciously. "What does that mean?"

"*Mitzi* will be coming up with me after work."

"No kidding? Mitzi? How'd that come about?"

"I guilted her into it," I confessed. "I thought it would be good for her."

"With no thought whatsoever for *my* well-being, I notice." Kim plumped the pillow behind her back.

"You can handle it if anyone can. You are one amazing lady." As I said it, my words caught in my throat. It is so true.

"Thanks, but right now, being a 'lady' isn't much fun. For once in my life, being a guy looks pretty good." Kim waved away my protest before I even spoke. "I know, I know, it can happen to them, too, but not as often as it seems to happen to us."

"The surgery must have affected your mind."

"Think about how much easier it is to be a man. Wrinkles make them look weathered and full of character but they make us look old. A man never has to wax his legs. *And* no one cares if he wears the same clothes three days in a row or has only three pair of shoes."

She had a point.

"And they don't have to worry about whether or not their husbands will think they're beautiful anymore." Her voice cracked, and I could hear the fear behind her cheerful facade.

"Oh, Kim." I pulled up a chair so I could face her, hoping that something brilliant and comforting would come to mind, but nothing did. Instead, I watched her face crumple in misery.

Dear God, give me the right words....

Finally I took her hand and asked her the question that had popped into my mind. "Why do you think so little of Kurt?"

That startled her out of her despair. "Kurt is the love of my life!"

"Then why do you think he's so shallow as to even care about an incision or an 'unmatched set'? Kim, you caught this in time. You're here. Do you think he's concerned about anything other than that?"

She was silent for a long time. Maybe I'd put my mouth in gear before my brain.

"When I met Kurt," she said softly, "I knew that he was the one God wanted for me. There was never a doubt in my mind—and there hasn't been since. He's an honorable, loving Christian man, the kind I wasn't sure existed until I met him."

"Made in heaven," I murmured. "And if God picked Kurt just for you, then he will certainly withstand this."

"Is my faith so weak that I forget so easily?" she murmured.

"Now you're looking for something else to worry about," I chided. "'Fix your thoughts on what is true and honorable and right. Think about things that are pure and lovely and admirable. Think about things that are excellent and worthy of praise.' Give it to God and let Him deal with it. You've got too much to do to waste time on something He's already handling."

"You're right. He *is* handling it. You're here, aren't you?" Kim smiled at me and wiped a tear from the corner of her eye. "I have so much to be grateful for."

That was when I choked up.

★ ★ ★

I was deep in thought by the time I reached the office. My conversation with Kim had forced me to think about my own life. Was the man wearing God's stamp of approval for me closer than I'd thought? Eric has always been tender, charming, absentminded and utterly undependable when an airplane was involved. The same little-boy quality that makes me care for him so much is exactly what drives me crazy. Is that what God has in mind?

Matt, on the other hand, is everything I've ever dreamed of—handsome, debonair and charismatic—but I still haven't let down my guard around him, afraid that he might be too good to be true. It's only been a little over a month since I met him. I have a tendency to hold people at a distance until I really get to know them. Maybe it's time to throw all caution to the winds and not analyze everything to death. It's tempting, very tempting.

Or maybe I'm acting like Kim—looking so far out into the unknowable future that I'm not seeing what's in front of me right now. Has God already answered my prayers and I just haven't noticed? The thought makes me feel oddly queasy.

There's no time for introspection once I walk through Innova's door into the Land of the Self-Absorbed.

I was early today. Only Betty was in, sitting at her personal laptop, staring intently at the screen. She was so busy operating her mouse that she didn't notice me immediately, and when she did, she flinched as if I'd caught her trying to blow the office safe. That, of course, told me exactly what she *was* doing.

Betty is addicted to eBay. I discovered it the day the UPS man had me sign for eight packages from all parts of the country. I had a sneaking suspicion they weren't all office supplies. Then Betty let it drop that she collects antique music boxes. She can't just walk into any old store and pick up a few, but there are pages of them online. She's careful never to do her bidding on office time, but I have caught her in the back room during her lunch hour doing something furtive on the computer, keeping one eye on the screen and the other on the clock.

I tried to buy something online once, but learned immediately that it wasn't for me. I had my eye on a pair of sandals, the kind the shoe store said had been discontinued. But there they were, online and NIB (New In Box). So I set my alarm for 2:00 a.m., thirty minutes before the auction was to end, and skulked over the monitor until it was time to make my final bid. Finger poised, eye on the clock, at 2:29 and 3/4 I pushed the Enter button and made my bid. I was about to start celebrating my purchase when I saw that someone with the moniker Emelda2 had outbid me. No doubt Emelda had high-speed access and had gotten in under the wire. No only did I not get my shoes, I was wiped out the next morning at work.

I'll leave the bidding to Betty.

Harry accosted me in the hallway and gestured me into his office. I studied my little Chia Pet on the way in. Like the ceramic ones, his head looks much better with a full crop.

He didn't waste any time on pleasantries. "What's going on with you and Lambert? Why is he so interested in you?"

I'm hoping it's my charm, wit and grace, but if Harry hasn't noticed that I have some by now, there's no use explaining. "We've had dinner, that's all. He's a very charming companion."

Harry snorted emphatically. "Something's up. He's too curious about you."

A little tingle of pleasure raced through me. "Really? Why do you say that?"

I wanted Harry to reply, "He keeps wondering which you prefer, sapphires or emeralds." But what he said instead floored me. "He keeps asking about your background and your education. I find it very odd."

Me, too. What am I, a horse whose teeth need to be checked before Matt makes an offer? Then again…maybe he wants to take me home to meet his family! It didn't bother my fantasy one iota that he'd never said a word about it to me. I would have drifted off into a meet-the-folks scenario, but Harry, scowling at me as if I was a clue in a murder mystery, kept me grounded. It was a little strange, a man wondering how many degrees I had.

"Watch it, Whitney. The guy is smooth. He's a great client, but there's something about him I don't trust." That statement didn't bother me much. Harry has always thought Gandhi and Mother Teresa were up to something, too.

I doodled as I fielded telephone calls today. Mostly I drew large peanuts, cashews and the occasional filbert. Then I started to draw a sketch of Matt's face. The conversation with Harry had inspired my thoughts. I drew a little chart on the scratch paper. On one side was a list of Matt's wonderful qualities. On the other, I listed his not-so-desirable traits.

The good traits were easy—charming, intelligent, handsome, independently wealthy, urbane, great dresser, good kisser (it was only a friendly peck on the cheek, but I could see the potential). He brings gift baskets to the office, laughs at my jokes, makes me feel as if I'm the only person on the planet when he's looking at me, tells me every time he comes in that I look even lovelier than I did the time before, buys Godiva chocolate, none of the waxy stuff…. The list could go on and on.

The other list was more difficult to fill. The objectionable traits included his proclivity for travel and work, his single-mindedness where Lambert Industries are concerned and, probably most important, how little he says about himself.

Though never secretive, Matt is difficult to maneuver into personal conversations. Our discussions always circled back to business—his philosophy of business, his obligation to his employees, his theory about keeping morale up in order to keep the plant functioning smoothly. All good stuff, but not the juicy stuff.

I, on the other hand, will tell anyone anything. "An open book," Dad calls me. What's to hide? I don't want any deep dark corners in my life that I'm reluctant to discuss.

I know Matt has older sisters, a retired military-man father and a homemaker mother. One thing I don't know much about is his faith. He glosses over that just as he does everything else that doesn't involve his business. Because I want it to be so, I've assumed he is a Christian. He hasn't said he's *not*. But it seems odd he doesn't talk about it more.

And, probably more important, *why haven't I asked?*

"Let's get this over with." Mitzi slung her purse over her shoulder and cloaked herself with an air of delight usually saved for eviscerations and bloodlettings.

"You can't see Kim with an attitude like that." Mitzi, on a bad day, could glower someone into cardiac arrest.

"Oh, don't worry. I'll be all charm with Kim." She glared at me. "You, on the other hand…"

"This is good for both of you. Kim will be so pleased you took the time to stop. Besides, it's time you learned how to visit someone in the hospital."

"I won't do it again. I'm not fond of ill people." She turned her pert nose up at the thought and shuddered elegantly. Mitzi has everything it takes to be truly beautiful except for the personality. I'm not giving up on her though. I may have to mine deep, but I know there's a heart of gold in there somewhere.

I ushered her out the door and toward my car.

"Are you kidding? I can't ride in that!" She stared at my little red Volkswagen as if it were a tarantula. "We'll have to take my Mercedes."

The seats of Mitzi's Mercedes felt like butter, and her stereo system sounded like the New York Philharmonic. The get-up-and-go this machine has on the freeway made me wonder if this would be the *last* day of the rest of my life. Mitzi drives as she lives, like the Queen of the World. As far as I could tell, everyone going slower than she is a moron and everyone going faster is insane. Mitzi, who varied her speed between forty and eighty mph during the drive, managed nicely to bridge both categories. We did, however, make it to the hospital ten minutes sooner than I believed possible.

It was a good thing, too, since Mitzi spent the entire trip grilling me about my love life.

"How often do you and Matt go out for dinner?"

"That depends on when he's free."

"And this Eric guy?"

"When he has money in his pocket and notices my refrigerator is empty."

"Hmm." Mitzi studied me from the corner of her eye, and I knew what she was thinking. But Matt and Eric weren't Mitzi's foot-obsessed husband. I'm sure that after a hard day in the podiatry department, he probably *needed* to go out for dinner and submerge his stress in a bowl of bouillabaisse. Matt and Eric are different, that's all.

Mitzi staged a hissy fit in the hospital lobby—something about smells, germs and ugly uniforms on the nurses who walked by—but she pulled herself together by the time we reached Kim's room.

In fact, she was downright nice. After a few minutes of pleasant chatter, Kim sent me a questioning gaze. Where was the real Mitzi? Who was this impostor who sounded interested in someone other than herself? Should we send out a search party?

As I listened to them visit, I felt a giddy high. I *knew* Mitzi could do it! God created us to be better than we usually are, kinder, more generous and thoughtful, more loving. And Mitzi was proving it. All those qualities are in her in abundance, in a well she hadn't tapped yet. Cool.

I've heard that we use less than twenty percent of the potential of our brains. I'm sure it's similar with our spirits, our energy and our lives. We're living only a fraction of what God created us to be. Imagine what would happen if we thought with our whole brain and lived lives with our whole selves the way He'd planned!

"My personal shopper says that I should never wear pastels, that they wash me out," Mitzi said. "But I could see you in a shade of warm peach. You're still a little pale, but peach would bring out your eyes and warm your skin tone. What color lipsticks do you have at home?" She dug a tube out of her purse, pulled the top off and flashed it at Kim. "Now, *this* is the color you need...."

Kim was having fun, I could tell. As they discussed whether her face was oval or round and whether or not she should have her eyebrows reshaped, I sat back and relaxed. It was a good sign that Kim was thinking about her wardrobe and makeup instead of her incision. My thoughts drifted, and I didn't realize for a moment that Dr. Andrews was standing in the doorway observing our cozy little scene. Kim and Mitzi were so intent on the *Vogue* magazine Mitzi had brought that I was able to jump up and get to the door before he stepped into the room. I had a question to ask.

In the hallway, however, after smelling that woodsy cologne he wears, my equilibrium shifted and I stumbled and stammered to get it out. "I know I'm not family...well, I *am,* practically. I was just wondering..." My tongue stuck to the roof of my mouth, and I knew I was making a mess of this. But the empty feeling in the pit of my stomach made me continue. "If there's anything you can say to me that wouldn't be a breach of confidence...you know. *Is she going to be okay?*"

He smiled at me. Those Crayola indigo eyes lit, and the pleasant little lines at their corners crinkled. A warm flush coursed through my body. What an incredibly handsome man. It didn't hurt either that he had a bit of silk covered with Pluto figures tucked into his jacket pocket. Handsome *and* approachable, Pluto seemed to say.

"I can't break confidence," he agreed, "but I can say this. As Kim's friend, I want you to make sure she buckles her seat belt from now on, because she's more likely to have a car accident than she is to have a recurrence. There are never guarantees, of course, but Kim's situation is the best I could hope for."

"Thanks. That's what I needed to hear. I'm Kim's seat-belt police from now on."

"I see how much you two care about each other." He looked directly at me, and it was as if no one else existed. "Have you been friends for a long time?"

"We both joined Innova about the same time, but sometimes we wonder if we aren't really sisters accidentally separated at birth." I wanted to say more, but my brain wouldn't cooperate. I think I was drugged by that heady aftershave he was wearing.

"Shall we go and talk to Kim now?"

For an instant I didn't want to share Dr. Chase Andrews with anyone—even his patient.

"Ah, sure," I mustered. After all, Matt is my man of the hour.

When we walked in, Kim smiled, and Mitzi, who has an eye for good-looking men, had to pick her jaw off the ground. Immediately she was interested in all things medical, not just feet.

She purred like a kitten when introduced to Chase and was just about as endearing. She was the cat and he was the cream and she didn't want to waste a drop of him. Of course, kittens also have claws, the part of Mitzi I see all the time.

"Now, who is this?" she asked coyly. Suddenly I saw what Dr. Foot might see in her—big violet eyes open wide, rimmed with unbelievably long lashes, a flirty pout on her lips and someone a hundred percent interested in the man to whom she's talking. For Mitzi, Kim and I suddenly didn't exist.

To Chase's credit, he was unflappable and unerringly cordial. He shook her hand, introduced himself and turned to Kim. But Mitzi wasn't finished with him.

When it became quickly apparent that Mitzi was determined to dominate the situation and squeeze every bit of personal information she could out of Chase with a rapid-fire string of questions, I said our goodbyes and towed her to the parking lot.

In the car, she turned on me with a vengeance. "Why didn't you tell me her doctor was so gorgeous?"

"Would it have made a difference?"

"He certainly improved the hospital scenery." Her highly glossed lips protruded in a pout. "And now she's getting out, and I won't have the chance to visit her here again."

"Don't you mean you won't have the chance to visit *him* again?"

"Is he single? Maybe *you* should try to get to know him."

"I don't want to develop an ailment just for that...."

"He's Kim and Kurt's friend. Why don't you have them set you up?"

"Mitzi, I don't even know his romantic status!"

"Find out."

And that, as they say, was that. Mitzi had made up her mind to find me a man.

Imagining Mitzi and my mother *both* working on my behalf made my blood run cold.

October 29, later

"Do you want a smoothie, Whitney?"

I watched Mom dump soy powder, flaxseed, orange juice, a few aging strawberries, an overripe banana, part of a carton of blueberry yogurt and a splash of rice milk into her blender and whiz it into a pale gray pulp. She eyed the mixture, added two ice cubes and blended it again before pouring the stuff into a tall glass. I shook my head frantically to stop her from pouring me a glass, too.

"Are you sure, dear? It provides three of your five daily fruits and vegetables, dairy and—" she looked at the gelatinous mass "—probably some whole grains or something."

"I'll chew mine, thanks." To prove it, I grabbed an apple off her counter and bit in. When I got an entire chunk of rubber in my mouth, I spit it out. "Since when did you start eating fake fruit?"

She smiled at me as if I'd just paid her a huge compliment. "I *told* your father it looked authentic! He said no idiot would mistake those apples for real, and now I've proved him wrong!"

"Thanks to his 'idiot' daughter."

"Don't blame yourself, Whitney. I paid six dollars for that apple. It *should* look real. For that, it should also *taste* real."

I'm never quite sure what goes on between my parents when I'm not around. I know they have a lot of fun together when Mom isn't flashing hot and cold, but placing bets on fake fruit? It's a scary path they're on.

"How's the diet going, Whitney?" Mom slurped on her smoothie and came up with a pale blue mustache.

"Fine, unless there were a lot of calories in that apple. I've been drinking so much water that I don't have time to be hungry, and the trips to the bathroom involve more exercise than I've had in weeks."

I was raised with a quirky little habit (one of hundreds, probably). Everyone in my family likes to read while they're in the bathroom. One of my earliest memories is the sound of my dad's voice as he pounded on the door of "The Library."

"Quit reading and come out. I've got to shave or I'll be late for work!" Then he'd go in there and finish the crossword puzzle he'd started, and my mother would do an impatient little I've-got-to-put-my-makeup-on dance in the hall. Needless to say, I grew up thinking the only way to take care of certain bodily functions was to read my way through them. Even at thirty, I still need reading material in the bathroom or I feel my time is wasted. That's how I once found myself reading the tag on my underwear informing me it had been made in Portugal. But I digress....

"You're much too concerned with your weight," Mom said as she slugged down her drink.

Fact is, my slacks are beginning to close at the waist and I feel lighter in my step. The exercise program is sticky, however—although my mind is growing more accustomed to the concept, my body has so far refused to participate. I'll have to talk to Tansy at our next meeting. Maybe she knows a way to shift me out of neutral.

"You'll never guess who I saw today," Mom said slyly.

The hairs on my arms stood up, warning me of imminent danger.

"Natalie Hammer and Carol Martin. You remember them, don't you? You played with their sons when you were little. You *do* remember Jackson and Martin, I hope. I saw pictures. They've turned into very handsome young men. Both single."

How *could* I forget those two nasty little boys with the ridiculous names? Jack Hammer and Martin Martin. I doubt their mothers will ever realize what dirty tricks they'd played on their sons with those monikers. They're probably scarred for life.

"Sorry, Mom, not interested."

"Fine. There's always Pastor Bob." I looked at Mom and saw the same resolute, dogged expression that I'd seen in Mitzi's eyes. Unless I quit my job and moved to Siberia, I'm in for a bumpy ride.

Lord, I'm confused. Life doesn't make sense. I know You're in charge and as long as I trust You to work things out according to Your plan, things will turn out for the best. Jeremiah is a life raft for me and has kept me from sinking. 'I know the plans I have for you,' says the Lord. 'They are plans for good and not for disaster, to give you a future and a hope.' Frankly, right now I just don't get it. Kim, who should be enjoying her husband and son, is talking about radiation and doctor's appointments. Harry, who hasn't noticed much of what I do for ages, is suddenly eyeballing me as if I'm invaluable and ready to jump ship. Mitzi's decided to become my friend, which, frankly, is more complicated than having her as a co-worker. Mom's memory has diminished as her hot flashes have increased and Dad's uptight.

And about that prayer for someone to spend the rest of my life with? Well, I'm more mixed up now than I was when there was no one in the picture. Matt is fabulous, but we're just getting to know one another. He's an astute, charming businessman and has great taste in suits. He's also pushing pretty hard right now. He's invited me out for dinner twice this week. I want him to be "the one."

Maybe it's Eric who's holding me back. He's the world's biggest sweetheart. Since there's been no airplane activity lately, he's offered to cook dinner, wash my car and make me a spinach malt so I won't fall off my diet. He's really sorry he let me down and is trying to make up for it. And then there's that ridiculous string of "possibilities" Mom keeps suggesting.

I'm exactly the same person I was a year ago, only then men seemed as scarce as good hair days. And, I hate to admit, I'd probably trade them all for an evening with Dr. Chase Andrews, who, Kim says, is on a sabbatical from women. According to Kurt, he was pretty burned by someone and is so not interested in dating.

Lord, there You have it. Guide me through this maze and show me Your direction. Heal and protect Kim. And let me be Your light in the Innova office. We need You in every heart, not just mine.

Oh, yes, and please bless that cute little guy in my Sunday school class who told me on Sunday that poor Moses died before he ever reached the Equator. He's also the one who loves to sing "Joshua Fit the Battle of Geritol" in music class.

Thanks for being here for me—now and forever. Amen.
Whitney

NOVEMBER

CHAPTER 7

November 1

leth·o·lo·gi·ca: The inability to remember a word you want to use.

Mom has a serious case of lethologica. She calls me "Frank" and has been referring to Dad as "Whitney." She's also announced that she was going to do a load of clothes in the dishwasher, asked me to hand her the ketchup instead of mustard when she was making potato salad, and couldn't think of her sister's name when she tried to tell me who was coming for a visit.

I printed information off the Internet and checked a couple books out of the library so that Dad could assure himself that this is normal for a menopausal woman and that he didn't have to look into commitment procedures just yet. On the other hand, if she keeps reading those medical books, I might suggest it.

"Do you think I've been bitten by a deer tick? Look at my neck. What do you see? It's a tick bite, isn't it?"

I stare at her shoulder that is remarkably smooth and shapely for an older woman.

"I don't see anything."

"They're very small. Look closer. Do you want a magnifying glass? Is there a rash? It's a very bad sign if there's a rash…."

She's begun adopting a disease of the week. This started at the same time as hot flashes, when she realized that she wasn't as young as she used to be. Now she's trying to stave off every possible health problem.

"Oh, here it is, I've got it." I plucked a practically invisible speck from her shoulder and held it out to her. "Gravel. Did you and Dad walk around the lake this morning? He probably picked something up and then put his hand on your shoulder."

She blushed. "Oh, that father of yours."

The expression on her face reminded me that my mom is a knockout. I keep forgetting that since she's first and foremost my mother. The pink flush made her eyes sparkle. She wears her hair in this improbable bob that would make me look as if I'd been attacked by a little Dutch boy with a hedge trimmer, but on her the style looks wonderful. Her eyes are disproportionately huge in her face and her nose has exactly the right tilt. And, until this menopausal thing started, she'd put all her wacky energy into being impulsive and funny. Until recently, it had been a huge compliment to hear the words "You're just like your mother." Now I wonder if that means I'll accidentally put my shoes in the refrigerator.

I hugged her.

She reached to smooth my hair out of my face as she has since I was tiny. "Whit, darling, you are such a wonderful gift to your father and me. God is good."

"Even if I'm single and stay that way?"

"Of course. We just want you happy, in whatever form that takes."

But I knew Mom could imagine only one form of happiness for me.

November 2

"Have you worked anywhere but Innova, Whitney?"

Matt and I were sitting on a bench at the Mall of America watching Christmas shoppers. The air around us was a hum of conversation and laughter interspersed with those hokey Christmas songs I'm sick of by December 1. How many times can you listen to "Santa Claus Is Coming to Town" before you hope he his misses his flight and ends up in North Dakota instead?

We had several packages between us—a wedding present for Leah, who for some reason actually thought she'd use a home-size cotton-candy machine in her new married life. Leah gave up drinking tea because she doesn't like to heat water. She's hoping that when she says "I do," Betty Crocker will be downloaded into her brain.

I purchased T-shirts, shorts and socks for Dad. That's a family tradition that started when I was five and my mother took me shopping for his present for the very first time. I could get the biggest bang for the buck in the underwear department, and now, no matter what else I buy for him, he's disappointed without his Fruit of the Loom.

Matt ordered engraved leather planners for everyone in his office and purchased a pen for himself that cost more than I'd spent on all my purchases combined. I could hear screams from Camp Snoopy and the sounds of little kids begging to go on the rides. Oddly enough, I felt soothed and calm, like an island in the storm. I was so relaxed I felt the marrow of my bones melting. We had a bag of chocolate-coated coffee beans and part of an uneaten funnel cake from the theme park on the bench between us. I was hoping to spend the rest of the afternoon in a movie marathon to complete the relaxing, mindless day.

But Matt had other ideas. He began grilling me with questions. Where had I said I'd gone to school? What was my major field of study? Had I interned at any noteworthy companies? Done any advertising campaigns he might recognize? Was I good with Quark, Excel, PowerPoint, etc.? Had I read the series of business books on which he'd based his theory of business management?

Borrrrring. There was buttered popcorn waiting. I'd given up carbs for two days just so I could justify an afternoon at the movies.

I tried turning the tables on him to see how he liked it but got monosyllabic answers like "Harvard," "MBA" and "Warren Buffet."

"So what's this about?" I finally asked. "Do I need a résumé to get into foreign films these days?"

"Just wondering." Then he turned those bone-melting green eyes on me, did a Vulcan mind meld with my brain and made me forget he was irritating me. "I want to know everything there is to know about you, Whitney. You do understand that, don't you?"

I bought it for a few minutes before coming to my senses. "Then why don't you ask me more about my personal life?"

"I want to know it all."

"Okay. I'm an only child with the world's greatest—and oddest—parents. I like to play tennis and water-ski, my favorite color is red and if I had to be stranded on a desert island with only three things, I'd take a Bible, a working telephone and an unlimited supply of animal crackers. Then I could call someone on the phone to do airdrops of food, a bed and a library full of books."

I watched his expression with something more than idle curiosity. It was time I discovered what Matt thought about the Bible. God's been on my case about it all week. I know how God works. Questions about Matt's faith kept popping into my mind. I'd run into the verse in 2 Corinthians 6:14 "You are not the same as those who do not believe. So do not join yourselves to them…." not only in my personal devotions but on the Christian radio station as I drove to work *and* in Sunday's sermon. God is not shy about making a point, but I do have to be consciously listening to Him to hear it.

"Really? Very interesting."

How's that for a response?

"So what's the most 'interesting' part?" I'd hoped we'd have this discussion somewhere other than on a bench near Camp Snoopy, but beggars can hardly be choosers.

"I had no idea you liked animal crackers so much. Have you considered trying honey-roasted peanuts as an alternative?"

I smacked him lightly on the arm. "Be serious!"

"What if I am?"

"I'm a Christian, Matt. It's what I'm all about. If need be, the only thing I'd take to that island is my Bible."

"I think that's wonderful. I really do." He smiled at me with one of those disarming grins that always make me lose track of my thoughts.

"Do you understand what that means?" I finally stammered. "Are you a Christian, too?"

I felt more than heard a little gap between my question and his answer. "I grew up going to church, Whitney. My family never missed a Sunday."

It didn't occur to me until tonight as I was brushing my teeth that that wasn't exactly the answer I'd wanted to hear.

November 3

The last person I'd expected to meet at Kim and Kurt's house was Dr. Andrews, but there he was, sprawled on Kim's couch, holding a coffee mug and yelling, along with Kurt, at the television. The Vikings were playing the Green Bay Packers, intense rivals since the early 1960s, before I was born.

Kim put a finger over her lips. We watched them fill the family room with testosterone for a moment before tiptoeing past the doorway into the formal living room.

"You're either doing great or not so well, considering that your doctor is making a house call," I commented and flopped into a chair.

"'Great,' so the doctor says." Kim looked more like her old self, but there were still dark rings under her eyes and I could tell she hadn't been sleeping well. "Kurt and Chase have fallen into their old friendship as if weeks instead of years have passed, and I'm loving it for Kurt's sake. Without Chase as my doctor, Kurt would have had a nervous breakdown by now. Chase keeps assuring him that what I have is treatable now, and nothing like the death sentence of forty years ago."

"And you?"

"I'm not always so sure." I saw how much this brave face was costing her. "I'm so afraid sometimes. My own body has betrayed me. It's logical that if cancer cells develop in one place, they can do it in another. Part of me wants to go through every sort of treatment available and knock this thing out of the ballpark. Another just wants to close my eyes and hide under the covers until it all goes away."

"That doesn't sound like a very practical idea."

"I suppose not, but having to go in for radiation every single day for six weeks isn't easy." Her head drooped, and I saw her weariness. "By the time I dress the baby, take him to a sitter, drive to the hospital, spend an hour there and get home, I feel like I've climbed Mount Everest. Every bone in my body aches with exhaustion. Chase says a lumpectomy and radiation are as effective as a mastectomy for the early stages. I know we need to kill any cells that still might exist after surgery. I know I can't get away from it, not that I'd want to, but..."

"How many weeks of this do you have left?"

"Four or five."

"Can't they do it all at once?"

"Chase explained that when radiation is done over a longer period, the cancer cells become inactive while allowing the healthy cells to daily repair themselves. Otherwise it would do too much damage to my healthy tissue."

"Does it hurt?"

"The area is a little tender and swollen. Sometimes I'm stiff." Her faint smile grew lopsided and wobbly. "Plus, I'm tattooed with ink so the radiation therapist knows where to aim!"

"Trendy."

"Very funny. They're pinpricks on my skin. Chase says he'll lighten or remove them when I'm done. Never miss a monthly exam, Whitney. If I hadn't..." She paused to regroup. "I'm such a mess and I don't know what to do...."

"I'm praying for you," I offered, helpless to do anything else.

"I'm glad *you* are."

Kim said this so strangely that it caught my attention. "What does that mean? That someone else *isn't* praying for you?"

"Yeah. Me. It feels as though my prayers stop at the ceiling and bounce back to me like so much reflected light. I don't think I'm getting them up there anymore. It's as if a heavenly blockade is preventing Him from hearing me."

"I doubt it's a 'heavenly' anything. If something is making you feel like that, Kim, I have a hunch it's coming from the other direction."

She sighed and rubbed the tops of her thighs with her palms. As she did so, she rocked slightly back and forth to comfort herself with the motion. She'd lost weight and I could see her bony collarbone in the scooped neck of her shirt.

"You can't trust your feelings. Faith is about believing when you *don't* have any proof," I reminded her.

Her expression was anguished. "Maybe we're deluding ourselves," she whispered. "Maybe He doesn't exist at all."

I was speechless at first, something rare for me. "But… can't…it's…I mean…" Then I blurted, "But God *does* exist! I know He does, and you do, too."

"Do I?" She stared at her fingernails. "I've been known to be wrong."

Was this what "crises of faith" looked like?

"Have you talked to anyone else about this?" I finally ventured.

"Everyone tries to 'tsk-tsk-tsk' me out of it, like it's a minor mood swing I'm having. It makes me so *angry!* Can't anyone see how difficult this is for me?"

She clenched and unclenched her fists. I wanted to reach out and stop her but instead I allowed her to vent, rant and cry until the rage, anger and fear spilled out and she seemed empty of any emotion at all.

Then, suddenly, crazily, she burst out laughing.

"You have no idea how much better I feel!"

I gaped at her, dumbfounded.

She wiped the corner of her eye on the hem of her sweatshirt. "I've been staying cheerful and not expressing my fear or frustration because I don't want to upset anyone, or make them worry. I don't want to cry around Wesley, and Kurt is such a big teddy bear that it would send him into a tailspin to know I've been stuffing it all inside. I needed to *explode!*" She wiped away another tear. "Thanks for listening and not trying to 'fix' anything. That's what I've needed."

"Hey, that's a skill of mine—not being helpful, I mean. Call me anytime you don't want something repaired." I moved to her side of the davenport and hugged her.

Hugging Kim is like hugging a skeleton in a sweatshirt.

"You know," I joked weakly, "maybe Dr. Andrews could do a fat transplant. You could use a little more these days, and I have some to spare. What do you think, should we ask him?"

"Ask him what?" The topic of our conversation stood in the doorway looking at us.

Oh, great. The last thing I needed to do was call his attention to my thighs and tummy, my ripest spots for a fat harvest.

Fortunately, his eyes went directly to Kim. He was sizing up the situation, including the tear tracks on Kim's cheeks.

He sat down, calmly leaned back in the chair and crossed his arms over his chest. He looked straight at Kim with a grave expression. "I have a mastectomy patient who says that removing her prosthetics and throwing them against a wall is very tension relieving. Since you don't need prosthetics, maybe you can use Nerf balls or something."

Kim's jaw dropped and I burst out laughing.

"It's almost as good as tears for getting the emotions out."

"Hear that, Kim? Just what the doctor ordered."

"Chase, quit kidding," Kim chided, but I could see a slight smile on her face.

"No kidding involved. You're like a kettle left on the stove to boil. If that kettle is ignored, one of two things will happen. It will either blow its lid or scorch itself to the stove. You're in danger of the same thing—blowing up or burning out. You need to find ways to release the pressure and the tension that's inevitable at a time like this. Sounds hokey, but keeping your mind busy and your body engaged will help you get through this."

I fell a little bit in love with him at that moment. A man who could understand a woman's emotions so fully—and commiserate so effectively—had to be one in a million.

"You aren't going to tell me that I'm 'lucky' that things have turned out as well as they have and that I should shape up?" Kim asked sharply.

"I'm certainly not going to tell you to 'shape up.' I'd be worried about you if you weren't working through this." Then he looked at me with those searing blue eyes. "I'm pleased that you have a friend who's obviously willing to hang in there with you."

Kim took my hand and gave it a squeeze. "I know. She's the best."

Chase looked at me a long time before nodding. "I can see that."

November 4

It was difficult to get up this morning after spending the night pursuing Dr. Andrews through my dreams. Was it even legal to be that handsome, charming and intelligent? It was certainly risky for my personal mental state. Sneaky thief that he is, he'd stolen my heart.

I have no business having a teenager's crush on my best friend's doctor. Especially one who, according to Kurt, has sworn off women. That's volunteering for heartache. Besides, I have perfectly good men in my life already.

In fact, there were messages from both Matt and Eric on my answering machine when I got home after a late night at work. Eric wanted to know if I would go help him pick out wool socks and a new stocking cap for his trip up north, and Matt had called to say good-night.

What more could a girl want?

November 5

twit: **1.** A pregnant goldfish. **2.** Me, when I get embroiled in Mitzi's schemes.

Mitzi was lying in wait for me at the office door this a.m. Her eyes were gleaming and her feral expression told me she'd hatched an idea and was ready to spring it on the world, or—more specifically—on me.

As I hung my coat in the closet, she thrust a handful of papers into my face. "Here, this should help you figure it out."

"What's that?" I asked cautiously. Once before Mitzi had

asked me to figure something out, and I ended up on the floor under her desk trying to guess where the wires she'd pulled from the back of her computer tower belonged. It will be a long time before artificial intelligence will be able to overcome incompetence. Another time, I ended up working a plunger in the ladies' room.

"About men. I can see that you're not good at them, but at least this will give you some guidelines." She shoved the paper at me again.

I didn't know you could be "good" at men. The first woman on earth had blown it with her man over an apple. How could I be expected to be an expert on a creature so confusing?

Just then, Harry launched out of his office with a list of things for me to do, and I had to put down Mitzi's mysterious offering to work on those projects. Since Harry's perm is growing out, it has taken on a life of its own. Some days he appears to have stood in a gust of wind and his curls are all blowing in one direction. Other days he looks like a "before" poster boy for hair conditioner and needs to tame his frizzies and broken ends. We're wondering now when he'll reperm. Bryan says that Harry's hairdo has become our office mascot, and we'll miss it if it grows out. There's something bizarre but true about that observation.

I didn't get to Mitzi's notes until lunchtime, when I ate a tuna salad with pickles and low-fat mayo at my desk. I really shouldn't eat tuna in the office, because it smells like a fishing boat for the rest of the day, but my only other choices for protein this morning when I packed my lunch were a piece of string cheese or a pale, very jiggly glob of tofu. Tofu scares me. It reminds me of brains in a lab jar. Still, I buy it, intend to eat it and throw it out over and over again.

It's interesting that Mitzi avoids work at all costs when she's actually a very good typist. She'd hardly made any mistakes at all on the manifesto she'd created for me.

Mitzi, generous to the core, had devised a point system for ranking men.

HOW TO RATE MEN:
What to Look For and What to Avoid

Characteristics	*Number of Points*
Good-looking	4
Drop-dead gorgeous	5
Financially stable	3
Wealthy	5
Broke	-3
Good teeth	2
Clean fingernails	1
Hobbies that involve motors, guns or engines	-3
Hobbies that involve me	5
Chews with mouth open	-20
Owns a home	3
Rents an apartment	1
Lives with parents	-3
Good shaving cologne	2
Attentive	3
Remembers your birthday	2
Brings flowers on ordinary days	2
Is taller than you	2
Is shorter than you	-1
Good listener	3
Watches TV while he listens to you	-2
Says "Just a minute" when you ask a question	-1
Doesn't hear a word you're saying	-3
Likes to give jewelry	3
Likes to give advice	-2
Can cook and does	3

Can cook and doesn't	-3
Can't cook and does	-4
Wears suit and tie	2
Can't match clothing	-1
Insists on picking up all tabs; refuses to "go Dutch"	4
In medical field	5

Hmm. Just running down that list and picking the characteristics that apply most, Matt gets a 29, my father a 27, Dr. Andrews a 28 (could be higher, but I don't know that much about him) and poor Eric a 2. Eric's good teeth, clean fingernails and good looks just couldn't outweigh his forgetfulness, apartment living, finances and love of engines.

I did, however, pencil in a final rating, Christian…100.

"Mitzi, this list has nothing to do with personal characteristics like kindness, compassion, gentleness…."

She waved a hand in the air. "That's all the stuff you get hung up on, Whitney. This is about all the stuff you'll *miss*." She preened a bit and added, "My husband is a 44."

Ick. Too much information.

"Thanks a bunch, Mitzi. Now, do you have those letters I dictated typed?"

She looked at me as if I'd lost my mind. "Of course not. I was *busy*."

November 6

Leah called to say she's bringing the bridesmaids' dresses and a seamstress to Kim's house for a try-on session soon. I questioned the wisdom of it but she insisted. I'm a little worried. If I expect the event to push *me* into a period of deep depression, what about poor Kim?

The thought of having to try on my butter-daffodil sunflower-colored dress drove me to do something I should have done weeks ago. Join a health club.

News flash: Joining a health club is the stupidest idea I've ever had. Except, maybe, for that can of spray-on hair I bought late one night after eating Haagen-Dazs until my brain froze. I was only trying to help Dad, knowing how self-conscious he is about that teeny-weeny bald spot of his.

But back to the health club—what was I thinking? Had I momentarily forgotten everything I know about fitness clubs? The concrete, the sweat, the muscled men in embarrassingly tight clothing? The women who work out in more makeup than I own? The meat-market atmosphere full of bulgy-bicepsed, pumped-up, toned, tanned, taut, trim, twenty- and thirty-somethings?

And that's how I felt before walking through the front door.

Mom says I can't let poor body image or low self-esteem rule my life. Easy for her to say. I came upon her doing yoga today, and if I hadn't caught her in time, she would have put the heel of her foot on the back of her head just to see how it felt. She says if Madonna can do it, why not her? I told her she couldn't do it because she wasn't Madonna. Neither did I want her to join the circus as the Human Pretzel attraction on some sleazy midway. Most of all, I didn't want to drive her to urgent care to have her untangled. Oh, yes, and I'd give my eyeteeth to be able to do the same thing.

Everyone in a health club is either peppy, cheery or wears a do-or-die look of grim determination. Bernard, the hulking body builder/trainer who was assigned to me, was of the do-or-die group.

"Before we do a body-fat analysis, let's just get your height and weight, shall we?" I stared, fascinated, at Bernard's biceps, which were nearly the circumference of my skull.

"But I hardly know you," I bleated. Other than the people at EEAT, I haven't told anyone how much I weigh since sixth grade.

He roared as if I'd made the funniest joke on the planet and pointed his finger at the scale. I had a sneaking hunch I hadn't just signed up with a nice fitness coach. I'd signed on with The Terminator.

I didn't like the unintelligible gurgles Bernard made as he examined my statistics. When he sighed and clucked his tongue like my grandmother always does when she disapproves of something I'm doing, I sensed immediately that I was in trouble. And when he came at me with calipers and electronic sensors for my upper arm to make doubly sure he'd read things right, I knew I'd regret anything that happened to me from this point on.

"You have very high body fat for a woman of your height and weight," he said sadly.

"You mean my weight's okay but I'm over-fat?"

"We have our work cut out for us. You haven't been getting enough exercise."

Flabby. Flab, flubber, blubber. It all boils down to one thing—Orca on a treadmill. I felt the flesh on my arms jiggle. Had I developed a wingspan instead of triceps?

"Can you help me?" How pathetic I sounded! Of course he could help me. He's charging me enough to make me into Wonder Woman.

Bernard's idea of "help," however, is more like basic, garden-variety torture. I sat in on a spinning class and came out feeling like my bottom had been imprinted with a bicycle seat. I thought I'd get a hernia lifting weights and then discovered that I *wasn't* lifting weights at all, but just the bar to which the weights will be added. I did crunches with Bernard holding my feet and barking orders. By the time Bernard and I were done, my legs had turned to rubber and I was leaning on a wall to keep from falling.

I should have quit right then and there, but he already had my check, and his gold front tooth intimidated me too much to ask him to return it.

November 7

"Are you ready for this?" I asked Kim as we sat at her kitchen table waiting for Leah to arrive with our dresses and the woman who was to "fit" us. "Are you sure you're up to it? You're awfully pale. I worry about you."

"It will do me good to have a distraction. No matter how many times I throw those silly Nerf balls you foisted on me, I keep wondering…what's going to happen next?"

Kim's worrying about radiation, about Wesley, about her housework and just about everything else these days. It's so unlike Kim, whose favorite scripture is Matthew 6: 25-34. She recites it anytime I'm anxious over something. "I tell you, don't worry about everyday life—whether you have enough food, drink and clothes….Look at the birds. They don't need to plant or harvest or put food in barns, because your Heavenly Father feeds them. And you are far more valuable to Him than they are. Can all your worries add a single moment to your life? Of course not…. And if God cares so wonderfully for flowers that are here today and gone tomorrow, won't He more surely care for you? You have so little faith!… So don't worry about tomorrow, for tomorrow will bring its own worries. Today's trouble is enough for today."

I think she's even worrying about worrying.

"You've just had surgery. You're having radiation. Is it any wonder you get down sometimes? Kim, depression can make you—"

"I'm not depressed!" Her temper flared. "How many times do I have to tell you that?"

Hot button. I never learn. I just keep pressing it. "I didn't mean to…" It's easy for me to talk. I wasn't the one who'd had all these changes in my life.

To my relief, Leah burst into the house in a swathe of dress bags followed by the small woman she introduced as her tailor. Leah was radiant. An honest-to-goodness natural blonde with blue eyes and porcelain skin, Leah is the epitome of the classic Scandinavian woman. Surely her ancestors lived along the fjords of Norway and rode the Viking ships. Of course, there are a lot of Scandinavians in Minnesota, but I'd guess there are few more beautiful than Leah.

Engagement does something wonderful for a woman. It's an ideal time, really. She knows she's loved and wanted, has a great party to plan, gets a new dress and doesn't know enough about her soon-to-be roommate's bad habits to be upset by them. Besides, she suffers from temporary fiancé blindness, and he can do no wrong in her eyes. Too bad they can't treat the condition with glasses. Some women might change their minds before the wedding if they got a glimpse of reality.

When Leah pulled my dress out of the bag, I didn't know whether to laugh or cry. It was the color of free-range-chicken egg yolks and sunflowers with a touch of pumpkin thrown in. I suppose I was so stunned when I'd seen it before, I'd blanked out the exact hues.

Still, my heart warmed when I glanced at Kim. Even she had to fight back laughter. Maybe this whole ordeal would cheer her up.

"Aren't they great? This one's yours, Whitney." Leah spread out a flouncy, ruffled dress made with enough fabric to clothe the Statue of Liberty. She eyed my dark hair and eyes and pale complexion. "I hope it works with your coloring."

There isn't a two- or four-legged creature on the planet who has coloring compatible with this color. It's only good for Halloween and Thanksgiving floral arrangements, right there with the tiny ears of decorative corn, mini-pumpkins, gourds, asters and marigolds. Which, I suppose, made some sense, as Leah had planned the wedding date just before Thanksgiving. I look great in red and love mistletoe. Why couldn't she have waited until Christmas?

"The florist is doing amazing things with fall leaves in the arrangements, and we're doing horns of plenty as table decorations. Won't that be sweet?"

Darling. I've never had the opportunity to blend with sumac before.

"This is nice," Kim said as she came in from the other room where she'd slipped into her dress.

On her, it was. She's been too nervous to eat. Her waist is absolutely tiny. And, to my amazement, she actually can wear yellow next to her face without looking jaundiced.

Leah squealed and clapped her hands happily. I took my turn in the bedroom and came out wearing the twin to Kim's dress.

Occasionally I've seen identical twins who look the same except one, somehow, seems prettier than the other, as though one twin is a caricature of the other, the same yet very different. Well, that's Kim and me. Kim looks like a princess in her dress and I look like her ugly stepsister.

"Aren't the dresses cute?" Leah gushed. "Whitney, let's see yours…oh."

Maybe it was the way I'd humped my shoulders or the pained grimace on my face, but I knew I was not nearly so "cute" as Kim.

Friend that she is, Kim raced over and pulled at the flounce tickling my ear. "It needs alterations, that's all. Once it's fitted, the dress will be lovely."

"You think so?" Leah said hopefully.

"Absolutely. And, Whitney, stand up! There. That's better."

By the time the tailor had clucked, fussed, mumbled something about opening a couple tight seams and promised me I'd be delighted on the wedding day, Leah went home happy. I received instructions to work on my posture and my expression and, best of all, the dresses went back into the clothing bags where they belonged and were left with the seamstress who would alter them. I trust that she will make me into a lady-in-waiting.

November 8

Talk about lady-in-waiting! Waiting for the phone to ring, that is.

I don't know what Matt and Eric have been doing for the past couple days, but neither has called me. They'd both warned me they were going out of town, but I'd hoped that *one* of them would pick up the phone to say hello. There was a time when Eric and I were seriously dating that I would have spent the duration of his absence obsessing about why the phone hadn't rung. Once I gave that up as totally unproductive, it improved my outlook immensely. I even got a life.

I'd be more upset about being neglected if Kurt hadn't called me with a request.

"Listen, Whit," he began. "I want to get Kim out of the house for the evening...."

"Sure, I'll baby-sit."

"No, I want you to come with us. I thought we could maybe...double-date...or something."

"That sounds nice, but there's only one of me."

"Can't you call Eric or that nut-roasting guy you've been talking about?"

"Out of town."

Kurt was disappointed but not discouraged. "Okay, I'll figure something out. Just be ready to go somewhere tomorrow night. Maybe we can catch a movie and dinner. Kim needs to get out, and I've already got the sitter."

"You're a good man, Kurt. She's lucky to have you."

"I'm the lucky one, Whitney. Kim's problems have made me realize how blessed we are. I didn't know how much I took for granted until now." There was a catch of emotion in his voice that made tears come to my eyes. To love and be loved so much...awesome.

"What do I wear to 'go somewhere'?"

"Whatever is comfortable, I guess."
With that bit of fashion advice, we said goodbye.

Lord, I'm feeling jumpy tonight. The aches and pains I've attributed to Bernard and his systematic, high-speed plan to get me into shape, but my heart feels edgy, too. It's…uneasy…as if something big or bad or surprising is about to happen. I've become complacent recently, feeling self-satisfied with the attention I've received from Matt and Eric. I'm much more attentive to You when I'm in trouble than when things are going well. Sorry. Without Your forgiveness and Your Son, I'd be…it's too devastating to think about. As I write this, I feel better. It's all about where I focus my eyes. When they're on You, the edginess goes away, for I know that no matter what, You're in charge, that You love me and that You'll never let me down. Kim's very blue lately, and I'd like Your advice on what to say to her. She is depressed, even though she won't admit it. Will You give me the right words at the right time, God? And thanks. I'm feeling much calmer already.

Reverently and with gratitude,
Whitney

CHAPTER 8

November 9

On my way to work there were several lanes closed this morning, which provided me with the opportunity to sit even longer than usual in rush-hour traffic. I don't mind. It's the one time I get to go slow on the freeway. I usually leave for the office an hour or two before we open, so I wasn't worried about being late. Plus, it's at least as entertaining as the morning news.

I'm boggled by what drivers do in their cars during rush hour. Checking teeth for lipstick marks in the rearview mirror is one thing, but doing hair and putting on makeup? Spreading jelly on a bagel, fixing a cup of tea in a traveler's mug from a stash in the cubbyhole and reading the *Star Tribune?* Once I saw a man spill coffee and change shirts on the Bloomington strip during a big crunch. Good thing he hadn't taken his laundry out of his car the night before.

It's a sign of the times. People used to expect delays. Now we're insulted if someone offers to send information by anything other than e-mail, fax or first-day air. ASAP used to mean get it to me "as soon as possible." Now it means "Get it to me yesterday."

When I got to work, Betty, who has never been seen with a hair out of place in the last ten years, was looking down-right messy. Her hair still had a flat spot in back where she'd slept on her salon "do," and she was wearing the same jacket she'd worn yesterday. Betty maintains a calendar for her clothes so that she never repeats a garment in a four-week cycle, so something was up.

She had eBay on her personal laptop and an auction was only seconds from ending. She was in a dead-heat race to the finish with a buyer named RabidShopper. The bid was going up in increments on a gilded music box and time was run-ning out.

"What time did you get here?" I asked.

"Shh. I'm trying to concentrate."

"She was here when I came," Bryan offered as he handed me a cup of coffee. "I think she's been here all night."

"You've got to be kidding!"

"Look at the garbage can under her desk. A pizza box, a pair of panty hose with runs in them, a No-Doze box and ten empty cans of Diet Coke. You tell me she didn't spend the night."

"Were you under her desk snooping?" I didn't know which dumbfounded me more, Betty pulling an all-nighter or Bryan acting like a television detective.

"It's an addiction, plain and simple," our resident Freud de-duced. "Where else can you get a heart-pumping adrenaline rush without moving anything but your mouse finger?"

"And why are you here so early?"

"I finished all that stuff you dumped on my desk yesterday."

"Oh."

I felt guilty…until he added, "So could I get off at noon today?"

Just once, I wish he'd look me straight in the eye when he talks to me. I suspect Bryan has low self-esteem, or none at all. Because his eyes dart everywhere but to my face, I always feel he's holding something back or not telling the whole truth. But maybe that's too much to ask of a man whose primary excitement is hiding from conflict in the men's room and looking in ladies' garbage cans. And he is a good assistant, when I can catch him, so I shouldn't complain too much.

I glanced at my watch. "I doubt you can finish the projects I have for you before twelve."

He sighed, sounding very put-upon, and scooted to his desk knowing full well that I'd make every effort to give him his wish.

People always tell me how "nice" I am. I just do unto others as I want them to do unto me. Harry doesn't always aspire to that theory, however, and today dumped a huge project on my desk. Since Betty was sluggish and in mourning over the loss of the music box to RabidShopper and couldn't help me, it was nearly six-thirty when I finally arrived at home. That left me fifteen minutes to get ready for my night out.

I took Kurt at his word and went casual. Jeans (which felt loose!) and a stretched-out but oh-so-comfortable fisherman knit sweater that did nothing for my figure but make me (I think) look cuddly and picks up amber glints in my dark eyes. I pulled my hair into a ponytail, ran blusher and gloss over the appropriate spots and got to the door just as the bell rang.

"Hi, Kurt…" I began. But I was staring into the beautiful sapphire-like eyes of Dr. Chase Andrews. He was dressed casually, too, casually à la Ralph Lauren, that is. Fine-wale corduroy trousers, a fabulous cream-colored sweater with suede on the elbows over a russet, green and gold plaid shirt and a brown belt with gold buckle shaped like Porky Pig. All he needed was a glistening bay horse about seventeen hands high at his side, a Great Dane by his feet and a riding crop in his hand to be the perfect country gentleman. I, in my baggy getup, wouldn't have been hired as his stable boy.

"Wha…" My mouth flapped open and stayed that way.

"I hear we're going to cheer Kim up tonight. Kurt called and asked me to pick you up. Apparently Wesley's babysitter is late. I hope you don't mind."

I didn't, of course, and minded even less when I saw his Volvo SUV with every bell and whistle known to automobile fanciers. The ideal carriage for the country gentleman and his…me.

Pretty much speechless for the ride to Kim's, I petted the creamy leather seat and pinched my thigh to make sure I wasn't dreaming. Chase was comfortable with my silence, not realizing, I suppose, that I'd actually *lost* my ability to talk and would probably need either medication or therapy to get my tongue moving again.

He was, in fact, utterly relaxed, humming along with the radio and smiling at me occasionally as if he'd had lots of speechless women cowering in the front seat of his vehicle wondering what glorious lightning strike had transported her into this alternate universe. Or maybe he had.

I kept sneaking peeks at him as we rode. I'd never studied his profile before and, to my delight, it was a piece of art, perfectly proportioned. I hadn't realized there were faces like that that weren't gracing the pages of *Gentleman's Quarterly* or *People* magazine's Most Beautiful People edition. And what made him even more attractive was the fact that he doesn't seem to know how good he looks.

He hummed and bobbed his head in time to the music, sometimes mouthing the words to the song and making faces as he did so. He especially got into character when Elvis's "Won't You Be My Teddy Bear?" played. Have I mentioned lately that I'm crazy about Elvis?

Fortunately, Kim's isn't a far drive from my place, so we arrived without my discomfiture being too apparent. Had I known it would be Chase Andrews on the far side of the door, I would have taken considerably more time with my hair, clothes and makeup—like a week or two.

Kurt appeared tense when he met us at the door. He and Chase exchanged a weighted look, communicating without words. Kim and I do that sometimes, but it was especially gratifying to see this bond between the men. It occurred to me that God had brought Kurt and Chase together early in their lives so when Kurt needed a great doctor and supportive friend years later, there would be one waiting in the wings.

Sometimes, when I'm contemplating the bigness of God, I imagine Him as a divine chess master, looking at the world and anticipating events centuries ahead of the current situations in which we find ourselves. It helps me to remember, when I become dissatisfied in my own life, that God's already seen my needs and has lined up a next move for me. Still, it's my job to call on Him to reveal what that might be and to take action. God isn't pushy. He's willing to wait for us to ask for help.

God is all about relationships. He wants to have one with each of us. He sacrificed a lot when He gave us free will. I can see His point, though. He wants us to come to Him because we want to, not because we have no other choice. Not being puppets, we get to fling ourselves into bad choices and stupid decisions for as long as it takes to discover the real answers for life.

Kurt and Chase clapped each other on the back the way guys do, and I noticed that Chase, though more trim, was nearly as tall and solid as Kurt. To get away from all that masculinity, I headed toward Wesley's bedroom, where I knew Kim would be. She has a difficult time leaving Wesley with a sitter. She feels much worse about it than Wesley, who loves the grandma-like lady down the street who comes in to watch him.

Wesley was already snoozing in his crib, looking angelic and smelling of baby powder and no-tears baby shampoo. The sitter was beside the crib in the rocking chair looking at him with such sweet pleasure that I guessed she'd be watching him sleep long after we left. Kim was the only miserable one in the room.

"Hey," I whispered.

"Hey, yourself." She touched the sitter's shoulder to indicate she was leaving, and we backed out of the baby's room. Kim shut the door softly.

Then she wiped her hands across her eyes as if wiping away a fog and smiled at me. "Surprised?"

"Flabbergasted. Why didn't you tell me the dazzling Dr. Andrews was going to be my escort?"

"Kurt planned it all. I'm as out of the loop as you are." She smiled mistily. "He's so sweet to me."

"You don't look very happy about it."

"I don't know what's wrong with me, Whitney. I've never felt this way before. Chase says that everything is fine physically, that I'm doing even better than expected and that my prognosis is excellent. But mentally I feel like I'm walking around under this big, ominous cloud."

"Kurt's right. You need to get out. Where are we going?" We linked arms and returned to the living room.

"Your guess is as good as mine."

Neither of us could have guessed our destination was a karaoke contest at the zoo to raise money for their species survival plan. It's a program to ensure the continued existence of endangered species and someday reintroduce them into their natural habitat. I couldn't have picked a better outing myself.

Although I didn't mean for it to happen, Chase picked up the tab not only for my entrance fee into the zoo, but for the unique smorgasbord-like supper we had as we grazed through the food booths set up for the occasion.

I did mental battle with the images of Tansy and Bernard being shocked as I munched deep-fried cheese curds, a gyro, an ear of buttered corn and a large paper cone full of oven-fresh miniature chocolate chip cookies. I knew I shouldn't be doing it. It wasn't good for me, it certainly wasn't honoring my body and Chase was seeing me in full gluttony mode. My only pitiful excuse is that it was over two months since I'd been to the state fair, and it was going to be a long time until I could have anything like this again. Some people are experts on fine dining. I am a connoisseur of fair food.

There's nothing like the food at the Minnesota State Fair. You can watch waves of people chewing on gigantic turkey legs wrested from Volkswagen-size turkeys, swirls of cotton candy big as thunderclouds, pork chops on sticks, plates of blooming onions and funnel cakes, crispy sugared elephant ears, mini-doughnuts, potato skins, buffalo burgers and more. Even the health-conscious people usually sport white mustaches from the all-you-can-drink milk booth. For a guy with a flat stomach and washboard abs, Chase ate pretty well himself. We had a definite linking of the minds at the caramel-corn booth.

All was going swimmingly except for the expression on Kim's face. Poor Kurt was beside himself. He kept offering her food, suggesting she sit down, stand up, go to the rest room, listen to the music the band was playing or anything that might snap her out of this mood. To each suggestion, she'd nod weakly and take wooden steps to obey him. Not exactly what he'd had in mind. Finally, in a desperate plunge to make her laugh, he signed all of us up for the karaoke contest.

I, unfortunately, was standing behind a door when God gave out musical talent. Yet to my delight and dismay, the idea of me singing and making a fool of myself in public seemed to cheer Kim considerably.

"I can't do this! Kurt, are you out of your mind?" I lunged for the front of his sweater to shake some sense into him just as Chase caught me by the back of my stretched-out hood.

"Oh no, you don't. If I'm about to ruin any shred of credibility I have with Kim, then you do, too."

I turned to my dear, trusted friend, the one who wouldn't let me down. "You wouldn't let that happen, would you, Kim?"

She broke into her first genuine smile of the night. "Of course I would. In fact, I'll sing with Kurt if you and Chase do a duet."

Big deal. Kim and Kurt sing in the church choir. Even little Wesley can cry on key.

"No." *Just say no.* Isn't that how we teach kids to stay out of trouble? Apparently even that doesn't work when your friends are determined to have you make a fool of yourself at karaoke.

We got to pick our own music, according to the promoters who were happily raking in money from the reckless participants. Kurt and Kim picked a favorite gospel song sung by Elvis, "You'll Never Walk Alone." The only song that Chase and I could agree on, because we both knew the words, was the enchanting Sonny and Cher classic "I've Got You Babe."

Kurt and Kim got a standing ovation and I saw several people wipe tears from the corners of their eyes when the song ended. It would be the epitome of understatement to say Chase and I made a slightly different impression.

It didn't help that as we mounted the stairs to the stage, he put his hand at the small of my back to help me up. Startled, I stumbled on the last step and skidded face downward toward the microphone.

His touch was less exhilarating the second time, when he shoved his hands under my armpits, hoisted me upright and dusted me off. Fortunately, the deluded audience, under the influence of too much sugar, thought I'd tripped on purpose.

Sonny and Cher had been a comedy act, too. The only thing I could think of to be grateful for was that I've been attending EEAT and there was less of me to lift.

I might have been able to "talk" my way through the song by keeping my eyes on the prompter and mechanically reading the words, but Chase grabbed my hand and made me face him. He wanted us to look authentic. That left me frantically moving my head back and forth between the words on the prompter and looking lovingly into "Sonny's" eyes.

The most Cher-like thing about me is my long dark hair. It fell in a rather nice blanket across my shoulders because Kim pulled out my ponytail fastener just before I mounted the stairs. About halfway through the song, I remembered to start shaking my head and running my fingers through my hair just like Cher.

Chase's voice is remarkably good. He imitated Sonny perfectly but occasionally threw in something that was more James Taylor. With his easy charm in front of a crowd, they went wild. At least that's what I'm assuming made them wild. I suppose it could have been my fingernails-on-chalkboard responses to his vocalizations.

It was the longest three minutes of my life. At the end, when Chase was taking bows and hissing at me to bow with him, I let my hair fall completely over my face in shame. The only redeeming part was getting a glimpse of Kim clapping and laughing until tears rolled down her cheeks.

"You *do* sound like Cher!" she squealed after Chase toted me off the stage. "That wonderful gravelly quality. I had no idea!"

Me, neither.

After sharing something as intimately embarrassing as our duet, I completely gave up any attempt to impress Chase Andrews. I'd never see the man again, that was certain. It was a wonder that he hadn't run off the stage to call a taxi, pack his medical practice and start anew in a different city and state. The amazing part was that he'd actually seemed to enjoy it.

We stopped at a coffee shop for some decaf lattes and a rehash of the evening. My pratfalls were a highlight, along with my Cher-hair, Chase's voice and how "cute" we looked together. Then Chase and Kurt fell into one quiet conversation and Kim and I into another.

"Having fun?" Kim waggled her eyebrows in Chase's direction as if to add *with him?*

"Absolutely! It's been the opportunity of a lifetime! It's the first time I've mortified myself more than three times in a single evening. A new personal best."

"Be serious."

I took Kim's hand. "It's been great. The company is wonderful, Sonny and Cher probably upped donations to the zoo by three hundred percent and you're smiling."

"It's been a while," Kim admitted. "I don't know why it's been so hard to smile lately. Everything feels so…heavy. Even getting up in the morning is an effort. And showering? Sometimes I don't get it done until noon or just before Kurt gets home. I should be grateful I could be helped, and instead, I'm…numb."

I didn't know what to say. The diagnosis and surgery had been hard and scary, but this melancholy seemed to be taking her personality away.

Proverbs 18:14 came to mind. "The spirit of a man will sustain him in sickness, But who can bear a broken spirit?" Even then, in the days of Solomon, depression and hopelessness took a costly toll. Before I could speak, Kim changed the subject.

"He's nice, isn't he?"

"Yes. Very." I meant it with my whole heart.

"Chase has been such a good support for Kurt."

I stirred the liquid in my cup. Kurt and Chase were so involved in their own conversation that we were invisible to them. "Why is he still single? Never mind, I shouldn't have asked that."

"Chase was engaged and there was a nasty breakup—didn't I tell you? He's too much of a gentleman to say much more." She shook her head in amazement. "Who could pass up a gem like him?"

Who, indeed? *Not me.* A girl can fantasize, can't she?

We fell silent, sipped our lattes and, without intending to do so, eavesdropped on the men's conversation.

"So you caught them?" Kurt's voice was a soft but ferocious growl, and he and Chase leaned toward each other across the table, heads close together.

"They weren't exactly trying to hide."

"And neither of them could even tell you to your face?"

"If I'd walked in on them like that, I'd have…"

"Pounded him into the ground?"

Kurt cleared his throat. "I would have felt like it."

"So did I, but something got a hold of me and told me I'd regret it later."

"What *did* you do?"

"Told him to get out, that Claudia and I needed to be alone." Chase gave a humorless chuckle. "He didn't like that. Neither did she, come to think about it."

"Funny about that." Kurt's eyes were narrow and his expression one of barely controlled fury.

"I keep asking myself *why.*" There was genuine stupefaction in his voice. "Why did she do it? The minute I caught them, she became contrite and remorseful, as if being with another man while wearing my ring was some kind of accident."

"She apologized?"

"Over and over. Said she loved me and only me. That he was just a lapse of judgment, a stupid mistake."

"Some mistake," Kurt snorted. "Dating another man when you're engaged to be married is stupid, all right, but she knew what she was doing."

"Where did we go wrong?"

"Maybe 'we' didn't go wrong—just her. She's not worth it, buddy," Kurt said, his voice low. "You don't want anything to do with a woman who'd chase around behind your back."

"She was the first woman I'd really cared about in a long, long time." Chase ran his fingers through his hair until it spiked on top. "I should have seen it coming...there must have been something. I'm not blind. What did I miss?"

"Cheaters cheat. Just be grateful it happened before you said 'I do.'"

"She'd already ordered the wedding invitations," Chase marveled. "I suppose I should be glad she didn't have them engraved 'But I really love one of our groomsmen.'"

Ouch. Even I, who wasn't supposed to be listening, winced at that.

"Forget 'em both."

"You're right." Chase was completely unaware of the eavesdropper beside him. "And if I can live without her, then I can live without any woman in my life. There's no way I'm putting myself through this again."

"You aren't ready now, but maybe someday someone amazing might come along."

"Claudia *is* amazing. Beautiful, a brilliant chemist, good with kids and animals, generous, lovable...what more could a man want in a woman?"

"Fidelity," Kurt said bluntly.

It hit me like a Mack truck that somewhere in my mind I'd been sending up a little cheer that now there might be a chance for me. How tacky and how small! I need a cage for my imagination when it runs wild like that.

I'd perspired like a waterfall singing that dumb song. In my damp wool sweater, hair gone berserk, makeup free, middle-management, much-improvement-needed state, what did I have to offer him? Even though EEAT was working pretty well these days, there was no angular, model-thin visage in my future. I'd probably still look like the girl next door when I was eighty. Besides, Chase, whether he'd admit it or not, was obviously still in love with the woman who'd run off with one of the bridal party. And I'm crazy about Matt.

I slammed the door shut on that particular fantasy.

"Maybe it's for the best. Claudia took a lot of my time and attention," he was saying. "This way I can concentrate on my work. That's really what my life's about. The gifts I have are for healing."

"She never much liked your being at the hospital all the time, did she?"

"Hated it." Chase gave a humorless laugh. "I thought she'd get over it. But it doesn't matter now. I know what I have to do—concentrate on my work."

In a weird way, I was relieved. I didn't like the way thoughts about Chase kept cropping up in the middle of my relationship with Matt.

Kim and I glanced at each other as the guys stirred from their intense conversation. She shrugged her shoulders as if to say, "Now we know."

We *do* know. Even poor Cupid won't get an arrow through Chase's freshly grown armor.

"You guys ready to go?" Kurt gathered the dirty cups at the end of the table. What a guy. He even cleans in public.

"It's about that time." Chase looked at his watch, which *didn't* appear to be one of those fake Rolexes you can buy on the street. "I've got a heavy appointment load tomorrow."

"Me, too," I said. We're kept busy covering Kim's job while she's gone, but there was no way I would tell her that. She needs to be at a hundred percent before she comes back to that stress. And, I thought as we said goodbye, that could be a very long time. The cloud she'd fought her way out of for a few hours was back. When she hugged me good-night, I felt tears on her cheek.

★ ★ ★

On the way home, Chase was quiet, thinking, no doubt, about his conversation with Kurt.

We were almost to my place when I mustered the courage to ask him what was on my mind.

"Do you think Kim's all right?"

"Haven't you discussed it with Kim?"

Oh, he's good. No patient-doctor confidentiality breach here.

"Kim and Kurt both said things were moving along as well as could be expected. I'm not talking about that. I'm talking about her *mood*. I know Kim grew up in a family where weakness wasn't tolerated. I'm not sure how close she is to her family now, but she's still got that 'stiff upper lip' mentality, even though she seems depressed to me."

"It happens," he said cautiously. "Thanks for caring and for speaking up. I'll be watching."

"Kim's not a complainer," I warned. "I get the idea she believes depression is weakness, something she should be able to handle by herself."

"That's like someone trying to 'handle' diabetes. The fact is, sometimes the body become chemically unbalanced and needs to be straightened out medically. A few months of medication can make a big difference. There's no shame in that."

His practical, matter-of-fact approach made me feel better. Depression isn't just about pulling yourself up by your bootstraps. For Kim to ignore this wouldn't be any smarter than for her to have overlooked that lump. At least I'd spoken my concerns to someone who could help.

Why, Father, is life so complicated sometimes?

Chase shook my hand at the door to my apartment, and I noticed Mrs. Clempert poke her head out to see that I was all right.

I was fine, of course, other than being slightly affronted that this most delicious man treated me like a kid sister.

November 10

Kim has become one of the walking wounded. Worse yet, she can't see how hurt she actually is. Though I've seen it coming, depression has blindsided her completely.

It's become a daily ritual for me to stop at her house on the way home from work. We sit at the kitchen table and feed Cheerios to Wesley, drink hot chocolate and talk. I tell her the latest Mitzi story and give a brief report on the state of Harry's hair. She describes what she and the baby have done during the day and cries.

"I can't figure out what's wrong with me, Whit." As Kim ran her fingers through her hair, I noticed that she'd chewed her nails to the quick. "I should be loving every moment I spend at home with the baby. I should be so thankful to God that the cancer hadn't spread to any lymph nodes. I should be grateful for my wonderful husband and my friends—you, Chase—you've all seen me through. Maybe it's because I'm so tired all the time."

Who was she trying to convince? Me, or herself?

"There are a lot of 'shoulds' on your list," I observed. "What do you *want* to do?"

"Sleep. Stand in the shower and bawl. Watch game shows without turning up the volume." Kim smiled weakly. "I'm not coping very well, am I?"

Not well at all.

She straightened her shoulders into a determined set, just as she did every day when it was time for me to leave, as though she'd absorbed enough of my energy to carry on. "I'll just have to pray harder, that's all."

(Translation: "If I were better or different or praying harder, this wouldn't be happening to me.")

"This isn't your fault, Kim. You've been through some tough times—your hormones and emotions must be rocketing all over the place...."

"I'll work on it, Whit. Don't worry about it."

Work on it? This wasn't a sewing project to be dragged out of a closet and hemmed. The way she hit the wall so quickly after surgery, I'm not sure it's something she can fix by herself. What is she thinking?

CHAPTER 9

November 11

woofies: Well-off older folks

I stopped at my parents' house after I left Kim's hoping to find a little calm after an insane day at the office. Mom was cooking soup—gallons, no, oceans—of soup. The entire house was a sauna. The windows had steamed over and her hair lay flat against her head.

When I walked in, Dad handed me a loaf of cranberry bread and a knife. "Butter's on the table. Eat this."

"What happened here, a culinary convention?"

"The freezer went out and we didn't know it. We're trying to save everything we can." Mom checked the kettles on the stove. "Hand me those thawed carrot medallions, will you? And the package of beans, too. Then I think we've used all the vegetables."

As she moved away from the stove, Dad opened the oven

door to reveal a half-dozen roasts. "They're done. Want to put the turkey in now?"

"How long has this been going on?" I asked, marveling at their cool heads and the vats of browned hamburger on the counter.

"I called your dad and told him to come home early. We've been cooking ever since. Four or five hours, wouldn't you say, Frank? I hope you're hungry, Whitney."

I couldn't eat an entire freezer full of food, not even in my pre-diet stage.

Mom saw the horrified look on my face. "Don't worry. We've called the church for a list. We're taking meals to all the shut-ins."

I sometimes envy my parents' approach to life. They take it as it comes—happy times or sad, a defunct freezer full of food or a broken-down car in the middle of the freeway—it doesn't matter. They just deal with it and go on. Come to think of it, what other choice do we have?

November 12

Every day is another spiral downward for Kim. The harder she tries to pull herself out, the lower she feels because nothing is working. I'm on the sidelines watching someone I love fall inch by inch into a deep well and feel helpless to rescue her. Occasionally she's able to grab on to something and fight her way to the top of the pit, but she hasn't the strength to hang on. Then she tumbles even deeper into the abyss.

I keep throwing her lifelines to take hold of, and sometimes they check her fall for a little while.

"Hey, Kimber! Want to run?" I stood on her doorstep, jogging in place. I'd pulled my hair into a whale spout on top of my head and slipped into my exercise clothes after work. I felt the way I had as a child, knocking on doors and hoping to find someone to come out and play.

Kim opened the door and stared out at me as if I were a complete stranger. The house was so dark behind her—curtains pulled and lights off—that she blinked and had to squint at me to see my face.

"Maybe tomorrow. It's too cold today."

"How about now? You've got on sweats and tennis shoes. Grab a coat. Just a spin around the block?" She didn't have Wesley as an excuse to say no. Kurt told me that because Kim was sleeping so much, he'd started taking Wesley to the grandma-lady down the block for part of the day. That Kim hadn't protested spoke volumes.

"I don't think…"

I don't delude myself into thinking I know how she feels, but I do know one thing—she's usually more upbeat after a run than before. "You'll feel better. You always do. I'm not leaving until you run." I've become accustomed to her resistance.

She sighed as if greatly put upon, grabbing her sunglasses off the foyer table. "You are a pest, Whitney Blake."

I grinned and set off at a slow jog. We didn't talk much except for some desultory chatter about the office. Otherwise we just plowed along, making our way through the now-familiar route of park, lakeside and road. Our course was four miles from the time we left Kim's to the time we returned. It usually took her that long to shake off the melancholy and invite me inside for something to drink.

"Better?" I panted, seated at her kitchen table, holding a glass of water with both hands.

"A little." She gave me an owl-like glare and then turned her gaze to her hands. "Betty called today. She asked how I was, but I think she really wanted to know when I'll be coming back to work."

"Oh?" I've learned to be noncommittal with Kim. No prodding, no judgments—she has plenty of those on her own.

"While I was talking to her, it was as if a big cage dropped from the sky and trapped me. I feel as though I'm smother-ing when I think of going back to the office."

"Then don't feel obligated. You have sick leave coming. Use it." Kim is barely making commitments as to what she'll eat at the next meal. Promising to come back to Innova is too big for her in the state she's in. She'll have to work up to that.

"Listen, kiddo," I said, wary of wading into deep waters, "maybe Chase could help or send you to someone...."

"No!" Her eyes flashed with more light and spark than I'd seen in days. "This is about me, my emotions and God. Chase deals with my body, not my head. I have to pray more and be more self-disciplined about this, that's all. It's mind over matter. I've just been...tired...."

"You can remedy how you feel through an act of will?"

"I wasn't brought up to run to a doctor for every little thing."

Every *little* thing? Being so paralyzed that she couldn't work or take care of her son? So exhausted and blue that sometimes Kurt found her still in bed when he came home from work in the evening? It didn't feel all that small to me.

Dear Lord,

I pray for Kim. She's doing so well physically and falling apart emotionally. She's stuck with the idea that there's only one way for her to conquer this. But I know that You work in many and mys-terious ways. I don't know how You'll heal her, Lord, but I do know You can make it happen.

Beseechingly,
Whitney

November 13

Snow! I woke up today to a softly falling curtain of snowflakes drifting past my window. Despite the fact that it's come too early for me, it was beautiful, and the perfect reason to sleep in. Matt, however, had other ideas.

He arrived on my doorstep at 9:00 a.m. wearing a stocking cap, mittens and cross-country ski boots. "Come out. The snow is perfect."

I looked at him bleary-eyed and suspicious. This was totally out of character for Matt to take a day off without good reason. Was *I* that reason?

I like snow as much as the next person. I love looking at it. I've never claimed to enjoy being out *in* it.

"Don't you have work to do?"

"Not today. It's a snow day. Come skiing with me."

For once, I wished he were working. "I don't have cross-country skis."

"We'll rent some. Dress in layers. I'll drive."

He took me to a park I wasn't familiar with that was, thankfully, void of crowds. Apparently not all of Minnesota wants to leap out of bed and onto a pair of matchsticks at 9:00 a.m. on the first snowy day of the year. Cross-country skiing reminds me all too much of the home ski machine I traded for four massages, two eyebrow waxes and a facial at my friend Roxy's salon.

My protests turned out to be a good thing, as Matt went down on bended knee to secure my boots for me. Secretly I could dream of it happening again someday when we're not skiing and he has a ring in his hand. I could have sat there all day, in fact, and was quite unwilling to get up when he said it was time to ski.

"I'll just sit here and watch you," I offered.

"Nonsense. This will be fun." He held out his hands to me. The cold had reddened his cheeks, and he looked remarkably healthy and fit. He was hard to resist, but I managed.

"I'm not good on cross-country skis. They're too narrow for me."

"So you like downhill?"

"I didn't say that. They're too narrow, too. I do best *after* skiing, sitting by the fire with hot chocolate and a blanket over my knees."

"You're such a joker, Whitney. That's what I love about you." He flashed a big white smile and pulled me to my feet.

But I wasn't joking. I shuffled a few yards to the beginning of the trail and looked out across the vast whiteness. This was what it must have been like for Lewis and Clark as they forged through the West—danger, excitement, dread, never knowing what was around the next corner…. Then a little girl and her father swooshed gracefully by us. The child had the rhythmic skiing motion that I'd never acquired. Okay, so maybe it wasn't *just* like Lewis and Clark.

"I'll lead," Matt said. "You follow."

He usually didn't get so excited about things other than peanuts, so I decided to humor him. "Yessir." I watched him push off, waited a moment and trundled along behind him. Fortunately he had his back to me and couldn't see my clumsy maneuvers. I was actually feeling pretty good about myself, when I noticed Matt had disappeared down a sloping incline. Now, I don't know much about skiing, but *slopes* are meant for downhill skiing, and they are definitely not for me.

Truthfully, it wasn't as difficult as I'd thought it might be to get down the hill. It hurt a little when my backside hit the ground, but the fabric of my ski jacket made a great makeshift sled. Thankfully my skis popped off and I dropped my poles, so I didn't have to worry about them during my descent.

I lay very still at the bottom of the hill, hoping that Matt wouldn't notice I was missing and would leave me there. Even freezing to the ground on the spot sounded easier than having to get up and try again. Matt did perceive that I'd gone astray, however, when no one behind him responded to his shouted questions.

I was still lying there when he returned.

"Are you okay? Did you get hurt?"

The concern in his eyes was lovely, but I waved him away with a mittened hand. "No, I'm enjoying it down here. Close to nature and all that. Go and have fun. I'll be here when you get back."

He put his hands on his hips, and his ski poles stuck out behind him. "Whitney, why didn't you tell me you don't cross-country ski?"

"Who says I don't?" I protested from my horizontal position. "Maybe I'm just not very good at it!"

The morning was not wasted, however. Matt took it upon himself to soothe my bruised feelings. We never mentioned other parts, the ones that were bound to turn black and blue. He took me out for breakfast, and we spent the day watching old movies. He was so sweet, and it was very romantic.

I just love skiing.

November 14

I hadn't planned to go to Kim's tonight because I had a date with Bernard, and Eric had promised to meet me after my workout, but Kurt called me at the office today and asked me to check on Kim after work. He's doing some day trips right now and is getting home late at night. Though he didn't say it, I know he's afraid to leave her alone that long. Today was the first time I've actually wondered if he's afraid she'll harm herself. The thought makes my blood run cold.

The house was sealed up tight. Curtains drawn, the morning newspaper still on the front step, a forlorn wreath of fall leaves Kim had hung out in October limp and battered hanging on the front door. If I hadn't known better, I'd have thought the house was vacated.

Knowing Kim doesn't always answer her door these days, I gave the doorbell a perfunctory ring, dug out the key Kurt had given me and unlocked the door.

"Kim! Kim! It's me, Whitney. Where are you?"

The silence had an airless quality, as if the entire house were holding its breath. I dropped my jacket, keys and purse on the first chair I ran across and hurried toward the back of the house. I could barely see at first as my eyes corrected for the darkness. In the kitchen, the dishes from the past few meals were stacked or strewn on the counter. A loaf of bread in a plastic bag was left open to dry out. The orange-juice carton, still half-full, was room temperature on the breakfast counter. The family room adjoining the kitchen looked ghostly. The television was on, muted, as the newscasters chatted and smiled into the void. The flickering light from the screen only enhanced the eerie feeling in the room.

"Kim?" Heart pounding, I made my way to the bedroom, hoping I'd find her there, sleeping peacefully. She wasn't there or in her bathroom or the walk-in closet.

I found her in Wesley's room, in the rocking chair I and the rest of the office had chipped in to buy for her and the baby. A glider, it slid back and forth in complete silence as she stared at the empty crib.

"Kim, it's me, Whitney."

She barely stirred. "Hi."

"What's up?"

Gliding. Back and forth, back and forth.

"Where's Wesley?"

"Down the street."

I sat down on a small painted stool by the crib. "Isn't it nice to have someone to watch him so close by."

Back and forth, back and forth.

Kim had a photo album in her lap. Several others lay beside her chair. I picked up the loose photos scattered about and reached to flip on Wesley's Humpty Dumpty lamp. Kim shielded her eyes from the light.

They were old photos, black and whites—a soldier in uniform, with the word Korea jotted on the back of the picture and a stern-looking couple straight out of *American*

Gothic. I found Kim's parents' wedding picture and several of groups of laughing young people at a picnic.

"Who are these people? They look like they're having a great time. This lady looks a lot like you. Any relation?" I held the picture up and Kim's gaze barely shifted.

"My aunt Corrine."

"I didn't know you had an aunt by that name." Not that I know everything about Kim, but we've talked about our families enough that I should have known she had an aunt. "Who are the others?"

"My mother's family mostly." Kim sounded like an automated prerecorded response.

Needing to keep her engaged in something other than a staring match with Wesley's crib, I gathered all the albums and stray photos together. "Let's go into the kitchen. I'll make some tea and we'll spread these on the table. You can tell me all about them."

If I was waiting for an enthusiastic response, I didn't get one. So, being enthusiastic for both of us, I took her by the hand and towed her to the kitchen.

"Want some soup?" I put the photos on the table and went to the cupboard. There were a dozen cans of condensed cream of tomato soup, four cans of tuna, an old bag of marshmallows, crackers, a jar of pickle relish and a package of lasagna noodles. Not exactly gourmet fixings. Not waiting for an answer, I dumped a couple cans into a pot, added milk and put the pot on to heat. After filling her teakettle and digging out the tea bags, I sat down on the bench next to Kim. "Now, let's see who we've got here…."

There was an odd disconnect between the pictures. All the young people were smiling or engaged in some sort of playful activity. They appeared to be an exceedingly happy group. But the older family members all looked as though they'd been engaged in a pickle-eating contest. Puckered and sour with squinty eyes and ramrod-straight posture, they not only appeared to be from a different generation, but almost a different species.

"Your parents are really cute." I was surprised at the wide grin on her mother's face. I'd met Kim's mom only twice, but she looked as tart and disagreeable as her older relatives now.

"Things change," Kim said, and then returned to staring at the photo without seeming to see it.

November 15

Another unplanned visit to Kim. After work, on a whim, I made an impulsive turn onto the street that leads to her house. If I hadn't forgotten my cell phone at home, I would have called first and known what I was walking into.

Anyway, Kim was home—and totally out to lunch.

"What happened to your hair?" I gasped when she opened the door. It had been chopped off and was ragged and spiky in spots, flat to her head in others.

"Hmm." She ran her fingers through what was left of her beautiful hair. "It was bugging me, so I decided to cut it."

"With what? A blender? Or a Weedwacker?"

"That bad, huh?" She stood aside to let me in. She was still wearing her pajamas.

"It has possibilities. After all, you look great with short hair, but I think a little professional help might be in order."

"That's what Kurt says. I just haven't found the energy today to make an appointment."

I followed her into the living room and opened the curtains, only to be surprised again. Kim is a fastidious housekeeper, the kind that can spot a speck of lint on the floor at thirty paces and is constantly using the sleeve of her shirt to buff stainless-steel appliances. I'd never seen so many fingerprints on her windows and coffee tables or so many papers and toys scattered on her floor. And never, ever, had I seen an overturned cup of coffee bleeding brown caffeine stains across her carpet.

"Sorry about the mess. I don't have the energy to pick up around here."

I followed her to the couch and curled up on one end while she did the same on the other. "Are you all right?" It was obvious that she wasn't, but what else could I say?

"I guess," she said vaguely.

"And?"

"Oh, nothing."

"Kimbo," I warned, using the pet name Kurt sometimes used.

"I'm just really annoyed with Chase, that's all." From the tone of her voice I knew she was more than just annoyed. She was furious. "He's got it in his head that I'm depressed. He even tried to give me a prescription for medication."

"What did you do with it?"

"I threw it in the trash, of course."

I went to the wastepaper basket near the writing desk in her living room. There was the prescription, crumpled into a ball. I pressed out the wrinkles and set it on the fireplace mantel. "You need to get this filled."

"Oh, Whitney, not you, too! Kurt and Chase have been ganging up on me, and now you. I'm just a little down in the dumps. I've been through a lot. That doesn't mean I'm mental, does it?"

"Hardly. What does 'being mental' have to do with anything?"

"Why don't any of you believe I can lick this?" She ran her fingers through her close-cropped hair. "Have you forgotten what Jeremiah said? 'Oh, Lord, You alone can heal me.' Where's my faith if I don't trust Him with this?"

"He's the Ultimate Healer. He answers prayers in the way He knows best." I put my hand on her arm. "Kim, you allowed Chase to do surgery. You didn't resist that. What's the difference?"

A stubborn expression settled on her face. "I'm not exactly sure, but I know it's different. My uncle suffered from 'depression.'" She said the word scornfully. "My grandparents believe he didn't recover because he never turned himself completely over to God. He didn't trust enough." There was pain in Kim's eyes and a perplexing deadness. "He *could* have pulled himself out of it. I know he could have. The family's always said so."

Hadn't we gotten anywhere with her? No wonder she was so conflicted.

"Oh, Whitney, I don't want to be like him! He suffered so much and had so little joy in his life." She sounded terrified.

"Then listen to Chase and your husband."

She shook her head slowly, obviously confused. "No, I can't. My grandparents and parents always said..." She looked at me uncertainly. "There's no other way...is there?"

The blight of mixed messages. As well as I've known Kim, she never told me that depression ran in her family— or that, unfortunately for her uncle, neither her parents nor grandparents believe in depression. *Malingering, spoiled, self-indulgent, lazy.* The words she'd learned to associate with depression were so unfair. So was the idea that she could "quit babying herself," "buck up," "face the music" or "snap out of it." She'd already judged herself and been found wanting.

"Did you come here to cheer me up or bring me down?" she asked finally. "Because I'm feeling plenty down on my own."

"Sorry about that. Let's change the subject."

"What do you think of Chase?" She forced animation into her voice. "Yummy, huh?"

"Good as chocolate," I said without enthusiasm.

"I had no idea that he'd had such a traumatic breakup with his fiancée. I do know he's very dedicated to his work, but that certainly wouldn't stop him if he had a woman like you...."

"Like me? I don't think so. I'm not his type. His Claudia is blond, brilliant and beautiful. Besides, he's sworn off women for good."

"An amazing brown-eyed brunette, dazzling, radiant, intelligent, clever, smart, funny, witty, stunning, elegant, loving, generous, loyal, faithful…not to mention those long, gorgeous legs…."

Who was she looking at, anyway?

As if she could read my mind, she added, "And a self-deprecating sense of humor that deflects all compliments. You are too modest. Which, by the way, you can stop at any time. That diet is working, and you're the only one who looks at you and sees the word Chubby in neon letters flashing over your head."

"So you've seen them, too?" I blurted.

"Knock it off, silly. You need to accept how incredible you are."

I left Kim's feeling both better and worse. At least we'd talked about her depression. And she'd said some lovely things about me that I was going to take to heart. But we hadn't solved a thing. Kim is still blue and I'm still single. And the insecure imp in my brain keeps reminding me that I'm over thirty and still alone.

Lord, You were in on the conversation between Kim and me. What's Your position on all of this? She thinks her faith is weak if she can't conquer her depression with faith and prayer. I know You can heal all things. I believe that You've given us good doctors, medications that work and the responsibility of caring for our own bodies. Are we unfaithful if we believe that You use means other than miracles to help us? Or if we think like Kim and assume there's only one way to get things done, are we putting You in a box that's way too small for the wonder of You? Will You help me here, Lord? What do I say? What is Your will and what isn't? She's thrown me for a loop here, God. Untie me, will You?

Trying to figure it all out,
Whitney

CHAPTER 10

November 16

"Well, well, look at you!" Bernard greeted me with a smile and a weird expression, as if he'd won the Great American Bake-Off and I was his prize pie.

"What about me?" I looked down at my usual uniform of gray sweatpants, white T-shirt and tennis shoes. The only thing that had changed was that I'd purchased a new white T-shirt because the other one had stretched out.

He reached out and pinched my upper arm in his meaty fingers. "Definition. Muscle. It's starting to show."

"It *is?*" I'd practically forgotten why I'd come to him originally. Now, with both work and Kim tugging at me, a sweaty session with Bernard makes me feel better. I'm glad I didn't back out of my sessions the first time I saw that gold tooth.

"I'm very pleased with your progress. You?"

"I haven't had much time to think about it." I stuck my fingers into the waistband of my sweats and realized there was *lots* more room in there than there'd been a couple weeks ago. Crunches, no doubt.

As we worked—or, more accurately, as I worked and Bernard watched—I told him the whole story about Kim and her surgery, her handsome doctor, the way she'd been acting lately, her reluctance to take any medication and her fear that her faith wasn't strong enough.

He listened impassively, as he always does to my ranting. I get loose-lipped when I'm in pain. Talking to Bernard is like talking to a warm brick wall. I always feel better afterward and know that whatever I've said is going to stay right there, with him.

Today he surprised me by sitting down on the weight bench next to mine. He weaved his fingers together as his hands hung between his knees. "I have some books you can borrow."

"On depression?" I think of Bernard only in terms of brute strength, not emotions.

"I got into fitness training and weight lifting because of my own bouts of depression," he said. "Exercise is a good tool for managing it, but it's not always enough. Normally I work with people I know have this problem. I'm not even sure how you got on my client list."

God, that's how. Planning moves to help me way ahead of what I even know I'll need. He already knew I'd need someone like Bernard down the road. What a glorious Lord I have.

When I left, Bernard called after me, "Get out a tape measure and see how you're doing."

I smiled but didn't commit. Any encounters I've had with my own measurements have always left me frustrated. It's hard to be a size-eight mind in a size-twelve body.

November 17

Matt called tonight. He's been acting very interested in me lately. Flowers. Dinner invitations. Even theater tickets.

"Business is hopping," he began, almost before saying hello. "I never expected to see growth like this, but this idea to begin marketing a new line of organic nuts to the health food industry was a flash of inspiration. Whitney, I'm going to have to add staff, roasters and packing machines. This is going to take my little company to the top!"

"That's wonderful." I wasn't as enthusiastic as I tried to sound. I'd hoped for something about "us" before business.

"Listen, Whit, I don't have time right now, but I need to talk to you. I've missed you. What are you doing this weekend?"

It's a good thing he couldn't see the face I made. "I'm bridesmaid in a wedding."

And I will be imitating an exploded yellow squash.

"Do you have an escort?"

Suddenly my heart was in my throat and my pulse pounding so loudly in my ears it was deafening. "Actually, no…" I hadn't really thought about that, other than it might be a relief to go alone and not let anyone else see me in Highway Department yellow.

"I'd love to accompany you if you'll have me."

Single men usually avoid weddings like the plague. Did I mean so much to him that he'd do that just for me?

"Sure…of course…absolutely!" Leah, eager for me to have a date, had assured me not to worry if I wanted to ask someone after I'd RSVP'd.

"I'm looking forward to it. Besides, it's time we do a little talking about our own futures."

Talk about our "futures"? Did he mean our future *together?*

"*He's* taking you to the wedding?" Amazement dripped off Mitzi's words like icicles off a roof.

"Is it such a surprise?"

Mitzi's incredulity didn't faze me. Matt's invitation simply confirmed what I'd been suspecting but hadn't dared put into words. He was interested in me. Really interested. Like let's-start-planning-a-life-together interested. Granted, I haven't known him that long, but maybe when it's really right it happens like that. He always tells me how lucky Harry is to have me and what a great head I have on my shoulders. Sometimes he even tells me what great hair I have on my great head. And eyes. And smile. I've never been one to count my chickens before they're hatched, but this time it feels right. The handsome, smart, successful Matt Lambert cares about *me*. Just writing that makes a warm tingle throughout my body, and my lips start to automatically curve into a smile.

November 18

The labels in my kitchen confuse me. Why is lemonade made with artificial flavor and dish soap with real lemons? And if I can shrink a wool sweater in the wash, why don't sheep shrink in the rain? Procrastination, I've noticed, is a great opportunity to ask some of the world's most profound questions.

I made lemonade, Jell-O, tuna salad and a weird low-calorie recipe for muffins that looked like hockey pucks to keep my mind off what I was about to do, but Bernard's voice continued to echo in my mind. "It's time to get out a tape measure, Whitney. We need to record your progress."

Tape measures and I have never gotten along. Especially when someone is trying to touch one to my hips.

Due to extremely bad timing, my mother rang my doorbell just as I was about to edge the plastic messenger of doom around my backside.

"Whitney, why are you dressed in a leotard? Have you been exercising?" She blew in like a gust of wind, dumped some packages on my couch and pounced on the tape measure I'd dropped on the floor. "Taking measurements? For the wedding?"

That was aeons ago. Those numbers had contributed, in part, to today's reluctance. "No, just curious." Bernard, not me.

Mom eyed me with that terrifying I-can-read-minds look she always had when I was a teenager. Even if I'd been prone to troublemaking, which I wasn't, I'd have been scared out of it by that expression alone. "You're thinner."

"Really? You can see it?"

"Yes, I can. Can't you?"

"I thought so, but…"

"Whitney, you are the only person in the world who sees yourself as overweight. The women I know would love to look like you!"

They probably hadn't grown up with a mother who felt "bloated" at a hundred and five pounds.

"It's probably my fault," Mom sighed. "But when I was young and scrawny, I was sure I resembled a plucked chicken and hated it. I've always tried to ignore my size and not think about such things. What I obviously *didn't* do was teach you that God designed every one of us individually. And no matter how we may look on the outside, if we're right with Him in our hearts, we're perfect."

Mom crossed her arms over her chest and bobbed her head as if to say, "So there."

"Oh, all right, you do it." I gestured toward the tape measure. "I've wasted too much time worrying about how I look. I quit."

Mom beamed at me and looped the tape measure around my waist.

"Hmm…aha… Okaaay…."

She clucked and hummed and wrote the numbers down on the slip of paper holding my BB (Before Bernard) measurements. The page was just out of my line of sight and Mom didn't give a hint as to what she was finding. Impatient, I grabbed the paper from her hand. "Okay, if I haven't lost anything just tell me…."

I blinked. Twice. And a third time. She'd done something wrong. "Do it again."

"Those are the correct measurements, Whitney. You're the same size you were when you graduated from high school."

I lurched for my jeans and pulled them on. "I can't be. Look at this waistband!" I pinched the fabric and pulled to show Mom that, although I didn't need rubber bands anymore, these were still my size. But they weren't. When had that happened? Not only did I not need rubber bands anymore, it was time to buy a belt—or new jeans.

"What's your secret, Whitney? This is amazing!"

"No secret. I exercised, wrote down what I ate, gave up refined sugar, flour and..." I almost felt silly telling her the rest. "When I wanted something to eat, instead of just stuffing it in and thinking about it later, I asked myself two questions. The first was, 'Am I actually hungry?'"

"And the second?"

"'What does God think of this? Even when no one else is watching He still is.'"

"Like not tossing garbage on the sidewalk instead of walking it to the trash or helping ourselves to extra pens and paper clips from the office just because no one is there to see you?"

"Exactly. That question put an end to my eating a pint of double-chocolate almond-fudge ice cream at bedtime. In fact, once I got the hang of it, it's become almost—" Was it me saying this? "—fun. But that's what being a Christian is all about, isn't it? Deciding what you're going to do about your beliefs every day for the rest of your life."

I have to tell Tansy this. She'll be delighted.

November 19

I couldn't quit staring at it. I'd moved it from the kitchen table to the sofa table and back to the counter. Was it really mine?

The graceful glass sculpture of two elongated figures dancing was something I'd admired when Matt and I walked by
the jewelry-store window in which it was displayed. The
fluid elegance of the piece was enchanting. I'd made him wait
while I'd admired it revolving slowly, light catching the glass
and sending out shimmering rainbows of color. And now it
was here, in my kitchen with a note that simply said, "For
someone who loves the dance. Matt."

When the phone rang, I flinched. I hated to tear my eyes
away from the amazing gift Matt had sent.

"Hey, Whit, what's up?"

Eric always sounds so cheerful on the phone. That's why it
was so difficult to have the conversation I had with him today.

"Do you have time for dinner? I've got a job interview
at four and there's an art show of historic airplanes at the
Mall of America I want to see, but we could grab something between…"

"Not tonight, Eric."

"What's wrong? You sound bummed."

I felt bummed—bummed and dishonest. I kept my eyes
on the figurine. "You know, Eric, that you are one of my best
friends in the world."

"You're one of mine, too, Whit."

"And maybe we should just keep it that way."

There was silence at the other end of the line, then, "What
are you trying to say?"

"I don't know. I am absolutely crazy about you as a human
being, and there was a time when I thought someday, we
could, you know…." I sucked in a lungful of air and plunged
in. "But everything has changed. It's not fair to you, Eric, because I really don't think it will happen." There, I'd said it.
"I want to be upfront with you. I don't want to be in your
way if you meet someone wonderful…."

I don't want to pretend that I'm waffling with indecision
any longer. Truth be told, I'm not choosing between Eric

and Matt. I think Matt's the man for me. And exactly why did I feel as if I needed to cut Eric free even before Matt and I had talked this through? Because it feels honest, that's why. It feels truthful and respectful. It's the answer to "I'm a Christian, so how do Christians act?" We're as open and sincere as we know how to be—no game playing, no manipulation, no using someone else for our own purposes. I've realized that I've been thinking of Eric as my "reserve," in case something goes wrong between Matt and me. Eric deserves more than that. He should have the perfect woman for him in his life—an honest-to-goodness angel.

Sometimes honoring God is very complex and exceedingly painful.

"Whitney, I'm not going anywhere. Even if you make the worst decision of your life and pick that good-looking lunk who sells peanuts over me, I'll still love you."

"I just felt it needed to be said," I stammered. "I want things truthful and straightforward between us."

"Okay, I get it," he said cheerfully. "Whatever you say. You're still the best, no matter what."

I felt better. I want to honor God in the little stuff, the stuff only I know about, like the contents of my heart. I'm glad that bit of housecleaning is done. At least now I'm not giving Eric any false hope.

November 20

I had to virtually *drag* Kim to Leah's bridal shower. She made up a million excuses for not going. She can't leave Wesley with a sitter again. She doesn't have anything to wear. She has dark circles under her eyes. She doesn't want to discuss her surgery. Radiation is making her miserable.

But the "old" Kim, the one before depression set in, would have been there anyway, in a heartbeat. I usually hung back at events like this. I didn't grow up in a gushy, mushy family and I'm a little uncomfortable with too much effusiveness. My parents had always emphasized Matthew 5:37. "Let what you say be simply 'Yes' or 'No'; anything more than this comes from evil."

It's the whole syrupy, sentimental factor that makes me uneasy. Leah's new mother-in-law gushed about how wonderful it was to have Leah in the family. Leah's mother cooed about finally having the son she always wanted. The bridesmaids prattled on about how "in love" Bradley was with Leah. Everyone thought the dresses were "precious," the invitations, "artsy," and the location of the reception—a very pricey country club—"so chic." I felt a little nauseous from all the sweets before I'd even had lunch.

Complaining aside, I'm really delighted for her. Leah is a wonderful person and deserves every happiness. And, if the truth be told, I *might* be a little jealous. After three dozen stories about the fawning affection Bradley showers on Leah, it occurred to me that no one ever fawns over me. I don't make guys mushy and weak in the knees.

Granted, Matt is generous to a fault, but he's always rather businesslike about it and he keeps a fair distance. His style is definitely affectionate yet reserved. Sometimes it feels as if he's wooing me, but without the romance. And Eric is like having a life-size teddy bear around—cuddly, nonthreatening, secure. Neither ever fawns. Nor have either of them ever fussed over and coddled me as Bradley does Leah. Still, they've both said things I've wanted to hear. And Matt *is* taking me to the wedding and it's his idea. That makes up for a whole lot.

"Aren't you going to help make Leah's hat?" Leah's sister Emily thrust a big straw beach hat and a glue gun into my hands. "We're putting all the bows from the packages on the brim so she'll have a reminder of today."

No. Say it isn't so. Leah's home is decorated in an Asian motif—shoji screens, a slender vase containing a single flower, a dining-room table only a few inches off the floor. Where on earth would she put this hideous thing? I guess that's what boxes, closets and basements are made for. I attached an ugly violet bow with a squashed ribbon streamer into the atrocity and hoped Leah would still speak to us once she saw what we'd done.

I hung close to Kim at the shower. I'm allergic to party and parlor games, so it was no loss when I didn't participate in the contest to see how many kitchen appliances I could spell with the letters of Leah's and Brad's first and last names.

Everyone asked how Kim was doing. She put on a happy face, but I know she was crumbling inside.

When I picked her up for the shower, I knew immediately by the state of her house. Kim has always been an immaculate housekeeper. Sometimes she carries a bottle of spray cleaner hooked over her waistband, like a holster, and stuffs a cleaning rag in her back pocket, so if she sees fingerprints, she can put them out of their misery right away. She's the Doc Holliday of germs, quick on the trigger.

When her house is untidy, the way it was again today, I know she's really down. Dealing with this alone isn't working, but she's the only one who refuses to see that.

The shower food included every appetizer known to humankind. Tiny sausages in hickory barbecue sauce, bacon-wrapped water chestnuts, miniature tortilla wraps, sandwiches the size of Post-it notes, skewered fruits and veggies and suspicious things that looked as though they contained ground liver. Urrgh.

Halfway through the gift opening, Kim handed me Leah's third crystal cake cover and rolled her eyes. "Does Leah bake?"

"Not that I know of, but she doesn't iron, either, and she's already received two of those. Maybe she'll start."

Everyone was chattering about the gifts and the wedding. No one was paying attention to us. Kim looked at me with narrowed eyes. "Do you want to hear what Chase and Kurt have been up to?"

I was surprised at the little flip I felt in the pit of my stomach.

"They're rebuilding an old car! Can you believe it? They barely have time away from their work to sleep, and now there's an old Camaro dismantled on my garage floor. They've reverted to their teenage years."

"I can't picture it. Skilled surgeon's hands on a carburetor? Does Ralph Lauren make clothes for that?"

"They're having fun, that's all I know. Kurt says it gets Chase's mind off Claudia. He really loved her."

I tried not to think about that. Instead I thought about Matt. He was the one going on the "dry run," as Mitzi called it. If a guy can get through a friend's wedding without panicking, she claims, there is a pretty good chance that he'll make it to his own. She's probably right. I've never known a commitment-phobic man who's agreed to take a woman anywhere near a wedding.

Thinking back on today makes me wonder why I didn't say more about Matt to Kim. It might have cheered her up. She wants me to be as happy as she is with Kurt. But I'm not ready yet. What could I say? "Matt's sounding serious.... Matt wants to talk to me about something big in our lives.... Pretty soon Matt and I will be an item.... Will you be *my* bridesmaid?" It's all too premature. His gifts, the tender looks, the fabulous dates are great, but I want to wait until he's not only shown but *told* me how much he loves me.

November 21

The Wedding Day.

How can one petite bride with no particular motivational skills get so many people to do her bidding? I can't even figure out how Leah talked me into renting a van and driving all the bridesmaids to the beauty salon to have manicures, pedicures and our hair done by 7:30 a.m. I know she paid for this as a treat for us, but when the alarm rang at 5:59 a.m., I found myself thinking another hour's sleep would have been gift enough.

I'm the only person in the group who's able to get up early and be cheerful about it. It was like wrestling grizzlies to wake everyone for our appointments. Julie hung up on me four times before I screamed into the answering machine until she got out of bed. To Kim's credit, though she didn't look delighted to be roused from sleep, she seemed willing to insure Leah's day was special. It took hours to rotate us from washbasin to hair station to manicure booth to the enormous pedicure chairs. I felt like Dorothy and her friends going through the assembly line of pampering and repairs when they arrived at Oz.

When we were all shaped, painted and sprayed, Leah strolled in to have the same royal treatment. She had been sleeping for the last four hours and looked divine. Someday it will be my turn, I hope.

Though not much of a dreamer, I do already have some guidelines already worked up for my big day.

1) I will not torture my attendants by forcing them to wear ruffled satin pup tents in colors not meant to be near the human face.

2) We will all go to the store and pick something matching off the rack. I'll marry in the spring, at prom time, when the stores are full of party dresses.

3) I will not have a bridal shower every two weeks for the three months prior to the wedding and will not force my husband-to-be to sit through a his-and-hers ordeal where he has to smile happily about my receiving a contraption for paraffin dip to keep my hands silky smooth and I have to be overjoyed at fishing poles for two.

4) I will not let either myself or my parents go into debt over my wedding.

5) The first name on the guest list will be God. If He's there, it's bound to be a success.

At two o'clock I decided to try on my dress. I didn't have to be at the church until four, and since Matt had agreed to pick me up at 3:45 p.m., there wasn't much else to do. I wear very little makeup, but I always take extra time to do my eyes, because Kim says they're the focal point of my face. Still, I can't spend all afternoon putting on mascara. Neither can I figure out how to get it on without having my mouth hang open. Leah wants us to wear false eyelashes, but I can only see myself with two big goopy spiders crawling down my cheeks. Thanks but no thanks.

I've become accustomed to the yellow dress as it's hung in my closet. It's been growing on me—like a wart. I imagine myself as a single black-eyed Susan in an entire field of flowers. That's pretty much what I'll look like, too. Leah has ordered so many flowers for the front of the church, it will be a miracle if the crowd can find the bridesmaids among the floral arrangements.

The dress felt smooth and heavy in my hands as I took it off the hanger and unzipped it. I stepped into it gently, careful not to make any more wrinkles than necessary. It slid silkily around on my shoulders as I zipped it up. The zipper glided easily into place. I forced a smile onto my face and turned slowly. "Mirror, mirror, on the wall, who's the fairest of them all?"

Not you, lady. Why are you wearing a hot-air balloon?

The dress was enormous! What had the seamstress said she'd do to it? Surely not make it into a taffeta circus tent! Something about letting out a couple tight seams... But that was before I'd gotten serious about EEAT and Bernard. I had no idea that fifteen pounds and pumping iron could make this much difference. Had I been so determined to block the entire thing from my mind that I never even considered trying it on? The dress made me look as though a huge yellow mouth was swallowing me whole.

I did what any sensible, thirty-something successful businesswoman would do. I called my mother.

"Quit blubbering, Whitney, I can't understand a word you're saying."

As soon as she understood my predicament, however, she came to the rescue. "I'll be right over."

She arrived on my doorstep with her tapestry sewing kit and my dad in tow, lugging her sewing machine, a steam iron and an attitude.

"The Vikings are ahead," he muttered accusingly as he lumbered through the door, as if I'd intentionally planned this crisis to conflict with the game.

"You can watch in the bedroom," I said. "There are baked chips in the cupboard and salsa in the fridge."

He beamed at me as if I was the perfect daughter and disappeared.

"What have you done to yourself, child?" Mom demanded.

"I never even thought of trying it on," I wailed, bizarrely unhappy that I looked better than I had in years. "I remember the seamstress saying she didn't like how the fabric pulled at the seams…."

And all that time, I was growing in the other direction!

"Let's turn this dress inside out and see how many seams we can take in."

Mom and Dad left at 3:40 p.m. Matt arrived at three forty-five having no idea that basting stitches, safety pins and an excessive amount of masking tape held together the woman who met him at the door. If I could get through the wedding without anyone knowing what Mom and I had patched and pasted…

Now I was *glad* Leah had chosen something with ruffles. They hid most of the radical, hit-or-miss tailoring we'd done. The whole thing was one big flounce anyway—no one would notice that I had a few more. But if anything gave way, the whole dress would slide off my shoulders and onto the floor. My only insurance against humiliation was that I was wearing my best underwear and most concealing slip.

Matt walked in wide-eyed, staring at my dress, my face, my hair. "I had no idea."

"About what?" I ventured cautiously, holding on to my precariously slipping confidence. Could he tell what Mom and I had done?

"That you could be even more lovely. Whitney, you are dazzling."

"C-come in. I'm almost ready," I stammered, giddy with pleasure.

"First, open this." He handed me a velvet jeweler's box. My stomach fluttered as I lifted the lid. Inside, resting on a bed of velvet, was a delicate gold necklace strung with a petite yellow diamond.

He took it from the box and held it toward me.

"I was hoping this would be right." Matt's breath was warm on my neck and shoulder as he looped the necklace around me and hooked it in the back. If I were a cat, I would have purred. Then he stood back and studied me. "Perfect. Just like you."

One glimpse in the mirror at my shining eyes, my upswept hair with gentle tendrils falling loosely around my face, a diamond winking at my neck and a tall, dark, handsome man standing beside me, and I knew this would be an evening to remember for the rest of my life.

For the first time ever, in my long career as a bridesmaid, I was actually almost as interesting as the bride. Well, not me alone, exactly, but *Matt* and me. He'd worn a black suit with fine tailoring, white shirt and a patterned tie of black and sunflower yellow. We looked as though we'd been planning our ensembles for weeks. That alone charmed me beyond belief. He'd paid close attention to what I said and did. He's always made me feel he was hanging on my every word, but this was proof positive that he actually had been.

I floated through the wedding and reception on a cloud almost as high as the one Leah and Brad were riding.

Unfortunately, by the time the last dance came around, I could feel some of Mom's work starting to shift. I was relieved when The Big Moment finally came. Not the vows, not the food, but the throwing of the bridal bouquet. Though I'd attended dozens of weddings, I'd never caught the bouquet. Of course, I'd never had a man like Matt at my side, either. He'd kept my punch glass filled all evening, brought crudités for me to nibble on and even offered to massage my feet when I complained about my Marquis de Sade designer shoes. This was my evening and there was no way I could miss this catch, literally or figuratively.

Grateful for Bernard's coaching and some newly found athleticism, I stood in the rear of the pack, directly in front of the bride but separate from the pressing crowd. I tried to look uninterested in the bouquet so I wouldn't be perceived as a threat. As the women huddled in, making fools of themselves (I've done it a dozen times myself), I stood nonchalantly at the back, watching and waiting, glad to have some inside information that most of the others did not. Leah had been the pitcher for a woman's softball league while she worked in our office—there would be none of this wimpy, girlie toss of the bouquet for her.

As the chattering and excitement increased down front, I knew I'd judged her correctly. Instead of just holding the flowers over her head and giving a limp-wristed toss, she wound up as though she was going to strike someone out. As if in slow motion, the bouquet left her hand, sailed over the heads and scrabbling, clawing hands of the mob and fell gracefully into my open hands.

The whole room screamed. I heard Kim's voice yelling over the din. "Finally!"

Then everyone descended, laughing and offering congratulations. As they did so, my eyes went directly to the edge of the room where Matt lounged by the wall. His arms were crossed and he looked as relaxed as a sated panther sleeping in the sun. He was smiling slightly and enigmatically. When I caught his eye, he gave a long, slow, glorious wink.

Yes, indeed, this was a night to remember. And there was more to come....

After waving the bride and groom off in their rented limo, we said our goodbyes and walked to Matt's car. We drove directly to my place, but when he opened my car door, he said, "Can we walk? The park is beautiful under the stars."

Moonlight kissed the area like a gentle lover. The air held only a whisper of breeze, enough to make a faint rustling in the topmost branches. The water, smooth and silvery as a giant looking glass, made only the barest slapping sound against the beach.

And in the midst of all that romance and beauty, I found myself praying.

"Thank you, thank you, thank you, Lord, for the beauty around me. I feel You out here tonight, as if You're walking with me....

It was true. He was with me in a way I'd never felt before, present, tangible, comforting. My relationship with God contains a quality of friendship and support, a "knowing" that comes over me sometimes. I don't always understand it at the moment, but later, looking back, I realize that He's held me up, cheered me on or kept me from falling even though I hadn't even recognized His presence at the time. And He was here tonight, keeping me safe.

As Matt led me to a park bench nested under a canopy of trees, a new prayer came into my mind.

He's going to propose! He is. I feel it. This is it! Is he the one for me, Lord? Show me! It feels so right. Is it Your plan, too, Lord? If it is, make it so.

It seemed an almost extraneous prayer, because I knew, just *knew,* that my answer would be yes.

Matt took my hand and gazed at me. I couldn't read his expression in the darkness, and it was unsettling that I couldn't see his eyes. Without looking into them, it was as though I didn't know him.

"I have something important to ask you, Whitney. I hope this is the right time. I've been building the courage to say this…."

Yes, yes! I squeezed his hands encouragingly.

"I know how loyal, dependable and trustworthy you are…."

That golden-retriever thing again?

"…and I've seen how much Harry counts on you…."

How did Harry creep into my marriage proposal?

"But nothing would mean more to me than having you at my side like that. You are a one-in-a-million woman, a treasure, a real find."

Here it comes!

"Whitney, name your price. I want you as my right hand in Lambert Industries. I've never had a relationship with another woman so fulfilling, so stimulating. You're brilliant, charming and warm. Delightful in every way. Our tastes and sensibilities are similar. We both love beautiful things and fine art as well as being together. You understand how important my business is and you can support me in all of it. Friend, business partner, soul mate…you're all of it to me. Will you make the jump? Will you come to work with me?"

My mouth froze open, like a carp wrapped fresh, quick-frozen and stuck in the deep freeze.

He sensed my hesitation and added, "A corner office, two great views, plenty of perks, great health insurance, your own car. And a terrific retirement package…"

That's what this had been about? Sammy Davis Jr.'s rendition of "What Kind of Fool Am I?" played in my head.

I had no idea what was going to come out of my mouth, but I opened it anyway. Giddy, borderline hysterical, disembodied laughter spilled out.

Matt, thickheaded and myopic as I'd just realized he is, took that as a good sign. "I'm glad to hear you're pleased. This is big for me, Whitney. I've never trusted anyone as much as I trust you or invited anyone to be so close to myself in the operation. Lambert Industries is my life, and you are very special to me. I want to share that with you."

I gaped at him in wonderment, an amazing serenity coming over me as all the pieces of the puzzle fell into place.

In a bizarre, fantastical way, Matt *was* proposing! He'd offered me the best of what he had to give. How was I to know it was his peanut-roasting factory? I knew of men who ate, slept and breathed their work, but this was the first one I'd encountered who was having a love affair with it! Not only that, he suffered from a terminal case of type-A, priority-confused, I-love-my-work-more-than-anything CEO-itis. If I hadn't been so devastated, I might have been flattered.

The only thing that kept me from crying was the laughter.

"Matt…ah…listen, I've got to go in…I…"

"Don't answer me now, that's fine. I can see you're excited but I want you to sleep on it. I'll call you tomorrow. Just say yes, Whitney. Together we can make Lambert Industries into something extraordinary." More marriage-like words. Words about his first and best love—Lambert Industries.

How I got to my apartment is a complete blur. As I sit here now, my dress and my life falling down around my shoulders, I feel numb, embarrassed, dim-witted and the world's poorest judge of character.

But the tranquility I felt earlier hasn't gone away. Much as

I try to whip myself into a frenzy, I can't. I don't want to. I don't even feel all that bad. Matt was right—I am good at what I do for a living. I'm also a good friend, honest, loyal and pleasant—all those characteristics that suddenly don't sound so bad. And I didn't lose Matt to another woman. No woman could compete with his true love, nor could God compete with mammon in his priorities. What Christian woman would *want* to marry such a man? Not me.

And, miraculously, I feel safe and supported. God is with me. He's been here all along. I prayed and He answered. He said no.

Matt isn't the man for me, and God knew it all along. I'd ignored the obvious signs, made up stories around Matt's attentiveness and charm and fantasized myself all the way to the altar. And now, lesson learned, I felt Him sustaining me and allowing me to regroup.

Okay, Lord, now what?

I'm embarrassed, ashamed to face my friends. Thanks for at least restraining me from telling everyone and their sister about Matt. You handle my love life (or lack of one) from now on, please. I'm not doing it anymore. When the right one comes along, the one You send, drop him into my lap and just let me know. I don't want anything that's out of Your will, including a mate. Just let me know, Lord, when Mr. Right is coming down the pike. And please help me make it through the next few weeks without falling apart.

Very single and all Yours,
Whitney

November 23

Wait for the Lord's help. Be strong and
Brave and wait for the Lord's help.

—Psalm 27:14

★ ★ ★

Fortunately the Lord didn't let me wait long for His help. I needed to be both strong and brave this morning in order to call Matt and decline his offer when my words weren't garbled and my mind on spin cycle. God provided both. I heard the confusion and disappointment in Matt's voice, but, gentleman that he is, he didn't press me. Though there was heavy question in his voice, he allowed me to save face. Part of me wanted to tell Matt my foolish assumptions and the notion I'd harbored that we were romancing not job interviewing. But I can't go there yet. Maybe never.

"He *what?*" I thought Harry's head might rupture when I told him what had happened with Matt. His face was the color of beet borscht and little veins stood out on his nose and forehead. His eyes bulged until I could see white all around the irises and his grown-out Chia Pet hair looked as though it had been electrified. "Why, that low-down, backstabbing, sneaky, employee-stealing thief! How *dare* he ask one of my employees to leave this company for him? I didn't think you were a flight risk, but with an idea-hamster like him I should have known. I wrote the software that doubled his business! I should have charged him ten times—"

"Thanks for asking how I'm doing, Harry." I slumped into a chair. "Now that I've been totally rejected, I mean."

I hadn't planned to tell him that Matt had broken my heart—or at least a piece of it—at the same time he imploded the rest of my life, but once I began to relate to Harry what had happened, he started drilling me with questions. Then, when I started to cry, he handed me tissues and got me water from his own personal stash, none of the cheap grocery brand, but the designer stuff in the fancy bottle. Since I'd been wallowing alone in my own personal misery since the wedding, any kindness at all was bound to loosen my lips. I sang like a bird. I told him everything, from the wretched yellow dress to the masking tape that held it together. I described the bouquet toss, my glorious catch and the fiasco that followed. The only thing I held back was that I'd also been mentally planning my own wedding.

"What a scum-bum. Leading on my favorite employee like that besides. I'm going to drop his account...."

Wait a minute. "Harry, did you say that *I* am your 'favorite employee'?"

"Of course. Haven't I told you that a dozen times?" He scowled at me and looked ill at ease.

"No. Not even once."

"Well, I thought it, then." He peered at me as if seeing me for the first time in months. "Things will change around here, I promise. I haven't been very good at expressing my gratitude for what you do, Whitney, but I will from now on. People tell me all the time that they wouldn't do business with Innova if they had to work with me. The clients *love* you, Whitney. Sometimes they act like I have a personality disorder or something."

The customer is always right.

"And a raise, you'll definitely be getting a raise." A number fell out of his mouth that nearly made me faint. Harry offered me more money than I'd ever dreamed of earning and added perks like an extra week's vacation and a cell phone for which I wasn't limited to four hundred minutes a month. *And,* he said, he'd get me a program with no roaming charges! Did he know how to cheer a girl up or what?

It took my foggy, tear-logged, dejected mind a few minutes to realize that Harry was saying these things because he thought I actually *might* jump ship and go to work for Matthew Lambert.

He obviously knows nothing about a woman scorned.

"Thank you, thank you, Harry," I babbled, overwhelmed anyway. "You don't need to—"

"Of course I do! I couldn't lose you, Whitney! You're family!"

Family? I thought of Bryan and his aversion to conflict, Betty and her three hundred useless music boxes, and Mitzi, who was at this moment scouring the personal ads for me. Granted, sometimes we're a cast of clowns, but we're also kin. We've been together a long time. We understand and tolerate each other's weaknesses, foibles and flaws. And though you'd never know it to talk to us, we'd go to the mat for each other anytime. Interesting. Harry and crew had been here for me all along. God, as He often does, uses the most unlikely candidates to do His work.

What's more, I'd felt a tingle of joy at Harry's words. Matt may have knocked me down, but I hadn't broken.

"You'll stay?" Harry asked hopefully.

"Of course. I wouldn't work for Matthew Lambert if he were the last man on earth."

"You wouldn't?" A lightbulb went on in Harry's head and I saw him processing the thought. Maybe that big raise hadn't been necessary after all…. I held my breath when he spoke.

"You really won't leave?" He sounded disbelieving. "He made you a good offer."

"But I chose to stick with you."

There was more silence while Harry chewed on that. "Then you really do deserve a raise." He stuck out his meaty hand to shake mine. "I'm glad you're on my team, Whitney."

Amazing how, in the midst of my embarrassment and misery, Harry was there, giving me a hand. I'd been infatuated with the idea of a handsome, wealthy, charming boyfriend—perhaps I was more smitten with that than I was with Matthew himself. The proof is that, despite how lousy I feel, I've already started to recover from the blow. If I'd really loved Matthew and not just the *idea* of Matthew, I wouldn't be out of bed yet. Still, I told Mitzi to tell Matt I was "unavailable" when he called and made up my mind to screen my personal calls for a while.

November 24

I'm sure there's a lesson in this, Lord. Help me learn it right away so I don't have to have another go at it later. Once is definitely enough.

Maybe it's this—I ignored the possibility of Matt and me being unequally yoked. I thought I'd work that part out later—on my own. But You aren't to be put off. You come first. I didn't trust You to handle it because I was afraid I might not get what I wanted. See what a dandy job I did on my own?

I'm reminded of Abraham and all it took to build his trust in You. It didn't happen overnight, but one incident upon another of Your proving Your faithfulness. Eventually, Abraham formed the kind of trust in You that allowed him to sacrifice Isaac just because You asked him to. He knew God had never failed him before, so he trusted You wouldn't fail him in that, either—and look how it turned out!

Like I told You before, I'm leaving this whole dating/romance/marriage thing in Your hands. But, if the guy You've got picked out for me is really ugly, could he at least have a great personality? Just kidding.

With her sense of humor coming back,
Whitney

November 26

Yesterday was Thanksgiving. I didn't think I'd be able to eat a thing, but of course I was wrong. It was, in fact, one of the *better* Thanksgivings I've ever had. Kim, Kurt and the baby were invited as well as a pair of grateful college students Mom had met during her morning walk. Their car had broken down and they were waiting for one of the students' fathers to drive in from Wisconsin and rescue them. They didn't expect help to arrive until at least 5:00 p.m., which left plenty of time to eat with us. Kim looked better than she had in a while. She sure knows how to pull herself together. Unfortunately, she has a difficult time making it last.

There'd been a little excitement before I and Kim's family arrived. My father had been assigned by Mom to take care of the turkey. This is a new development in my family. Mom is attempting to get him to take over some chores, but this probably wasn't the best day to teach him to cook.

He'd set the alarm for 5:00 a.m., staggered to the refrigerator, plopped the twenty-pounder into a big roaster and gone back to bed. When Mom got up at seven and smelled a strange odor coming from the kitchen, she knew immediately whom to blame. In his sleep-deprived state, Dad had forgotten to remove the plastic wrap and netting from the bird or wash it before he popped it into the oven.

Mom spent some time on the turkey hotline, but neither she nor the turkey volunteer could figure out a way to rescue the bird without disfiguring it and making it look hideous and unappetizing on the serving plate.

While my mother was talking turkey, Dad slunk out of the house and cruised the streets. It was with some pride he returned triumphant, having bagged a new entrée. That's how we came to have lovely orange-glazed Cornish game hens stuffed with wild-rice dressing, green beans almandine and garlic mashed potatoes with our pumpkin and pecan pies.

All in all, we had much to be grateful for and we showed God our thanks the best we could.

DECEMBER

CHAPTER II

Those who become Christians become new persons. They are not the same anymore, for the old life is gone. A new life has begun!
—2 *Corinthians 5:17*

December 1

It's the last month of the year, Lord, and it's going out in a whimper. The year of the Romantic Blunder—I'll be glad to see it in my rearview mirror.

I'm hanging on to 2 Corinthians 5:17, my verse for the upcoming year. *A new life has begun!* My life is two chapters—before I accepted Christ and after I accepted Him. I love knowing that the life I led before accepting Him is behind me. I'm choosing to look at this year the same way. It will be past soon, a closed book and the year ahead is one of possibility and hope.

Unfortunately I'm still prone to dwell on the negative. The mess with Matt is like losing a filling in my tooth. Until it gets fixed, the tip of my tongue is drawn to the crevice. I keep touching the empty spot, feeling it gingerly to see if anything has changed, drawn by some macabre impulse for this weird entertainment at my own expense. Pretty soon my tongue is raw and sore on the tip and the filling is still gone.

Looking back (my favorite hobby these days), all the signs that Matt didn't care for me as I did for him were there. He treated me like a princess whenever we were together, but he was busy or out of town so often that our actual evenings together were fairly few. Because I'm not an advocate of pre-marital intimacy, I appreciated his lack of physical advances, and when flowers arrived, they usually came with a card that said, "You're the best" or "Thanks for your efforts in my be-half." Not exactly love notes, but who cares when someone sends dozens of roses?

How did I ever think that I could commit to a man whose favorite color, food and music I didn't know? I had stars in my eyes, all right—and their light blinded me to the facts. I knew nothing about his faith or lack of it—and didn't care. He told me he grew up "going to church," as if that made him a Christian. I wanted it so badly I accepted it without question. Well, I grew up going to ball games, and it didn't make me a Minnesota Twin any more than standing in the garage made me a car.

I thought I had a handle on the whole thing until today when Mitzi breezed in as I was eating a low-cal TV dinner in the break room, and reminded me again what a blind, ro-mantic fool I'd been.

"I talked to my friend Joanie whose cousin works with a lady who knows Matt Lambert's secretary!" Mitzi snapped her gum for emphasis. "Small world, isn't it? They went to school together."

I put the dinner back in the box, knowing that after she said whatever was coming next, I wouldn't be hungry anymore.

"Well, being *very* discreet, as I always am…"

Uh-huh. Megaphone-Mouth Mitzi. Discreet is her mid-dle name.

"…I mentioned that I knew someone dating Matthew Lambert…."

I know Mitzi. No doubt she said something delicate like, "What's the scoop on this Lambert guy, is he a womanizer or what?"

"And you will *not* believe what she told me!"

I could feel a migraine—although I've never had one before—coming on.

"He is congenitally charming, and every woman who meets him is crazy about him!"

What a relief, I'm a member of the majority party.

"But *he's* not the least bit interested in settling down. According to Joanie's cousin's friend's friend, all he cares about is building his business. He was engaged once to a woman who didn't like all the time and attention he put into Lambert Industries, and when she told him to pick between her and the company, *he picked the company!*" Mitzi loves rolling out a good, gossipy story.

She looked at me speculatively. "It's a good thing you two broke up before you did anything silly, like fall in love." Then she uncovered her dish of sushi and delicately began to eat.

It was that diamond necklace that really fooled me, I decided. Why wouldn't a girl think she was special to someone who gave her that? But to Matt, I *am* special. I'm great at my job. And to him, that's reason enough to woo me to his company in any way possible. No wonder I got confused. I'm not used to that. I've had to practically sit on Harry to make him give us our Christmas bonuses.

December 2

I'm having trouble keeping my spirits up. Part of the problem is that I miss Kim terribly. I miss the funny, playful, energetic friend who disappeared again after Thanksgiving. I can't go to her house and count on being cheered anymore. Instead, I struggle to keep both of us from sinking lower. Her fears of the cancer returning, of Wesley's future, even of Kurt's continued love are wrapping ropes around her and they are tightening fast. That the fears are of her own invention doesn't matter. They've trapped her anyway.

I stopped at her place after work today and found her in the living room watching Wesley play on the floor. The television was turned to a medical channel and she was watching a surgeon lift a flap of flesh and fold it back to reveal the muscle and a bloated tumor beneath. I dived for the remote and turned the program off.

"Why are you watching that stuff?"

"It's the real world, Whitney. Bad things happen. You might as well face it."

"Facing it and putting it on Replay are two entirely different things. Remember 'Think about the things that are good and worthy of praise. Think about the things that are true and honorable and right and pure and beautiful and respected.'"

"Whatever." She picked up the remote and turned the surgery on again, this time without the sound.

I went to the foyer table to pick up the letters I'd seen there. "You haven't even opened your mail." I carried it to Kim and attempted to hand it to her.

She brushed my hand away. "You open it."

"Shouldn't you or Kurt do that? It's none of my business...." I separated the bills from the ads and made a third pile for anything that looked personal. I handed her the third pile. "At least read these. I see there's a letter from Wyoming. It must be your parents."

"I'll read it later."

"You aren't interested?"

"They're always the same. Nothing ever changes."

"Nobody lives reruns, there must be *something* new they want to tell you."

Kim made a face. "Daddy is busy with his business, Mother has volunteered to bake for some event, they're at church twice on Sunday as well as Tuesday and Wednesday nights, the dog has learned to dance on his hind legs and everything is wonderful."

"Right." I opened the letter and attempted to hand it to her.

"You can read it to me."

Realizing she meant it, I unfolded the lined paper and began.

Dear Kim and family,

How is darling Wesley? Getting big, I'm sure. We'd love to come out and see him, but your father has been so busy lately that he barely gets a day off. I'm spending a lot of time in the kitchen these days. The church is sponsoring a large gathering at the end of the month and they've asked me to be in charge of the food. We've ordered much of what we need, but I've committed to making all the baked goods for the afternoon tea.

It's a good thing we have our church events Tuesdays, Wednesdays and Sundays because that time requires us to stop working for a little while.

You should see Peppy these days. He's such a clever little dog. He's learned to fetch your father's slippers. Of course, small as he is, he can only carry one at a time.

Everyone here is just fine. We are so blessed.

Much love, Mom

I stared at Kim, and she smiled faintly at my puzzlement. "Everything is always fine at my parents' house. Nothing bad is allowed to happen there. If something unpleasant does happen, it's swept under the rug and doesn't really exist. Problems are never to be spoken of or written about and certainly not aired publicly."

"Kim, did you tell your parents you had surgery?"

"Yes. They said they're praying for me. My parents aren't good at things like illness."

"No one is."

"No? Maybe not, but my parents even have a hard time *believing* in sickness and disease."

What an odd thing to say. "Why?"

"They aren't good at admitting problems that anyone—especially family—has. I don't want to go into it, Whit. It's just better if I don't, okay?"

I let it go, but couldn't shake the feeling of sadness that had come over me. Kim was obviously not fully sharing what was happening to her with her parents. For whatever reason, she was trying to carry the load alone but for Kurt and me. It makes my heart hurt to think about it.

December 4

Free puppies: half Siberian husky,
half neighbor's fault for letting his dog
off the leash.

At thirty years old, successful in my career, back in the smallest jeans I've ever worn, I sat at home on a Saturday night reading the classifieds. How pathetic is that?

I was so happy when the phone rang that I knocked over a lamp and a can of diet soda to get it by the third ring.

"Hey, Whitney! What's up?" Eric's cheerful, familiar voice was music to my ears. It hit me just how much I'd missed seeing him around since we'd had our "discussion."

"Not much. I'm glad you called."

"I wanted to tell you about my new job. It's really cool, Whit. You are now talking to the assistant manager of an aviation museum! It's unbelievable. I get to talk, think and look at airplanes all day long!" Head in the clouds, he rambled on happily about his duties, the size of his office and the fact that he'd eaten his lunch today in the cockpit of a World War II bomber.

I was about to ask if he wanted to come over for popcorn and a movie when he said, "And I meet the most interesting people."

The little hairs on the back of my neck tingled and my skin begin to itch. "What kind of people?"

"Schoolkids on field trips. Old pilots. They come in to look around and end up spending hours talking about their flying days. Artists sometimes come to sketch the planes. And there's even someone there every day doing research for a book she's writing."

Ping! So that's why my intuition had kicked in.

"She has a degree in avionics. I've never met anyone who knows so much about planes. Did you know…" He rattled off obscure facts about airplanes in the 1950s.

No, I didn't know anything about that. I know that babies are born without kneecaps and that mosquitoes don't like fabric softener, but those scintillating items of interest don't hold Eric's attention.

A wave of sadness nearly toppled me as I hung up the phone. Eric didn't know it yet, but he'd found the girl for him. I heard something in his voice that had never been there for me. This was the one for him. There wasn't a doubt in my mind.

In a turmoil of mixed emotions—happy for him, sad for me—I turned back to the ads. There, under Miscellaneous was advertised the perfect gift to give Eric for the mood I was in.

For Sale: Parachute. Never opened.

Used once.

Just kidding!!!

December 7

> *Pride will destroy a person. A proud attitude leads to ruin.*
> —*Proverbs 16:18*

★ ★ ★

There's no doubt that I'm in the lowly and oppressed crowd these days and feeling very humble. I'm hanging on to Proverbs 29:23, though. "A man's pride brings him low, but a man of lowly spirit gains honor."

I'm looking at life through a gauzy veil these days. I've slept until my eyelids won't close, made mashed potatoes, roast beef and tapioca pudding until comfort food doesn't comfort me and scrubbed my bathroom with a toothbrush until the Comet and my knees gave out. There is no way to keep busy enough to forget what happened with Matt.

I've come to the conclusion that maybe he betrayed me and maybe he didn't. I really believe he gave our relationship all he had to give. The disappointment and disillusionment I feel are with myself. I should have known better.

Then again, maybe I should cut myself some slack. I haven't been sleeping well at night. I've been waking up to this strange, unsettling noise. Tick, click, tick. Every time it happens I sit bolt upright in bed with my heart pounding and my mouth dry. Going from feast to famine in the relationship department has shaken me more than I dreamed it could. It's certainly blown the top off any insecurities and doubts I have about myself.

This morning we sat in the break room discussing the football game (why do people talk about sports at work and about work at sports events?) when I told Mitzi, Betty and Bryan about my restless night.

"Are there cockroaches in your dream?" Bryan asked hopefully. "I used to have dreams about cockroaches…."

"No cockroaches, Bryan." I'm always a little alarmed by Bryan's Kafkaesque dreams.

"Have you seen a doctor?" Betty asked.

Not nearly enough of one.

Mitzi, for once, didn't offer an immediate opinion. Instead she slowly ate a single grape and looked thoughtful. Hmm. Mitzi and thoughtful—another word combination I never thought possible in a sentence.

Finally, as she popped the cover back onto her Tupperware and burped it gently, she said matter-of-factly, "It's perfectly obvious to me what you're hearing."

We all stared at her and said in unison, "It is?"

"Certainly. It's your biological clock…tick, tock, tick, tock, time is running out, tick, tock, tick, tock…."

Betty snorted coffee out her nose and sprinted for the bathroom as Bryan remembered a vitally important memo he'd forgotten to send. But Mitzi stayed put, staring at me with a pitying expression in her eyes. "Tick, tock," she droned like a demented clock.

"Uh-uh. Nope. Nada. Nix. No, no, no."

"Get a grip, Whitney! You just turned thirty, you broke up with the man in your life…"

The *men* actually—she didn't know about Eric.

"…and there are no prospects in sight! Tick, tock, tick, tock…"

Ridiculous. It couldn't be. Could it?

"You are a very loving, maternal person, Whitney. You don't have a mean bone in your body, you care about people just the way they are. You aren't critical or competitive and are nauseatingly nice. I suppose it's your beliefs that make you that way. You *want* to love. It's in your nature. Why wouldn't you worry about finding someone to love?"

I actually heard gears slicking and shifting in my head as I stared at Mitzi. She'd read me like an open book. Self-centered, diva-ish Mitzi was not so self-absorbed as she let on. She'd looked more closely into my heart than I had into hers. I'd misjudged her. Another lesson come home to roost. Would I ever stop learning the hard way?

Then she stood up, patted my hand and solved my problem for me.

"If you can't have a man, Whitney, you should at least have a cat."

December 23

"Ho, ho, ho!"

Kim's front door was unlocked, so I walked in, my arms full of gifts. I deposited my packages on the foyer bench and heard Kurt and Kim talking in the kitchen. They weren't exactly keeping their voices down, either.

"Kim, you can't listen to them! They don't understand what's going on with you. They're never going to understand! You know how it was with your uncle Jim and the others."

"My parents and grandparents love me!" Kim protested, her voice high-pitched.

"I've never said they didn't. I'm saying that your family has always denied that problems like this exist and it's caused a lot of pain over the years. I don't want you to go through the same thing...."

"What if I agree with them, Kurt? What if I think my father is right? Maybe there is something wrong with me spiritually. Maybe I'm just not good enough, faithful enough...."

"Who can be 'good enough'? 'All have sinned and fall short of the glory of God.' Being depressed isn't a sin."

"My father says that if I'd just pray more..."

"I know, I know 'God will answer.' What if He's already answered? What if He gave us an amazing doctor who understands these kinds of things and is willing to help you? What if God wants to work through Chase this time?"

Kim broke into sobs that nearly tore my own heart in half. "Kurt, I don't know what I believe." Her voice grew muffled as he undoubtedly took her in his arms. "I'm so scared."

I silently backed up, opened the door and rang the doorbell to warn them that they weren't alone.

Kurt came to the front, his face ragged-looking and etched with pain. He wiped his own tears away when he saw me. "I'm glad you're here," he whispered. "I need help. We called her parents to wish them Merry Christmas and it went all wrong. Talking to them makes her more depressed *and* guilty. Can't they see how much she needs their compassion and support?"

"What did they say?"

Kurt scuffed his foot against the floor while choosing his words carefully. "Whitney, there's a history of depression in Kim's family and a lot of broken lives, but no one will talk about it. No one has acknowledged it for three generations. Her grandfather was very adamant in his beliefs that depression is *always* caused by unconfessed sin. He never allowed room for the thought that depression is also an illness. There are family members suffering and getting lost along the way."

"So if they pretend it doesn't exist, then maybe it will go away?"

"Exactly."

When Kim walked into the foyer, I was shocked. Although she'd been steadily losing weight, today her collarbones protruded so sharply through her skin that it looked painful and her eyes were as red and sore-looking as boils. Ironically, she'd come through the surgery just fine, but the emotional aftermath was killing her.

"You brought presents." The simple statement, delivered in an expressionless voice seemed to exhaust her.

"I know you're going to Kurt's parents' for Christmas. I wanted to be sure you had them before you left."

"Let's open them now," Kurt suggested in a falsely bright voice. "And Whitney can open hers from us."

Kim nodded and turned toward the living room like a robot.

"Sorry about that," Kurt said. "Nothing much gets her excited these days...even the baby. I'm scared, Whitney. Really scared. I can't force medication down her throat or haul her to counseling only to have her sit silently for an hour. She's an adult, she needs to be willing to get treatment."

"Prayer," I murmured, the only solution I had.

"We've been bombarding heaven," Kurt murmured, "and we'll keep on."

Wesley made a gurgling sound and yelled "Da-da!" from his crib.

My eyebrow must have arched, because Kurt hurried to explain. "He's figured out that I'm the only one who comes to get him now. He's almost quit asking for 'Mama.'" His shoulders slumped. "I don't think Kim's even noticed."

I removed my jacket and bent to pick up my packages. I also nearly fell headfirst into the decorative ficus tree when the front door swung open behind me and slammed me in the backside.

"Sorry. I didn't know you were there." It was Chase, carrying presents of his own. "Are you okay?"

"Fine. You hit me in my most padded spot." I took his gifts so he could shake the snow off his boots and Road Runner stocking cap. Did the man ever run out of cartoons to wear? He was the only person I knew who could wear a designer suit and Daffy Duck tie ensemble and make it look cutting edge.

"I thought I'd drop some presents off before Christmas."

"Me, too." I tipped my head toward the living room and rolled my eyes.

Kurt had put up a tree. It was obvious that he had decorated it, because there was an overabundance of unbreakable fabric balls and edible popcorn strings around the bottom of the tree. The top of the tree was fairly sparse except for a few lights and clumps of old-fashioned tinsel flung here and there. On the very top was a listing angel hanging to the tree-top by her toes. Her halo was skewed but her expression was beatific. She didn't seem to mind hanging at a ninety-degree angle off the tree.

"We did the best we could," Kurt said as he returned with Wesley, "didn't we, big guy?"

Wesley shoved a chubby fist into his father's mouth and giggled.

"New trick," Kurt said, extricating the baby fingers from his own mouth. "Cute, huh?"

Kim, who was seated on the couch, didn't even turn her head to see what her baby had done.

"Why don't we open our gifts right now," Kurt suggested, his voice artificially bright. He glanced at Kim, but she said nothing.

We made a jolly party, at least as cheery as we could be with one of the participants barely acknowledging that we were there. Kim brightened momentarily when she opened Chase's gift to her, a soft lavender cashmere throw that she promptly flung around her shoulders. Wrapped in the fluffy lilac knit, her eyes like violet jewels in her pale face, Kim looked ethereal and wraith-like. It only reminded me of how fragile and delicate she is right now.

Chase gave Kurt an amazing tool set, which promptly initiated a conversation about the overhaul of the old car in Kurt's garage. And, for the baby, he'd purchased enough building blocks for Wesley to open his own construction business. Wes immediately began attempting to stack blocks in tidy rows, an infant prodigy in the building world, and I marveled at how carefully and suitably Chase had chosen the gifts.

I, however, am no slouch in the gift department, either. By the time we were done with Wesley's gifts, the child had disappeared among them, surrounded by stuffed toys and the wall of blocks the guys built for him to knock over.

Chase sprawled on the floor helping Wesley design a cage for his new zoo of stuffed creatures. As they did so, they made faces and engaged in a most sincere exchange of baby talk. Chase, sleeves rolled to his elbows and barefoot, lay flat on his belly. Wesley, who loved the eyeball-to-eyeball approach, occasionally leaned over to grab Chase by the hair and squeal delightedly.

As I watched, my stomach muscles tightened and a wave of longing rolled over me.

Why isn't there someone like him for me, a good man who's also perfectly handsome, perfectly prosperous, perfectly charming and perfectly ready for fatherhood? And why don't Santa's elves live in my apartment building? Because Christmas elves and perfect men are both fantasies, that's why.

Chase is likely a workaholic with a little black book so full that he's had to divide it into twenty-six volumes, A-B-C, and so on. And I'll bet he leaves dirty laundry in the bathroom, eats onions and garlic on weekends and…and… I couldn't think of any other flaws Chase might possibly have except, of course, that he's sworn off women forever. That, itself, is a biggie.

When I returned from my daydream, Kurt had opened his gag T-shirt, and the only gift left to hand out was the impulsive, last-minute one I'd decided to give to Kurt and Kim. The envelope didn't look like much, but it was a big deal for me. Being half-afraid to be alone with Wesley for an afternoon—what if something went wrong?—I didn't want to be responsible for a plumbing leak or a broken arm. It had taken all my courage to offer them a weekend away while Auntie Whitney took care of the home front.

Kurt read the card and broke into the biggest smile I'd seen from him all evening. "This is *exactly* what I've been wishing for! I just didn't know how we could swing it." He jumped to his feet and gathered me in a bear hug. Into my ear, he whispered, "Maybe this will help."

Kim smiled and some of her old zest came back. "You? Baby-sit for an entire weekend?" She knows what a nervous Nellie I am with such great responsibility. If I ever have my own children, I will buy a home within walking distance of an emergency room or urgent care center, build them a padded playroom and sterilize all their toys.

"You two need to get away. I put a list of B and Bs in the envelope for your escape." I knew I'd scored a home run in the gift department by the look on Kurt's face.

After our goodbyes, Chase and I found ourselves staring at each other over our cars in the driveway.

"D-doing anything special for the holidays?" I stammered, suddenly dumbstruck.

"Not really. There are a lot of people in our clinic who have young families and like to be home, so I offered to be on call. Unfortunately, Christmas is a tough time of year for some people and it's usually very busy."

So he'd managed to insulate himself into a protective cocoon for the holidays, too busy to think, too needed to feel alone. I found myself wishing for a cocoon of my own.

December 24

Christmas Eve.

The midnight service always brings me right to the core of the meaning of Christmas. What it must have been like for that young mother, in pain, ready to give birth, riding on the back of a rough donkey stumbling over rocks and stones.

And Joseph…poor guy. What must have been going through *his* mind? *This is God's kid we're having? Yeah, right… yet somehow I accept it. But the guys back at the carpentry shop are never going to believe this….*

The story all seems so tangible on Christmas Eve. I can feel Mary's weariness and Joseph's desperation at not finding them a place to stop and rest. I can envision the humbleness of the stable and smell the earthiness of the animals. But I can also imagine sweet hay and warmth radiating from those furry bodies. It's right, somehow, that Jesus was born with God's other miraculous creatures on watch. I can visualize the gentle, luminous eyes of the cow, the bright dark eyes of the sheep…such beauty in a place so unlovely. Sometimes my heart feels too big for my chest when I think of it.

And the songs! "Silent Night," "Away in a Manger," "O Little Town of Bethlehem" and that triumphant chorus, "With angelic hosts proclaim," or, as the boy in the pew beside me sang so sincerely, "With the jelly toast proclaim—Christ is born in Bethlehem."

December 31

New Year's Eve. The one night of the year—other than Valentine's Day—I really long for someone special in my life. It doesn't seem right to be at a party when the mirrored ball falls in Times Square and not have someone to grab me and plant a lovely "Here's to a great New Year" kiss on me.

It also doesn't seem quite right to be celebrating the festivity and romance of the beginning of the new year with the people you see at the office every single day.

"Cheer up, Whitney," Mitzi cajoled from a lushly padded seat behind the vast table at which we were sitting. "Don't worry, I'll make sure you have a man in your life by next year at this time. If nothing else, we can run an ad in the personals."

What's worse, really? Not having a date for New Year's Eve? Spending it with my officemates because Harry had an unexpected outbreak of generosity and decided to fund our holiday party on this most celebratory of evenings? Or knowing I am on the top of Mitzi's charity list for an entire year?

At first, I'd thought the idea of having our office party on New Year's Eve was dreadful, but once I'd surveyed the staff and discovered that *no one* had other plans, it was almost a relief to have something special to do. Harry picked one of the nicest hotels in the city for our party. The ballroom was filled with people enjoying music, lobster bisque, prime rib and Cornish hen, broccoli au gratin and a dessert table that defied description. I know, because I tasted everything on it.

Betty and her husband, Dick, had spent much of the evening visiting with old friends they'd run into at the buffet table. Mitzi and Dr. Big Foot played toesies under the table while Bryan and his date, a girl named Jennilee, who seemed every bit as skittish as he, discussed such important matters as where the butter knife should really go and whether it was smarter to order your soda with or without ice. Harry and his wife, Clarise, made sure everyone had full plates, full cups, fresh water and turns at conversation with them.

Harry was entering the new year with a fresh perm, tight and curly as a brand-new scouring pad. We all complimented him on how good it looked and actually meant it. Just like so many things I don't initially like, I can grow to love it. It gives him a playful quality that no one had noticed before, and anything that made Harry more appealing was a definite benefit to us. And everyone was being wonderful to Kim and Kurt, who had been invited to join us even though she was still on leave from the office.

"You look great, you know," I told her when we escaped to the bathroom to refresh our lipstick. "Who'd ever think—"

"That I'm the mess I really am?" Kim put on lipstick without even looking in the mirror.

"That you've been through a tough time and are going to come out on the other side."

"Whatever."

"Kim, it's a brand-new year. It's time to look ahead."

She turned to me with a distant expression, her features flat and her voice resigned. "To what? Maybe I won't even live through this year."

Her words struck me so hard that I stumbled backward. Caught behind the knees by a chaise longue, I half sat, half fell onto the cushions. "What?"

"You heard what I said. Am I the only realist here? Whitney, I've had cancer!"

"And your very accomplished doctor is delighted with your prognosis. He believes you're going to be fine. Why don't you?"

"Chase doesn't know everything. No one does." The hopelessness and despair fed by her depression were dragging her under. Pretty soon she'd be shoveling dirt on her own grave.

"You can't go on this way. What can I do to help?"

"Do whatever you like. It doesn't matter." She moved toward the door of the ladies' lounge as indifferently as if we'd been discussing recipes instead of her life. "Nothing matters anymore."

Considering the direction the party had taken for me after Kim's disturbing statements, I thought there was nowhere to go but up. Ha! Was I wrong!

At five minutes to midnight, everyone gathered at the center of the ballroom floor under a huge netting full of black and silver balloons. They would fall at the stroke of midnight and people would lunge at them as if money were floating from the ceiling. In some sense, it actually was. A dozen of the balloons held vouchers for trips to take in the new year—Barbados, Rio, Sydney, Alaska and Maui, to name a few. I saw Harry, Bryan, Mitzi and her toe doctor hunkering down for the lunge to find the winning balloons. There'd be none of that ridiculous kissing, hugging and good wishes from my crowd at the stroke of midnight.

As I stood there, remote and detached from the hubbub and the clamor, I felt a tug on the arm of my dress. I turned around to see Eric and a lovely blonde with glowing porcelain skin, a sweet smile and pale lemon hair falling around her face in long, natural waves. She looked like an angel in her demure white gown.

"Hey, Whit! I didn't know you were going to be here," Eric said, his arm firmly glued to the woman's tiny waist. "Great, isn't it?"

"Yes." I struggled to sound excited, but my stomach was doing weird things. "Fabulous."

Out of the corner of my eye, I could see the digital clock on the big screen counting to midnight. Only one minute left until this year was history.

"I'm really glad you're here, Whitney, because I want to introduce you to someone very special. Whitney, I want you to meet the woman I'm going to marry, Allison Lund...."

The ball fell. Cheers erupted. And Eric's words were muffled as he placed his lips over the upturned mouth of the woman in his arms. A black balloon floated by, and I caught it and hugged it to my chest, the closest I could come to an embrace. When it popped, it revealed a slip of paper. On it, it big curlicued letters were the words *You are a winner! A Romantic Round-Trip Vacation for Two to Hawaii—Happy New Year!*

"Happy New Year, Whitney," I muttered to myself, totally alone in a crowd full of couples.

JANUARY

CHAPTER 12

January 1

And then there were none.

Eric's fiancée is perfect for him—beautiful, sweet and crazy in love with him—his angel. Allison Lund grew up with a military pilot as a father, two brothers who fly for big airlines and a mother who thinks it's perfectly reasonable to have her family building an airplane from a kit in the garage just for the fun of it.

I'm so happy for Eric that I could just cry.

I could just cry anyway, because right now my life is one big mess. Kim is better one day, low the next. The two men I had in my life are long gone. Tansy doesn't expect me to show up at EEAT every week (a happy/sad thing) unless I feel like it, because I've reached my goal weight and I only have to weigh in monthly now. And Mitzi has designated herself my new best friend.

How did this all happen? Back in September, I wanted to meet a marriageable Christian man, lose a few pounds and make an upward movement in my career. I met men, all right, but look how that turned out. And I lost weight on what I now call the "obedience diet." I fed less on food and more on His word, especially those about gluttony, obedience and honoring Him in all I do. I'm astounded how willful I am sometimes, but it made a difference. Then there's Bernard. He's got big plans for me. I'll need to let him down gently. He talks about bouncing a coin off my abs and me training to enter a bodybuilding contest. Any coins I have go right into my purse. He must be hurting for clients.

In spite of the fact that I received a huge raise and did many of the things I set out to do, I feel self-pity knocking at every door. I've thought of eating myself into a stupor, but that's a thing of the past. I'm beginning to appreciate the body God gave me. I won't throw that away.

I've found the verse that's going to carry me through the year.

> *Why am I so sad? Why am I so upset?*
> *I should put my hope in God. I should*
> *Keep praising Him, my Savior and my God.*
> —Psalm 42:11

So here it is, the New Year, a blank slate. What do I want to write on it?

January 5

It is impossible to baptize a cat. I know. I've tried.

This is one of the lessons most indelibly printed in my brain from childhood. I came out of that particular sacrament sopping wet, with tooth and claw marks on my arms and face that didn't heal for weeks and a pet that avoided me for the better part of a year.

It is as impossible as trying to *bathe* a cat.

Sometimes I astound myself. I actually took Mitzi's advice. If I can't have a man, the least I should have is a cat, she said, and I listened. I need something in my apartment that's overjoyed to see me when I get home…not overjoyed, exactly, cats being what they are…but at least he stands up to see what's for supper. Sometimes he even rubs against my leg, purring and winding himself in a figure eight through my ankles. I've noticed however, that he chooses only to do so on days I'm wearing black. He must innately know that hair sticks better to black than to denim.

His name is Mr. Tibble. Don't ask me why. That was the name on the cage at the humane society, and not wanting him to have to adjust to everything being new, I thought he might as well keep his name. On his information card it said his owners were moving abroad and couldn't bring him along. It said he's "regal, independent, vocal, decisive and has a good appetite." Come to think about it now, those aren't highly sought-after qualities in either cats or humans, but it's too late. He's now part of my family, and I love him in spite of himself.

Mr. Tibble, on the other hand, has not yet decided if he wants to keep me. He sits on top of my refrigerator and stares at me with accusing gold eyes, as if I were the source and not the solution to all his problems. I am also beginning to believe that his owners really didn't have to leave the country. It was the only good excuse they could think of to get away from Mr. Tibble.

Even though I've had him only three days, he's already taking his share of my bed (the center), sharpening his claws on all vertical surfaces including my legs, drapes and couch and is singing arias in the middle of the night just because he feels like it. From all accounts, it's just like having a man in the house. He doesn't like water, discipline or cheap food. He does like watching television, shedding fur and the most expensive gourmet cat food on the grocery-store shelves.

I had to have someone—something—to take away the sting of seeing Eric with his lovely new woman. Though I didn't want him for myself, it hurts to know that he's no longer an option. Still, when I hugged them both, said congratulations and wished them all the happiness in the world, I meant it. Then I came home and cried myself to sleep.

On January second I went to the humane society and adopted Mr. Tibble. Talk about jumping out of the frying pan and into the fire.

I only told my parents the news about Eric yesterday, and what I'd feared might happen did. Mother went into "find Whitney a date" mode faster than Mr. Tibble can ruin a pair of panty hose. It took all my powers of persuasion to convince her that Pastor Bob, the youth pastor, is *not* my type, and she *must not* sign me up to chaperon the youth group's rock-a-thon. Besides which, there just might be a new man in my life and I'd tell her more when there was something to tell. Of course, she has no idea this "new guy" is a cat named Mr. Tibble.

January 8

I awoke to the sound of the telephone. It was Kurt. He sounded both relieved and anxious. "Listen, Whit, I want to cash in on that Christmas present you gave us—a weekend of baby-sitting for Wesley. Are you free this weekend?"

"I can be," I argued. "What's up?"

"Chase was here last night. Kim's agreed to give medication a try. She's not happy about it, but Chase was very persuasive. She's promised to give it six months."

I felt relief sweep through my body.

"He says that she'll probably be ready to start weaning herself off it by then anyway." Kurt drew a deep breath. "I'd just like to get away alone together for the weekend and come back fresh. We've agreed not to look back anymore but concentrate on the life ahead of us. Maybe a couple days away would help us start on a clean slate."

I've never been so delighted to baby-sit in my whole life.

January 10

Kim, of course, isn't quite as happy about this turn of events as Kurt. I stopped over after work tonight, and she was packing a bag for the weekend and grumbling.

"I don't see why we have to leave the baby at home. Surely that B and B has a crib available."

"When he could be here in his own home with me, who will play with him for hours on end, spoil him relentlessly and teach him to throw his shoes in the toilet?"

"Well," she said with a smile. "That is pretty irresistible. Are you sure you'll be okay?"

"Positive. You have nothing to worry about. I repeat, nothing."

The phone rang. Kim made no move to answer it, so I did. "Hello, Easton home, Whitney speaking."

There was a protracted pause before the caller spoke. "Oh, hello, Whitney. This is Pastor Bob calling from the church."

For a moment, I thought my mother had talked him into asking me out but then I realized that couldn't be—he had called the Eastons, after all.

"I'm doing some house calls today for our visitation pastor, and thought that if Kim was home, I'd stop by to see how she's doing." There was a question in his voice.

"Yes, she is. Would it be soon?"

"In the next half hour, if that's convenient. But I don't want to interrupt your visit...."

"No danger of that," I assured him.

"Good. I'll see you in a few minutes."

I hung up the phone and looked at Kim. "The new pastor is stopping over to say hello. Will Kurt be home for dinner?"

"No, he's working late."

"Then I'm inviting myself. Soup sound good?"

Kim waved me toward the kitchen. "You know my house better than I do. Fix whatever you'd like."

While I set the table, Kim joined me, carrying Wesley in one arm and the photo album I'd seen before in the other. She settled Wesley in his high chair and curled onto a chair to look at the photographs.

As I dished up the soup and brought crackers and spoons to the table, Kim held up a snapshot. "This is my uncle Jim only two weeks before he died."

I looked over her shoulder. I don't know what I'd expected—an ill man perhaps—but Uncle Jim was a broad-shouldered, robust young man with dark hair and an infectious smile. He had his hand on the shoulder of a small girl who looked adoringly up at him—Kim, no doubt.

"What a good-looking guy." I stared at the grainy photo, captivated by the energy and personality radiating from him, even after all these years. "What a shame. Car accident?"

"Suicide."

I sat down heavily. "Him? But he looks so happy!"

"He had to," she said bluntly. "My grandparents wouldn't have it any other way. My uncle had some problems. When he was doing well, he was the most delightful, amusing man in the world. But when he wasn't..."

"When he wasn't...?"

"He had 'moods.' When he was in a mood, he'd disappear for a while. Not at first, of course, but near the end." She sighed. "Grandpa kept reminding Jim that his emotional problems stemmed from his lack of faith. Because, of course, if he'd had enough faith, he wouldn't have had those problems."

"That's a convoluted way of thinking."

She didn't respond. The doorbell was ringing.

Pastor Bob was on the front step. I grabbed his hand and pulled him inside. In a low whisper, I gave him a sketch of what Kim and I were discussing and what had been going on.

"Help me, will you?"

"Whitney? Who is it?" Kim called from the kitchen.

When Kim saw Pastor Bob, a guy with a receding hairline and a soft pouch just starting at his waistline, the strangest thing occurred. She sat up and smiled.

Not only did she smile, but she managed to sparkle. For a minute I thought my best friend had become Dr. Jekyll and Mr. Hyde, then it dawned on me. That was how Uncle Jim had managed to look so happy and high-spirited only days before he took his own life. Neither Kim nor her uncle wanted people other than their closest confidants to know how much pain they were in. I looked at Uncle Jim's photo and his wide smile. What a dreadful game he'd had to play.

Pastor Bob, forewarned, was wise enough to figure out for himself that Kim's animation was forced, an act of will without genuine feeling behind it.

"So, Kim," he said casually, "Kurt says you're doing well physically. How are you doing emotionally? Have you been depressed?"

She recoiled. "Frankly, in spite of my husband's and friend's opinions, I'm not sure I believe in depression. I was taught that it's the result of sin."

"You mean depression is a character problem? A sin rather than a sickness?"

"I suppose." Her gaze darted around the room as if looking for a way out.

"Those are hard words," he commented softly. "And a very harsh judgment on people who suffer from depression."

"My grandfather told us that true faith would bring us true healing."

"I see." Bob didn't press the question any further.

I could see he was genuinely concerned about Kim, and I liked Bob better by the moment. "Will you eat with us? It's just soup from a can and crackers from a box. It's not much but…"

"Thank you, I'd love to." He looked at me over Kim's lowered head and I saw compassion in his eyes. God had sent us a gift to help get us through.

"Let's sit in the living room. I built a fire. And I already have dessert planned."

"Whitney, you don't have to stay and baby-sit for me," Kim began.

"I'm not baby-sitting. I'm enjoying myself."

"Me, too," Bob said.

Dessert was roasted marshmallows, candy bars and graham crackers.

Bob cooked marshmallows in the fireplace while I constructed the s'mores and Kim fussed. "I've never done this before. The carpet…"

"Then it's time." I laid a perfectly roasted marshmallow on the graham cracker she was holding and topped it with a large square of chocolate and another cracker. "Carpets can be vacuumed. Moments like this can't be replaced."

"You're a free spirit." Strings of marshmallow dripped out Bob's mouth until he looked as if he'd had his mouth stitched shut with thick white sutures. "You have a unique sense of humor and don't take yourself too seriously."

"That's part of it." I dipped a napkin in my water glass and handed it to him so he could scrub his face. "There are things I'm very serious about, like my faith, and I'm trying to let God handle the rest." I almost added, "He's been slow in the mate department," but managed to control myself.

I don't know when he became just-plain-Bob, instead of "Pastor Bob" to myself and Kim, but the comfort level in the room rose swiftly. Bob must have felt it, too, because he chose to say something that startled both of us.

"I've struggled with depression all my life."

"You?"

"Ministers are human, too," he said bluntly. "I knew God could heal me, but He didn't—not in the way I'd expected." He leaned back in his chair. "I asked Him for a miracle, a lifting of the darkness in me. Instead, He sent me to read Paul."

He looked at Kim's expression and chuckled. "I know. It didn't seem very helpful to me either at first. Paul wrote in 2 Corinthians, 7:5-6, 'We were afflicted on every side; conflicts without, fears within. But God, who comforts the depressed, comforted us by the coming of Titus.' I don't believe healing comes in just one form."

"What do you mean?"

"Sometimes people pray for physical healing and it doesn't come. But that doesn't necessarily mean they aren't believing enough."

"No, but…" Kim frowned.

"Perhaps the healing is spiritual or emotional, or maybe it is healing a rift between that person and God. We put God in a pretty tight box if we don't give Him credit for being able to save us in spite of ourselves. I believe He's stationed people all around us who are ready and waiting to provide what we need—and we don't even give Him credit for that wonderful gift."

"What do you mean?"

"When my car breaks down, I don't fix it myself. I call the auto club and have it towed to a repair shop so an expert can work on it. I'm grateful for those who helped me, and I don't feel bad that I couldn't fix it myself. Sometimes our bodies and our emotions are a little like our cars. They need repair. We know where to call for help. It doesn't mean God couldn't miraculously make my car start, but it's just as miraculous to me how He provides others who can meet my needs."

He had Kim's full attention.

"I find it interesting that in the case of Paul, God used another man to bring Paul comfort and healing. We are remarkable, multifaceted beings, rich in mind, body and spirit, and live in a fallen world where every part of us is challenged every day. I thought that if I prayed hard enough about my depression, I'd be freed. I threw myself on God's mercy and waited for my miracle clinging to the knowledge that He had not abandoned me, that apart from God, I was nothing."

"'All have sinned and fall short of the glory of God,'" Kim murmured.

"'Not that we are competent in ourselves to claim anything…our competence comes from God,'" I added softly, quoting from 2 Corinthians 3:5.

"Then He sent my Titus, to comfort me—in the form of a very wise doctor."

Kim stiffened and leaned forward.

"No one is impervious to sickness, not in this world," Bob said gently. "That comes in the next. For now, sometimes we have to turn to another of God's miracles—doctors and the medical treatment they provide." He paused when he saw Kim's eyes narrow.

"Has Wesley had his baby inoculations?"

"Of course."

"Then if you believe that is beneficial to him, why can't medicine be beneficial to you? Just as our bodies suffer from so much humanness, sometimes so do our minds."

After he'd gone, Kim was quiet, but it wasn't the deadened, anesthetized silence of before. Somewhere in her a flicker of hope and the flame of her old self had been fanned.

January 25

Mr. Tibble here.
My new pet Whitney is behaving badly. All she wants to do is

lie around and sleep. Doesn't she realize that's my job? I've tried to awaken her by walking across her face, singing ("Caterwauling," my previous pets called it) and even tantalizing her with my catnip mouse. Nothing has worked. I'm getting worried. She always gets excited about the catnip mouse. Even my last-ditch effort to engage her was futile. Barfing a hairball never failed to get her moving—until today.

She's not even fussing with my food or worrying about why I'm so finicky. So far I've managed to reject beef, chicken, fish and shrimp flavors. Why hasn't anyone come up with something mouse-flavored? Doesn't anyone know anything about cats?

This lassitude is intriguing. A refreshing change from all that "Here, kitty, kitty, kitty" stuff I usually hear. I felt the need to investigate it further. Lay down on her chest and stuck my nose near hers. Very pleasant. She smells good. Also chewed the buttons on her shirt, played with her hair and fell asleep on her leg. That, at least, inspired enough energy in her to shake me off.

This must stop. I'm receiving no tuna treats, no brushing (I like it but would never let her know that) and she's begun encouraging me to drink out of the toilet. Puleeese. Haven't I suffered enough?

Mr. Tibble, signing off

CHAPTER 13

January 26

"Mary Poppins at your service." Or was I Maria, the failed novice from *The Sound of Music?* I felt very Julie Andrews-like as I stood on the front steps of Kim and Kurt's house, bag in hand, ready to baby-sit. Or maybe I was Nana, the sheepdog from *Peter Pan,* assigned to take care of the children. I had to pick a role model quick, because I could hear Kurt's footsteps coming down the uncarpeted hall.

"Good, you're here." He grabbed my hand and pulled me inside. "Kim's in the kitchen. I want to get her out of here before she changes her mind. She's already told me once today that she sees no reason for us to get away without the baby." With no time for questions he towed me into the kitchen where Kim was shuffling several lists scattered across the table.

"Come on, honey, we have to leave. The way traffic is on Friday afternoons, it's going to take us an extra hour to get out of town."

"I'm not so sure...." She definitely did not look like a woman happy to be going away for a romantic weekend with her husband. "I haven't gone over my lists with Whitney. I have to tell her that FedEx is picking up a package, and the food in the fridge—"

"She can read. Let's go." Kurt threw an arm around me and gave me a squeeze. "I can't tell you how much this means to me, Whit. Wes has been sleeping about twenty minutes, so you'll have at least an hour before he wakes up."

As he was towing Kim out the front door, she turned to him. "Kurt, aren't you going to tell her?"

But instead of answering, he gave me a friendly wave and whisked her out the door. I sat down at the table and started to read Kim's instructions.

She'd drawn a sort of flowchart in half-hour increments, outlining Wesley's day. The child has more activities scheduled than I have recorded in my PalmPilot for the entire week. Just looking at it exhausted me. I tiptoed into the living room and stretched out on the couch. No use allowing Wesley to be the only one enjoying a nap.

Half an hour later, I woke with a start. There was laughter coming from the baby's room. Wesley was giggling and chuckling to himself, apparently having a dandy time. What a good baby, able to entertain himself like that.

Mentally I wrote my script for Kim's return. "That child is a little angel...cheerful, happy...."

I opened the door and rewrote the script.

Wesley looked up from this source of entertainment to give me a grin. His fine hair stood out around his head like a halo, and the benevolence of his smile should have melted my heart. But...naked as a little cherub, he sat in the middle of his crib examining the contents of his diaper. Wesley had learned to master the sticky tabs on his disposable diapers and, in doing so, had struck...well, it was definitely not gold.

He gurgled a greeting and held up the treasure he'd found.

Not again! It wasn't fair. This was the second time there was no one to hand Wesley off to, no parent who, by virtue of the job description, had to take cleanup duty. This one was mine, all mine.

I gingerly picked him up under the armpits and, with my arms straight out, carried him into the bathroom. He squealed and kicked with delight as I settled him on a big terry-cloth towel and ran the water for his bath. I deposited him, towel and all, in the tub.

This time I stripped my clothes off, tossed them over the toilet tank and, in a manner of speaking, dived in. A rubber duckie, a plastic sailboat and a tsunami later, Wes was clean and I was stripped down to my bra and panties.

"I wanted to wash my hair anyway," I assured Wesley as he tugged on one of my damp curls. I pawed through the stack of clean laundry on the counter and found a pair of Kurt's cotton shorts and a shirt that hung past my knees like a really ugly housedress. My drawers were drooping as much as my spirits.

I was so busy dressing Wesley that I almost didn't hear the doorbell. Federal Express, no doubt.

"Come on, big guy, let's go." Stepping over the puddles, I padded to the door. I glanced in the mirror and winced. Wesley, enamored with my long hair, gave it a tug so hard it brought tears to my eyes. That's why I flung open the door and yelled "Ouch!" into Chase's face.

"Whitney?" He sounded unsure. I can't imagine why. Was it because I looked like the sister of the Creature from the Black Lagoon? Or did it have something to do with wearing an oversize shirt that made me look as if I was walking around in a pup tent?

"Is everything all right?" He smelled of woodsy soap and something deliciously citrus, probably Issey Miyake. "Have you been crying?"

I thought of the mess in Wesley's crib. "No, not yet, but it's probably coming." Then I added bluntly, "What are you doing here?"

"Didn't Kurt and Kim mention their plan to you?"

I recalled Kim's parting words, "Aren't you going to tell her?"

"What plan?" I asked suspiciously.

"The only way Kurt could get Kim to leave Wesley was by promising her that I'd check on the two of you as often as I could. Fortunately, I have someone covering for me, so I'm able to be around all weekend."

He put his index finger under my chin and closed my mouth for me. "Kurt thought it would be good if you didn't have to do everything alone, and Kim said that she might be able to enjoy herself if she knew there was a doctor in the house."

In the house?

He saw the expression on my face. "Not literally, of course, but it's no problem for me to hang around until the baby falls asleep."

"Thanks for the vote of confidence, Kim," I muttered.

"Don't take it personally. She's still fragile. If it makes her feel better…" An odd expression flitted across his features. "The house smells funny. Did Kurt say anything about septic problems?"

"Not exactly." I patted Wesley's bottom.

Suddenly a man on a mission, Chase followed our damp trail into Wesley's bedroom and the adjoining bath. I closed my eyes and waited.

To his credit, he didn't say a word. He just came out of the baby's room with an odd smile on his face, walked over to me and took the baby out of my arms.

"Discovering ways to entertain yourself, I see, aren't you, buddy?"

Wesley beamed like a lighthouse.

Chase turned to me. "Need a little help?" He handed Wesley back to me, took off his jacket, unknotted his tie and hung them over a chair by the front door. "Do you think Kurt has an old work shirt I can use?"

That was how Chase Andrews and I came to be working in tandem, he with a bucket of water and cleanser, scrubbing the rails of the crib, while I washed baby sheets, clothes and the panels of the curtain from the window by the crib. Wesley held court in his high chair, slamming a spoon against the tray and squealing sounds so high-pitched I was sure all the dogs in the neighborhood would soon be barking at the back door.

"Do you think I got carried away?" Chase asked when we finally sat down at the kitchen table. "I hope Kim doesn't mind that I did a little extra cleaning."

"A little extra? Wes's room smells like a surgical suite. I'm sure even Kim's never cleaned it that thoroughly in her life."

"Well, you did all the laundry and washed everything but the ceiling in the bathroom."

"It felt good to do something concrete for her," I admitted. "Besides," I added, suddenly shy, "it was fun. It would have taken me forever to get all that done without you."

Okay. The man had already proved he could clean, tend a baby and keep his head in a messy situation. He's compassionate, gentle and has a great sense of humor. His former fiancée must be deranged.

We were both silent, and I was grateful for Wesley's nonsensical burbling.

"I'm going to fix dinner. Would you...?"

"I'd love to." He stood up and headed for the freezer section of the refrigerator. "If I'm not mistaken, Kurt owes us a steak for this."

Wesley conked out between his mashed potatoes and his tapioca pudding. I put him to bed, and when I returned to the kitchen, Chase was building banana splits. He had chocolate, whipped cream, pineapple preserves, cherries, strawberries, marshmallow cream, nuts and a half dozen other toppings spread across the counter.

This man knows his ice cream.

"I can't!" I wailed. "Do you know how many calories there are in one of those things?"

He glanced over at me and shrugged. "I wouldn't think that would bother you. You should probably gain a few pounds."

Of all the words a man can say to make you love him, those must be the best.

"Where were you when I started dieting?" I muttered.

He chuckled and put the lid back on the fudge sauce. "When magazine publishers quit using teenagers as models for the ideal adult woman, and everyone stops buying into all this surface-beauty stuff, then women will realize what normal really is. More chocolate sauce?"

Happily, I took my banana split to the table. Doctor's orders.

After dinner, Chase didn't seem in any hurry to go, and I was certainly not in the mood to let him. It was he who suggested a game of Scrabble. Talk about waving a red flag in front of a bull, or in my case I suppose, a heifer. He'd found the only competitive bone in my body. Fortunately for him— and unfortunately for me, words kept turning up to throw me off my game.

"G…E…N…T…L…Y. That's six plus a double letter on Y plus ten points to start. Okay, Chase, your turn."

"A…L…L…U…R…I…N…G. Eight and a double words score makes sixteen. Are you writing this down?" He looked up at me. "Tell me about your job, Whitney."

"Nothing much to tell. I'd rather hear how you decided to become a surgeon. B…R…I…D…E. Ooooh. Triple letters on both B and E. Sixteen points!"

"H...U...G...G...E...D. Double count on the G and E. Fifteen-point total. It seemed like the right thing to do—heal people, help them live longer lives." He looked at me expectantly. "Your turn."

I was having a little trouble concentrating, noticing the words that were appearing. "W...A...N...T...E...D. Triple letter on the W. Sixteen points!"

"Good one. L...I...K...E. A measly nine points."

My numbers were stacking up. "Okay, I've got one. T...O...P...P...E...R. Six points."

He looked confused. "Like a topper on a pickup truck?"

"Sure, or on a cake. You know, like a wedding...cake." I hadn't meant for that to come out.

He seemed blissfully unaware of my loss of composure as he spelled out H...Y...M...N for a double letter on the Y and sixteen points. Then I looked at my letters and I felt my ears redden. The word I needed to spell was right there in front of me. D...E...S...I...R...E.

By the time the game ended, my cheeks were as hot and rosy as a burning coal. Chase hadn't seemed to notice the theme of our Scrabble board.

Chase glanced at his watch. "I'd better go. Why don't you think of something you'd like to do tomorrow to entertain the baby."

"Think?" Me? There wasn't a single thought in my head other than this man couldn't be real. He was too perfect. It wasn't until he'd walked out the door that I realized he'd made plans for Wesley and me to spend much of the weekend with him. Not that I mind, but despite what the game board read, I really don't need another man in my life whose interest in me is purely platonic.

January 28

I never think of myself as the motherly type, but when Wesley started to fuss at 3:00 a.m. this morning, there was something truly remarkable about rocking his husky little body as he sucked his thumb and burrowed into my chest. It left an ache burning inside me, an unfilled space I hadn't known I had. Just stroking that soft head and watching him suck the thumb he'd already managed to callus put an exclamation mark on what I already know so well. There is a God and He makes miracles. I was holding one.

The phone rang just as I saw Chase pull into the driveway. It was Kim, sounding homesick.

"How's Wesley?"

I watched Chase come into the kitchen, spring the baby from his high chair and tickle him under the chin. Wesley squealed with glee.

"Is that him? Is he okay?"

"Couldn't be better. He and Chase are bonding."

"Are you angry?"

"No, I'm glad they're bonding."

"About us not telling you, I mean. We trust you, but he's a doctor. Whit, if anything went wrong…"

I didn't argue. If we'd had to invite all of the Mayo Clinic to camp in the backyard while they were gone, it would have been fine with me.

It wasn't anything we discussed or planned, but Chase and I fell into an easy camaraderie that precluded conversation where Wesley was concerned. It was as if we could read each other's minds. We reached for diapers, juice and toys simultaneously, until I felt uneasy about the way the brush of his hand burned against my skin.

Because it was ten degrees below zero, we decided to stay in and keep warm. The only movies in the house were Wesley's, but Chase didn't seem to mind and I've never really outgrown cartoons. Wesley, of course, fell asleep on the couch before the first credits had rolled and snored with that kitten-like purr babies sometimes have.

As Chase ate popcorn and cheered on Cinderella, I watched Wesley sleep. It was a slippery slope I'd stumbled onto these last few days, and it alarmed me how far and how fast I'd fallen for this man. Don't I ever learn from my mistakes? What about the lesson I'd learned with Matt? It's pure folly to fall in love with an unavailable man.

"You're deep in thought," Chase observed.

"I didn't realize it showed." I'd been so lost in my own thoughts that I could hardly find my way out.

"What's going on in there?" He brushed away a strand of hair that had fallen over my shoulder.

The thing on the top of my mind bubbled out. "Chase, are you a Christian?"

"Yes, I am."

Simple, clear, delivered without a moment's hesitation. Not "I always go to church" or "I was brought up that way" or any of the other subtle dances people do around questions that make them uncomfortable. I've always had a sense that when people answer that cautiously, they're really asking themselves the same question.

I had so much on my mind when Kim and Kurt returned that I left the house without scolding them for not trusting me to baby-sit for Wesley without help. Of course, as it turned out, I had a much better time with Chase present than I would have had without him. That, however, is information Kim will never hear from my lips.

FEBRUARY

CHAPTER 14

February 2

Today was a total waste of makeup.

"I've solved your problem, Whitney!" Mitzi, waving a newspaper in her hand, bolted into my office with such energy that papers fluttered on my desk.

"My only problem is Mr. Tibble," I retorted. "He shreds my drapes and sleeps on the kitchen counter while I'm gone. I'm holding you personally responsible for that.'

"So many cats, so few recipes," Bryan murmured as he went by.

Much as I complain, the cat is growing on me—like warts.

"*The* problem. The one you always have."

"Oh, that one." I turned back to my computer screen. Almost immediately, a set of bloodred artificial nails holding a newspaper advertisement replaced my lovely blue screen and colorful icons.

"Don't be difficult," Mitzi ordered in an audible hiss. "I'm the one who can help you make something of this miserable life of yours."

Miserable? Boring, maybe, but my life is hardly miserable.

"This is the answer to your prayers!"

I glanced at the newspaper. *"HastyDate! The latest in speed dating! Meet 15 men in only two hours. Find your own TruLove and have time left over for lattes! Sign up now, we're filling fast for our Saturday, February 4, event. Reserve your spot, find your man. Make checks out to HastyDate...."*

"I pray a lot, Mitzi, and I can guarantee you this is not on my list. Now, if you'll excuse me, there's a trade show coming up and I have a lot of details to—"

"Trade show? You can't think about that now. You haven't been out on a date since you refused to work for Matt Lambert! You aren't as young as you used to be, my dear. There's no time to lose."

I envisioned my youth on a fast slide down the toilet as Mitzi spoke. Unfortunately, no matter how hard I try, there is a little teeny-tiny part of me that agrees with her. The closest things to romance in my life recently have been the books on my bedside stand.

I looked more closely at the article. "People actually *pay* to go to these things?"

"We live in a very busy society, Whitney. We have our groceries and dry cleaning delivered, high-speed Internet and cleaning ladies. Who doesn't move at high speed these days?"

"Thanks, but no thanks, Mitzi. Nice of you to suggest it, but it's not my thing."

"It doesn't have to be your 'thing.' It's just a way to get you out there and circulating. Think of it as practice. You're probably rusty at making small talk with men. Besides, I've already registered for you and paid the fee. Think of it as a belated Christmas gift. It's at the Radisson. I'll drive you there and wait in the lobby." She glared at me menacingly. "And I don't wait in lobbies for *anyone* so you'd better not disappoint me."

I suppressed the urge to salute as Mitzi turned on her stiletto heel and stomped away. Unfortunately this is one Christmas gift I can't return for credit.

February 4

Apparently I wasn't supposed to get myself out of the HastyDate ordeal, because everything I tried failed.

Not only didn't my parents need me for anything, they didn't even want me around tonight. Mother, feeling like her old self, had arranged an evening out with the Martins and the Hammers. When I really needed her, she'd planned her own excitement.

"You're a big girl, Whitney. Go, have fun, leave. And be thankful you have a friend who cares so much about your happiness."

That's a new perspective on the situation—Mitzi as a benevolent, loving friend. Maybe she is, in her own inimitable way. That isn't going to help me get through tonight.

"You can't wear that dress! It makes you look like Martha Washington!" Mitzi sat on my bed and censored every bit of clothing in my closet. "Too baggy," "too pale," "too bright," "too ugly."

Everything is loose-fitting—except, according to Mitzi, a little black dress I'd purchased as an incentive the last time I went on a diet. It had been twenty dollars on the "Final Clearance, 80%-off" rack at Marshall Field's. I tried it on, it did fit and, though I'm loath to admit it, Mitzi's right. It does look good on me.

Although I fought her at every turn, by the time she dragged me out of my apartment and into her car, I looked great. Even my thick, willful hair cooperated with her. I protested the entire time she was doing my makeup, but with only one pound of eyeliner and two gallons of lip gloss, she managed to make my brown eyes large and smoky and my lips full and luscious. Not bad for a girl who wanted to stay home and watch the special on rescue dogs on the Animal Planet.

On the way to the hotel, Mitzi insisted we stop at Kim's and show her my transformation. As we pulled into the driveway, Mitzi commented on the SUV parked by the garage.

"Well, well, what have we here? Did the Eastons get a new car?"

"No. That belongs to Dr. Andrews."

"Ohhh. How nice. We'll get to see him again." She sounded inordinately pleased.

Kim answered the door. Her skin had a little more color and her eyes weren't puffy from crying—good signs. In fact, she smiled when she saw me. "Whit! You're fabulous. Where did you get that dress?"

My reception in the living room was equally gratifying. Kurt whistled and Chase's eyebrows arched in surprise. They both jumped to their feet to greet us. And Wesley, who was playing on the floor, clapped his hands until he lost his balance and fell over.

"What's the big event?" Kurt asked. "And who's the lucky guy?"

"Guys. Not one. Dozens." Had I ever felt more foolish than I did at this moment? Probably, but this was in the top five.

"I registered her for HastyDate. It's the latest way for singles to meet men." Mitzi whipped the advertisement out of her purse. "Want to read about it?"

"So you pay money and all get together in one place and rate each other? Ouch." Kurt winced. "Painful. Good way to get a battered ego." He looked at me sharply. "Not you, Whitney, but there will be a lot of guys there setting themselves up to get hurt."

Interesting, isn't it? That's exactly what I'd thought about the women.

Mitzi had me pirouette and strike a pose to show off my dress. I didn't try to fight her, even though I felt like a poodle at the Westminster Dog Show. Then she went into a huge lecture about my makeup and how she had applied it. I could see Kurt and Chase trying to keep from laughing. I didn't blame them. It was hard for me to keep my mouth shut, too.

When Kim asked Mitzi into the other room, I dropped onto the couch next to Kurt. "Save me," I pleaded.

"You'll probably have a great time."

I looked at him through narrowed lids.

"Well, an okay time, then."

"Optimist," I accused. "If she wasn't so convinced that this is a good thing she's doing, I'd be gone right now. But she actually thinks she's doing me a favor!"

"She's doing someone a favor," Chase said enigmatically.

"Really, who?"

"Those men who've paid good money to come to Hasty-Date. Just seeing you will be worth the fee."

I felt pink from my torso upward until my face was on fire. What a gallant thing to say. "Thank you."

"My pleasure." He turned to Kurt. "What kind of friend are you? You never got me hooked up with HastyDate. Then I could be interviewing Whitney, too."

Kurt hooted. "Yeah, right. You're the guy who told me you were done with that stuff altogether, right?"

"Oh, yeah. I forgot for a moment in the presence of a beautiful lady." Chase stood up and winked at me. "I'm going to say goodbye to Kim. I have to stop at the hospital."

He paused in front of me. "I hope you have a wonderful time tonight, Whitney, and that you meet the man of your dreams. But be careful. Don't let anyone break your heart."

My heart is tough, I thought as I watched Chase leave the room. But if anyone could do it, it was him.

★ ★ ★

"I have some instructions for you." Mitzi dragged me into the ladies' lounge and eyed me doubtfully, as though she had a very slow learner on the end of her leash and wasn't quite ready to set me free to run about on my own. "With every guy you meet tonight, pay him a compliment."

"What if I don't like anything about him?"

"Find something. His cologne, his smile, his watch."

"Hello," I practiced, "what a lovely toupee you're wearing. It matches your eyebrows perfectly."

"You aren't trying." She glared at me, reminding me that it was her money I was wasting.

"Nice tie. Did they have more? What a great gift it would make."

"Much better." She consulted the recipe card in her hand. She'd made a list of things to teach me so I didn't make a fool of myself.

"Don't forget your body language. It's very important that your words and your body language agree."

"You mean I shouldn't put my hands over my eyes and tremble when I'm telling this guy how handsome he is?"

"Lean forward a little. And smile. Nothing big or fake. Just enough to show him you're interested."

This had gotten entirely out of hand. If Mitzi hadn't been so generous (in her own mind, at least), I wouldn't have gone through with it. But she was truly excited for me. The least I could do was show up.

"You have a great smile, so use it. Did you use that whitener I gave you? Good."

Being friends with Mitzi involves a lot of extra work, I've discovered, most of it on me. Her theory is that you can't improve on perfection, so we never look for flaws in her but take a magnifying glass to mine. Still, I have to admit, I've grown to like her. She's feisty and funny, a survivor. From what I've gathered, her childhood wasn't great, but she made the best of it. If there's a way to turn Mitzi on to God like she's turned on to fashion, trends and gossip, she'll be awesome for Him. I'm working on it and she's listening, but she's not going to commit to anything she's not sure about. That's why, when she really meets Jesus and builds a relationship with Him, she'll be faithful to the end.

Mitzi interrupted my thoughts to tell me to reapply my lip gloss between every suitor.

The hotel ballroom was wearing more jewelry than I was. HastyDate occupied the main event room, which dripped with crystal chandeliers, velvet flocking and mirrors. Unfortunately, all the lush beauty was twenty feet above my head. What was beneath it was not pretty. The enormous room was filled with white linen-covered tables. At each table were two chairs that sat facing each other—sort of an adult boys-against-the-girls challenge left over from grade school. The women were told to sit at "their" chairs all evening while men came to them, rating cards in hand, spent ten minutes discussing the secrets of life and love and moved on to the next woman—a foreshortened version of my life lately. At least with these men, I knew they'd be moving on quickly and not get my hopes up.

Mitzi, who'd managed to bully her way into the ballroom saying that without her I'd never participate (absolutely correct), gazed around with interest. I could practically see her mental gears turning and hear her checking off the Hasty-Daters as they milled around. "Yes. No. Maybe. Good possibility. Are you kidding?"

"Isn't this great?" Her eyes were shining. "Think of how efficient this will be!"

"Efficient" isn't a big requirement in my social life. I like store clerks, waiters and deliverymen to be efficient. Not once have I ever imagined myself whispering in someone's ear, "Darling, your efficiency thrills me."

I've accidentally gathered a collection of "Worst Night of My Life" stories—Leah's wedding and New Year's Eve among my co-workers. How could I possibly choose the most awful? Tonight would definitely be one more to add to the list.

I found my table by the tented cardboard name card, "Whitney Blake #8." My own card had a list of participating men and the numerical order in which they'd be arriving to interview me. Very well organized, these HastyDate people. Beside each name was a box in which to write "yes" or "no." If I didn't feel any chemistry or wasn't interested, I was to write "no" in the box. If I'd be willing to see the guy again, I was to write "yes." I could have filled the thing out immediately, but that seemed a little rude.

There were a few slots to check for each person such as "smoker/nonsmoker," "animal lover" and lines left open for my own comments. At the bottom of the sheet were some added instructions: "What is most important to you in a relationship? Be sure to ask questions to which you really want to know the answers." Examples: "Do you like loud music?" "What is your occupation?" "Where did you go to school?" "What do you see in your future?" "Are you dating anyone else right now?"

Mitzi had warned me about this, so I had my own list of questions prepared. One question, actually. "Are you a Christian?" I figured that would speed up the process for me. And there might actually be some long, pleasant silences in which we were both frozen mute by the sheer ridiculousness of what we were doing.

As Mitzi wandered off to check out the appetizers, I stared morosely at the crystal pitcher of water on my table. It was filled with icy water, and the outside of the carafe was sweating profusely. It wasn't the only thing sweating in that room, that's for sure. There were men pulling on their shirt collars and several with beads of sweat on their foreheads. Dating—

especially the HastyDate way—is nerve-racking business. Fortunately my sense of humor and spirit of adventure had begun to kick in.

A short, wiry-haired man leaped onto the makeshift stage. "Welcome, HastyDaters! This may be the most thrilling night of your life. I know my first HastyDate event was that for me. It's where I met the lovely young woman I'd like to introduce you to right now—" imaginary drumroll "—my new bride, Francine!"

Everyone clapped. Francine looked lovingly at her husband. It was so sweet, I got cavities. Apparently HastyDate hires anyone who finds TruLove at one of their events to work for the company. Two other successful HastyDater success stories followed. The last time I'd felt so much encouragement was at a high-school pep rally. One couple even had photos of their new baby blown up on a screen that glided down from the ceiling. A corporate sigh settled on the room, "Awwww...."

Visions of that first love nest together—the one with stainless-steel appliances, matching BMWs in the driveway, two perfect children (one boy, one girl), a perfectly trained dog and a pool—got everyone's juices flowing. When the bell rang, the men left the starting gate and plunged toward the first woman to whom they were assigned.

My lucky suitor, a computer programmer/grocery shelf stocker (computers are in a slump) named Gordo (short for Gordon, which he said sounds wimpy) dropped into the chair across from me. Either his glasses were steamy with excitement or he was simply overheating. Gordo must have been an efficiency expert once, because rather than depend on the flimsy sheet handed out by HastyDate Inc., he'd recorded all his questions in a ring-binder notebook, which he immediately flipped open.

"Do you want to go first?" he inquired. I could tell from the way he was drumming his fingers on his notebook that he wanted my answer to be no.

"I'd like you to be first." He put a little check in his note-book, and I knew I'd scored a point for something—intelli-gence, deference or obsequiousness.

"Age, height and weight, please." The man has a death wish. Most women will part with information on their height without too much trouble, but the other questions were social suicide.

"Educational background?"

He was pleased to hear I had a master's degree.

"Current employment and previous jobs?"

My long tenure at Innova was also in my favor.

"Type of music you like best?"

"Country-western." I never listen to it, but I couldn't help myself. I needed a few bad scores on his sheet or he'd be call-ing me to ask me out.

Unfortunately, he was pleased by my answer.

I needn't have worried, because I went downhill from there. Gordo doesn't like any food cooked by human hands. His favorites are Twinkies, Little Debbies and nacho chips with that yellow cheese "food" poured on top. Give him a Mountain Dew and he's in epicurean bliss.

Cats make him sneeze, perfume makes him sneeze, dust makes him sneeze. He wouldn't even have time to carry on a conversation in my apartment between all the achoos and geshundheits.

And he isn't a Christian.

Next.

Mark, Stan and Trent were nice enough guys if you were trying to put together a softball team, but not much in the conversational department. To Mark, everything I said was "cool." Stan loved my hair—said it reminded him of his sis-ter's (just what a girl wants to hear). And Trent, well...

"Where have you been all my life?" was his opening gambit.

"The upper Midwest, mostly."

He slapped his leg and laughed as if I'd just bested Jay Leno. After that, I was unable to say anything at which he did not hoot and holler with hilarity. I was beginning to feel conspicuous, when the HastyDate master of ceremonies rang the bell, our signal to exchange partners. From the corner of my eye, I noticed that Mitzi had carefully planted herself between a heavy velvet curtain and a potted palm, unobtrusive but strategically placed so that she could tune in to any of several conversations. At least *she* was enjoying herself.

A tall man with stooped shoulders and a defeated demeanor skulked to my table. Here, at least, my maternal instincts were allowed to flare. He looked much more miserable than I.

"Hello." He had brown eyes that were heavy-lidded and drooped at the outer corners. The skin on his cheeks sagged into what would no doubt turn into jowls as he aged. In fact, as I studied him, I realized that *everything* about him sagged. Only the little name tag on his shirt looked perky, and even that was bent on one corner. "I'm Walter. You don't have to talk to me if you don't want to. Nobody else does."

He'd paid good money to be ignored. Now *that's* the epitome of hopeless.

"Don't you have some questions for me, Walter?"

"Why?" He looked at me suspiciously, as if I had something up my sleeve. "You don't really want to know about me, do you?"

There's something I believe with all my heart: God designed each one of us for His purpose—and God doesn't make junk. Therefore, I had a much more benevolent view of Walter than he had of himself.

"Not in a 'dating' sense. I'm not planning on dating anyone I meet here tonight. I was forced to come by my meddling, underhanded, sneaky, know-it-all so-called friend. But I'd still like to know about you as a person."

As if I'd tossed a scrap of meat to a starving dog, he snapped it up.

"I'm a mechanic. I work on mostly foreign cars. Cars I'd never be able to afford for myself in a million years. That gets discouraging after a while, you know?"

Everything, I discovered, was disappointing in Walter's life. His wife had left him because she was bored with him. She didn't even make the effort to help him be less boring. She left with no other explanation and no remorse. It didn't surprise me a lot when Walter told me she'd run off with a contortionist from with a traveling circus.

Oh, Lord, this hurts my heart. Open people's eyes, let them see what they're doing to themselves and to others. Whatever happened to fidelity and faithfulness? People aren't to be used up and discarded. Show them how You love—unconditionally. Help them to get it into their minds and hearts that Jesus loved them so much He died for them. Once that happens, they'll never look at another human being the same way again. And heal the hurts we inflict on others as a result of our own selfishness. Heal Walter. Amen.

By the time Walter left my table, I felt sad. The evening was barely half over, and I'd already experienced the ultimate in pathetic and the ultimate in outlandish.

I realized that to take any of this seriously would be a total waste of resources. I decided to get into the festivities of the evening.

I met a great cop from the narcotics squad who didn't have time to meet any nice women, a sweet fellow still recovering from hernia surgery and several genuinely pleasant men who did nothing for me. I wasn't fond of the pompous little guy who reminded me of Napoleon Bonaparte or the newspaper reporter who was there to get the "scoop" on what really went on behind the closed doors of a HastyDate event. And my last potential prospect for love was a very nice man who was still obviously devoted to his former girlfriend.

"Now it's as if I never existed," Ryan said morosely. "She's seeing half-a-dozen other guys and thriving on it. She's having more fun now that she ever did with just me."

"Then why do you want her back?"

"I still love her," Ryan said. "I'm the one who broke it off, but I still love her."

If nothing else, I have a listening ear.

"She stepped out on me. She'd go out again after I'd dropped her off and said good-night. She told the other guy she worked a late shift."

Okay, that's appalling.

"Why can't I get over her when she hurt me so much?"

To my shock and dismay, I turned teary, too.

"I'm so sorry. I don't know." All I could think of was Chase. Is he still in love with his fiancée? And if he is, why does it matter to me? I'd signed off on him as soon as I'd heard he was down on women.

Or had I?

We were blubbering and holding hands when the final bell rang. Ryan squeezed my fingers and whispered, "Thank you, Whitney. You're going to make a great girlfriend for some lucky guy."

"And you'll heal. I'll say a prayer for you, okay?"

He nodded sweetly and leaned close. "May I?" Gently, he placed a kiss on the top of my head.

As soon as he left, Mitzi bolted toward me rubbing her hands and smirking. "Saved the best for last, did you? What a cutie! When are you going to see him again?"

"Never, same as the rest of the guys I met here tonight."

"Are you completely nuts? That last guy was darling. I know some weren't your type, but all of them?" She glared at me. "You're being too fussy."

"I don't think so. I only had one requirement for any of them, one little question."

"And what was that? 'Are you a billionaire?'"

"No. 'Are you a Christian?'"

"Terrific. I'll bet that was a real conversation starter. Couldn't that have waited for later?"

I thought of Matt and shook my head. "Nope."

"Did you have any luck?"

"A few. A cop and a couple more who didn't fall out of their chairs when I asked the question."

"A cop? Masculine, tough and tender, law-abiding. Are you sure you won't change your mind?"

Impulsively I stood up and threw my arms around Mitzi, my new self-appointed friend. "Positive. But I love you for being concerned and for bringing me here." I was surprised to hear myself saying it, but I meant it. "It was a real...experience."

"I *knew* you'd like it!" She took me by the hand and led me toward the door. "I'll just have to start watching the paper so we know when they sponsor another. You have to start reading the personals and singles ads, you know. I can hardly believe how careless you are about your love life...."

I just let her ramble as I breathed the good night air in the parking lot. Getting out of HastyDate was like escaping from prison.

CHAPTER 15

February 5

mid·den: **1.** A dunghill or refuse heap; **2.** Refuse that indicates the site of a human settlement; **3.** Current state of my apartment; **4.** Perhaps the current state of my life.

I can't get Chase out of my mind.

I keep rehashing Ryan's words about his girlfriend: "I still love her." How could he? He'd been betrayed, cheated on and deceived, given no respect or consideration whatsoever—yet no matter how much she'd hurt him, his love had not diminished.

He'd reminded me of Chase—blue eyes, athletic build, gentlemanly, courteous and, although not breathtaking like Chase, definitely good-looking, a disconcerting déjà vu. Both Chase and Ryan ooze with loyalty, faithfulness and commitment. They're the kind of guy who says he'll take his bride "for better or worse" and mean it.

Okay, I'll admit it, maybe I have been entertaining the idea that Chase would get over the old girlfriend and notice me as more than Kim's best friend and Wesley's baby-sitter. I've imagined him glancing at me and really seeing me for the very first time.

Everyone tells me they love me. But nobody loves me the way I want to be loved—with the passion Kurt has for Kim, that Dr. Heel-and-Toe has for Mitzi and Betty has for eBay.

What's wrong with me? I'm in better shape now than I was in high school. I'm intelligent, successful in business, well traveled and have what others say is a dry-but-witty sense of humor. Lately fear and self-doubt have crept into my thoughts like insidious weeds, choking out the positive things I know to be true. Even though I see it's happening, I don't know how to stop it. I keep bailing my boat, but I'm getting swamped anyway. Maybe I'm like Peter walking on the water—as soon as I glance away from God, I sink.

It happened to Kim. The surgery and her fear of not being able to raise Wesley to adulthood turned her inside out and brought up a whole host of family issues. Fear and frustration are slippery slopes. Once you start sliding downhill, gaining momentum, it's hard to stop.

The other contributor to the "midden" of my life is Mr. Tibble. He's a toilet-paper, string-and-mischief addict. Every night I come home to find something new untied, broken or strewn across the floor.

I am an admitted toilet-paper freak. I buy a twelve-pack of double rolls, extra soft, every time I see them on sale. My idea of a household crisis is running out of toilet paper. Besides the obvious uses for it, I use it to remove makeup, apply makeup, blow my nose, clean the bathroom counters, mark pages in books, pick gunk out of the shower drain and, in a really desperate circumstance, to tuck under my bra straps for that gentle lift that doesn't make me look like the Hunchback of Notre Dame.

There was a time in my life when I used several rolls a

week to stuff my bra (no longer necessary, thankfully). And in third grade I won a prize for best costume while wrapped in my favorite tissue and masquerading as a mummy.

In a cruel twist of fate, I've adopted a cat as crazy about toilet paper as I am. Mr. Tibble, in his first week in my home, learned to paw open the cupboard under the bathroom sink, bat the rolls of paper stored there into the room, find the sealed end (something even I can't do) and drag the entire roll throughout the house. He's done this four times. A double roll each time.

Once I put the toilet paper under lock and key, he started untying every knot he could find—the ones that kept the cushions on my chairs, the ribbons I'd so proudly added to the silk-flower bouquet on my coffee table, the pull cords that raise and lower my curtains and the loopy fringe hot-glued to the underside of my couch just as I'd seen done on the Home and Garden Channel.

The cat is creative, I have to give him that. Every time I take away a source of entertainment, he finds a new one, such as emptying the kitchen counters of bric-a-brac with his paws and tail or sleeping on top of the television for its warmth and falling off and undoing every wire behind the set. He also prefers to sleep in a nest of freshly dried clothes or on my pillow—while I'm using it.

I've done more damage control since Mr. Tibble arrived than I have in the last four years.

February 6

Mitzi, dying to discuss the HastyDate fiasco with me, insisted on taking me to lunch. By the end of the soup course and before the entrée was delivered, she was already thoroughly disgusted with me.

"What do you mean, you don't want to do it again? I watched you. The men seemed very eager to get to your table. Sometimes they even left the previous table early to stand in line."

"Mitzi, the lady next to me was interviewing them on their opinion on environmental issues. If a guy said he ate meat or didn't know anything about the rain forest, she began to twitch. And the woman before that had twelve children she didn't want to raise alone."

"So one person was a little odd. What's that? There were plenty of appealing women there as well."

"Of course there were, but some were very shy, and others wouldn't talk to men unless they had a full head of hair. I wasn't exceptionally popular, I was just…safe."

"You're fighting this for a reason, you know." Mitzi popped a bite of bread into her mouth.

"Maybe it's because I don't want to meet a man that badly. Have you thought of that?"

"Maybe it's because you've already fallen for someone and just won't admit it." She buttered another bit of bread carefully before adding, "Like Kim's doctor."

Huh? For a minute there I'd actually believed I knew what was going on in Mitzi's mind, and then she threw me a curveball. She'd managed to put her razor-sharp bloodred fake nail on my sorest spot. I hate it when she does that. Just when I think I totally understand her, I regain consciousness.

"What makes you say that?" I struggled for nonchalance and got something closer to feigned indifference.

She gave me a look so sharp it could have sliced bread. "I'm a woman who knows love. I can see it, I can feel it in the air. And you, my dear, have fallen big-time for the inaccessible doctor. Haven't you figured that out yet?"

I'm obviously a slow learner.

"If you're right, big emphasis on *if,* what am I supposed to do about it?"

Mitzi thought so hard I actually began to believe she had an answer for me.

Then she looked up, triumphant. "Wear tight shoes!"

This is advice for the lovelorn from the podiatrist's wife? "Tight shoes?" I echoed helplessly.

"Of course." Mitzi stuck a wad of money in the leather folder the waiter had dropped off and stood up. "I always wear tight shoes when I have troubles. It's the best way to forget your problems. All you can think about is your feet."

February 9

> *I look at the heavens, which you made with your hands. I see the moon and stars, which you created. But why is man important to you? Why do you take care of human beings?... You put him in charge of everything you made. You put all things under his control.*
>
> —*Psalm 8:3–5, 6*

Today I organized my life. Not my life, really, but my closet. A person has to start somewhere.

There would be three classifications, Keep, Give Away and Toss. I have supported the plastic storage-bin industry far too long. I started with my clothes. That was fairly easy as things either fit or they didn't. That left me with a wardrobe of three-year-old clothing, as that was the last time I weighed what I do now. It also left me in a predicament. My new rule for clothing is this—if it makes me look lumpy or trapped in the last century, it goes. After weeding things out by that standard, I was left with a pair of jeans, two pairs of black slacks, a black skirt and jacket, three identical shirts in black, cream and gray and a sarong that was bunched up in the bottom of my closet from the last time I'd been to the pool. And, of course, my sweats.

I could live with that. It would mean two trips to the dry cleaner's a week, but with a couple more shirts I'd get by. My mistake was turning around and looking into the give-away box that held the history of my life for that past four years. My green sweater, the one I'd worn the day Wesley was baptized. And the beautiful pink dress I'd bought to wear to a wedding and on which I'd accidentally spilled punch. The unstained part of the fabric was still so pretty, surely it was a shame to waste it. Maybe I could make something out of it—place mats? Little jewelry cases like the ones they sold at boutiques? Barbie clothes? And the buttons! I'm always losing buttons. I'd just remove them and keep them in another storage box for those times when someone I knew needed a button.

It wasn't until I'd taken everything out of my give-away box and sorted it into materials for crafts, quilts, stuffed animals, jewelry pouches and rag-rug weaving that I remembered that I hate sewing on buttons, don't do crafts, and don't make quilts, stuffed animals or jewelry pouches because I don't have a sewing machine. And I haven't the foggiest clue as to how to weave a rug.

I'd wasted an hour by the time I got all the clothes back in the give-away box and moved on to my shoes.

Clutter, I've decided, is a metaphor for an out-of-control life. God had a plan when He created Earth. Six days to get it all done and a seventh to rest. Light and earth and sky, plants, the moon and stars. Birds, sea creatures and animals came next. Then man and woman, those who would be in charge of the rest. It was done in perfect order. He didn't start with man and woman and then have to figure out where He'd put them. He planned land for the animal and seas for the fish and prepared land and sea first, so the living things would have a home.

It's really so simple. Approach life the way God does, first things first. Keeping that in mind, the closet was done in record time.

Question: Why am I at home on Saturday night cleaning closets?

February 14, Valentine's Day

"Whitney, are you doing anything for dinner tonight?" Mom sounded excited, which, in retrospect, should have warned me to beg off before she had a chance to invite me over. I had, after all, purchased a spendy can of cat food for Mr. Tibble and planned to serve it to him out of a crystal goblet, just as they do on television.

"Mr. Tibble and I have some fine dining planned. Then I thought we'd watch some old movies I rented." Mr. Tibble is especially fond of Marilyn Monroe and Katharine Hepburn.

"Let the cat watch them alone. You can come to our house for dinner."

"I don't know, Mom. I'm not sure I want to say I spent Valentine's Day with my parents."

"You'd rather say you spent it with a cat? Be here at six-thirty, Whitney, and don't wear those gray sweats."

I hung up and looked down at my legs—how had she known I was in my gray sweats anyway? Of course, I did have three pairs—light, dark and intermediate—I suppose the odds are pretty good she'd get it right. Maybe they should go into the give-away box, too, but I'd wrenched enough things out of my own grasp for this week.

I was feeling good about myself as I stood at my parents' front door in a slim skirt and fine-gauge sweater that hugged my newly found curves. I'd managed to dash into a store, find something I liked and, with the clerk's permission, wear my new purchases out.

There was laughter coming from the kitchen as I knocked. No one heard me, so I opened the door and stepped inside. The house smelled wonderful, like roasting meat and fresh bread overlaid with the sweet aroma of a homemade dessert, maybe cherry pie. Mom likes Valentine's Day. She's a real romantic at heart. When I was a child, she sent heart-shaped peanut-butter sandwiches with raspberry jam in my lunch or made sure I had a "red" meal that day. It was the only day of the year I got stewed tomatoes, cinnamon candy, maraschino cherries and red licorice for lunch...thank goodness. She's also made it a tradition to cook a huge meal for Dad. It usually involves ground round patted into the shape of hearts, plenty of ketchup and, if she can get it this time of year, watermelon.

"Hello! I'm here! Did you start the party without me?" I called, surprised Dad wasn't at the door to greet me in his traditional red shirt.

"Oh, there you are!" Mom popped out of the kitchen in a sequined headband with two glittery antennae-like hearts attached by coils of wire. She appeared to be impersonating a Valentine insect. "Look, Bob, she's here!"

My heart took a quick elevator ride from my chest to the basement. "Bob?"

Pastor Bob walked sheepishly out of the kitchen, his scalp as red as Dad's shirt beneath his pale, fine hair.

I'd been set up and had walked into the trap with the innocence of a new babe.

"Mom..." I suppose I should have told her that we'd gotten to know each other at Kim's, but it felt like breaking a confidence.

Bob's a trouper. Clearly he'd been set up before and he knew how to make the best of an awkward situation. He winked as he handed me a beautiful box of chocolates wrapped in velvet and ribbon. "Friends?"

Definitely friends.

February 16

I will never understand how a two-pound box of candy can make me gain five pounds. It's just not right.

Eric stopped by tonight. He was grinning from ear to ear

as he thrust another box of candy into my hand. This, how-ever, was a bright scarlet heart full of Gummi Worms.

He had news he wanted to tell me in person.

"Whit, you're the first person to know, even before our parents."

His eyes were glistening with delight and I knew this had something to do with Eric and his Allison.

"We're getting married in the fall."

"Oh, Eric…." Genuine tears of happiness came to my eyes. "She's a lucky woman. You deserve the very best."

"*I'm* the lucky one." Eric grasped my hands in his and looked intently into my face. "If it hadn't been for you, this wouldn't be happening."

"I didn't do anything."

"You loved me enough to be honest with me." He chewed his lip, searching for words. "You know you've always had a very special place in my heart. We both felt it, Whit. I think there was a time when we could have made it—as a couple, I mean. It took a long time, but I'm finally doing what you asked. I'm growing up—no more following air-show circuits, no more goofing off.

"I think I might have hung around until that Matthew guy was history if you hadn't laid it on the line and been honest with me. You cared enough to tell me that you didn't want to string me along. I know how hard it was for you. You can't fool me. I saw your eyes."

Eyes—windows to the soul—it must be true.

"I've spent my adult life going where the wind blows me, and you were the gust that blew me into Allison's arms. If you hadn't told me waiting for the number-one spot in your heart wasn't going to work, I'd probably still be hanging out, riding the air currents, getting nowhere. Because you thrust me out of my comfort zone, I knew it was time for things to change. I found a job I really wanted." A soft, blissful smile came over his features. "And I met Allie. Now I know what you meant about waiting for exactly the right one to come along. Thanks, Whitney, for waking me up."

I'd done all that? "I h-had no idea," I stammered.

"You're the one who says it all the time, Whit. 'God works in mysterious ways.' By working in you, He worked in me."

Suddenly it was so clear. Obedience, even in the small things or in the things I really didn't want to do, brought blessings that spread ripples like a pebble tossed into a pond. God wanted me to tell Eric the truth because He had great plans for him, plans that involved Allison, not me.

"Hey, Whit, don't cry! I didn't mean to make you cry." Eric was scanning the room for a tissue box.

"I'm crying happy, silly. Not sad. The tissues are in the kitchen."

When he returned with the box and I'd managed to turn the waterworks down, I said, "You have no idea how much this means to me. You've given me such a gift."

He didn't question me. Maybe that's what I love most about Eric—he does read my eyes and see my soul.

"There's more," he offered.

"I can't take much more!"

"Allison and I have talked it over. If her pastor agrees with it, I'd like you to be my best man...best *woman*. If not, then Allie wants you to be her maid of honor. What do you think?"

I was stunned. "She agrees with that?"

"You bet. She knows all about us and is as grateful as I am that you're in my life."

Allison *is* an angel.

"Nothing would please me more."

"Great." An enormous grin spread across his face. "Now, are you okay with a top hat and tails? You're not going to be fussing that they make you look fat, are you?"

February 27

A quiet two weeks.

I've been mulling over the amazing twists and turns my relationship with Eric has taken and thanking God for the remarkable outcome. Eric will be in my life forever in a way that's comfortable for both of us, and with a bonus besides— his beautiful wife. Who could have predicted that?

Kim is lying low. The medication is taking hold slowly, but she's feeling *some* improvement. Better yet, she and her parents have been talking. Nothing too heavy, she says, but it's looking good. They've started looking up and forward instead of back. They're finally praying together as a family for *God's* best answer for Kim, and relying on Him to give them the solution. It has lifted a weight from all of their shoulders to give God the burden He wanted to carry all along. Knowing God's will in order to be obedient may be hard at first. One has to listen very carefully for His direction. The good news is, from my experience I've learned that it gets louder the longer and more prayerfully you listen.

Betty is going through withdrawal from eBay. She's quit bringing her personal laptop to work to use on lunch hour and breaks. Her fingers tremble on the keyboard on her desk, and I know she wants to sneak into the break room for just one glimpse of those music boxes. She says she signs on only three times a day now—before and after work and at bedtime. It's progress, but I'm sure she'll feel better when she's kicked the habit completely and detoxed her system. There's a patch for nicotine addiction. I wonder if they make something for people like Betty.

Business at the office has been amazing. We're expanding soon and hiring more software geniuses. Harry is smiling all the time, and I got another bonus. I'm giving my check to a mission that provides intercessory prayer for people. We all need all the prayer we can get.

Mitzi is lying low. I think she's composing personal ads for me, but I'm not asking. Some things it's best I don't know.

Even Mr. Tibble has been behaving. He greets me at the door with a loud purr and has only unrolled the toilet paper three times. He eats his food willingly, shares my pillow with me instead of hogging the whole thing and entertains himself with his mouse. Frankly, I think he's planning something.

It's weird, really, how well things are going. I'm glad, but there's a part of me that wonders if this is some kind of calm before the storm.

MARCH

CHAPTER 16

March 1

This March definitely came in like a lion. Not only did it snow outside, but I had my own personal storm today. I shouldn't have gotten out of bed this morning. As soon as my feet hit the floor, things began to go bad. The electricity was off in the night, and my alarm didn't ring. The warm water gave out shortly after I'd poured shampoo on my head. Traffic was sluggish because of the weather. There are only two seasons in Minnesota, winter and road construction. We're always in one of them, and they're both miserable. Plus, it wasn't until I got to work that I realized I was wearing one navy shoe and one black shoe.

Bryan had the day off, so I was behind before I started, and by noon I'd unintentionally insulted everyone in the office. I suppose I should have been happy about that. No one was speaking to me unless they absolutely had to, and the silence was a nice change of pace. When I told Mitzi that her jacket had "a lovely brocade pattern" around her hips, I didn't mean she had big hips, but that was how she took it. And I didn't intend to offend Betty by saying her desk looked as messy as mine. I just meant she had a lot of work to finish by five, not a comment on her housekeeping. Offense was in the air. Even Harry was upset because I didn't tell him I liked his new tie, one with miniature computers and dancing mice that he considers hilarious.

Between my concern about Kim and my nonexistent social life, things have taken a nosedive. Rats! Airplane terminology always reminds me of Eric. I didn't appreciate how much I'd miss his company when he started spending time at Allison's house instead of mine.

It was Kim's call, however, that put the frosting on the cake.

"Whit? Can you talk?"

"Sure. I took an early lunch today." Even that—a pickle and Swiss cheese sandwich and a few pitted prunes—was nasty. I *have* to go shopping for groceries soon. "Are you okay?"

"I'm fine." There was a pause on the other end of the line. "And I think I actually mean that."

"You don't know how happy that makes me."

"My lows aren't quite so low as they were," she admitted. "And my parents are doing their best to be supportive. I'm adjusting to the antidepressants and Chase has convinced me I'm not dying any time soon. I think I'll make it, Whitney."

"You just improved my day one hundred percent."

"I'm sorry, then, that I might ruin it again. I wanted to let you know so it wouldn't come as a complete surprise. Chase asked us to have dinner with him and Claudia a week from Saturday. I know you like him, and after that junk with Matt and..." Her voice trailed off. "I just thought you should know."

The lion had roared.

"Ah...great. Have fun."

"You're okay with it? Kurt and I have been hoping you and Chase would get together, that someday he'd decide to date again, but this...we can't figure it out."

"It's a surprise, all right." I kept my voice neutral. What had I expected? That Chase would wake up and discover the woman of his dreams right under his nose and the woman would be me? I was the one who needed to wake up. I'd fantasized Matt all the way to the altar and now I was guilty of doing it with Chase.

"Looks to me like they're making moves toward getting back together, but Chase is cautious. He wants Kurt and me there as a buffer, to make sure that it's purely a social evening with no heavy relationship talk. I told Kurt I didn't want to go, that I wanted to see you and Chase together, but like Kurt said, Chase is a big boy, he knows what he's doing. Sorry, Whit."

Not nearly as sorry as me. Well, at least the worst of my day was over by noon. There was nowhere to go but up.

March 2

I have given up men for Lent.

I will not be thinking about them or dating them, and I will look at and speak to only the male of the species when necessary to retain my job, repair my car or tell my father I love him.

Last year I gave up chocolate and I thought I'd die before I could dig into the chocolate Easter eggs on my desk. This should be easy compared to that. *Just kidding!!!*

It's not such a bad idea, though. Until I turned thirty, I rarely thought about marriage, child rearing, a lake cabin or a minivan. Since my birthday, it's all been mounting in importance and I want it to stop. It's a weed in my garden, being thirty. Twenty-nine was never like this.

I will tell Mitzi tomorrow that I'm on sabbatical from relationships. I will give her time off from studying the personal ads for hours, from researching lists for dating services, from scouring the Internet for online singles' chat rooms. I find it ironic that when I ask Mitzi to do something in the office, she's usually resentful and unwilling. Now that I've told her that I do not want her to try to hook me up with someone under any circumstances, she's turned into an avid researcher for my cause. I've been handling Mitzi all wrong. Next time I have things for her to do, I will tell her *not* to do them under penalty of death. She'll have them done in no time.

March 3

Got together with girlfriends from high school. Had a blast. All married.

March 4

Had lunch with Erica, Sammi and Jodie, my housemates from college. Fun. All married.

March 5

Gave party for customers and suppliers to say thank-you for business. Nice. Everyone married.

March 6

Leah invited bridesmaids over to see her wedding gifts and honeymoon photos. So-so. Everyone married, engaged or seriously involved.

March 7

Have quit going out with friends and acquaintances. It's best for now. Have decided to seek friendships with other thirty-something single women.

March 8

Have decided to stay home and learn to quilt.

March 9

Don't like quilting. Reminds me too much of a puzzle. Quilt may be metaphor for my life. Mr. Tibble loves it—has unrolled all my thread.

March 10

If I don't get out of the house soon, I will go insane.

March 11

Have gone insane. Matt called today, said he wanted to talk, to clear up the misunderstandings between us. He asked me to go out for dinner. Not only am I insane, I'm a mad and crazy lunatic. I said yes.

March 12

Today's burning question—what does one wear to meet the man who accidentally and unintentionally broke my heart—or if not my heart, my feminine ego—because he wanted a business partner instead of a wife?

I didn't call Kim tonight to ask her how I should dress for dinner with Matt. That would mean I'd have to tell her I was going out with him.

It isn't all that big a deal, really. Matt deserves more than a garbled "No thanks" and the transfer of his files to another division. Harry wanted to drop him as a client, but I wouldn't hear of it. I'm the one who misinterpreted his motives. I'm the poster girl for misinterpretation.

Matt called the office every day for a month after I declined his offer. It wasn't that I liked avoiding him, but it took me a couple months before I could even bear to think of how deluded I'd been. Now, four and a half months later, I can handle it.

I really dressed for the occasion, putting on all the armor of God. It was my own version, of course, but symbolic enough for me to remember that no matter what, God would be with me, protect me and carry me through.

So stand strong with the belt of truth tied
around your waist. And on your chest wear
the protection of right living. And on your feet
wear the Good News of peace to help you
stand strong. And also use the shield of faith.
With that you stop all the burning arrows of the evil one.
Accept God's salvation to be your helmet. And take
the sword of the Spirit—that sword is the teaching
of God. Pray in the Spirit at all times. Pray with all
kinds of prayers, and ask for everything you need.
To do this you must always be ready. Never give up.
Always pray for all God's people.

—*Ephesians 6:14–18*

My belt of truth was actually a wide leather sash that made my waist look small and reminded me that I'm designed perfectly for God's purpose. On my chest was the beautiful silver cross my grandmother gave me when I accepted Christ. The shoes were the strappiest I own, to represent the humble sandals of the Carpenter. The shield, a beaded purse with a New Testament tucked inside. My helmet? My salvation, the gift I carry in my heart every day of my life. And the sword of the spirit, a slim silver pen given to me the day I graduated from college, a symbol of the written word of God, the training manual by which I live.

As I dressed with purpose and care, I thought of each of these amazing bits of protective covering that together give me the knowledge that with God's help I can defeat anything that anyone might throw at me. It was with a grateful heart that I went to meet Matt.

He was standing in the doorway of the restaurant waiting for me. As I drove up, I watched him shift from foot to foot and rub his hands together to keep them warm. He looked nervous. There were lines of tension etched in his face that I hadn't noticed before, but he's just as handsome as ever.

"Whitney!" His face lit when he saw me and I took a gulp of air. This was going to be hard, very, very hard. Or not. I sent up a petition for God's expectations to come true, not mine.

"Hi, Matt."

"You look wonderful," he stared at me. "Beautiful."

"You're looking pretty sharp yourself."

He took my hands. "I've missed you."

"Let's go inside, shall we?"

He'd reserved a table tucked near the fireplace. Just like Matt, to do things right. After we'd ordered, a cavernous silence hung between us. When we spoke, it was at the same time.

"Listen, Whitney, I don't know…"

"Matt, I know I've been…"

"Who goes first?" he asked when we both sputtered to a stop.

"You," I said. I needed to collect myself.

"I'm still not quite sure what went wrong with us, Whitney. I've relived that night a hundred times and never figured out what I said that scared you off. I never meant to do that. In fact," he added ruefully, "I thought I was doing everything right."

"Oh, Matt." How had this man and I gone so wrong?

"Much of the responsibility is mine. We weren't communicating. Or, maybe we were both listening but hearing only what we wanted to hear. Looking back, I can see what you'd intended, but at the time…"

His eyes, dark and troubled, searched my face and it was very clear to me why I'd fallen for him. But I'd picked myself up now and I wasn't falling again—for anyone.

"What did you hear me saying? What was it that was so wrong?"

I felt heat blister my cheeks. How humiliating to admit this to him, but I could hardly keep it a secret. I heard in my head the words from 2 Corinthians 8:21 that my parents spoke so often in my childhood. "We are trying to do what is right. We want to do what the Lord accepts as right and also what the people think is right." Granted, those were the words Paul spoke about being trustworthy about the money with which he and his companions were being entrusted, but it rings true so many times and in so many ways in my life. Do what is right. It's right to tell Matt the truth.

"Matt, you were so generous to me—the gifts, the flowers, the necklace. I would never have accepted them if I'd thought they were part of a plan to lure me away from Innova."

"I show my appreciation to everyone who works for or with me," he said, his brow furrowing. "People need to hear 'Thank you, job well done.' Hiring Innova has been one of my smartest moves." His expression grew remorseful. "Frankly, I do know why you responded as you did and I don't blame you."

"You don't?"

"Of course not. You're a woman of integrity, Whitney. I've regretted ever trying to get you to move to Lambert Industries. I should have known you wouldn't leave Harry. It was a low-down, underhanded thing to do. If I'd been Harry,

I would have dropped my account. I'm so sorry. Please accept my apologies."

It would be so easy to be gracious, to tell him this was exactly why I'd been upset, accept his apology and close that door behind us. So very easy. And wrong.

"Matt, I agree with you one hundred percent about going behind Harry's back, but that's not what upset me at the time."

Now it was his turn to be puzzled. "Then what did I do?"

Here was the moment I needed that armor. "Matt, I thought you were pursuing me. Not in a professional sense, but in a personal one."

It seemed like hours for him to take in what I'd said. "I…uh…I didn't mean…well, I can see why you thought… you are so beautiful…I did consider…the gifts…I never thought about it like… If Lambert Industries weren't so demanding…. No wonder you wouldn't speak to me. I wouldn't speak to me, either!"

He scraped his fingers through his hair and groaned. "I am a complete and total idiot and I am so sorry."

I saw the pain on his face and put my hand on his arm. "It's not the end of the world, Matt. I misinterpreted your gestures all along. I guess I wanted…more."

"And I was so consumed by ambition that I didn't even see."

An entire drama seemed to be playing out on his face and in his eyes, but I couldn't tell what he was thinking.

"This isn't the first time I've been blinded to what's really important, Whitney. I've been guilty of it before."

"You don't have to tell me…."

"I want to. I was engaged to be married to a woman I'd known for a number of years. It seemed all right, she seemed happy enough to me, but I really wasn't looking. Lambert Industries was in a very seminal stage then, and it demanded all my time. I didn't even notice that our relationship was crumbling until she confronted me one day and told me to pick, either the company or her. I was dumbfounded. I hadn't seen it coming. Of course, I didn't see it coming because I was hardly ever with her."

I waited as he collected his thoughts.

"I wanted to talk about it, to get counseling, something, but she was completely fed up with me. She insisted I had to decide that moment, her or the company."

I realized I was holding my breath. Although I knew the outcome, I wanted to hear his side of the story.

"She wouldn't relent. 'Choose,' she kept saying. 'Choose.' And because I knew I couldn't make a commitment like that without talking about our feelings and the situation and perhaps seeing a counselor, she felt I'd opted for the business and she ended our relationship.

"It left me reeling, Whitney. The way I submerged the pain was by digging even deeper into the company. Growing it in leaps and bounds. And by closing myself off to personal relationships in my life." He made a sound almost like a chuckle. "And look what I passed up."

"It's still in you though," I told him softly. "You treated me like a queen. The romantic, tender man is too strong in you to keep him suppressed forever. You even gave me a taste of what it would be like to be loved by you."

"You are the most remarkable woman I've ever met." He sounded awed. "Where do you come from? How did you get the way you are?"

"I can tell you what motivates me, Matt, but first I have a question to ask you. Are you a Christian?"

It took some time for him to answer.

"At one time," he said thoughtfully, "I probably would have said, 'Sure, why not?' I've seen the inside of a few churches and tried to be 'good.' I've always figured that was enough to count me as a Christian." He stared at me. "But since I met you, I've begun to realize that isn't it at all. I'm not sure what's involved, but there's way more to you than just going inside a special building and being kind to others. I think I need to learn more about it."

I put my hand on his and murmured, my heart full, "I have some Good News for you, Matt. The very best."

What might have been a disaster was a magical evening. The hurt and anger I'd felt at both Matt and myself bled out of me and was replaced by a calm and serenity like I hadn't experienced in weeks. Matt, too, could feel it.

"You know, Whitney," he said as the waiter laid the dessert menu on our table, "your brand of Christianity is different from what I'm accustomed to. In you it's…alive, a growing thing…it's real."

"There are lots of Christians just like me, with a relationship not only with other people but with God."

"I think I need to find some of those people for myself."

Okay, heart. Try not to burst. Not my will, but Thy will, O God. And His will is far better than anything I could imagine.

"Coconut-cream cake, cherry tarts, kiwi-strawberry cheesecake, nutty chocolate-fudge cake, fruit and cheese, caramel apple crisp topped with vanilla-bean ice cream…." Matt read his menu while I drooled on mine. "What do you want?"

"All of it and none of it. If I don't watch my waistline, nobody will."

"If they don't, they're crazy. How about sharing?"

"I'd love to."

He studied me intently. "Chocolate, I think. With ice cream on the side. And decaf with real cream. How'd I do?"

"Perfect." It was not only his ordering that had been perfect. Once over the rocky spots, Matt and I had begun to get to know each other as we should have months ago. He told me his favorite color, his mother's maiden name and what size shoe he wore. I fessed up to loving old movies, rain on the roof and going barefoot. We compared upbringings, childhood stories and favorite foods. And we both admitted feeling completely at peace for the first time since Leah's wedding. I couldn't have asked for more.

Regrettably, I got "more" anyway.

The waitress had served our coffee and gone back for the cake when I saw them come in. From my vantage point by the fire, I could see Kim clearly and a stunning blonde with a thick mane of hair that she kept tossing away from her face like a movie star. Both Kurt and Chase displayed impeccable manners seating the women. Fortunately, Chase sat with his back to our table. Unfortunately, Claudia was seated so that I could see her every expression.

And what an expressive face she has. Even from a distance I could read several emotions—adoration, love, devotion—all aimed directly at Chase. There was something else in her face as well, something that appeared and disappeared depending on whether Chase was looking toward or away from her, the real truth under the mask, I suspect. Cunning.

What had Kim said? That Claudia and Chase were "making moves toward getting back together." Oh, yes. Someone was making moves all right. If Claudia's eyes and demeanor were windows to her soul, then Chase was as good as married. *Predator* and *prey* were the words that came to mind.

"What's wrong, Whitney? You aren't eating."

Matt's voice drew me back to my own table—and my own business. "I just saw someone I've met before, that's all."

"Do you want to go over and say hello?"

"No. They're very engrossed in each other. I don't want to interrupt." I smiled at him, grateful for his consideration. "Thanks for asking."

"I'm not the cad your experiences with me might lead you to believe. I was actually raised rather well. The one-track mind I developed myself." He picked up his fork. "You aren't eating, Whitney. I do believe I'll have to feed you." He scooped a bit of the fudge drizzled on the plate, caught a bite of cake and raised it to my mouth. I closed my eyes and savored the sweetness.

I picked up my fork and returned the favor. That's how Matt and I came to be feeding each other tiny bites of cake when Kurt and Chase arrived at our table. I saw them hover, one over each of Matt's shoulders, with wide eyes and gaping mouths. They were even more surprised to see me than I was to see them.

"I didn't know you were going to be here tonight, Whit," Kurt said. Translation: If I had, we would have gone someplace else.

I glanced casually around the dining room. "Oh, there's Kim." I waved. She stared back, shocked.

"Have you eaten yet?" Matt asked politely, blissfully unaware of the lightning bolts whizzing between tables and around his head.

"We'd just ordered when I saw Whitney over here."

"Have you both met Matt?" I inquired, thinking Mom would be so proud of my manners under pressure. And without waiting for an answer, I reintroduced them.

The scamp in me was actually having fun. At least I looked as though I was able to have a meaningful relationship, even if, truth be told, I wasn't sure I knew how. The other part of me was alternately seething at Claudia's disapproving expression because Chase had left her side, and moaning inside, bewailing the fact that he was with her instead of me. Terrific, I thought, now I'm developing a split personality. That means more mouths to feed.

Kurt and Chase didn't have anything to say, but neither did they seem inclined to leave our table. "You look great tonight, Whit," Kurt offered. "Nice outfit."

Nice *armor,* I corrected silently.

"Just out having fun?" I asked, needing to fill the awkward void.

"Yeah, sure, fun. Sort of." Kurt was miserable. He had too much information—my thoughts about Chase, Claudia's thoughts about Chase, and Chase's as well, whatever they might be. He was standing in the middle of an uncomfortable triangle—a Bermuda Triangle of relationships. He was sunk no matter what he said or did.

Matt pushed away from the table and picked up the check. "I'll just go to the front and pay this while you finish the last bite of our dessert. I'll be back in a minute."

Ahhhh, breathing room. What a gentleman to give me some.

"Are you going to stop and say hi to Kim?" Chase asked.

"No. You tell her hello from me. I'm sure you all have a lot to talk about. I'd hate to interrupt." Matt, get me out of here! my brain screamed.

At that moment he returned with our checked coats in his hand. "Are you ready to go?" He turned to the other men with an enigmatic smile. "Whitney and I have spent some time apart. We have a lot of pleasant catching up to do. We're getting to know each other all over again."

"Nice to see you," I added. "Say hi to Kim."

I kept my head high as I walked through the restaurant, oozing refinement and panache. My finest performance. Outside the restaurant I let down my guard. I had to release some of the steam that Claudia had set to boiling in my skull, so I bent over, rolled a snowball and stuck it down the back of Matt's neck. The friendly snowball fight that ensued was very invigorating.

At home, I allowed myself to fall apart. I picked up Mr. Tibble and put him on the ottoman across from me and poured out my story.

"You should have seen her, Tibbs. She is plotting, scheming and conniving to get Chase back at all costs. She knows that he's a good catch, and now she's remorseful about letting the big fish get away. How bad is that?"

Mr. Tibble lifted his head at the word *fish,* so I knew he was listening.

"He's a surgeon, Tibbs. A brilliant, skillful doctor. I hope some of that translates into savvy where Claudia is concerned. But why do I care? It's not my business. *He's* not my business."

Besides, Matt asked me out again for next weekend and I accepted.

Lunatic. I'm a certifiable lunatic.

March 13

"Tell me everything!" were the first words out of Kim's mouth this morning.

"When did you start getting up at dawn?" I yawned. "Hang up and call me when it's daylight."

"Don't you dare hang up this phone, Whitney. If you do I will come over myself and haul you out of bed."

"Put the coffee on when you get here, will you?"

"Whitney!"

"Okay, okay." I sat up in bed and yawned, disturbing Mr. Tibble, who'd curled up next to me. "What do you want to know?"

"Everything. Don't leave one single thing out."

"Oh, I can't promise that," I said coyly. "Can't a couple have some privacy?"

"You aren't a couple. Are you?"

"I have no idea. Matt and I went out to discuss the misunderstanding between us. We got clear on what happened and then we had a delightful evening. How did your dinner go?"

"Unsatisfactory information, Whit. Are you two, like, dating?"

I zipped my lips.

"So you aren't dating?"

"I didn't say that, either." What does our next meeting count as? Follow-up? A recheck at the doctor's office? Then the ten-year-old in me added, "I'll tell you more if you tell me more."

"Like I said, we were the shield between Chase and Claudia and any awkward conversations. Chase was testing the waters between them."

"And Claudia?"

"Oh, she's already in the water, swimming like mad. She wants him back in the worst way, Whit. It just oozes out of her."

"Groomsman dumped her, huh?"

"Apparently. She's pulled out all the stops where Chase is concerned. She would have eloped with him last night if he'd even hinted that they might get back together."

"What does Chase say about the whole thing? I thought he'd given up women forever."

"He's a perfect gentleman, you know that. Whatever he's really thinking, he doesn't say. He did tell us that Claudia called him and begged to patch things up."

"How do you like her?"

Kim's silence on the other end of the line told me everything I wanted to know. "Never mind. If you can't say anything nice, don't say anything at all."

"All I can say is that she feels a little…desperate, like she'll do anything to get Chase back, no matter whom she hurts. Now it's your turn. What happened between you and Matt?"

"We put a lot of issues to rest, Kim, and I'm so glad. We decided not to look backward, but to look ahead. And we had a great snowball fight."

"What *is* ahead for you?"

"I don't know. I'm not sure I want to know. Right now I'm just grateful for enough foresight to get me through the day. I'm not counting on anything from Matt. I've already fallen into that trap and won't make that mistake again. I've been more concerned about turning thirty than I realized. It's time to get back on track. After all, even if I could, I'd never buy a minivan."

Kim, dear friend that she is, understood exactly what I'd meant.

CHAPTER 17

March 15

Mitzi is a stalker.

I tried all day to avoid her, but she appeared around every corner eyeing me suspiciously like Mr. Tibble does when he thinks I have his catnip mouse. I did my best to avoid the places she might trap me alone, but I had to go to the bathroom sometime.

When I returned to the hall, she was there, arms crossed over her chest and foot tapping. Knowing better than to make a run for it, I turned around and went back into the ladies' lounge and flung myself onto the nearest couch. "Okay, Mitzi, you finally caught me. What is it?"

"I should be asking you the same question." Her violet eyes were flashing. "You've been hiding something from me. Something has changed in your love life, I can tell."

Why is it that I continue to think that Mitzi can't surprise me again? Does the woman have spies?

"What makes you think that?"

"I'm a good judge of character. I read faces. It's written all over yours."

"Why can't you read my face when I want you to complete a project or shorten your breaks?"

"That's not interesting," Mitzi said airily. "I'm indifferent to boring emotions."

"And boring work?"

"You've got that right." She rubbed her hands together with anticipation. "So, what's happened? You either met or were disappointed by someone. I'm not sure which." She scrutinized me the way she usually inspects herself in the mirror, with an alarmingly intent gaze.

"Maybe both," I admitted. Why try to keep it a secret from matchmaker/mind reader Mitzi? She'd already weakened my will. Why not just cave in and confess before she started turning the screws?

"Aha! Tell Mitzi everything."

I confessed to having dinner with Matt, but she had to drag out of me that Chase had returned to his former fiancée.

"So the handsome doctor is unavailable and the handsome businessman is now obtainable."

"We're not talking rental cars here. I'm just telling you how it is. It doesn't matter to me because I'm no longer interested. I've moved on."

She eyed me skeptically. "Then you won't mind if my husband and I ask you to join us and a colleague from his clinic for dinner on Saturday? He's a new doctor, single, and has just recently moved to the Cities. It's time he got acquainted." Then she smiled sweetly. "I'm serving mahi-mahi. Come at seven and we'll eat at eight."

"Mitzi, I can't do that."

"No? So you *are* still interested in the doctor. Good choice. Or is it Matt?" Then she sat down across from me and I saw something unfamiliar in her eyes. "Whitney, I like you. I know everyone here thinks I'm a fluff head and sometimes

I am, but there are a few things I do know. One, there is nothing better than finding a soul mate. I can say that because I found mine. Two, there's nothing worse than settling for less than one. If either of these guys is your soul mate, then they're worth fighting for." She looked at me with such compassion and wisdom that I reached out to hug her.

She accepted my hug gracefully and then added, "And if neither of these jokers are right for you, come to my house on Saturday. Podiatrists give the best foot massages."

Sometimes after talking to Mitzi I have whiplash.

March 18

"You're going on a cruise?"

"A second honeymoon," Mom said happily. "And it's all your father's idea."

"What came over him?"

"We'll be gone ten days, so you'll have to look after the house." Mom paused. "Honey, are you okay?"

Even the condensed *TV Guide* version of my love life, or lack of it, concerns my mother. She told me once that people were deluded to think that child rearing ended when the children turned eighteen or graduated from college or got married. Once a mother, always a mother. And, boy, is she good at it.

"Have time for a progress report?" Kim's voice sounded strong, cheerful and, best of all, normal.

"Of course."

"I had a good checkup. Chase says I should go back to work whenever I feel like it."

"Do people ever feel like working? At Innova, I mean?"

"I've missed it. I've even missed Harry and the rest of the zoo. I called him today, I'm going to start part-time and see how it goes. Our sweet little neighbor has agreed to come in mornings for a while."

"Can she handle it?" I picture the small white-haired lady toting Wesley. He's in a growing stage and seems to double in size every time I see him.

"Oh, sure. Wesley loves her and it will be good for him to be in his own home."

There was a long pause on the line. Unspoken thoughts hung in the wires like icicles, but neither Kim nor I voiced them. She wanted to tell me what she'd gleaned from Kurt about Chase's status with Claudia these days. And I desperately wanted to satisfy my curiosity, but so far had managed to zipper my lip. Chase's love life is none of my business, I reminded myself, knowing full well that should the opportunity arise, I'd happily make it so.

Kim weakened first. "They went to the theater last night."

There went any faint optimistic hopes. "Is the wedding on again?"

"I have no idea. Chase is totally mum on what he's thinking, but he's certainly given Claudia every chance to convince him that it should be. By the way, how's Matt?"

"Practically standing on his head to make amends."

"And?"

"And we're…friends. He's trying to focus less on business and more on the rest of his life, but it's a challenge for him." Four months ago I would have been euphoric at the transformation and now…I've changed.

That big clock Mitzi insisted was hovering over me has quieted down. I'm at peace with whatever is in store for me. I've given it to God, and I'm trying very hard not to wrench it out of His hands this time. He doesn't need my help. All He wants is my respect for His wisdom.

"I'm still sorry, Whit. I thought you and Chase would have made a great couple. Maybe that's just my selfishness talking,

two of my favorite people in the entire world being together—what fun we'd have!"

Eager to be off the subject I'd already spent too much time
dwelling upon, I said, "Speaking of fun, have I told you what
Mom and Dad are doing this week?"

March 21

Spa Sunday.

After church, I came home and filled the tub with water,
seasoned it with scented Epsom salts and a drop of lavender
oil and immersed myself up to my chin. When the water
cooled, I refilled the tub again. Then, when my toes and fingers looked like white raisins, I reluctantly pulled myself out
and began the ritual I'd been waiting all week to begin. Face
mask, teal green, grainy and could be used in place of plas-
ter of paris. Pedicure, pumiced, painted and pampered toes
and feet. Manicure, aromatherapy, and an hour spent doing
nothing at all except listening to whale calls and ocean waves
on the CD player. By four o'clock I was so relaxed that any
more self-indulgence would have made me comatose. By five
o'clock I'd eaten the wholesome and nutritious, low-calorie, high-in-phytonutrients meal I'd prepared.

By six, I was dressed, with my hair done and makeup on,
sitting ramrod straight in a chair with my heart pounding as
if it was going to break out of my chest. At six-fifteen, I was
relieved to hear a knock at my door.

"Hi, Mrs. Clempert. What can I help you with?"

"Emma. Call me Emma, dear." She pushed past me and
into my living room. "We've been neighbors so long and
really never gotten to know each other. Is this a good time
for you?"

"Actually, it is. I've been feeling odd today, anxious, and I
have no idea why."

"A change in the weather perhaps. I know my rheumatism is acting up." She sat on my couch, her hands primly folded, and looked at me expectantly.

"Would you like some tea?"

She'd drunk three cups of tea and eaten half a box of Girl Scout thin mints before she got around to why she was really sitting here in my apartment.

"I was praying this morning," she began, "and I had an odd sense of foreboding." She looked at me sharply. "About you. Maybe not only you, but it's you I felt I should talk to."

"About what?"

"I have no idea. When God puts a face or a thought of someone in my mind, I've learned to act upon it. It's the oddest thing. Sometimes someone I haven't seen in years comes to mind, and I know from experience that I need to call him or her right away."

"Then what?" How curious that she was saying this now.

"And they always say, 'Oh, Emma, I'm so glad you called. I've desperately needed someone to talk to,' or they've told me something is wrong in their family or any of a number of things. And today you came to mind." She spread her age-spotted hands open in a bewildered gesture. "Here I am. What do you need?"

"I have no idea, but it's something." I told her about the groundless apprehension and anxiety I'd been feeling.

"Then it's time to pray," she said with assurance. "I believe God often puts a person or an idea in my head. When that happens to me, I know it's time to pray whether I know what's happening for them or not. Most times I hear later that they were in difficulty or need and yet somehow found the strength to get through. I believe God gives us the privilege of being intercessors for others, 'boosting the prayer numbers,' so to speak."

She looked at me calmly. "Feel free to call me a crazy old woman if you like. I won't take offense. And I won't change my mind, either."

I stared at this remarkable elderly woman in amazement. So that's what she did behind that locked door all day long! "I don't think you're crazy at all. I think you're right. Someone needs prayer and we're available to give it." I hesitated just a bit too long.

"And?" She leaned forward and her bright, clear eyes seemed to see right through me.

"I have sometimes thought you were just a little bit unusual...the locks and all."

A surprisingly hearty laugh burst from my diminutive neighbor. "Oh, that? You've noticed my locks then? I moved to Minneapolis from a farm in Iowa. My family worried so much, warning me that my life was in danger in the 'big city.' I promised that I'd be very careful, but they didn't quit worrying. Lo and behold, within three months, my two brothers, a sister, my daughter-in-law and four of the neighbors all sent me locks for my door. Rather than explain or hurt their feelings by sending them back, I just had them all installed. It creates a bit of confusion sometimes, as I don't always remember which I've locked and which I haven't, but I figure it out eventually. One day it must have taken me ten tries to get them all open at once. Good thing I have a telephone. If I ever get stuck in there, I'm going to call my cowardly brother and tell him off!"

We'd prayed for everyone and everything we could think of by the time the phone rang.

I leaned over and picked up the phone. "Hi, Whitney here...."

"Whit!" Kim's voice was frantic. "It's Wesley. He's had a seizure. He's turned blue."

"Have you called the ambulance?" My heart was pounding so loudly that I was sure Kim could hear it.

"Chase is here. He and Kurt were watching a college-basketball game. He's with the baby right now. Can you meet us at the hospital?"

"I'm on my way. Is there anything…" But she'd already hung up the phone.

With Emma's promise to keep on praying, I picked up my coat and purse and dashed for the door.

The hospital smelled the same—both abnormally clean and yet infected with illness, heartache and fear. The woman at the information desk took far too long to find and tell me where they were. "Still in the emergency room, apparently. It's through there." She pointed her pen in the direction of a set of double doors.

Kim and Kurt were in the hall. Kurt paced like a hungry lion in front of the examining room. Kim sat on one of a series of miserably uncomfortable-looking chairs bolted together along the wall. She jumped up and ran toward me when I walked in.

"Oh, Whitney, it was awful, just awful. I went in to his room to get him up from his nap and…"

"Slow down, honey, have you had any word?"

"Chase is with Wesley. He called a pediatrician and a neurologist from the ambulance, but he promised he'd stay with the baby until he knew what was going on. We've just been sitting here, waiting."

"Okay, so tell me what happened." Kurt walked over and gave me a hug. I rubbed his arm and let my hand drop to my side.

"I'd put him down an hour before, because he was so fussy and rubbing his eyes. Wesley is never crabby, but today he was crankier than I've ever seen him. I assumed he was teething. His nose ran a little and he was a tiny bit warm, but that's not terribly unusual for a young child. I made the guys a pizza and then went in to check on Wesley and he was…"

She lifted her clenched fist to her mouth as if to stop the words from spilling out.

"I could tell he wasn't conscious, but his eyes were open and rolled back in his head. He was stiff, and his little arms and legs kept jerking. At first I thought he might be dreaming. I put my hand on him to wake him, but it was as if I wasn't there. I screamed, and the next thing I knew, Kurt and Chase were beside me. Chase sent me to call an ambulance while he put pillows on the sides of the crib to keep the baby from thrashing into them."

Kim was shaking so hard that I thought she might fly to pieces before my eyes. Kurt put his arm around her. His face was completely gray.

"Did Chase say anything?"

"He was busy with the baby," Kurt interjected. "All he said was that seizures aren't necessarily unusual in the pediatric-age group."

"Maybe not in the 'pediatric-age group,'" Kim said wildly, "but they're unusual for my child!"

It seemed like forever until Chase walked out of the exam room. He was in jeans and a sweatshirt, much like the uniform Kurt wore for his sports-watching afternoons. His hair was mussed and his eyes somber.

"What? What?" Kim grabbed him by the front of the shirt. "Is my baby dying?" Kurt had to pry her off as Chase talked slowly and softly to her.

"A seizure can be much more frightening to watch than it actually is. It needn't be catastrophic, and with Wesley I doubt very much that it is."

"Will he be all right? His brain, I mean. It's not damaged?"

"The pediatrician has recommended several tests, including a computerized axial tomography and magnetic resonance imaging, which are very effective in distinguishing lesions in the brain. I suggested an angiography just to see if there were any vascular disorders, which I doubt there are. We'll do an electroencephalogram...."

Kim sagged in Kurt's arms, and I saw she was terrified.

"Chase." I spoke up, knowing that he hadn't even noticed me there. "Could you translate that into patient language?"

He shook his head as if to clear it. "I'm sorry. Kim, he's going to have a CT scan, an MRI and an EEG. Ignore the big words. You know what all those are and they're completely painless. He's very tired right now and may sleep right through them."

"You can't let him go to sleep! Look what happened when—"

"It's not unusual for a child to feel sleepy after a seizure. We'll watch him." He looked at her with such compassion that my heart ached. "And because I don't want you to worry, we may do a biochemical study just to make sure there's no metabolic basis for this. We'll take some blood and run it through. That should tell us a lot."

"But what do *you* think it—" Before Kim could finish, a nurse rolled Wesley into the hall in a metal crib with high sides. Wes was sucking his thumb for all he was worth and trying unsuccessfully to keep his eyes open. He was pink and beautiful and completely healthy-looking.

"You go with the baby. I'll be up after the tests are done," Chase said.

I started to follow them, but Kim pivoted to look at me. "Whit, find out what's going on, will you?" And then she turned to follow the winsome little Pied Piper in the crib.

We stared at each other awkwardly for a moment, but before we could speak, were interrupted by the two other doctors who had been with Wesley.

"They're going to do the tests," one of the men in white said. "He and the parents should be back to their room in less than an hour."

Chase turned to me. "We have some time. Kurt and Kim will stay with the baby. Want some hospital coffee? It has a reputation worldwide. Not for tasting good, mind you—an entirely different reputation."

"Sure." I felt as though I'd been playing crack the whip on ice, flicked this way and that, not knowing what was coming next. I needed to sit down.

The cafeteria was almost empty. Chase pointed me to a table and went himself for the coffee. He returned with two steaming cups of the brew, but also a mug of hot chocolate and a bag of caramel corn.

"You must have read my mind."

"It's not hard. It's written right there on your face." He sat down across from me, leaned back and sighed.

"Wesley?"

"I don't know for sure, but I believe it was what we call a febrile seizure. He'd been warm and fussy when Kim put him down, and now he's got a temp of almost a hundred and four."

He must have seen my eyes widen, because he hurried to continue, "Sometimes children will have a fever that rises quickly. When a child's temperature spikes like that, they're more at risk of having a seizure."

"What does that mean? For the future, I mean?"

"Since he's had one febrile seizure, his risk of having another is somewhere between twenty-five and fifty percent. If he didn't have neurological problems before, he has no increased risk of that in the future."

"And that's what you think it is?"

"Yes, but it's the other doctors Kurt and Kim need to talk to. They'll be reading the tests."

I sagged into my chair and felt tears leaking down my cheeks. "Thank you, God."

"Want to take a walk?"

"Please. I need to take the edge off this adrenaline rush. My heart is pounding like a drum."

"It's cool outside, but there's a long walkway that goes

between the buildings. It's a pretty good place to stretch your legs."

We walked from one end of the complex to the other, and I felt myself calming down with each step. As we turned to start back, Chase put his hand on my arm. "There's a visitors' lounge here that's seldom used. Want to sit down and talk?"

There was little to talk about, I wanted to say, but I wasn't quite ready to go back and pace the hall waiting for Kim and Kurt to return, either. It was a cozy little room with a coffeepot, television set and magazines. Chase sat in a chair and I took the one across from him.

Silence hung between us as we searched for something to say.

"Did you have a nice dinner?"

I looked at Chase, puzzled. "I haven't eaten yet. Kim called and—"

"I meant the other night. The night we ran into you at the restaurant."

"Oh, that. It seems like a long time ago now. Yes, I did have a nice evening." I hesitated before plunging in. "How about you?"

"Fine. Food was good."

"Not the company?"

He laughed. "The Eastons are always good company."

Another silence.

"Is that the man you're seeing now?" His voice was courteous, as if he felt he needed to make polite conversation.

Seeing? Even that felt intimate for the relationship Matt and I have right now. "No…yes…no."

"Which is it?" His eyes scanned me much as I imagined Wesley was being scanned right now. What could Chase see? What was his diagnosis of me?

"No. Nothing serious. I'm on sabbatical from relationships right now."

"Really?" He sounded as though his curiosity was piqued. "For how long?"

"I can't say. I hope I'll know when it's over."

"I know what you mean. I went through the same thing myself."

"'Went' through it? Meaning your sabbatical is over?"

He seemed not to have heard me. "Why? What's the reason behind your retreat from the opposite sex?"

That was a question that could take a month to answer, so I went for the condensed version. "I turned thirty in September. I didn't think I minded that big round number, but everything started to change for me. I lost weight, Kim got sick, I had some romantic…misadventures, got a raise, was adopted by an officemate as her official charity program, my boss turned into a Chia Pet, things like that."

"You have had quite a year." There was laughter in his voice—and something else. Relief?

"Closer to six months, actually, but I've always been an advanced achiever."

"I'll bet you have." His face was more relaxed, and his smile came easily.

"How about you? When does your sabbatical end?" I looked at him quizzically. "You didn't appear to be having time off the night I saw you."

"Neither did you."

I made a face. "Sometimes looks are deceiving. The past eight months have taught me that I'm going to wait until God tells me it's time for a new relationship, a job, anything."

"How will you know when a relationship is right for you?"

"I'll know. I'll listen, I'll pray and I'll trust that He can handle it all much better than I. Maybe the next thing I'll have to learn is patience." I squirmed under his intense gaze. "Does any of this make sense to you?"

"Perfect sense. As if I were on the same path. Sometimes we want people to be something they aren't. We want it so much that we don't recognize the reality of who they really are, warts and all."

He shook his head. "Now I'm the one not making sense."

His pager went off, and he jumped to his feet. "Wesley's done with his tests. Let's go down and see how the family is doing."

I trailed after him, consumed with curiosity. We'd both been talking in riddles—almost the same riddle, in fact.

When we got there, Kim and Kurt were being briefed.

"Treat a fever just as you always would. Use lukewarm sponge baths and acetaminophen. Always use the correct dose, and watch him."

"Is there any way to prevent this from happening again?" Kim was holding Wesley so tightly in her arms that he could barely move.

"Not necessarily. Even treating him this way round the clock doesn't mean he couldn't have another seizure." The doctor closed his file when he saw Chase.

"I'll let you take over," he said with a smile. "The little guy is going to be fine."

"Let's get out of here," Kurt said. "I'm spending way too much time in hospitals."

It took Kim forever to put Wesley to bed. She hovered over the crib, unwilling to leave. Finally I forced her to join the men in the kitchen.

"Maybe we could move the crib into our room," she suggested as she set a plate of sandwiches on the table.

"Kim, if there's anything you don't want to do, it's to become overcautious and to coddle him to the point that he thinks he's sick. He's not." Chase spoke firmly. "Watch him when he has a fever, and if it happens again, which it may not, just stay calm. Make sure he's not having trouble breathing and put him on his side so he doesn't choke. Don't stick your finger in his mouth or try to restrain him. Make sure he doesn't have any sharp object around him."

"That doesn't seem like enough."

"Call your pediatrician. He's one of the best. Or call me."

"What would we have done without you these past months?" Kim turned to me. "Or you?"

"We aren't going anywhere," Chase said as he looked at me. "Dr. Chase Andrews and Dr. Whitney Blake are on call 24/7 for you."

"You've got that right," I added.

Chase and I left together. He paused by my car, and for a moment, I held my breath, waiting.

"Thanks for being here today, Whitney. It helped." He paused, then shifted awkwardly. "But I've got to go. I told Claudia I'd be there at nine. I'm going to be late as it is. Take care of yourself, okay?"

Okay. Looks like it's up to me and God to do that. It's certainly not up to Chase to watch out for me. He has Claudia to look after.

APRIL

CHAPTER 18

April 1

March roared like a lion till the bitter end.

April has got to be better…doesn't it? Maybe not if today was any sign.

April Fools' Day is Innova's national holiday. We celebrate it with abandon. Bryan came in on crutches with a cast on his leg. Betty complained of a pain in her side that she was sure was appendicitis. Harry handed out bonus checks, and Mitzi announced that she'd been promoted to my assistant. I made decaffeinated coffee instead of regular and told them all there was a fast-moving virus going around that made people sleepy, lethargic and headachy, and that the survival rate was only about thirty percent. By noon, Bryan had a thermometer in his mouth, Betty was composing a last will and testament and Mitzi was conducting a survey to see who had the same-size foot as hers so she could designate who'd be inheriting her shoes. Harry, who is hyperactive anyway, didn't seem to notice.

It's our job on the first of every April to decide who is fooling and who's telling the truth. That's never easy, even on normal days, so it's particularly challenging when everyone is making an effort to tell the biggest-fish story.

I had to confess about the coffee early, because everyone was slipping into caffeine withdrawal and work slowed to a standstill. That took me out of the running. Bryan was next, because when he wasn't looking, Mitzi gave his cast a sharp whack with a broom. He didn't even flinch. Therefore, he had to show us how he'd split the cast and put tiny hinges inside for easy entry and exit. I don't want to think about what might have happened if his leg had actually been broken. Ouch.

At two o'clock, Bryan, who'd taken out his large bonus check to gaze at it for the tenth time, discovered that the account number on every check was actually Innova's telephone number. He was devastated that the check was not valid. He'd already made out his shopping list.

That left only Betty and Mitzi to be exposed for the frauds they were. When Betty rushed to the bathroom for the third time to throw up, we had a quick conference and decided she might actually be telling the truth. I was calling for someone to take her to the hospital, when she returned. Suddenly she quit clasping her middle, made a leap into the air that would have made a Dallas cheerleader proud and screamed, "Yes! I did it! April fools!"

Four down and one to go. Only Mitzi's April fools' joke remained to be exposed. At ten minutes to five, as Harry walked through the office, I said nonchalantly, "Harry, we've already figured out that Mitzi's been making this whole thing up about becoming my assistant. You may as well announce it, so she can quit the ruse and we can all go home happy."

Harry looked at me and blinked as he so often does when his mind is a million miles away. "Oh, didn't I tell you? I'm giving Bryan some new responsibilities, so he won't have time to help you. Mitzi *is* your new assistant."

We all laughed. "Good one, Harry!" "That's even better than Betty's appendix!" "You win!"

He looked at us blankly. "What's wrong with you people? It's not a joke. Whitney, Mitzi is all yours starting next Monday. Bryan, see me tomorrow, and for now start getting Mitzi up to speed on the jobs you do for Whitney. With Kim returning, we'll finally be back to normal."

I've been bamboozled, duped, hoodwinked and deceived. Mitzi is my new assistant. It's simply too much to comprehend.

Normal. What a simple word and a beautiful concept. Why is it that I've never experienced it?

After presenting Mitzi with the office traveling trophy we've dubbed Fools' Gold, a hideously ugly lamp with a court jester as its base and a garish lampshade that has all the former Fools' Gold winners and the years of their victory stapled to it, we ate the traditional celebratory foolish cake Betty always baked. It's really just an upside-down pineapple cake that I normally love, but it was hard to swallow today. Just as hard to swallow is the idea that Mitzi is my right-hand woman.

And I thought March was challenging.

April 7

Their children run and play like flocks of lambs. Their little ones dance about.

—Job 21:11

"I'm sorry your parents couldn't come to Wesley's birthday party." Kim handed me a cake with a big "2" on it.

"They were as well, but now that Mom's menopausal mania has subsided, they've been doing all those things they gave up when she started asking entire hotel complexes to turn down the heat. They're visiting her sister for a couple weeks. Dad's using the vacation time he's been saving to enjoy life."

"Kurt and I have decided to do the same thing. We've had two nasty scares this year and we realize that life is to be lived, not saved for later when the kids are grown or it's time to retire. Wesley is portable. We're going to make the most of it before he starts school."

I stopped in the doorway of the kitchen. "You sound like your old self."

"I'm finding her, bit by bit. God's been good to us." She studied me closely. "Have you talked to Chase?"

"Not yet. He's been on all fours in the family room giving Wesley horseback rides."

"He's great with kids, isn't he?"

"What are you getting at?"

"Nothing," Kim said. "Not a thing." A clamor went up in the other room. "Now what?"

I glanced at the cake in my hands. "Don't we already have one of these on the table?"

"That's just for Wes. None of the rest of us will want cake after he's done spitting on it, blowing out the candles and sticking his fingers in the frosting, so I decided to make him his own."

"He's not spoiled, not him!"

"If he is, it's thanks to you. Whit, were there any toys left in the store after you were there?"

"If it was pink, I left it behind. It's just too much fun watching him open gifts." Each time his mother handed him a package, Wesley's eyes grew wide and a grin spread over his entire face. He'd shred the paper and chortle with glee. Who could resist?

"Between you and Chase, the child is set for life." Chase had given the baby savings bonds to use for college.

After Kim left I stayed in the kitchen to gather my thoughts.

Life has been a roller coaster. Work is great since Kim came back. The office feels whole again. Bryan considers himself very important in his new position and retreats to the bathroom only occasionally. And Mitzi! She's been an absolute whirlwind. She has me so organized that I've been able to take on new projects. Harry is so pleased by the work we're accomplishing that he actually broke down and gave us real bonus checks. He's also talking hair transplants now, but we voted and it was unanimous—keep the perm.

And, the craziest thing of all, Bernard wants to train me to help him run a new class he's planning. It's for out-of-shape desk jockeys and he says I'm living proof that it doesn't have to be that way. I'm still considering it. Emma and I have been praying together once a week. I love visiting with her because she's got such a savvy take on things. She truly is what I want to be when I grow up.

Mr. Tibble has been asking for a new catnip mouse—or maybe it's a new kitten. I'm not sure yet, but he howls as if he's being abandoned to hungry wolves every time I leave the room and I feel very guilty. I guess he's decided to keep me.

"Whitney?" Chase stuck his head through the doorway. "Are you okay? They're almost ready to sing to 'Happy Birthday.'"

"Fine. Just taking a breath."

"I haven't seen much of you at the Eastons' lately. What's going on in your life?"

"I've been reconnecting with some old girlfriends and helping with the youth group at church. And I've taken on much more responsibility at work."

"Life is good, then?" He looked at me with those deep blue eyes as if scanning my soul.

"It is. What are you up to these days?"

"I'm on call a lot during holidays and vacations, so my weekends are as full as my weeks. It's good, though. No time to be bored."

"Doesn't Claudia mind your being gone so much?" If I were she, I would.

He gave me an odd look. "Didn't you know? Claudia and I aren't seeing each other anymore. She's moved to California to be near her sister."

"Are you guys coming?" Kim popped into the room, grabbed Chase by the hand and pulled him toward the festivities. "Whitney, Wesley's waiting for his cake!"

April 9

Mr. Tibble here.

My person is behaving very strangely. I've considered taking her to see her vet, but am having trouble convincing her she needs to go. Have eaten several noxious houseplants and thrown up on carpet but still we do not go. Wish her vet spoke cat. Then I could call him and discuss her condition. Her oversize Touch-Tone phone makes dialing easy. I discovered this after attempting to knock receiver off cradle as my afternoon entertainment. Answering party said, "Harrod's of London, may I help you?" This may have had something to do with long, animated call to the telephone company about bill later in month.

I am actually afraid for my own safety. She tried to drown me again, in that intimidating receptacle she calls "the tub." Not only did she immerse me, but doused me with foul concoction she called "shampoo." Fortunately she came to her senses in time and must have felt some remorse, as she wrapped me in warm towel and, when I was dry, fed me tuna. If she tries it again, it had better be caviar.

She has also been promising me a treat. Seems to have trouble deciding between a catnip mouse and a new kitten. Am not sure what word kitten means but it is familiar. I think it was my nickname in early youth.

If I hadn't grown to love this pet of mine, I'd get rid of her. She's very high maintenance.

Mr. Tibble, signing off

April 11

"So Chase and Claudia did split up. He told me things weren't going well between them and that she was going to her sister's. I had no idea it was permanent." Kim frowned. "I wonder why he didn't tell Kurt."

Kim and I were curled on the floor by the fireplace with Wesley, who was happily hammering on a little xylophone.

"Who said he didn't?" None of us had heard Kurt come in until he dropped into the chair nearby. "I forgot to tell you, actually. He let it drop while we were working on the Camaro."

"Car fog," Kim said gloomily, "can wipe out Kurt's memory faster than anything."

He shrugged. "I never liked Claudia very much. I don't suppose I'll miss her. Once, I heard her ask Chase why he and I were friends. She said she didn't think I was his 'type.'"

"You're everyone's type!" Kim yelped indignantly. "Especially mine," she added softly.

"Chase told her that he likes all kinds of people, and doesn't sort them into categories." Kurt smiled a little. "He also said she'd better get used to me and my family, because we were part of the package."

"Good for him!" Kim clapped her hands. Wesley, seeing his mother doing it, clapped, too.

Kurt frowned. "You don't suppose our friendship is part of the reason they're not still together?"

"Claudia is the reason they aren't together," Kim pointed out. "There are lots of wonderful women out there who aren't so selfish and social climbing." She looked pointedly at me.

Kurt caught the glance. "Oh, yes. That's another reason I didn't tell you. Poor Chase needs a break before you start trying to hook him up with someone else. He's pretty burned out right now, so leave him alone, okay?"

April 17

Now I've done it. I've really put my foot in it this time. I brought a kitten home from the humane society for Mr. Tibble. He's supposed to be a companion for Tibbs while I'm away all day.

Scram, the new two-month-old golden tabby, exhibits all the symptoms of a child on a sugar high. The people at the shelter gave him his name. He was underfoot so much and told to scram so often, he'd begun to claim it as his own.

When I came to the kitten room at the shelter, he awakened from a sound sleep, stretched every fiber in his tiny body and batted a paw through the wires of his cage until I held him. That did it, it was all over for me. I had to have him.

What sleight-of-hand trick occurred between the door of the humane society and my home, I may never know. All I do know is that a sweet, cuddly kitty went into that carrier and a spitting, hissing fiend came out.

I put Scram in my bedroom while I soothed Mr. Tibble, who yowled complaints at even the smell of the interloper. When I got back to the room, it looked as if it had been sent through a gigantic paper shredder. The curtain sheers had been used as Mount Everest, and my silk-shantung bedspread and throws had tiny hook marks and pulled threads from Scram's claws. My vanity was vandalized, and the pages of my open library book had been used as a claw sharpener, as had the cloth legs of my vanity chair. Two plants had been toppled, and potting soil spilled out across the rug.

As I stared at the mess, a furry torpedo shot out of the bathroom, skidded along the floor and plowed himself into the wall on the far side of the room. When I tried to pick him up, he dived under the bed and managed to sit just out of reach of my fingertips, hissing.

I shoved the litter box and bowls of food and water into my bedroom and shut the door. Tibbs and I will be sleeping on the couch tonight. My bedroom has been hijacked by something smaller than a can of hair spray.

April 21

Mr. Tibble here.

You'll never believe what my pet dragged home. It was nothing delectable like a freshly killed mouse. If she'd been hunting for big game and bagged a juicy rat, that would be one thing, but this! I'm beginning to suspect that she's been messing with my catnip. Pathetic. She didn't have bird feathers on her breath though. I know. I did a sniff test.

The little scoundrel got my pet so upset that we ended up sleeping on the couch. I did a little detective work once everyone else had fallen asleep. The odor on that box the little pest came in smells very much like the one in which I arrived. Hmm. Should I pity the poor fellow or eat him for lunch?

Mr. Tibble, planning his next meal

April 25

This day will go down in history as the day I became a vice president of Innova. No more schlepping tons of boxes in and out of trade shows. No traveling out of town unless I choose. No more crowded office without windows.

Once Harry realized that I was a valuable team player (Thank you, Matt Lambert!), he decided to make me so comfortable that I wouldn't dream of going anywhere else. Who am I to complain?

In fact, since the shuffling around of jobs, we're all doing better. Bryan's looked me straight in the eye twice today. Using reverse psychology on Mitzi works like a charm.

But if everything is going so well, why do I feel so flat?

Lord,

My gratitude to You is inexpressible. It fills my heart to bursting. You have answered prayers in unimaginable ways and carried my friends and me through some very tough times. "Thank You" seems so small in light of all You've done.

I have to admit there's still that one little pocket in my life that's empty, but I've come to think it's okay. I'd rather be single than badly married. I trust You're working on this for me, so I'm just tossing it out so You know I'm still waiting for an answer. No rush, Lord. I know Your time and my time are often very different.

Finally having turned all parts of my life over to You,
Whitney

April 30

Saturday night. Laundry done. Floors washed. Manicure repaired. Now what was I going to do for the next six hours? The phone rang and it was Kim, inviting me over to watch a special on Egypt's pyramids. Perfect. One old relic watching another.

The porch lights were on when I pulled up.

I was barely out of my car when Kim and Kurt emerged from the house pulling on thick sweaters. Kurt jumped into the car that idled in the driveway while Kim headed toward me.

"Where are you going?" I asked. "I thought you invited me over to watch TV."

Kim reached out and hugged me. "We did, but something's come up. Will you watch Wesley for a few minutes? He's sound asleep. The baby monitor is in the living room. You'll hear him if he wakes up. I've already put the food and beverages out on the coffee table. Help yourself. We'll be back."

"What's so important?"

Kim had already turned around and headed for the car. She waved a hand airily over her shoulder. "I'll tell you later."

And they were gone.

Weird. This was the first time ever that Kim hadn't left me with a list of instructions about Wesley that was as long as my arm.

There was a fire in the fireplace, music playing from speakers in the walls and the lights were all dimmed. Whatever they had to do must have been a real surprise, for them to leave like this. The pyramids were already on the TV screen, so I grabbed the remote and launched myself into the pillows to watch.

It wasn't five minutes before the doorbell rang. I couldn't remember turning the dead bolt but I must have locked them out. Groaning, I padded barefoot to the door and flung it open. "That was quick…."

Chase stared at me as if he'd just found an ostrich egg in a henhouse.

"What are you doing here?" I blurted.

"I could ask you the same question. I came to watch Wesley while Kurt and Kim are out."

"But she asked me to—" Before I could finish my sentence, Chase's cell phone rang. It was Kim.

"Hi, are you at our place yet?"

"I am, but there seems to be some sort of mixup. Whitney is already here baby-sitting."

"I know." I could hear Kim's voice clearly because Chase tipped the phone so that both of us could listen. She was unusually bright and cheery.

"Then why am I here?"

"To baby-sit Whitney, you thickheaded man! We invited her over for the evening and abandoned her. Keep her company for us, will you?"

"When are you coming back?"

"We have theater tickets and a late-dinner reservation downtown. Don't expect us anytime soon."

I grabbed the phone from Chase's hand. "What do you mean, 'tickets' and 'reservations'? You can't impulsively run out of here thinking theater tickets will just appear."

"Of course not, Whit. We've been arranging this for days."

"Then why—" Uh-oh. "You didn't…"

"Set you up? Of course we did. We couldn't leave you to your own devices any longer. You're both dying inside to talk to each other, and it's not happening. Tonight is the night. Whitney, don't you dare leave Chase alone with the baby. And Chase, I know you're listening. Do not, I repeat, do not, abandon Whitney. Oh! I have to go. I'm supposed to be looking for parking spaces. Have fun. See you *both* later!" And she hung up.

Chase and I stared at each other awkwardly. Finally, I remembered my manners. "Would you like to come in?"

Mutely he followed me into the living room, observed the romantic little setting and dropped onto the couch with a groan.

After a few minutes of silence that felt like hours, I said, "Well, this is embarrassing. What should we do?"

He looked around. "Eat? Enjoy the fire? Talk?"

"You mean it?"

"Of course. Why shouldn't we enjoy the evening together?" He patted the place next to him on the couch.

"Or maybe I'm being too presumptuous. I shouldn't assume. After all, I know nothing about your relationship with your friend Matt."

"There's nothing between Matt and me but friendship now."

"There was more once?" he asked, curious. I felt flattered that he cared.

"More or less," I answered vaguely. *Mostly less.*

"So, Whitney, what's your life been like otherwise?"

Whether he wanted an answer to the question or not, I told him everything. I told him about Mitzi as my new assistant, my promotion and even about that little fiend in kitten's clothing, Scram.

Then it was his turn.

"I suppose I was a fool to try it again with Claudia," he admitted ruefully as we shared the chips and dip. "But it seemed the right thing to do at the time."

"Was it?"

"I think it was. I finally saw Claudia through clear eyes. There's no way I could have married her. Our values and ambitions are too different. It would have been hurtful for both of us."

"Does that mean you're over her?"

"Romantically? Yes. But I'm still learning lessons from my experience." He stared at the fire. "I didn't really accept how important it was for Claudia to share my belief system. She was rowing away from faith while I was paddling toward it. We got stuck in the middle of the pond."

"So you're looking for someone who can travel in the same direction?"

"It can't be any other way."

Suddenly Chase and I had a million things to discuss.

MAY

CHAPTER 19

May 1

"Are you mad at me?" Kim's voice was small and worried.

"I should be." I tried to sound stern, but my mood was too contented.

"Did you and Chase have a good talk?"

I knew she was itching for me to spill it all, so it gave me great pleasure to string out her suspense for a time. When even I couldn't stand it anymore, I relented.

"Yes, we had a wonderful time."

"Just wonderful?"

"Amazing, fantastic, unbelievable."

"Tell me more!" I could feel her drooling for details.

"All I can say is this—we've made some plans for you and Kurt on Mother's Day, so keep it open."

May 3

Movie with Chase.

May 5

Dinner with Chase.

May 8

Walk around Lake Harriet with Chase.

May 10

Walk, dinner and movie with Chase.

Lord,

You planned it this way, didn't You? It wasn't until I turned my wish to have someone in my life completely over to You that You answered my prayer. I thought I'd done it a dozen times, but now I realize that I was still clinging to my own plans deep in my heart.

It's that trust and obedience thing again, isn't it? When I gave up my own ideas of how my life should run and asked You to take over the wheel, I got something more wonderful than I could have imagined. It's a paradox, all right. Not my will but Your will. Your will be done. And Your plans included Chase all along.

Awestruck by You,
Whitney

May 15

Mother's Day.

The sun was shining and the sky a cloudless blue. Music is played as some of the most amazing survivors in the world are gathered for the run of their lives.

"This is the best idea you've ever had, Whit!"

Kim came up to me pushing Wesley in the aerodynamic stroller she uses when she goes running. "A family marathon for everyone who cares about finding a cure for breast cancer. I can't believe how little I paid attention to it until now. I'm ashamed of myself. This is going to be a yearly event for us from now on. Right, Kurt?"

"Uh-huh." He was too busy corralling the rest of our runners to say more. The 5K was coming up soon, and he was determined to have every one of our little group present.

My parents had already been to the aerobic warmup, but were still doing jumping jacks and stretching out their legs. They were wearing the matching T-shirts I'd given them. Dad wore a billed cap that said Hers on it, and Mom's cap said His. Too cute. They're such baby boomers.

Emma had caught me leaving the apartment this morning and insisted she should go along to cheer us on. Even Leah and her new husband had come. I doubted they'd be much good in the race as they couldn't seem to quit looking at each other, but they could at least walk the circuit. After all, they'd made it down the aisle, hadn't they?

And Chase—gentle, loving, wonderful Chase—had taken on a job I wasn't sure he could handle. He'd put himself in charge of getting everyone from my office decked out with sunblock and proper shoes. It would be easier to herd cats.

Betty and her husband, who planned to walk the race, slathered on sunscreen, as did Harry and his wife. I was glad to notice she reminded him to put it on his scalp, which, despite the remarkable perm, is beginning to show signs of losing ground. Harry looks as if he's started molting. Bryan had come in a long-sleeved shirt buttoned tight at the collar and cuffs, jeans, tennis shoes and a hat that had looked much better on Indiana Jones than it did on him. No dastardly drop of sunlight was going to touch his sensitive skin. Even Bernard showed up.

It was really only Mitzi who was causing trouble.

Her husband, Dr. Achilles' Heel, wore brand-new running

shoes that made him look three inches taller than he actually is. His feet would be safe from even an explosion under the track. He's obviously practicing what he preaches in the podiatry department.

Mitzi, however, must be as unmanageable at home as she is at the office. She'd come to the race in high heels.

"You can't run in those!" her husband said.

"Who said I was running?"

"Walk, then. You can't walk in them, either."

"I don't remember agreeing to walk. I thought I was only here for moral support." She waved and gave two passersby a thumbs-up. "See?"

Wary of just such a thing happening, I'd brought several pairs of shoes from my mother's closet. She's the only one I know who wears Mitzi's size. Chase held up a pair of white runners. "How about these?"

"Are you kidding? Do you know how big white makes your feet look?"

"These, then." Mom's beloved blue-and-white tennis shoes.

"Ewwww. They look as if they've been used!"

"That's what happens, Mitzi, when you borrow shoes. They aren't all brand-new."

"I'm not wearing someone else's sweaty feet." She looked at the box Chase was digging in. "What else have you got?"

"You aren't on a shopping spree, Mitzi," Chase reminded her.

"Oh, you are so boringly persistent." She pointed her finger in the direction of the box. "I'll take those."

Chase pulled out a pair of slip-ons made to look like tennis shoes. Cute, but impossible for running.

"I like them. And the red matches my belt. Isn't that clever?" Mitzi pranced off.

"Clever," Chase muttered under his breath as he turned to me. "How do you do it, Whitney? How can you function with her as an assistant? If she were in the operating room with me, no patient would come out alive."

"It's an art form," I replied as he gathered me into his arms for a hug.

"Loving you is an art form," he corrected. "Mitzi is a test of willpower and sanity."

"You get used to her. I have."

"I'll take your word for it." He pulled away a little and looked into my eyes.

"I'll take your word on anything, Whitney. If you say it, I'll believe it."

"Then believe this. I love you, Chase."

I felt him tremble a little before he squeezed me tighter still.

May 31

It's full. I've used up all the pages in my *Whitney Chronicles*. Kim has promised to get me another. I hope she hurries. Chase and I have a big date tomorrow night that I may want to record.

I think he'll ask me to marry him. I know, I know, I've had that thought before and look where it got me. But God's doing a far better job with my social schedule than I ever did.

I do have one little tiny plan however. That balloon I caught on New Year's Eve—with the prize of two tickets to Hawaii? It wouldn't hurt to offer it up as a honeymoon plan, would it?